Vagina Mundi

BY WOL-VRIEY

Vagina Mundi

BY WOL-VRIEY

Burning Bulb

PUBLISHING

Vagina Mundi
By **Wol-vriey**

Burning Bulb Publishing
P.O. Box 4721
Bridgeport, WV 26330-4721
United States of America
www.BurningBulbPublishing.com

Cover designed by Gary Lee Vincent with the following licensed elements from Can Stock Photo, Inc.: csp9077683

Author Photo: Lolade Akinsowon © 2014

First Edition.

Paperback Edition ISBN: 978-0692262801

Printed in the United States of America

THANKS AND ACKNOWLEDGEMENTS.

Firstly, thanks to Gary Lee Vincent and Rich Bottles Jr. at Burning Bulb Publishing for taking on this project. You guys are totally the best! And, Gary, man, that's one incredible cover!

Now, a special acknowledgement: This book would never have been written except for a picture of Fabulous Raye Roeske's hair that I saw on Goodreads. Dark witchy locks spread out like they were alive . . . (Just the hair, everyone. Because this story is so odd, I don't want anyone associating any other character traits/experiences with the nice lady.)

And, NO NO NO! Mr. Rich in this story isn't Rich Bottles Jr.! LOL!

Of course, this page won't be complete without me thanking my lovely wife Victoria . . . for everything. Thanks, Darling!

And, finally, major thanks to all fans of my work.

(The catch here, is that this book has the word 'Vagina' in its title, so I'm wondering if all the people just mentioned would have been happier if overlooked.)

Peace, everyone!
Wol-vriey.
7/25/2014

DEDICATION

To all the WOMEN of the world: Unsung Goddesses all.

In the beginning, Woman gave birth to man – Femina.

PRELUDE: THE BALLAD OF HOLLY WOOD

Tongue me delicately,
Lick my clitoris.
Please,
Sex me at your ease.
Nibble me deliciously,
Like a mouse eating cheese.

If I faint from pleasure,
Bring me back to life.
With mouth-to-cunt resuscitation,
Between my spread thighs,
I don't want no penetration,
Tonight.
Cunnilingus rules,
Far and wide.
Man, my pussy's smoking hot,
Lick my most sensitive spot,
Suck me till I boil over,
(Till orgasm floods my honey-pot!)
Then cool off.

Tickle my lush pubic bush,
Finger-comb my pubic hair,
Spread my engorged labia wide,
Can you see the moisture there?
That should tell you I'm prepared.

Wet a finger with saliva,
Gently . . . slide it inside,
Have no fear . . .
Vagina's here!
Let Pussy be your guide.

Mouth-to-cunt resuscitation,
I don't want no penetration,
Tonight's not for masturbation,
Cunnilingus rules.
And afterwards, I'll do you too.

Oops, sorry! I almost forgot,
(Don't stop eating me, don't stop!)
Just what,
I'm here for.
While you unlock my vaginal door,
Permit me to introduce my self:
Better late than never,
As sometimes never lasts forever.
My name's Antonia 'Holly' Wood.
(Kate Rose's necklace was no good;
I drowned in a swimming pool,
While cruising in my ship of fools.)

Now that that sad bit's been said.
While you give me luscious head,
I'll tell you the story,
Of the pussies of glory,
Of the cunts of divinity.
Of vaginas good and bad,
Vaginas happy and sad,
Of Vaginas both sane and mad,
And of said vagina's owners, ha ha!

I'll advise that you acquire my taste,
You can't eat pussy in a haste,
If tried,
Your effort will just prove a waste,
And leave me unsatisfied.

Now . . . while you lick me,
Try to smile,

VAGINA MUNDI

Cos this tale between my legs,
Of money, love, and violence,
Of lust found, and lost happiness,
And a huge amount of deviant sex
Will take quite a while to tell . . .
A fact I know real well.

Now please suspend your disbelief,
And hear out my narrative,
Of how two hot courageous chicks,
Fought valiantly for relief,
From their crap circumstances,
Against all obstacles in their way.
From Chicago to NYC.
(Sing the chorus again please:)

Mouth-to-cunt resuscitation,
Enjoy me without reservations,
Lick me like it's your occupation,
Fill my vagina with sensation.

And if I die after I come,
It's okay—at least I had some fun.

From beyond the grave my spirit speaks,
It's a tale to stupefy the meek,
One to terrify the weak.
In which no one turned the other cheek!
Throw the first stone if you've no sin . . .
Let the drama begin!

PART ONE: CHICAGO GIRLS

Making money is sufficient justification for any course of action
–Monica 'Money' Rich.

CHAPTER 1

10 p.m. Renaissance West Building, Logan Square, Chicago, IL

With a hiss, the skylight latch crumbled to ash.

Raye froze. *Oops! That's much louder than I expected.*

She switched off the laser, then lay flat beside the opened skylight. Totally motionless. In her black jumpsuit, there was no telling her from the other rooftop shadows.

It was an atypical Chicago midsummer night, cold with a pre-fall chill. The air felt dirty . . . packed with industrial waste. A not-quite-smog that settled in the lungs like a premonition of bronchitis.

Raye stifled a cough. She waited one minute. Two minutes. Five.

Below her, illuminated in moonlight, the Kate Rose necklace glinted silver and emerald on a velvet cushion. Raye grinned. *Yeah, Bug gave me the straight dope alright. Ash, baby, one million dollars is ours!*

***

The Kate Rose necklace made the wearer bulletproof. Some believed the ancient illusionist's ghost was still stuck in it.

That was the story, anyway. The necklace had most recently belonged to porn actress Antonia 'Holly' Wood.

Holly, scared of being assassinated by ultra-feminists, hadn't taken the necklace off once in twenty years. She'd worn it through all her movies, including her most infamous—*Horse Sandwich.*

While filming *Horse Sandwich* (Holly Wood had been eating freshly shat horse poop on bread, while two men sandwiched her), four women with M16 assault rifles had broken into the studio and begun shooting.

Both Holly's male co-stars died in the attack. The horse had died too. Holly, however—face covered in horseshit—had wrestled one of the attackers' guns away from her. Then she'd killed all four women. Raye had seen the video . . . everyone had . . . bullets bouncing off Holly's head and body like she was Superwoman . . .

And then the genius of director (and Holly's husband) Eddie Fiddle. Eddie had survived both gunfire and ricochets by pulling Holly's two dead co-stars over himself for protection. Thus shielded, he'd kept filming, capturing the whole shootout.

Once the firing stopped, Eddie instantly forced Holly's mouth back into the horseshit, pulled down his pants and slid his penis up her anus. "Yeah, babe," he'd groaned while coming all over her pink buttocks, "You gave those animal abusers a real taste of their own medicine."

So porn history was made.

After Holly Wood died—by falling into an swimming pool while stoned and drowning—the necklace (and Eddie) disappeared.

Now it had turned up again. For sale to the highest bidder. The Chicago underworld grapevine had been abuzz for a week now with the news that Kate Rose's necklace was in town. The starting bid was fifteen million dollars.

Raye smiled. From what she'd heard, bids were already up to twenty-five million.

Raye wasn't greedy. One million was more than enough for she and Ash to bid goodbye to Chicago for good.

Bug had tipped Raye off as to the necklace's location.

Bug, Chicago's number one fence, was a massive white insect like a giant bleached cockroach.

"Logan Square. Renaissance West Apartments," Bug had said in its raspy voice, its faceted eyes glittering like black diamonds. "The penthouse. What's important to us is that there are no security cameras installed there yet."

Rachel Risk—twenty-eight, dark-eyed, brunette, a little on the plump side but definitely pretty—had smirked. "Bug, how the hell do you know that?"

"'Cos the guy who wants to buy the necklace from me owns the company contracted to install the cameras. And they're doing so *tomorrow* morning."

"Who's the guy?"

"Someone rich enough to kill an overly curious cat." The insect fixed Raye with a dark gaze. "Look, do you want to earn this million bucks or not?"

"I'm still here, aren't I? Keep talking."

"It's easy enough—"

"Then why aren't *you* doing it?"

The insect looked pained. "I would if I had your hair, Raye."

***

If I had your hair. Memory of the jealous longing in Bug's voice made Raye smile. Wasn't the first time she'd heard such.

She peered down into the skylight. Ten minutes now and no one had shown up to investigate. *I've been worrying for nothing.*

By silent inches, she opened the skylight. After a final peek down into the gloom below, she climbed through, let herself drop towards the floor.

CHAPTER 2

Rachel Risk's hair was alive. The dark locks caressing her shoulders like lovers' fingers were as much a living part of her as an octopus' tentacles were of that creature. Her hair was also as strong as steel and stretchable as rubber.

Now, as she dropped through the roof, her hair billowed above her like a parachute. It wove itself into four humanlike arms, their ends hands that gripped the skylight's rims, halting her descent. Two additional locks curled under her armpits, reducing the strain on her neck.

Raye hung there in space above the silver/emerald necklace, tense and wary, all her senses alert for alarms.

The room was silent as death.

There's no one here, she decided finally.

She dropped several locks of hair to the floor, where they propped her up like stilts. She floated there like a spider, an angel with woven pilus wings.

She dropped lower, stared warily at the necklace. The skylight illumination framed it like a spotlight beam. *This is almost too good to be true. I just pick this up and wave farewell to this city.*

She stretched a hand toward the necklace, then, deciding against touching it, extended a hair-hand instead.

The moment the brown hirsute fingers touched the necklace, the room burst into light. Simultaneously, a stream of bullets struck the hair-hand.

Raye grabbed up the necklace. *Oh, shucks! I should've known. Bug, you idiot!*

Quickly stuffing the necklace in her pants, she looked around for the bullets' source.

Hell no!

12

Three robogoons were emerging from holes in the wall. All three 'goons'—six-feet-tall and human-shaped, with ugly metal faces—wore pinstriped suits and porkpie hats. Completing their 1930s gangster vibe, each robot carried a Tommy gun with a round drum magazine.

"So you're the broad that wanna steal our necklace," one robot said in a rusty voice from 60s sci-fi. "You're gonna regret that, babe."

All three goons began firing on Raye.

***

It never occurred to Raye to put on the necklace. This wasn't the time to prove the legends right. Or wrong—for all she knew, Holly Wood's legendary shootout with the ultra-feminists could have been all special effects.

Instead, Raye did what came naturally—she cocooned herself in her hair. Faster than lightning, her brown locks dropped from above/rose from below to shield her from the flying bullets.

She fell to the floor in the brown egg, rolling across the room from the force of the gunfire pummeling it. Inside the egg, she blocked her ears with her hands to dim the noise.

The noise stopped. The hair cocoon stopped taking a battering. Raye split her hair for a look. The three robots were reloading.

She broke up the cocoon, formed HUGE fists with her hair instead. "Okay, bolt-heads, it's my turn."

The robogoons looked up from their reloading. "Just you wait," one said. "We'll—"

A massive hair-fist smashed into the speaker, demolishing him. The robot fragmented against the wall, his metal innards spraying everywhere. His limbs dispersed left and right. Oil splashed the wall behind him. His head flew away across the room.

The other two robogoons stared at their demolished colleague in surprise. Then both turned to Raye. "Die, human bit—"

Raye smashed both mechanical gangsters to bits with a barrage of hair-fist punches. Metal arms and legs, dismantled gears and springs rolled across the room. One goon's suit caught fire. The room filled with smoke.

A Tommy gun discharged as it hit the floor. The slug hit a wall; the ricochet punctured Raye's pants, just missing her right thigh.

"Screw you pieces of junk," she spat at the demolished machines.

Her breath came fast and furious, her pulse was racing. She'd not been expecting this at all. Hell no! And the noise . . .

This noise must have alerted someone. The faster I'm out of here the better.

She dissolved the massive brown fists, wove her hair back into ropes, and slung them up towards the skylight.

She grinned back at the room—
No one ever said making a million dollars would be easy
—Then hauled herself up and was gone.

CHAPTER 3

11:00 p.m.

Normally, Raye would have headed straight from Logan Square to Bug's Hyde Park apartment. Now though, she went home. Both to calm down after the recent excitement and also change her clothes.

The East 46th Street apartment she shared with her girlfriend Ashley Status was on the way over to Bug's anyway.

There was also the fact that, now the deed was done—now she had the necklace—Raye no longer felt in any hurry. *A million dollars right now is the same thing as a million dollars in six hours time. Money in the bank either way, honey!*

Driving her 'borrowed,' hot-wired Honda Prelude down through West Side, she pondered what had happened back in the penthouse. *What the hell? Someone knew I was coming? No, that's impossible . . . just Bug not properly checking the security setup there. Or, more likely, me being careless—I must have triggered some alarm.*

***

Once home, Raye dropped the Kate Rose necklace onto her coffee table.

She spread it out over the glass. The circle of emeralds set in silver caught the light beautifully.

For a moment, she considered not taking the necklace over to Bug, instead calling Ash, and the two of them heading out of town.

But no . . . Bug is tight with the mobs. If it sets them looking for Ash and me, there'll be nowhere in the US safe for us to live. No, not just the USA—there'll be nowhere safe on the planet. And what use is that?

She nixed the thought of selling the necklace herself. She'd keep to the deal—give Bug the goods, take the agreed payment. *We'll still be able to leave Chicago, leave the gangs, the goons, the guns, far behind.*

She grinned, her brown eyes sparkling with glee. It was still very good. *Oh yeah, baby. Ash and I are made now. One million clams!*

A warmth filled her crotch at the thought of the fun they'd have from now on.

Then, just as she was about to begin masturbating from sheer joy, the Kate Rose necklace altered. First, both silver setting and emeralds marbled with black lines, then the entire necklace turned ash-gray.

Raye watched the changes with a sinking feeling in her gut. She dared touch the sculpted gray circle; it crumbled to ash on the tabletop.

Damn! A fake? I just risked my ass for a fake!?

Before the thought was over, the gray ash that had recently been Kate Rose's necklace began evaporating. Raye watched it disperse into thin air. It felt like watching a million dollars burning up in a fire.

Oh no, this isn't happening to me.

She walked over to the bed, picked up her cellphone, dialed Bug.

Busy tone.

She dialed again. "Thank you for calling. You've reached Bug's voicemail box. Please leave your message after—"

She considered dialing Ash, then flung the phone on the bed instead. Ash had a date with Mr. Rich. The horny slut. Girlfriend would find out the bad news later. Then she remembered; she'd not told Ash about this steal. She'd wanted it to be a surprise. She looked at the coffee table—the only sign the necklace had ever been there now was a circular darkening of the glass like it had been scorched—and sighed. *Yeah, some grand surprise this turned out to be.*

Feeling heavy depression setting in, Raye walked over to stare out the living-room window at the South Chicago skyline.

In the cloud-filtered moonlight the low-rise buildings looked like dirty cardboard boxes stacked atop each other. The skyscrapers seemed many-eyed monsters feeding on them.

After a while of staring emptily, Raye again tried getting Bug on the phone to tell him what had happened. Again no success.

She figured there was no point in immediately rushing over to Bug's place. Instead, she turned on the TV, channel-surfed to an old 40s rom-com. Judy Garland and Gene Kelly in *The Pirate*. She watched without actually seeing the people onscreen, just using their happy voices as soundtrack to neutralize her misery.

CHAPTER 4

11p.m. The 5550 Apartment Building,
South Dorchester Avenue, Hyde Park

Mr. Rich, Downtown Chicago's criminal overlord, stood by his bedroom window making a phone call. The kingpin, dressed head-to-foot in clothes tailored from hundred dollar bills, was in a foul mood.

Mr. Rich frowned and spat into the phone, "Dougie, you louse, you screw with me just this once and the goons'll come visiting!"

A voice groveled on the other end of the line. His face cold as stone, Mr. Rich listened.

"I hear you, you weasel," Mr. Rich said when the line was silent again. "Now you hear me: Dougie, if my damn shipment ain't here shortly, you're history. Be the first time anyone in your retard family every achieved anything notable anyway."

He slammed down the phone, then turned to the robogoon standing by the door. "Al, get a carload of the goons over to Melrose Park. Dougie Sloane's bringing over a cargo of Montana snow.

The robot, a roughly accurate replica of Al Capone—plump, immaculate in a cream suit, and with thick black eyebrows and two long simulated scars on the left side of his pink plastic face—nodded. "'Kay, Boss." Al pointed past the naked blonde seated on the edge of Mr. Rich's bed to a metal door with a spyhole. "We'll need the money."

Mr. Rich snorted. "Forget the money for now. When Dougie shows, bring his ass over here. I gotta feeling the Montana crew are ripping me off."

"Old man Reuben wouldn't dare."

"His kids would. Pair of greedy bastards. Josh and Kyle studied accounting before their dad insisted they join the family drug trade."

Al Capone laughed, mechanical like radio static. "Heard that too, Boss. Also heard that he bitterly regrets it—word is, Old Reuben can't even wipe his backside now without one of the twins measuring the rectangles of tissue paper out for him and reminding him how bog paper costs money."

Mr. Rich grinned, then his expression turned frosty again. "I don't care how far back Reuben and I go . . . If his kids *are* ripping me off . . ."

He waved Al away.

"Have a nice screw, Boss," Al said as he opened the door.

Mr. Rich grunted. That was one problem with robogoons. They were an irreverent lot.

Al Capone left.

Mr. Rich turned from the robot to gaze out his bedroom window, his eyes roving past the vacant rooftop helipad, over the Chicago skyline. The skyscrapers and high-rises, squares of lambent light bound in concrete shadows, reassured him of his power over all.

He turned back to the nude woman in his bed . . . Ashley Status.

***

Seeing Mr. Rich was done with his drug-dealing and now had time for her, Ash spread her legs.

Mr. Rich's expression remained stony. He began removing his clothes.

Ash faked a yawn as she watched him undress. Her mind, however, was racing. She was as pissed-off as usual when here. *How the hell can anyone be so crude as to wear clothes tailored from money? It's disgusting. And Raye and I live on barely-have-enough street? Shit! Each of this guy's suits literally costs thirty thousand dollars, and there's his socks and shoes and . . .*

Mr. Rich stepped out of his money-tailored underpants and flung them over his shoulder. His penis was soft between his legs.

Ash admitted the kingpin was good-looking and in good shape. Fifty-five, no paunch, clear blue eyes, his dark hair graying around the temples. And immensely RICH.

So frigging rich he wears clothes made of money. And I . . . I'm just amusement . . . stress relief.

Mr. Rich frowned at the sight of Ash's vagina, the soft blonde bush framing the pretty pink slit. At the moment her sex did nothing for him. His penis remained flaccid.

Ash hid her disgust. She unzipped her upper right arm, took out a fifty dollar bill from its bicep purse. She rubbed the fifty dollars over her vagina.

Mr. Rich gasped in a sharp intake of breath. His hands began trembling lightly. Like a flag being raised up a mast, his cock slowly came to full erection.

Ash turned the note over, so he could see it was creamed with her vaginal secretion.

He smiled. It was an established routine/connection between them.

***

Ashley Status—thirty-one; pretty, blonde and blue-eyed; slim with small firm breasts, a tight backside, and long legs—met Mr. Rich several times a week to have sex.

It wasn't by choice. Ash had originally worked as a teller at Arlington Park, Mr. Rich's horse racing track. Six months ago, Mr. Rich had come by one afternoon to watch Desert Storm, a new purchase, run. After the new horse had won two races, the boss had decided to look around. He'd seen Ash paying out money to winners. She'd looked up. Their eyes had met. The boss had winked at her.

"Bring her up to the penthouse later," Mr. Rich had told Pretty Boy Floyd, another robogoon lieutenant. "She reminds me of an old girlfriend."

And that had been that. No one argued with the boss.

Ash didn't mind—being the boss's moll paid loads better than being a teller, even if the sex *was* freaky. She also got to travel out of town a lot.

Raye however was pissed off.

"It's only till he tires of me," Ash pointed out. "From what the goons say, Mr. Rich goes through at least two women each year." She kissed Raye tenderly, then grinned, gesturing around their apartment. "And we get to keep all this."

The brain upgrade 'mind-chip' that had enabled Ash keep perfect track of every financial transaction through the day while working at the racetrack was still in her head. The removable chip resided in a socket behind her right ear.

Al Capone had suggested that Mr. Rich have it removed.

"Leave it in," the boss had replied. "She can hook up to Pornopedia with it, download the Kama Sutra, keep me entertained better in bed."

Ash, prompted by Raye, had found other uses for the mind-chip. She'd upgraded it and bought several more, one of which illegally connected to Warpedia, the military version of Wiki.

Just like she'd found other uses for her muscle purses.

She'd initially had two: One in her left thigh (she was left-handed), that concealed/held a small Beretta Bobcat .22 pistol (in case her teller window was attacked), and the other in her right bicep, which held an emergency cellphone.

She'd since (without Mr. Rich's knowledge) had two more muscle purses installed in her other thigh and bicep.

***

Ash's gaze momentarily rested on the pictures of Mr. Rich's two children on the nightstand. His daughter Money, a beautiful redhead with arrogant green eyes, and his son Cash, who looked like his father—dark and handsome. (Cash was down in Vegas, overseeing the kingpin's casinos.)

The bedroom was large and opulent. One wall was almost completely papered over with money. A tapestry of tens, fifties, hundreds . . . mostly hundreds.

As always, Ash, raised dirt poor on an Ohio hog farm, was taken aback by the waste.

Almost two hundred grand on that wall and Raye and me are almost always broke?

Not for the first time, a feeling of desperation gripped her. A longing to be this rich. But how?

***

Ash continued rubbing the fifty dollar bill over her vagina.

"Yes," Mr. Rich gasped. "I'll get the money suit."

He turned around, walked briskly over to the door with the spyhole.

Ash got off the bed and followed him.

Mr. Rich peered into the spyhole with his left eye. The spyhole—the lock for his wall safe—scanned his retina then gave a beep of approval. He stepped back. The safe door swung open. Mr. Rich reached into it for the money suit hanging there.

Ash peered around him into the vault. She gasped. Like Mr. Rich's conversation with Al Capone had suggested, the safe was *full* of money, stacked bands of C-notes.

She quickly estimated the thickness of notes. *I'm looking at a million dollars in cash, minimum.* Her attention was momentarily caught by something else. *What's that hanging on the left? Another suit?*

Mr. Rich turned back to her, holding out the money suit. His normally stern face was flushed, like he'd soon get a nosebleed, his pupils dilated with lust. His erection was firm and throbbing. "Put this on, quick!'

The 'money suit' was, like all Mr. Rich's clothes, literally made of money. It was a full-body cat suit (complete with hood and mask) tailored to fit a woman's curves. A hundred thousand dollars, zipped and pasted together, rubberized and stitched so it fit like a glove. The bills lay atop each other a quarter-inch thick.

Ash pulled the suit on, then turned her back to Mr. Rich. "Zip me up."

Licking his lips, his body trembling, his eyes bulging, he did so.

The money suit covered Ash completely. It had finger and toe extensions, and perfectly placed holes for her anus and vagina.

She pulled the hood over her head. She hated the damn thing. The mask was designed so its face was fifty cut-out Benjamin Franklins. She was totally blind in it—no eye holes. There were, however, air holes for her nostrils, two tiny ones for her ears, and one for her mouth—this last expertly sculpted so it folded in over her lips.

Mr. Rich had no time for romance. Money was his one true love. Now, staring at the cash-coated woman before him—the fifty Benjamin Franklins regarding him back in place of her own face—he was in ecstasy. All he saw was MONEY with a mouth, a vagina, and an anus. Money waiting to be fucked.

"Oh, Money darling, you look absolutely gorgeous."

And blinder than a bat in daylight, Ash thought in the darkness of her cash cocoon.

"Come to me, Money darling," Mr. Rich said.

Ash still found it odd to be addressed as 'Money.' *That's the name of your daughter, old man. You're not imagining that I'm her, are you? Okay, and if he calls me Cash? He's thinking of doing his son?*

Following the sound of his voice, she walked toward the bed, swaying like a zombie, arms held out in front of her.

She stopped when she bumped her legs against Mr. Rich. He was seated on the bed's edge. He pushed her down to her knees. She felt in his crotch with dollar-clad fingers, took his erection into her mouth, began fellating him.

He was already dribbling pre-come. She licked it up, swirled her tongue around the throbbing penis.

This is obscene, Ash thought. *Super-powerful or not, this man is a total kook.*

Oblivious to her opinion of him, Mr. Rich put some music on.

Femina.

***

Femina. The sultry erotic singer was the underground rave of the moment. Her second album, *Pussy's Revenge*, was still number one on Billboard's MuXXXic chart six months after its release. Femina's first album, *Pussy Violated: Penetrated without Permission*, released eighteen months ago, was at number two. *2 4k or not 2 4k (Bedroom War of the Sexes)*, the singer's new album, was currently zooming up the charts like a rocket, and looked set to displace both its siblings within the next week.

Femina's sound was a weird mix of poetry, rock, rap, and conventional singing. A good number of her songs were simply her chanting or reciting jagged verse over a beat with a skeletal piano or guitar accompaniment. Several tunes had unbalanced verses and meter . . . Sometimes there was no chorus. Sometimes the whole song was a chorus, a numbing drone that seemed endless. Her rhymes were strange, sometimes so basic as to be seem infantile.

But their content . . .

Femina's lyrics were raw and violently sexual, leaving nothing to the imagination. Her albums were like recorded orgasms. No subject was too taboo to be broached.

Rape, suicide, fetishes, war, insanity, domestic abuse, necrophilia, gender politics, insecurities, murder—in Femina's songs all were obsessively sexualized, as if the singer was having the best sex of her life rather than detailing the darker side of human nature.

She'd been banned on countless radio and TV stations overseas, and even here in the USA there was massive pressure on her to tone down her 'message.'

"I sing about women everywhere," she'd said on *The Jerry Springer Show*. "Their plight is my plight; I feel what they feel. Too long have we suffered under the illusion that male might is right. I for one will never give up the fight for my woman rights, and I'll eternally strive, to bring my blind sisters into the light." Then she'd giggled. "But still, I like . . . to suck cock every night."

That was Femina.

Most ultra-feminist groups had issue with Femina's seeming stance that "woman must desperately love man to death, even as she hates him with her every breath," as she once put it.

***

Ash sucked Mr. Rich's penis. The music played on. The song was *Fuck Me!*, a soft, soulful ballad, with Femina's raspy voice floating in a hypnotic chant over piano and drum backing like a seagull gazing down on ocean waves:

"Yes, I feel like shit,
I often do,
It's not your fault,
Though I'm blaming you,
My sweet darling fool.
Don't look so scared,
You're always seem unprepared.
By now, you should expect,
My estrogen flares,

Those dark interludes,
(When I'm stressed out and vexed,)
Between romance and sex.

Cuddle me up in your masculine arms,
Whisper my name,
Dazzle me with your charms,
Back me into the bedroom,
Lay me down on our bed,
Rip of my panties,
And spread my legs,
Start giving me head.
Today looks nicer already,
Oh yes!

Fuck me!
Make me feel better!
Fuck me!
Make me feel better!"

A saxophone solo picked up the music after the first chorus. Ash smiled. She loved Femina's background singers, their three-part harmony like a female Bee Gees:

"Life is a bitch,
It's making me bitch,
Come on, scratch my itch,
Yes! With your penis!

I need to relax,
From filling out income tax,
Worries about this and that,
And how I'm getting fat.
Yes, I know you don't care,
If I'm fat or I'm thin,
But that's neither here nor there,
You don't live in my skin.

I've a lot on my chest,
And not just my breasts,
What? Can't you guess?
Well I'm sad and depressed,
And feel quite oppressed,

By this new government's,
Policies on health care,
Amidst 'rising breast cancer' scares.
I've got bills and bills,
Shopping credit card chills,
And just being a woman,
Man, you don't know how that feels.

But I know a sure-fire way to fix ALL my ills.

(I want you to . . .)

Fuck me!
Make me feel better!
Fuck me!
Make me feel better!

Orgasm is so nice,
When I'm in a foul mood,
It really helps me pull through,
Helps me not to brood,
Makes me feel oh so good.
Orgasm is so nice,
Just like sugar and spice,
like chop suey and rice,
Just like great chocolate,
Soothes my bad feelings away,
Makes me giggle again,
And again and again.

I'm dropping my panties,
Get your manhood out, honey,
Then put it away again,
Deep inside me!
Sex is so wonderful.
Makes me feel beautiful,
And I really need to feel beautiful,
After this horrid day!

Fuck me!
Make me feel better . . . !"

The song played on in the background. Mr. Rich grunted. He pulled Ash's mouth off his penis, jerked her up from the floor, and pushed her down on her belly on the bed.

Ash grunted with pain as he penetrated her anus. No lube as always. He'd told her he always intended to, but once she was incarnated like this, as Money, reason fled him.

And me? Once again, I forgot to lube my ass up first. Ouch! Ouch! Ouch! Damn!

He fucked her hard and fast. Harder and faster.

"Oh, I love you, Money honey," he groaned, lying his entire weight on her and holding and squeezing her tight, his fingers digging into her dollar-smothered breasts. "Oh, Money, Oh MONEY!!!"

Damn, talk about objectification. Under him, Ash felt like she'd burst. Totally unsighted, she felt like the walls of reality had closed in on her.

Her body flopped up and down on the sheets as he pumped. Her claustrophobia passed. Slowly, as always happened in this situation, arousal poked through her discomfort. Enough of a sexual spark to fan up to a blaze. She stuck a hand between her legs and pleasured herself to his thrusts.

His moans grew louder, his thrusts into her rectum became more violent. His body trembled on hers. Ash knew what was coming next.

"Oh, oh, oh, fuck, yeeeessss!"

His erection pulled out of her anus. Blind in her prison of cash, Ash rubbed her vagina fiercely till she came also and flumped down like a fish on the bed.

In the background, Femina rapped:

"Wrap it up even if it's clean,
Yeah, slip on your artificial skin.
C'mon, hurry up, man! I'm tired of waiting!
It's bad manners to keep a lady waiting!
Put your penis in . . ."

***

Mr. Rich had waited until the last moment, until he'd felt the semen already bubbling up from his testes, before pulling out of Ash's anus.

He grabbed a hundred dollar bill and ejaculated on it. When it was creamed over, he grabbed another, then two more.

The orgasm felt great. They always did. Gazing down at Ash/Money, her anus still wider than normal, he permitted himself a cool smile. Nothing beat the feeling of making love to his wealth. He considered: *Maybe I'll simply have Ash wear the suit all day long,* then shook his head: *Can't do that. My empire won't run itself. As I always say: To have money, I've gotta make money.*

Mr. Rich picked up the semen-smeared bills. One more thing remained to be done before his come dried on them. He walked to the wall papered over with money and stuck the notes into empty spaces on it.

For a moment he regarded the new additions, then returned his attention to the woman in his bed.

Ash still lay on her belly, greenbacked buttocks up in the air, legs spread, anus a pink pit. Her fingers fluttered over her sex, wringing out the last tendrils of her orgasm. Her breathing was soft, like she was sleeping.

Mr. Rich found her dollar-obliterated form—each curve lovingly clasped by cash; woman as financial sculpture—gorgeous beyond belief.

He stroked his penis. It was still bone-hard. Any woman in the money suit had this effect on him—he could last forever. He walked back over to the bed. After wiping his erection clean with a handful of fifties, he stuck it into Ash's vagina.

He groaned at the velvety feel of her cunt around him. It looked like quite a few more bills would be gracing his money wall tonight.

CHAPTER 5

1 a.m.

Two hours later, her anus and vagina so sore she could hardly walk, Ash staggered out of the elevator on the ground floor.

Bugsy Malone, one of Mr. Rich's robogoons, had phoned to say they were on their way over with Dougie Sloane.

"Okay, baby, you gotta go," Mr. Rich said. "This business with Dougie might get ugly. If the Reubens *are* screwing me, I'm cutting off both Dougie's balls and mailing them back to Montana by UPS."

Ash had gulped. No way did she want to witness that. She'd pulled off the money suit, cleaned up and left. Not before noticing, however, that there was now at least another two grand plastered on the wall.

She was grateful for the chance to escape—the boss had been disgustingly potent tonight. *How come,* she wondered, *how come nice normal guys can't get it up more than once or twice at a time, and yet this man can go all night if I'm wearing that damn suit of his?*

She'd made the best of it though, reaching another three orgasms herself. Two while he fucked her pussy, and one more while she blew him. *Maybe I'm as messed-up as he is—I always get off too.*

While Mr. Rich was replacing the money suit in the safe, Ash had again noticed the second suit.

"What's that, Richie?" (He didn't mind her showing familiarity after they'd just had sex.) "Another money suit?"

"Yeah, I'm thinking of finding another girl to make it with you." His eyes turned inquisitive. "You live with a friend, don't you? What's her name: Raye?"

Ash nodded.

"How 'bout her? She like girl-on-girl action?"

"No," Ash said quickly, shaking her head. "She's straighter than you."

"And you?"

She shrugged. "You know me, Richie. I'm always game. Anything you want, I want."

His middle-aged face creased into a cool smile. "You're the kind of woman I like, Ash—too bad I'm not into getting married again." He sighed. "Too bad also about your friend. But I don't wanna force anyone on you."

"You could get me a call girl."

He shook his head. "No. I need a real lesbian, not a financial one. I don't just want to watch my money make love to itself, I want to see it *enjoy* making love to itself." He nodded to the door. "Now git, darling. Keep it in mind though—you meet a girl you'd like to ball and who feels the same about you, call me. Any hour, day or night."

***

Ash exited the lobby, descending steps past three robot guards.

The robogoons waved. "Night, Ms. Status."

"Would you like us to call you a taxi?"

She waved back. "No, don't bother. I feel like walking."

"You could get mugged, Ms. Status."

Ash laughed. "You're kidding, right? I'm the boss's woman; who'd be so suicidal as to mess with me?" She tapped her thigh. "Besides, it's just two blocks and I've got my gun."

The robo-gangsters laughed like grating metal. Ash walked on.

A few steps later she heard the screech of tires behind her followed by a minor commotion and spun around.

Mr. Rich's daughter Money was alighting from a black stretch limo. The beautiful redhead—her see-through plastic dress clearly revealing the body beneath it as being tattooed all over with dollar-bill signs—looked once dismissively in Ash's direction, then walked up the steps into the 5550 building.

What a family of freaks, Ash thought, turning to continue her walk. *It's a wonder her father doesn't screw her instead of me.*

Ash turned at the second corner she reached. She looked around to ensure no one was watching, then unzipped her left bicep and took out a two-inch-long model of a car. The model had a little tube like a drinking straw set into its hood. Ash placed the straw between her lips and blew a long breath into the tiny car. Then she threw it into the road.

The model car expanded to full size in fifteen seconds.

Ash climbed into the inflated car—a black Corvette Stingray C7 with the sunroof down—and drove off.

Driving, she tuned the radio to an alternative music station. As was the norm nowadays, the music playing was Femina, this time her latest hit: *Powerful.*

Ash relaxed into the song. After the relentless pounding her sex had just endured, and feeling helpless in the money suit, it was nice to listen to something empowering:

"My pussy is the best that you'll ever get,
Don't deny it, honey—it's your favorite pet.
Miles better than your hand on your cock, I bet.
Tasty like sushi, slippery when wet,
This silken squishy feeling that you'll never forget.
You want my sweet loving, honey? Get your ass in bed.
Now squeeze me and touch me with delight.
Well, you know how this slit feels, right?
Boy, I'm not virgin-tight,
But a loose woman is what you need tonight.

My vagina is fire burning up your woody,
It's the Hell you can't escape,
Inferno torturing your body.
You're chained to my pleasure,
My pussy's bound you in fetters,
And it don't really matter,
What measure I give ya.
Now, come and be good, come and be bad,
Just moan for me like it's the best come you've ever had.
Like I'm the last orgasm you'll ever have.

My pussy is powerful,
My pussy is powerful.

My pussy is the cat, you're the mouse in this house,
Play with yourself only when I'm out of town,
'Cos what I say goes when I'm around.
This isn't a debate, you've just been enslaved,
Now get down on your knees and lets misbehave.

29

My pussy wants to eat, it needs a little meat,
Feed it to me slow, do it like I please,
Now take it out and lick me so I'm nice and clean,
Okay, I'm only kidding, slide your bone back in,
And I'll bark like a dog while you pump come in,
And gasp and moan like you're my favorite sin,
No, don't pull out, when will you ever learn?
Rest on me awhile, then we'll start again.

My pussy is powerful,
My pussy is powerful.

CHAPTER 6

1:15 a.m.

"He *what?*"

"Yep. Mr. Moneybags suggested we both perform for him."

"He's an asshole."

Ash laughed. "Never forget the key word. *Rich*. He's a *rich* asshole who shits money."

Raye scowled. "Don't trivialize this. I don't understand how you can sleep with him and enjoy it."

"Would you prefer I say no? I'd be in a cement overcoat before evening. If he asked *you* to be his mistress, would you dare refuse?" She shrugged. "Maybe you would. With your hair, you're close to being Superwoman."

"You know what I mean. It's demeaning."

(For a moment Ash was tempted to get annoyed. This was the difference between she and Raye. Raye believed a woman's body was a holy temple, and male hands defiled it. Ash was more pragmatic. In addition to liking men more than women, all she asked was that her consent be sought before the use of her body by her lovers. Even when, as with Mr. Rich, it was pseudo-consent.)

"It's demeaning, the way he uses you," Raye repeated. (She and Ash had been together a year now, since their eyes locked while each buying shoes in Skyscraper Heels on West Belmont Avenue.)

"More so than being broke?" She looked Raye steady in the eye. "Oh no, girl, we've both already been down that route. Now look: we're not doing too badly here; let's not screw this up. Okay, so we don't have a lot

31

of money, but we've this cool pad, and we've got each other. Once Mr. Rich is tired of me we'll move on. And he's very generous to his exes, you *know* that. Besides, we've been together half a year now—our relationship's definitely close to its expiry date."

"Whatever. I still hate sharing you with that old—"

"What's *really* bothering you, darling?"

"This." Raye pointed to the faint dark circle still decorating the coffee table and told her about the evaporated necklace.

Ash listened in silence, her eyes cold. "Why didn't you tell me earlier?"

"You were already over at Moneybags' when Bug called me. Besides I thought it would be a lovely surprise."

Ash hugged Raye. "It *would* have been lovely." Her voice saddened. "And now we're back to square one."

"Yeah. Broker than the rats in that abandoned church down the street."

The pair kissed. Ash pushed Raye through the bedroom door. "I need you to eat my pussy."

Raye shook her head. "Uh, uh, darling. Not after Moneybags has just come in it."

Ash rolled her eyes. "I've told you he never comes in me. Only on hundred dollar bills which he then plasters on the wall."

"And he only ever does you when you're wearing a suit sewn from money?"

"Can't get it up otherwise."

"He's sick."

"Eccentric."

"Huh?"

"Sick rich people are called eccentrics."

While Raye mused over the difference, Ash stripped naked, lay back in bed and spread her legs. She reached her hands out to Raye.

"Please eat me, darling. I need some orgasms for pain relief. Mr. Rich's dick felt like it was made of stone tonight."

"That bad?"

"You've no idea. He'd still be slamming it to me if he didn't have to discipline some drug dealer."

Raye relented. She stripped naked and climbed into bed with Ash.

CHAPTER 7

1.20 a.m.

Like she knew Ash liked, Raye wove her hair into a multitude of arms and hands. Flowing like muddy water around her head, her dark locks twisted and twirled into limbs and fingers.

The hair-hands spread Ash's legs wide, held her motionless in place on the bed while Raye made love to her. They caressed her thighs, gently kneaded her sides, and rubbed and squeezed her breasts.

Ash squirmed and moaned, delirious with pleasure.

Raye tongued Ash's cunt. The sex opening was dark with bruising. She winced at a deep tear in the soft flesh: *Mr. Rich is a real rough son-of-a-bitch. And you, Ash honey, do you get off on the pain?* Raye hated seeing Ash like this, hurt, and yet somehow enjoying the hurt, like a latent masochist.

She licked the tender vagina to soothe it, loved it with her mouth, worked on giving her girlfriend as much pleasure as possible with her tongue. Ash, held spread-eagled and caressed by soft brown hair-fingers, trembled with delight.

"Oh, yesss!"

Raye couldn't understand how Ash needed sex so much. For herself, twice a week was fine, once even. Sometimes, she forgot about physical lovemaking altogether, was content to just lie in her lover's arms, enjoying their emotional connection. But Ash? *Hell no. All the time's too little for my honey here.*

Raye was suddenly pissed-off. Images of a thousand faceless men fucking Ash reared up before her. One after the other, ad infinitum.

Specters of all the men who'd been between Ash's legs, both before and since they'd met.

Oh, no, honey—

She slid two fingers up the moist vagina—

It ain't just Mr. Rich you're screwing on your own time.

Lips puckered tight around Ash's clitoris, Raye's suddenly mind filled with hatred, like God had opened up her head and was spooning in abhorrence. Oh, how she'd love to smash all those men to bits.

"Raye? Raye?"

Ash's voice was a strangled gasp.

Raye licked over the swollen clitoris, fingered Ash's cunt faster. *Yes, come for me baby.*

"Raye!"

Raye looked up from Ash's vagina. *Oh no!* Ash's face was purple, her tongue sticking out of her mouth.

Raye was horrified. In her rage, she'd unconsciously begun throttling Ash. Two hair-fists were locked around Ash's throat and squeezing hard.

Despite her struggles to breathe, however, a lustful glimmer filled Ash's eyes. She grinned down at Raye. Raye saw Ash's nipples were massively engorged—pink erections atop her milk-white breasts.

Raye gaped. *She thinks I'm strangling her as part of lovemaking. The dumb slut is about to come.*

Her own pleasant sexual buzz instantly died.

"Oh, Rachel, I love you."

Another wave of rage washed over Raye. She felt fiercer than a wounded lioness. She really felt like killing Ash for good, ending this nonsense once and for all.

The moment passed. Instead of murdering Ash, Raye loosened the grip of the hair-fingers ringing her neck. While Ash sucked in gasps of air, Raye resumed eating her.

Fifteen seconds later, Ash gave a loud strangled sigh. She stiffened; her vagina flooded with fresh moisture. She gasped, pumping her hips up, grinding her vagina deliciously against Raye's mouth, while Raye's hair kept her spread open on the bed.

Raye tongued Ash fiercely—like she could pleasure her to death—channeling her anger into the swollen clitoris.

She fucked Ash. She throttled Ash with her hair, till Ash went limp and silent.

Too silent. Raye hurriedly looked up again from Ash's vagina. She was horrified: *Have I killed her for real?*

But no; Ash was smiling down at her. Raye winced at the bruises around her neck. She winced deeper at the unaffected look of love on Ash's face.

She really doesn't suspect how angry I am with her?

Ash reached down her hands to Raye. "Hold me, darling. No one does me like you do."

Still disbelieving, Raye retracted her hair and slid up Ash's soft welcoming body.

CHAPTER 8

2 a.m.

"Something stinks, if you ask me," Ash said. "You called Bug yet?"

"Its number's dead," Raye replied sullenly. She was still angry.

Ash sat bolt upright in bed. "Shit!"

Raye looked up at her in alarm. "What?"

"Didn't it occur to you that Bug might be in danger too?"

"How d'you mean?"

"Someone might have tapped its apartment. That's how they knew you were going over to Logan Square. They set you up, then went after Bug."

Raye thought for a second, then sprang out of bed and began dressing. "You're right. We need to get over to Hyde Park now!" She regarded Ash worriedly. "You've got a fast ride downstairs, right? Not one of your pink showboats again?"

Ash pulled on a white tube top over her cutoff jeans, reached for her boots. "Souped-up Corvette Stingray. Fast like sci-fi transport. Still got ten hours usage left."

They rushed for the elevator.

CHAPTER 9

2.05 a.m.

The trip from East 46th Street to Hyde Park took three minutes. Down South Vincennes Avenue, onto East 50th . . .

Ash drove like she was at a NASCAR race, burning through two red lights.

"Cool it!" Raye snapped. "If the cops stop us, Bug is done for."

"Every second counts."

"It may already be dead."

"Meet my girlfriend the optimist."

"Shut up and drive, you."

Before Ash could retort, Raye flipped on the radio. Femina's husky voice floated out into the night.

"Ain't there anyone else on the playlists nowadays?"

Ash swung the Corvette in a tight curve round a corner. "I thought you approved of her."

The Chicago night streamed by them, a collage of lights and concrete. Moonlight reached them like strobe-lighting, sliced into shadow caverns by the high-rises they sped past. Sandwich strips of night and light. They rolled past a fallen-over plastic sculpture of a Big Mac burger.

Their hair flowed behind them in slipstream.

"I do approve of Femina. I really do. But I like hearing male singers too. Okay, so I don't want to bed them, but some guys have incredibly sexy voices." She wiggled against the leather seat. "Get's me so hot under the hood, you know?"

37

Ash nodded. "I like dick occasionally. But too much gags me."

Raye grimaced. "Slave."

"Dick isn't bad. It's the dicks they're attached to that's the problem." She spun the car around another corner. "We have an open relationship— you're welcome to some penis too. Actually, as much as you like; the trick is not to choke on it."

Lips pressed grimly together, Raye spat over the side of the car. This 'open relationship' thing was beginning to really grate on her nerves. Maybe she *should* have killed Ash back there. *I still can. No!* She forced her mind off her romantic dilemma and onto the music, Femina chanting *Pussy Anarchist*:

"I'm a pussy anarchist,
A live pussy anarchist,
Man, I'm really, really, pissed,
And you'll have to live with it,
Just fucking deal with it.

I love you, fucking love you,
Love fucking you too,
Even more than I fucking love you.
And yet, I don't give a shit,
I don't care one bit!
But don't you dare leave me,
If you ever leave me,
I stalk you till eternity,
You'll never, ever, be free!

I'm a pussy anarchist,
A horny pussy anarchist.
C'mon, give me a wet sexy kiss,
Lower, lower, lower, *lower,*
Now you're down with it.
Hit it! Yeah, hit it!
Lick my dripping slit,
French tongue action between my pussy lips.
Okay, stop—I need to go shit.
What? I can't just run off,
Now I've got you so hot?
Oh, that *isn't* your cellphone in your briefs?
Ooh, honey, it looks so swollen—so big!
What have you been feeding it?
Okay, so what do you want *me* to do about it?
Kiss it? Lick it ? Suck it?

Are you friggin' serious? *Worship it?*
I'm laughing over this,
Why are you looking pissed?
Hey! Hey! What fucking right do you have to look pissed?
This is my hot body, my ass, my tits,
I can do whatever the fuck I like with it.
That includes—refuse you sex!
Dude, do I look like a glory hole?
Don't give me that lost-sheep look, it's *your* meat pole,
Okay, I'm just joking,
You've really got my pussy smoking,
Hungry, hoping for a passionate poking.
Hang on though,
I really do need to go poop,
But I'll be back out in a bit,
To take care of us both.

Living with me,
Is your destiny,
You can't escape your karma, so . . .
Just adapt, with minimum strife.
Evolve, slot neatly into my stress-filled life.
You know the sex is worth paying the price.

I hate you, hate you, hate you,
I love you, love you, love you,
I hate you if you love me,
Love you if you hate me,
It's not my fault I'm confused,
I'm emotionally abused,
Gender abused,
Generationally misused,
Sexually misused.
Everyone keeps telling me what to do.
We live in an age of shifting truths.
Hey, people! Fucking just make up your minds,
(On what's right and wrong,
And the politically-correct way to be sexually inclined.)
Sometimes I just wish I was blind,
Dumb and deaf too,
So I didn't have to listen to you.
Stop fucking my brain,
There is no need to explain,

Again and again and again.
I get it!
I fucking got it even before high school,
(When bras and tampons became the golden rule.)
Who I am, who I'm not,
Who and what's cool, and who not to screw!
Fuckin' leave me alone to do whatever the fuck I want to do!
And hey! Yes you—the man I love! Totally fuck you too!

I'm a pussy anarchist,
A live wire pussy anarchist.
(Your personal hyperactive romanticist.)
I totally love you, but . . .
Man, I'm really, really, pissed,
And you'll have to live with it,
Just fucking deal with it.

My relationship with you,
Is perpetually in shambles,
You say living with me,
Is like sleeping on a bed of brambles.
Sure, I know I'm a rose with thorns,
But you *love* the way I fuck like hardcore porn,
Take the good with the bad, my lad,
Hands down, I'm the best woman you've ever had.
And don't you dare,
Take your cute ass off anywhere;
You fucking remain here,
And show me that you care.

What? I've got issues?
So? I know I got issues!
You are my fucking issue!
Fucking pass me a tissue!
(Hey! Now that you've made me cry,
You can at least wipe the tears from my eyes!)
Bad idea, that—letting you closer,
I can already feel your boner.

Oh, now you want to fuck me to sleep?
Fuck me to sleep?
Sex will relax me!?
It's medically prescribed stress relief?

I don't believe this shit!
Can't I just bare my tits,
Walk nude at home in peace?
Without you feeling obliged to feed me dick!?
Is this what you call a relationship?

Okay, Let's start again,
I'm having a bad day,
A really bad day,
What'd you just say?
I *always* have a bad day!?
Well, screw you, Jose!
Right now I feel like blowing it all away,
The whole hypocritical society,
Plus you and me.
You think I'm joking? Just watch and see!
I'm a time bomb, been ticking since puberty.
Hell hath no fury like angry pussy!
I've got more overkill than World War III!
What was that again?
'Not today?'
Hey, hey, hey, you—stay away from me,
Your pants are bulging,
I know what that means!
(With that lewd sneaky grin.)
Okay, but you'll make dinner,
If I give in.

Strong men don't run away,
They stay with you till their dying day,
Until their fatal coronary.
They let you kill them with passion,
Murder them with your indecision about fashion:
What not to wear,
And why you love and hate the latest trends in hair,
And . . . (Sing the fucking chorus with me!)

I'm a pussy anarchist,
A live wire pussy anarchist,
Man, I'm really, really, pissed,
And you'll have to live with it,
Just fucking deal with it.

I want to blow the world up and start all over again,
Turn men into women,
Women into men,
But I'm scared everything will just remain the same.
Hey, darling—I thought you could sense my pain.
You do? So how come you've a hard-on again?
Shit! Men! All you've ever got is sex on the brain.
Hey! Keep that fucking thing away from me!
Let me go!
NO! *I DO NOT* WANT TO COME AGAIN!!!

I'm a pussy anarchist,
Pussy anarchist,
A pussy anarchist,
I ain't taking no more shit!
I ain't taking no more shit!

"She does jerk off a lot," Ash said as the song faded.
"At least she's not a pussyfist like you," Raye retorted.
"Huh? What's a pussyfist?"

"A pussy-pacifist. Best definition?—You. A woman unable to resist even the most demeaning male kiss, eternally turning on every penis, wanting to be deeply pricked by it."

Ash sniggered to hide her displeasure at the unflattering appraisal. "Wow, darling, you're waxing poetic now?"

She concentrated on driving.

CHAPTER 10

2:08 a.m.

Bug lived in a old apartment block on South Woodlawn Ave. A squat ugly mass of concrete with a lot of broken windows and few lights. On one side of the building was a basketball court, on the other a gutted warehouse.

All the apartment's human residents had long left. Bug lived there with the occasional human girlfriend amidst its computers and geek paraphernalia.

Ash cut the Corvette's lights four blocks from Bug's building. Now the black convertible rolled slowly, an almost imperceptible chunk of the night.

"It looks more like an anthill each time I see it," Ash said, nodding toward the apartment block. "Only an insect would consider that thing home."

"Ssssh!" Raye hissed. "Pull over!"

Ash did, then looked at her. "What's up?"

She pointed up the road, at the front entrance. "You were right, the goon squad's here."

Ash squinted along Raye's fingers. Her eyes first caught the moonlight glinting off metal faces and weapons, then the goons' suited outlines. "Three outside." She patted her thigh. "We take 'em on?"

"Nah, there's bound to be loads more robos inside. We'll go round the back. The good thing is: if they're still here, Bug is most likely still alive."

"And being tortured." Ash had a sudden horrible image of a robogoon—Bugsy Malone or that psycho dwarf Baby Face Nelson—

sawing off the insect's legs while Bug screamed like a baby and spurted yellow goop from its wounds.

"We're wasting time. Let's go."

***

They snuck around to the back of Bug's super-dilapidated housing. There, Raye wove her hair into a ladder. They climbed it to a lit, open fourth floor window.

Ash couldn't resist a quip as they rose: "Oh, I love you, Rapunzel. Oh, Rapunzel, will you marry me?"

Raye grit her teeth, then she bit back her anger. "Keep quiet, silly. You'll give us away."

They reached the window. Stood there on her hair peering in.

Bug wasn't in any danger. The insect lay on the floor, its cyber-chip-studded head buried between the thighs of a similarly prostrate woman in a black pantsuit. Her head was totally covered by a black cowl with eye holes cut in it.

Her fly was unzipped—Bug was licking her vagina. Bug's body—six-feet-long and termite-white—twitched convulsively as it lapped the woman's moist sex. Its middle and lower legs kicked in knee-jerk-like reflexes. Its upper limbs trembled as they spread the woman's trousered thighs wide.

"We should have known," Raye said. "Bug is a total sucker for human pussy."

"You mean 'licker,' not 'sucker.' And you need to be more understanding. Not Bug's fault our vaginal secretion has a narcotic effect on its species."

The woman groaned, stroking Bug's head with gloved fingers. She raised her head off the green rug. Green eyes glistened through the holes in her black cowl. "Oh, you do it so well!" she gasped.

Bug pulled its thick flat tongue from her vagina. "You taste superlatively delicious, Miss Black."

"Don't talk!" she gasped. "Lick me!"

"Of course." Bug returned its tongue into her genital crevice.

From their vantage point on the hair-ladder at the window, Raye and Ash watched.

Raye scowled. "Okay, let me get this straight," she whispered. "We both rushed all the way over here to save this dumb insect's life, only to watch it having sex with its new girlfriend?"

"At least we've ringside seats. Personally, I wouldn't mind some of that tongue in me. Looks as large as a cow's."

Miss Black began coming. Loudly.

44

"She *sounds* like a fucking cow," Raye said.

"And *you* sound jealous."

"Jealous? Not me, honey. It offered to do me once. I turned it down."

Ash looked at the quivering black-cowled woman on the ground, her fingers trying to grip the floor in the throes of her orgasm, then looked back at Raye. "It did? *You did*? Why?"

"Why should I?" she whispered back harshly. "It's a mutated insect. Without those chips in its head, it's simply an overgrown cockroach." She shuddered. "Ugh, imagine a roach inside your holy of holies."

Ash gestured at the fucked-out woman. "*She* doesn't seem to mind much. I'd have enjoyed it too."

"Unlike you, girlfriend, I have high standards regarding who uses my vagina." Her eyes moistened slightly. "Only women I love have access to it."

Ash missed the implication, her blue eyes focused in thought. "You weren't tempted at all?"

"Sure I was. But nothing doing."

"Opinions change. You should have taken a rain check."

"I did. A permanent one." She laughed coldly. "It even offered me a bonus if I let it lick me."

Inside the room, Miss Black had stood up. She zippered her fly, then smoothed down her jacket over her large breasts. Once done, she sat in a chair facing the window.

Ash and Raye ducked out of sight.

Bug rolled over, lay on its back at Miss Black's feet. The insect was in a drugged stupor; its body heaved, its antennae and legs waved in the air.

Miss Black nonchalantly used Bug as a footstool, crossing booted feet on its pale segmented underbelly. She reached down a hand and stroked Bug's head with its myriad projecting chips like spark plugs.

"That black cowl of hers definitely makes her look creepy," Ash said. "Like KKK, but with the color reversed."

Raye started reeling in her hair, making the ladder descend. "Let's go."

Ash stopped her with a hand on her arm. "No, wait."

"What now? You want to watch it tongue her anus?"

"They're done. We'll wait till she leaves, then you tell Bug about the fake necklace." She leaned close to Raye. "Then we go back home and I'll give you head to make up for all tonight's bad shit."

Raye's expression softened. She kissed Ash, raising the hair-ladder again as their lips locked.

Ash gasped when they separated, her breathing fast. "Just you wait. I'll lick you better than Bug just did freaky-woman in there."

They waited and watched and listened.

CHAPTER 11

Femina – Trust

Who can I trust?
Just my pussy and my lust.
Oh yeah, I want to get fucked,
But not fucked over, or fucked up,
By my lovers and friends,
Family and employers . . .
Who want to shit in my ice cream.
Anyone who feels it's cool to piss me off.

Who can I trust?
My vagina's never let me down,
I know when it needs a helping hand,
When kitty needs a pat on the back to make me feel pretty as a princess.
I'm just—I trust my lust.

I just wanna fuck you, baby, not fuck you up.
I'll be your lovely cocksucker!
Suck your penis till you spurt,
All over my tits,
While moaning 'Holy shit!'
And pussy will have your second helpings for desert.

I know I should trust in God,

But there's so much disagreement as to what He wants,
So instead I'll just trust my cunt.
Penile insertion as religion leaves too much to be desired,
So I'll aspire for something higher,
No, lower . . . between my legs.
My fingers on my clitoris always tell the truth,
My own body never makes me beg.
(And when I come . . . I feel beautiful,
So damn good,
Like I'm one of those glossy chicks on red carpets,
In Hollywood.)
So I'll trust in myself,
'Cos then I don't need proof.
I'm terrified of trusting you.
I've no idea what you're gonna do,
Once we kiss and you promise to be true.

CHAPTER 12

2:30 a.m.

Bug finally regained its senses. It rolled over onto its legs, then scuttled up onto a sofa beside a stack of computers.

"You have no idea how incredible that was for me," it told the woman in black. "I could lick you for hours—we should transact business more often."

Miss Black laughed. "You're excellent too. I haven't had my pussy eaten that well for quite a while." Her voice altered subtly. "Ah yes, business. I'll remember you next time I've a difficult job to handle. Despite your reputation, I doubted you could so easily secure Kate's bulletproof necklace."

Raye froze on hearing her statement.

Ash tensed also. Not just because of what Miss Black had said, but also because, now that it was devoid of the sheen of passion, she realized Miss Black's voice was artificial. *She's wearing a voice modulator; she's not who she claims to be.* Bug wouldn't likely notice, nor would Raye, but Ash's mind-chip easily detected vocal distortions. Ash mentally recorded a sample of Miss Black's voice and uploaded it to an online records department for unscrambling. *Who the hell is she?*

"It wasn't nearly as difficult as I expected," Bug said. "The main problem was who to set up as the fall guy . . . or in this case more appropriately, fall *girl.*"

"Why bother? It's not like I'm going to be wearing it out in the open like Holly Wood did."

48

Bug stroked its left antennae with a forefoot. "For my protection after you've left with it."

It laughed. "Getting the necklace itself was easy: Infamous porno director Eddie Fiddle, Holly Wood's widower, was the seller. His reputation for being cheap played neatly into my hands—I simply bribed the robogoons watching the necklace. As I'd expected, Eddie was paying them peanuts to guard it, and they know it's worth millions, so—"

"Twenty-four million," Miss Black interrupted. "Too much."

"For something that makes you bulletproof? And I hear it protects from other harms as well."

"But twenty-four mil—?"

"Won't buy you a spare life."

Miss Black 'hmmphed' under her black hood. "And you also insisted on eating my pussy too."

"We both enjoyed that. And without reservation, I assure you you've one of the sweetest vaginas I've ever tasted."

Bug reared up and made an expansive gesture with its front legs, squirting a lemon scent into the air. "My real profit is twenty million. The extra four million was for the guards. Besides, I don't keep all my share either. About half goes for protection money, both to the mob and the cops. The fences' association also takes a cut. Now back to *how*. I gave the robots the fake necklace, they looped the CCTV camera feed for five minutes . . ."

Outside, hearing this, Raye gasped. "The son-of-a-bug assured me there were no cameras!" she whispered to Ash.

Ash squeezed her hand. "Keep listening." She felt Raye trembling with anger. *Oh no, Bug, now you've gone and done it.*

". . . Made the switch, and sent the real necklace over to me. Then, when my fall girl—a petty thief named Rachel Risk, tough for sure, but not much in the way of smarts—arrived an hour later to steal the fake necklace, they were to rough her up good, but let her escape with it . . . along with a few bullet holes, but nothing immediately fatal. CCTV evidence, blood, DNA, hair traces . . . everything would implicate her. And the necklace itself—"

"I don't like it," Miss Black interrupted, her posture suddenly tense. "Too simplistic. Investigators will soon realize the necklace is fake."

"They won't," Bug said emphatically. "It's set to self-destruct exactly an hour after human hands touch it. It'll evaporate—no one will believe she doesn't have it."

"She'll point them toward you."

"And I'll say she's lying." Bug laughed. "Push comes to shove, I'll simply claim I found it somewhere. Don't you worry your delicious vagina, Miss Black, I've got this all figured out. Besides, it's only a concern if she lives long enough to blabbermouth." The giant white insect laughed louder.

"None of this need bother you, madam. You forget that I don't even know who you really are."

"Hearing how you worked the robbery, that's a major relief." Miss Black got to her feet. "I'd best be leaving now. If this fall girl of yours—Rachel?—gets caught, I don't want to have to explain to anyone what I'm doing here."

"Not so fast," Raye said, shaking off Ash's restraining hands and showing herself in the window. "You don't leave till I get paid my million bucks."

The hooded woman looked at the woman framed in the window, then turned to Bug. "Who's this?"

"The aforementioned Rachel Risk. A dumb broad having a bad hair night."

Bug grabbed a semiautomatic pistol off the floor, then cackled at Raye, "Couldn't you just take a simple hint and die?"

Bug began firing.

CHAPTER 13

2:35 a.m.

Raye reacted instinctively. Immediately Bug grabbed the gun, her hair swept up from the ground, forming a shield between her and the bullets.

The slugs dented the wall of hair like nails being hammered into it. The force of their impact knocked Raye back, away from the window. The hair ladder, now reduced to a single immense stilt, swayed to and fro while she fought to get her balance back.

"You can't escape me!" Bug yelled. "Have some more, freak!"

More bullets pattered the wall of hair separating them. Anger surged through Raye.

"Raye! Help!"

Oops, I forgot Ash. She looked down. Ash had fallen when Raye dissolved half the ladder. She was now a floor down, her arms and legs wrapped tight around the brown pole to keep her from sliding lower.

"Sorry, honey." Raye wove a hair-seat for Ash, then pulled her back up. Gunfire still slammed against the hair-shield, but Raye had now anchored herself to the window above.

"We should get out of here," Ash said.

Raye shook her head fiercely. "Oh, no. Bug both set me up and now is trying to kill me? Time for some heavy payback."

"I'm not protected like you are."

"They didn't see you. Bug doesn't know you're here. Just keep out of sight."

"I've got my gun on me." A message alert beeped in Ash's head: *Upload analysis and voice-matching result.* "Check you later," she muttered, returning her attention to Raye.

"I thought you were scared of dying," Raye said.

Ash unzipped her thigh, pulled out her Beretta. "Yeah, I am. But I'll die with you, you know that."

Raye took time out from her anger. She blew Ash a kiss. "That's my babe."

Bullets pattered hard and hot on the hair-shield. The smell of burning came from it now. Behind it, Bug was laughing. "Hey, Raye, we can do this all night long! I got guns and ammo to spare!"

Raye scowled at Ash. "I am so going to *kill* that cockroach turd."

"Okay, but watch out for the goons. This noise definitely has them on their way up now."

***

Bug, intent on firing at the brown obstruction in the window, was shocked when the wall to its right exploded inward in a shower of bricks. Through the dust and debris, Bug gaped at the HUGE fist that had punched through the wall. The brown hand wavered in space, then withdrew.

Bug pumped gunfire through the new hole. Then it leapt back as another punch demolished the rest of the wall on that side of the window. This time, one of the flying bricks scraped Bug's back, furrowing a wet groove through the white chitin.

Nerves flaming with pain, alarm on its face, the insect scuttled over to Miss Black.

The cowled woman was already out of her chair, speaking into her cellphone. "Get your metal butts up here, Dillinger, we've got a situation."

"We're on our way," a robot voice replied.

"We need to leave here!" Bug said.

"Don't sweat it. My goons are on their way up."

Bug yelped as the wall to their left also suddenly disintegrated into chunks flying everywhere. It and Miss Black instinctively rushed the other way, toward the rear of the room, by the larger hole in the wall.

***

Ash behind her, Raye stepped through the new, smaller, hole. She'd mummified herself in her hair, wrapping her entire body in a brown cocoon with eye and mouth holes. She'd also run two locks down the length of her

52

arms, ending these in the huge hands with which she'd demolished the wall. This way, moving the hair-hands felt like they were her natural ones.

Raye saw Bug looking desperately out of the massive hole beside it.

Raye smirked. "No escape there, Bug. Except you jump. Then . . . Splat! Either way, you're dead."

"Let's not be too hasty now," Bug said, its abdomen heaving spastically with rapid worried breaths. "I just know we can reach some kind of agreement."

Raye cocked a fist. "You should have thought of that earlier, insect."

Behind Ash and Raye, a loud pounding came from the outside door.

"Be reasonable," Miss Black said in an even voice. "My robogoons are outside. There's no way you can get away. If you leave now . . . Ash? Ashley Status? What are *you* doing here?"

Ash looked back at Miss Black in confusion. "You know me?"

"Yes. What are you doing here?"

"Dammit, Ash," Raye said in irritation. "Not *another one* of your endless sexual entrées."

"But I honestly don't know her!"

Inside Ash's head, a reminder beep sounded. *Upload analysis and voice-matching result.* She ignored it again.

The door behind them burst open. Three robogoons spilled into the room.

Dillinger, in a white suit and hat, Tommy gun at the ready, yelled: "Okay, everyone, stop whatever the hell it is you're doing!"

Bug, however, hadn't seen them enter. It had taken the distraction of Miss Black's recognizing Ash and their conversation to grab an RPG-7 grenade launcher from behind a chair.

It trained the weapon on Raye and fired.

Ash knocked Raye out of the way.

Dillinger caught sight of the streaking projectile just in time and leapt aside, toppling through the hole in the wall and just managing to keep from falling by a single dangling handhold. The massive warhead smashed into the robogoon behind him, knocking the machine out into the corridor where he exploded into bits. Shrapnel from the explosion blew back into the room, knocking the third robot to the floor.

The felled goon attempted to get up. Then his back exploded. He fell forward again and lay still, his rear a burning mess of sparking wires.

Ash rushed over to Dillinger. The robot, natty white hat blown off his head, was attempting to climb back into the room. She put her gun to his bronze temple, pulled the trigger twice. Dillinger lost his grip, fell backward out of sight. A loud clang announced his hitting the ground four stories below.

Bug was scrambling to load another warhead into the RPG-7. Raye grabbed the insect around the middle in her right hair-hand. She lifted it off the floor, shook it hard so it dropped the weapon.

"Ouch, put me down!"

Raye lowered it, but kept the massive brown fingers wrapped around its body. The insect shook with fright, its mouth agape with terror.

Miss Black, standing to Bug's right beside the hole in the wall, grabbed up its abandoned gun and fired at Ash. Ash ducked behind Raye. Miss Black swung the gun towards Raye. Her green eyes widened in their black framing when the bullets ricocheted off Raye's protective coating of hair.

The gun clicked empty.

Holding Bug firmly in her right hair-fist, Raye grabbed Miss Black in her left. With the way her hair was woven down over her hands, she simply reached out and picked her up also.

She held insect and woman up side by side. "Now, you two—"

"Let me go or you'll regret it!" Miss Black shrieked.

"Okay, if you insist." Raye flung her out of the hole in the wall.

Ash watched Miss Black fly through the air in a smooth arc, streaking across the street to smash into a house on the opposite side, then fall limply to the ground, where she lay with her neck at an odd angle. Ash looked down. Dillinger also lay motionless on the ground.

"Goon and employer both out of the game," she told Raye.

In a peeling away like the melting of cobwebs touched by fire, Raye unwove her hair off her face and body, till only the HUGE right fist that gripped Bug remained of the brown shield. She scowled at the man-sized insect. "Guess this leaves just you and us."

"Please!" Bug begged. It was visibly sweating now, fluid beading on its face, literally stinking with fear.

Raye squeezed it till she felt its carapace just short of cracking. Bug winced with the pain. "Please—I'll burst!"

"Okay," Raye said coldly, "I'll let you pay for your miserable life. Where's the money?"

"I don't have it!"

"Don't lie to me! Miss Black said she'd paid you." She squeezed harder. Bug's shell creaked like opening a gothic mansion door in a horror movie.

"Ouch! Please! She paid me in stock!"

Ash gaped at Bug. "In stock!?"

Bug nodded emphatically, both its antenna wobbling furiously. "She offered me shares in a Vegas casino as payment. I accepted." It cringed at the furious look on Raye's face. "It's true! It's true!"

"I thought you said you don't know who she really is!"

54

"I don't. Her brokers and mine handled the transaction. Total secrecy was part of our agreement. If I even *tried* to discover who she was, the deal was off." Bug looked pleadingly at Raye. "I'm sorry, honest."

Once more a beep went off in Ash's head. *Upload analysis and voice-matching result.* Ash was tired of hearing the damn thing. *Download and play,* she angrily thought back at it.

***

Raye laughed coldly. "You know, Bug, you should really just have stuck to cunnilingus. Double-crossing's a fatal sport."

Bug cringed before her merciless eyes. "No, PLEASE. I'll make it up to—"

"Yeah. By eating my pussy from the afterlife. Hope your tongue's long enough."

She squashed Bug, tightening her hair-fist slowly so its shell cracked in excruciating stages, with Bug's innards squirting through the grip of massive brown fingers and falling as a yellow mess onto the green rug.

"Nooooooo!"

Bug screamed, then it moaned softly. Then its head popped off its neck and rolled away across the floor.

Raye opened her hand. The insect's remains—a pulped white obelisk with deep finger indents—stood upright for a moment, then toppled over into the mess on the rug.

Raye retracted her hair back to her head, stinky bug pulp falling off her locks as they shortened.

She smirked once at Bug's remains, then turned to Ash.

"Ash?"

Ash didn't reply her. She was staring out the smaller hole in the wall.

Raye joined her. The morning moon floated above the end of the street, big and round, setting off objects with stark, brutal clarity. "Ash?"

"We're in a trailer-load of trouble," Ash said, pointing at the motionless black-clad and hooded figure lying on a shattered concrete walkway across the street. "Miss Black *really* wasn't her real name."

Raye looked at her, not understanding. "What are you talking about?"

"Girlfriend, you just killed Money Rich."

Raye looked at her in horror. "Mr. Rich's daughter?"

"One and the same. No wonder she recognized me. I uploaded a voice-match sample and it came back positive."

Raye studied the motionless prone figure. "You sure she's dead?"

"Does she look alive to you?"

A clanking of metal alerted them to motion below them.

They looked down. Dillinger was pulling himself up off the floor.

"Behold the one that got away," Ash said.

The robogoon got to his feet. He shook himself off, then looked up at the window.

"You two broads are going to pay for this!" he yelled up at them, then re-entered the building. He was now limping badly.

"Let's go," Ash said.

"We should put him out of his misery."

"He's certain to call for backup before coming upstairs. And you know where backup's coming from, right? Daddy's gonna be mighty pissed that his little girl's dead."

Raye looked at Ash. "We're fucked."

Ash nodded. "Well said, darling. Best we leave town before we're gangbanged."

"I hate your way with words. Couldn't you put it better?"

"Honey, let's just go."

Raye took one last look at Bug's mashed corpse. "Yeah, let's. We'll head to our flat and get our things."

CHAPTER 14

2:45 a.m.

They made it safely back to their car and drove off up South Woodlawn. Then, at the East 51st Street intersection, Ash pulled over to the side of the road and killed the engine.

"Why'd you stop?"

"Try to guess. A hint—it's not good news."

"Huh? C'mon, I'm not in the mood for suspense."

"Okay. We go back to our flat, we'll likely be walking into a trap. Remember Bug set you up? There's likely robogoons awaiting us already 'cos of the necklace."

Raye slapped her head with a palm. "Oh, damn!"

"My vagina hurts just *imagining* how screwed we are."

"Stop saying that. I'm trying not to panic here."

"I'm just pointing out the gravity of our situation."

"So what now? We drive? Keep rolling out of town?"

Ash thought a moment. "We need money."

"We *always* need money. We should be the cast of *Two Broke Girls*."

"No, I'm serious. To escape the mob, we'll need a mountain of loot to buy friends with."

"Where do you think we'll find any at this time of night?"

Ash smiled. "Call this a suicidal gamble; but I know where there's close to a million bucks for the taking."

"I'm listening."

"Mr. Rich's safe."

Raye sagged back in her seat. "Now *you* need to use your brains. We just killed the kingpin's daughter and your suggestion is to go rob him?"

Ash was emphatic. "It isn't that complicated. Remember how I told you that Mr. Rich and I were interrupted during sex because of some Montana yokel named Dougie?"

"Go on. Convince me you're not mad."

"Well, the money to pay Dougie for the drugs is still in the safe in Mr. Rich's bedroom. I saw it. Stacks of lovely cash, more that enough to set us up. I know Mr. Rich. He'll have gone to bed. Even when the goons bring Dougie in, despite his sending me home for that reason, he'll tell them to keep him on ice till morning."

"Not if he knows Money's dead. You know how men behave when shit concerns their daughters. He'll be awake and looking for her killers."

Ash looked across the cold night street before replying. "That's the gamble of it: he might not know."

"Make sense."

"That Dillinger robot took a major knock to the brains when he hit the ground. He also looked up at *us*, not around the neighborhood. He'd have looked around if he'd seen Money Rich flying through the air. So we know he didn't. Also, *we* only saw Money's body when we looked from Bug's window; from the ground she's hidden by some overgrown hedges. Remember too, the robot didn't see us leave—we went out the window after he reentered the house to climb the stairs. So, as far as he knows, we're currently still holding Money and Bug captive in the room. He has two choices: Call in any more goons he has out front, or come in himself, gun blazing."

"You're saying he might not call Mr. Rich at all?"

Ash nodded. "He's a machine. They aren't called goons for nothing—intelligence ain't their strong point. The Dillinger won't call in until he's reentered the room where we supposedly still are and found Bug's corpse, then he still needs to find Money's body and go back down there and confirm that she's dead. Only then . . . And you saw how badly he was limping from his fall."

"How much time we got?"

"Not much. Twenty minutes . . . twenty-five max. If we get in, pull the battery from Mr. Rich's phone while I sweet-talk his dick to erection."

Raye nodded. "Okay, that makes sense. You're still missing something though."

"What?"

"Why the hell would Mr. Rich want to see you at three in the morning? He's already screwed you tonight."

Ash grinned. "That's the beauty of it. Remember how I told you he's looking for a girl to fuck me? How he wants to watch his money love itself? And how he suggested you?"

Raye's face twisted in horror. She waved her palms at Ash. "Count me out. I'm not putting on a show for your pervy moneybags."

Ash got out her cellphone. "Oh yes you are, babe. It's just to get the safe open. Then we split."

She dialed, put the phone to her ear.

"Hi, Richie baby, it's me, Ash the cash lady . . . Why this late? You said to call you immediately I found a girl . . . ?"

Raye listened to their conversation, a tight angry knot forming in her belly. She couldn't help it. Even as a ruse, hearing her girlfriend mutter endearments to a man pissed her off big-time. She realized, however, that this phone call had one guaranteed positive: If Mr. Rich had heard of his daughter's death, they'd know from this call.

Ash hung up, then hugged Raye tight. "I told you," she gushed. "He said to come right over, that the Dougie business has been resolved. No problem at all. He has no idea that Money's dead."

CHAPTER 15

2:55 a.m.

Ash and Raye stared at each other in confusion.

Mr. Rich—naked beneath a beige bathrobe—stared back, his expression stern as he held out the pair of money suits to them both. "Go on, go on, put them on quickly."

Ash and Raye hadn't considered the possibility of Mr. Rich being so turned on by the thought of watching them have sex that he'd have gotten the money suits out in advance. Behind him, the safe was shut again.

Faking smiles, they took the stitched-dollar suits from him.

"Put them on slowly," he said, undoing the sash of his robe so they saw his straining erection, the turgid blood-engorged cock. His voice was a strangled gasp. (*Wow, he really is up for this,* Ash thought on seeing how hard his penis already was—a first in her experience of him.)

Mr. Rich was trying hard to maintain control of himself despite his excitement. His face was flushed, his eyes betrayed his intense lust. Raye felt them stripping her naked, laying her out and raping her.

Mr. Rich got into bed and watched both women undress. He admired Raye's body—fuller than Ash's, but with smaller breasts and larger nipples. He gave up the comparison. He'd never met two women with exactly the same body. No matter how close the similarity, there were always differences. It was just like with men and their penises, he felt: everyone was different, comparisons were meaningless. The organs functioned just as well once the partners got naked.

Pussy always felt wonderful.

Ash, now naked, giggled at Mr. Rich. "Enjoy our rear view for a bit, Richie darling. My girl Raye is shyer than a mouse." She knew Raye was nervy; she needed to calm her down.

They turned their backs on Mr. Rich, bending over so he could see their vaginas as they pulled the money suits' leggings up their legs.

"We've got to get that safe open," Raye whispered heatedly.

"Let's go through with it, catch him unawares afterwards."

"We don't have time." She looked back. Mr. Rich was stroking himself slowly. She smiled shyly at him and turned back to Ash. "He's looking like he'll want to join in—he's cocked like a gun—and you told me money works like Viagra for him, he never goes down. He'll be humping us both till rush hour."

Ash frowned. "We hold him up, then? Okay, move behind me, block off his view while I get the gun out of my leg."

"You should have kept it in your purse like I said."

"How was I to know . . . ? Look, just cover my ass, willya?"

"Hurry up," Mr. Rich groaned. "You're taking too long."

Ash, busy slipping the Beretta out, giggled. "Sorry, Richie. Girl stuff. I just broke a fingernail. And Raye is insisting on sniffing my pussy first."

She placed the gun between her feet, then quickly rolled the money suit all the way up her body and slipped her hands into its arm holes. She grinned at Raye, who was already similarly dressed.

They zipped each other up, resuming their whispered conversation:

"How does the safe open? Combination? Fingerprints?"

"Eyeprint. Retina scan on that peephole."

"Okay, lets—"

The bedside phone rang.

Ash and Raye looked at each other, fear in their eyes. "They've found Money!" Ash gasped.

The phone rang again.

Ash nodded grimly at Raye. Both women spun round. Mr. Rich, a look of deep irritation on his face, was reaching for the phone.

"Don't answer it," Raye said coldly.

Mr. Rich paused. He looked over at Raye. "Though I can't wait to watch you both, it isn't for my money to dictate my actions." He reached again for the phone.

"She said not to answer it, Richie!"

Mr. Rich let the phone ring on. He turned back to the two dollar-clad women, giving a start when he saw the gun in Ash's hand.

Though his penis remained hard, the expression in his eyes turned cold. Deep lines set in his handsome face. "What the hell is this about?"

"We want the money in the safe," Ash snapped. "Just hand it over and we'll let you live."

Mr. Rich smiled mirthlessly. "A robbery? Are you two nuts? I run this city; where the hell could you escape to?" He shook his head at Ash. "Girl, I gave you credit for more smarts that that."

"So maybe I'm dumb. I'm a blonde, aren't I? Just get the safe open. We'll worry about staying alive."

"That chip in your head is addling your brains. Are you sure you didn't accidentally slot in some Pringles in place of the real thing?"

Ash, aware that the clock was running down, smiled tightly and jerked her pistol toward the safe. The phone stopped ringing and started again. None of them paid it any attention.

"Well, hurry up," Raye growled. "What are you waiting for?"

Mr. Rich laughed. "There's no money in the safe. You've both just screwed yourselves for nothing."

Ash's eyes narrowed. "You're lying! I saw it, earlier."

Mr. Rich continued laughing. "After you left—"

He stopped laughing. Raye had woven her hair into a massive hand and grabbed him around the neck, was choking him. "Stop your bullshit and get the safe open!"

"Help!" Mr. Rich yelled instead, confused by what she was doing with her hair. "Bugsy! Al!"

Ash shook Raye. "Let him go! Just carry him over to the safe and we'll force him to—"

Bang! Bang!

In the confusion, neither woman had noticed Mr. Rich pull a gun from beneath his pillow.

Raye felt a horrible pain in her belly. She looked down. Blood was welling from a pair of punctures on her left side, spilling down over the stitched dollars clothing her. She looked up at Mr. Rich, unsure how the gun had gotten into his hand.

Ash spun to face Mr. Rich. "Why the hell did you shoot her?"

They stood, guns pointed at each other; she worried, he sneering. The uncertainty was now gone from his eyes, replaced by a look of grim satisfaction. The hair-fingers were still wrapped around his neck, but their grip had slackened.

"You should rather worry about yourself, my dear," he told Ash. "Much worse is coming for you." His face turned ugly. "You dare steal from me!?" Specks of spit flew from his lips as he raged. "From me? Are you nuts? First, I'll have Al Capone break all your bones with his baseball bat. Then I'll personally yank out all your teeth with pliers and saw off all your fingers and toes. Then you'll wear this money suit day and night in this bedroom for the rest of your miserable life."

"Oh no, you won't," Raye gasped. "That ain't happening to her even over my dead body, and I ain't dead yet."

Face empurpled with rage, Mr. Rich looked at Raye.

Ash also looked at her. Raye was bleeding a lot. But, added to her worry over her girlfriend's injuries, Ash shuddered at the look in Raye's eyes. It wasn't just pain, it wasn't just anger. There was a scary component of ruthlessness in Raye's facial expression that Ash had never seen before.

Mr. Rich waved his gun at Raye. "No, you're *not* dead yet, are you? Best I fix that."

He fired twice, but Raye had already protected her torso with her hair. The bullets ricocheted harmlessly off her breasts.

Mr. Rich's confusion returned magnified. Astonished, he slowly raised the gun towards her face.

"You don't learn easy, do you?" Raye asked. She quickly tightened her grip around his neck again, then broke it—the snapping vertebrae sounded like a lock clicking open.

Mr. Rich instantly went limp as a rag, his puzzlement following him to the grave.

The phone started ringing again. Simultaneously, loud banging exploded on the bedroom door, followed by a chorus of loud metallic voices.

"Hey, Boss, you okay in there!? Mr. Rich!? Mr. Rich!"

"Shit! The goons heard the noise."

Ash peered worriedly at Raye. "You sure you won't die on me, baby?" she asked in a trembling voice.

Raye nodded, swaying on her feet. "Just get me to a doctor soon." She scowled, blood on her lips. "Okay, we stick to the new plan. Get the safe open. I'll watch the door."

More banging sounded on the bedroom door.

Ash turned to look at the safe. "I don't know why he had to prove difficult. He could just have given us the money."

"He's still going to." Forming a second hair-hand, Raye ripped Mr. Rich's head off his corpse and held it out to Ash. "Stop trembling and take it from me. It's our passport to a new life."

Shaking, Ash took the severed head and walked over to the safe. She walked like she was dreaming, sheathed in her suit of money. The cash-coated wall on her left was a financial mirror reflecting herself. She found it very odd how her entire life had fallen apart in the space of just two hours. *Damn! How the hell did this happen? All we wanted was some cash.*

She was aware of sounds behind her. The endlessly-ringing phone, the bedroom door splintering off its hinges amidst loud gunfire, robot voices, Raye's laughter and the sound of metal bodies fragmenting. More gunfire.

The loudest sound of all was the thumping of her own heart.

She raised Mr. Rich's head to the safe's spyhole. "I'm honestly sorry, Richie," she said, spreading his left eyelids open with trembling fingers. "I didn't intend for this to happen."

There was a soft click, and the safe swung open.
The phone stopped ringing.

CHAPTER 16

3:20 a.m.

Money Rich lowered her cellphone. She looked over at Dillinger. "Dad's not picking up his calls; it keeps going to voicemail."

Dillinger nodded. "Maybe he's asleep, ma'am."

"Dad?" She mused on that. "It's possible. He did have Ashley Status over earlier tonight. Their workouts last hours. But he's normally a light sleeper."

Money and Dillinger were standing in the driveway where she'd fallen, looking across the street, up at Bug's apartment. Moon to their right with daybreak around the corner, they peered into Bug's demolished living room through the two gaping holes in its wall.

"Good thing the necklace protected you from breaking your neck," Dillinger said. "Unlike me." The four-floor fall had damaged the robot a lot. When he moved now, there was a creaking of misaligned gears. He was also dripping oil from his groin—his left trouser leg was soaked with lubricant. His voice was noticeably slurred.

Money fingered the silver/green chain around her neck. "I honestly didn't know it could do that," she said, a thin smile on her beautiful face. She'd abandoned the black hood once Dillinger roused her. She tossed her head around, letting her red hair flutter in the light breeze. "Other than for a headache, I'm fine. Normally I should have broken every bone in my body."

Dillinger gave a metal laugh. "Too bad the insect didn't keep the necklace for itself then. You need to see it—looks like toothpaste with a head."

Money winced at the simile. Her body replayed her recent orgasm with Bug. "A total waste." She shrugged. "Shows it don't pay to be overconfident . . . or careless." She laughed. "That girl—Raye—is good. Find out who she is. I want her for my personal bodyguard."

"Yes, ma'am."

She looked at Dillinger. "Are your boys repairable?"

The robot shrugged. "So, so. Gotti's finished; rocket blew him halfway to Mars. We need to order a replacement. Lucky Luciano's in better shape; a few new resistors and capacitors and he'll be back on his feet again."

Money nodded. "Come on, let's get back home, I need to take a bath. I also have check on Dad. Hope the old guy hasn't had a coronary and kicked the bucket." She grinned. "Though if he has—means I'm in charge, Cash has no stomach for bloodshed."

"You'll make an excellent boss, ma'am," Dillinger said.

She laughed. "Keep licking my ass like that, and I'll make you my chief lieutenant."

"Al Capone won't like that."

"Al can go rewire himself."

They set off for their car.

CHAPTER 17

3:20 a.m.

Ash stared into the safe in bafflement. *What the . . . ?*

"The safe's empty," she dully told Raye over her shoulder.

Raye, once again cocooned in her hair, smashed another robogoon to bits. The others retreated down the corridor. Ash and Raye heard the robots yelling at each other, their voices like cars being crushed.

Raye blocked the doorway off with a weave of hair. "What the hell do you mean, empty?"

Ash turned to face her, holding up a single sheaf of hundreds in each hand. "Two hundred Benjamins; nothing more." She stepped sideways so Raye could see for herself.

Raye looked into the safe. It contained only Mr. Rich's head. She looked back at her girlfriend, her eyes wide with pain and disbelief. "You mean we've just risked . . . destroyed our lives . . . for a mere twenty grand?"

Ash stared back in equal confusion. "*There was* money in the safe earlier. I don't know what—"

An explosion blew the hair shield Raye had draped over the door to bits. Raye ducked out of the way as a projectile streaked into the room and blew out the opposite wall. Like a replay of the scene in Bug's apartment, the bedroom filled with dust.

"Shit, they've got rocket launchers."

Her stomach on fire, she stumbled over to Ash, who was looking around the room. "Maybe it's under the bed; maybe—"

"Snap out of it," Raye gasped. "Lets just get the hell out of here! They're bringing up the heavy artillery. My hair can't defend us against this stuff."

Another rocket streaked into the bedroom. The hole in the opposite wall widened, dust and concrete blew outward over the rooftop helipad.

Ash frowned at Raye. "You want heavy artillery?" Before Raye could deliver her weak retort, Ash turned her back to her. "Unzip me."

Raye unzipped the money suit. "Ash, I'm so weak now I can hardly stand up. We need to leave like before yesterday. You got parachutes in your arms? We jump from here before the goons rush in—"

Ash peeled the suit off down to her waist, then rolled it down her legs. "I got better than parachutes, honey, don't you worry." She unzipped her right thigh, fumbled around inside it.

"Ash, I need a doctor."

"We're going, baby, right now."

"Hey, you two broads! Let Mr. Rich go right now and we won't kill you!"

"We can't!" Raye yelled back. "You lunkheads just killed him with your rockets!"

There was silence while the robots pondered that.

"That's smart thinking" Ash said without looking up. "Now you've totally confused them." She finally pulled a miniature rocket launcher out of her thigh, along with a tiny crate of rockets. She straightened up, placed both to her lips at once and blew into their inflation tubes.

Raye nodded as the metal tube and rocket pack expanded. "Darling, you're a walking bag of tricks."

Ash quickly showed Raye how to load the inflated weapon with its shells, then kissed her wetly on the lips: "Try not to die just yet. Give the goons a taste of their own medicine while I get our transport set up."

Dragging the rocket launcher along, Raye staggered over to the wall by the bedroom door. She leaned against it, breathing in labored gasps. Her hair dangled to her feet in woven bloody ropes she was too weak to control. The money suit was soaked red down into her crotch and thighs. *I look like I just laid down in my menses*, she thought.

Out in the corridor the robot gangsters were deep in muffled metal conversation. Huddled together, not looking her way. Raye glanced once across at Mr. Rich's decapitated body, blood-red without a head, white vertebrate poking from ruptured neck meat. She winced at a stab of pain, then coughed up blood and dust.

She lifted the metal tube onto her shoulder, aimed out the bedroom door.

"Hey, robos! I've a present for you!"

"Hey, broads!" came the replying metallic yell. "We don't believe Mr. Rich is dead! Hand his corpse over as proof!"

"What? Are you machines serious?" Raye fired. Fire streamed out behind her, the rocket streaked forward through the doorway. The corridor exploded into a mass of flame. One explosion set off another, the floor resounded with detonation.

Raye staggered sideways, collapsed on the bed. The pain in her belly was now a blade slicing through her guts. Her eyesight was dimming. She looked over at Ash, gave her the thumbs up. Then her eyes narrowed. "Ash, you slut, why are you fisting yourself in the ass? We need to get out of here!"

Ash looked back in embarrassment. "I'm not fisting myself, our transport's stuck up there."

After giving a resigned shrug, Raye collapsed back on the bed. She looked out through the demolished wall. The full moon was beautiful against the inky black sky. Soft radiant white, as fetching as a bride on her wedding day. A night for lycanthropes, Raye felt. Despite her pain, romantic twinges flittered through her. A warmth spread in her crotch.

She grinned. *Oh, Ash. Be so sexy to die together now with the night so beautiful— like werewolves in love. Holding each other tight, while the world explodes to pieces around us.*

The lust wiped from her eyes. *But if we're gonna die . . .*

She reached for the discarded rocket launcher, began loading another shell into it while stealing glances at Ash, who was now squatted over, straining furiously like she was trying to defecate.

"Come out, you!" Ash growled. She grimaced at Raye. "Damn! I think Mr. Rich jammed my rectal zipper with poop!"

Raye got the rocket launcher loaded again. She managed to get up, stagger four steps—

"Hey, bolt-heads! Here's some more medicine!"

—discharge it down the corridor, then collapse back onto the bed. The corridor resounded again with shrieks and explosions.

Floating on a cushion of dissolving pain and seemingly approaching death, Raye's mind shrilled with the question: *Where the hell did that million bucks Ash saw get to?*

CHAPTER 18

4:00 a.m.

"I can't believe something as little as that almost caused a gang war," Dillinger said as Money Rich drove their blue Mercedes down South Kimbark Avenue.

She chuckled. "See what I mean about you machines not being infallible?"

The robot nodded, his handsome bronze face somehow managing to convey amusement. "The scale was badly calibrated?"

Money nodded. "Not *one* scale; *six* of them—a factory defect. For two months they've been under-weighing everything by twenty percent. Old Reuben found out because the house scale broke down also and he needed to crosscheck the weight of a parcel for his wife. The twins—Josh and Kyle—are down in Vegas at the moment, so he did it himself using one of the coke scales. Scale read five kilos at home, at the post office the parcel weighs in at four.

"Next day, same thing happens again with another of Mrs. Reuben's parcels. The old guy uses another coke scale and gets the same error, so he calls the company. They tell him there's a problem with that batch—some screw that balances it out wears out too early. He checks all the scales they got; all the ones the chemists are using are fucked."

Dillinger nodded, light glinting off his nose and mustache. "But if so many scales were bad, how come we never noticed before now? The weight should differ, right?"

Money pushed a strand of wind-blown carmine hair out of her eyes. "Nah. Remember they cut the coke for us. The bad scales were only affecting what they weighed out, not the final mix. The guys cutting the blow always weighed out the right final amount—it was just too diluted, was all. But our dealers had begun complaining about the cut percentage. Dad didn't first believe them, I mean he trusts Old Reuben, if not the scrooge twins. But then Tony Marconi complained bout his dog."

"His *dog*?"

Money nodded while shifting gears. "Big Tony's our biggest New York buyer. He's got this female Doberman called Bitch. Used to be a police sniffer dog, till she accidentally fell into a mass of coke in a dealer's den and got addicted. Tony bought her from the pound before they put her down, and now uses her to test coke he buys. If the coke's okay good, the dog will lick your anus; if it's very good, she'll suck your balls. If the coke's crap, the seller's ass gets bitten good and hard."

Dillinger laughed. "You ain't serious, ma'am."

Money burst out laughing too. "I've seen it happen. Bitch bit a Chicano dealer so hard in the ass once, they called the guy 'Crater Butt Jose' now—dog ripped out a whole chunk of meat from his right buttock and ate it." She slapped the steering wheel hard, accidentally triggering the horn. "But back to the main story: Uncle Luigi Rossi, our New York connection, sends Big Tony six kilos of coke. Runner's name is Joey. Bitch sniffs the blow and goes loco on his ass. Sinks her teeth in so deep, it takes three guys to pull her off. Joey goes straight from there to emergency at the nearest hospital. Big Tony immediately calls Dad to complain."

"Possibly because no one would deliver his coke anymore," Dillinger said.

Money laughed louder. "Bitch has never been wrong before, so Dad knows there's definitely something wrong with the cocaine. The original plan was to get Dougie Sloane in here and put the screws to him till he talked, but then Old Reuben called two hours ago and explained what's happened. Dad said he was sweating on the phone like he'd got a fever."

"He don't want Mr. Rich thinking he was intentionally cheating him."

She smiled, her jade eyes ice cold. "No, he doesn't. He knows we'd eat him, his two skinny geek kids, and his overweight wife for breakfast. Grind them up as sausage for Big Tony's coke dog."

She made the final turn onto East 56th Street. "Anyhow, the old guy apologizes for the error and promises to make up the difference on the next shipment. So Dad calls Al Capone and Bugsy and tells them not to rough Dougie up or bring him back anymore, then he sends Baby Face and Pretty Boy after them with the money. One point two million in cash."

"Too bad it didn't turn into a fight," Dillinger said. "I wouldn't have minded a trip to Montana to kick some ass. I also got an old girlfriend back there, name of Metalya . . . Hey, what's that?"

"What?"

The robogoon pointed a metal finger up ahead at the top of the 5550 building. "Looks like fire in the boss's penthouse."

Money looked at the red-orange glare on the high-rise roof. Fire with smoke billowing over a dust cloud. She realized its implications, taken in concert with her unanswered phone calls to her father. Horror spread like nightfall over her face. "Damn!" She floored the gas pedal. The blue Mercedes sped forward like a panther.

CHAPTER 19

4:10 a.m.

After what seemed an interminable period spent floating between life and death, Raye found the strength to sit up again and reload the rocket launcher.

She glanced right. Ash, with a triumphant yelp, was sliding an object out from between her buttocks.

"Oh yeah, finally!"

Raye gaped at the white cucumber-shaped object emerging from Ash's anus. "What is that?"

Ash grimaced as it popped free. "Combat helicopter." She giggled apologetically. "My arms and legs were full of cars."

Raye gaped at the model aircraft. Both it and Ash's buttocks had a thin coating of blood on them. "Honey, have I told you lately just how incredible you are?"

Ash didn't reply. She was already walking toward the demolished portion of wall while fiercely blowing air into the helicopter's 'inflate' straw.

She flung the miniature aircraft out onto the helipad. As always, like a cat, the inflatable landed right-side-up. They watched it expand like a balloon pumped with air. Twenty seconds later, a full-sized AH-64 Apache helicopter sat on the helipad. Gleaming black like a forgotten part of the night; propellers that looked sharp enough to shave with.

Raye looked from the helicopter to Ash, her expression doubtful. "Baby, this isn't a racecar. Are you *sure* you can fly this thing?"

Ash shook her head. "Don't have a clue how to." She grinned at the other woman's disbelief. "But there's always Warpedia."

She unzipped her right arm and ruffled through its bicep muscle-purse for a moment—

"Where the hell is this thing? Oh, here you are!"

—then quickly flipped the panel behind her ear open and switched her normal girly-pink internet chip with an ominous looking red-and-black one.

She flicked the panel shut, stood frozen for a moment while the war chip initialized, then looked at Raye, her warm blue eyes suddenly ice cold.

"I can fly it now. Let's get the fuck out of here."

Loud noise alerted them to the arrival of a new batch of robogoons.

Raye staggered to the bedroom door and discharged the rocket launcher out into the corridor again. Then she dropped the hot metal tube and stood propped up by the wall, too weak to make it back over to the bed.

Amidst the confusion following the subsequent explosion, Ash (who was still naked), rushed over to Raye and woman-handled her out through the hole in the wall. Skin goose-pimply from the cold pre-dawn air, she dragged Raye across the helipad and heaved her up into the Apache's front, co-pilot seat.

Ash shut the cockpit door on Raye, then ran back into the bedroom. She grabbed Mr. Rich's twenty thousand dollars off the floor and ran out again.

"Can we go now?" Raye asked groggily as Ash climbed in behind her.

"We've already left," Ash said, flicking switches in a blur.

The rotors began spinning. The Apache lifted off the rooftop. Ash turned it east, toward the rising sun. They floated off across the sky toward Monroe Harbor.

She looked back once. Several robogoons stood in the hole in the bedroom wall, pointing after the chopper.

Ash was relieved that they'd not thought to use the discarded rocket launcher. The robots clearly felt the chopper was out of range. *Either that, or they're scared of accidentally blowing up the surrounding buildings if they miss us. Or even of hitting the helicopter and then it slamming into a building.*

Their reluctance also saved her the bother of blowing the rooftop to bits. (She'd heard the Apache's Hellfire missiles packed quite a punch—she was almost disappointed not to have a chance to try them out in a firefight.)

She forgot the robots, peered forward at Raye in the chopper's front seat. Her face fell—her girlfriend stared back dully, half-comatose in her catsuit of bloodstained dollars.

"We made it, honey," Ash said.

"We did? Then why does my belly still ache like I'm in Hell and Satan's fucking my navel?"

Ash grinned. "You're okay if you can still wisecrack like that."

She yelled out the cockpit window: "New York City, here were come!"

"After I see a doctor, Ash! Only after I see a doctor!"

"I'm only joking, darling. Once over the lake we're first stopping in New Buffalo to get you patched up."

Raye coughed weakly. "Hurry this machine up."

Ash was alarmed by how pale Raye suddenly looked. She stopped joking and concentrated on piloting the helicopter across Lake Michigan, the dark expanse of water now approaching them at a rush.

CHAPTER 20

Femina ft. Soraya Vagina – The Prodigal Tongue.

Intro (The Players / Summary):
Your tongue travels,
Across my landscape of wonders,
To my palace of delights,
Where Queen Clitoris holds sex court each night.
Lick on, you prodigal son,
Swirl over me with your tongue,
Deep and long.
Prodigal sojourner,
Long left home to roam,
Border to border,
Wallow in sexual loam.
(Happier than pigs in mud, many miles from home.)
Traveling far and wide,
From lady-side to lady-side,
Your erection,
Your masculine perfection,
Your lust to thrust,
Biology: ego or pride,
Won't be denied,
So come inside.
But wait, mate,
Not yet, pet,

Though I'm most definitely wet,
Keep travelling across me,
By your own admission,
I'm quite the sight to see.

The Starting Line:
Kiss my eyes,
Feel my eyelids flutter like butterflies.
Softly, softly, lick each eyeball!
Yes! I said *lick* them!
Purge them of the impressions of previous men.

Next, tease my throat,
Like you're a vampire.
Nibble my sweet neck veins,
But draw no blood,
Cause no pain.

On my belly, back to the whore:
Clean me like I'm dirty clothes.
Knead me, massage me with your fists,
Wash me with your spit,
Scrape the dirt off me with your teeth,
Then swallow it.
Yeah, that's the shit,
I like it,
When you lick my back,
Like that,
Smoothly slurping from shoulders to ass-crack!
Now take it right up back,
Nice and slow,
Up my spine and down below.
Chew on my ribs,
Like they're barbecue.
Run your tongue between them,
Like feet walking among sand dunes.
I swoon,
From the pleasure.
You're good,
A national lingua treasure.
Back and forth across my waist,
I sense your haste,
But cool it! Dude,

Enjoy this nude,
To the max,
Sex my back.

Mount ASS:
You're getting all of me, see?
More than I'm sure you want or need,
But I see you're needy, and weary,
(Traveler,)
And I'm not greedy—I'm sharing.
Now suck on each gluteal mound,
Ooh, yes!—my sensation abounds,
I gasp as the chills resound,
And squirm around.
Oh, Fuck! Doctor,
Later you'll inject me with penis-cillin,
And cure my love infection,
But suck my ass first,
Chew on it . . . blow on it,
Assuage my sensual thirst,
Then give me another burst.

Nude Interlude:
Turn me over,
Lover . . .
Flip me on my back,
Now, renew your oral attack.

Tits:
My breasts,
Twin mammary Everests,
That your tongue scales,
Slow as a snail, leaving a saliva trail.
Your trip across my bust,
Mustn't be rushed,
Suck each nipple slowly,
Like they're holy,
And you're scared to offend,
The deity living on each alabaster peak as you ascend,
Then descend again.
Suck me like I'm Mother,
And when I shudder in a flesh earthquake,
Make obeisance to my nether lake.

Lick each breast cone like it's ice cream,
Nice and slow, dreaming, that's the way it goes,
Make me flow like honey across myself,
Like I'm somewhere else.

My Navel:
Time unravels like a spool of thread,
I feel I'm dead,
When you give me body-head.
As your tongue traverses my abs,
Six pack or expanse of flab,
I resist the urge to grab,
You in return, pleasure you in return.
Rather I control my fire and slow-burn,
Roasting like mutton in your spit, as your tongue turns,
On my belly button.
The delicious feeling!
I'm reeling,
Far off in space, and yet in this same place,
Floating between floor and ceiling,
Watching you kneeling over me,
Licking me.
And you go lower . . .

Pubic Furrest/Bush Blues:
My hair grows,
Thick like winter clothes,
Wild like me, tickling your nose,
Making you sneeze,
Yet you still inhale me deeply;
Can't get enough of my stuff.
It doesn't matter the color of my hair,
Down there,
I know you don't care,
You never stop and stare,
You sweep through,
A knight charging to a rendezvous,
Fighting dragons without hesitation,
Jousting to reach your lower destination.

Cunt and Cervix:
There's a river flowing deep and wide,
Bubbling up from my soft insides,

Irrigates my ass and thighs.
Lick it! Make me squirm with female pride.
Mardi Gras in my ass!
Stroke your tongue,
Long and strong,
Across the gaping pass.

Anus:
Tongue my ass,
No I won't fart,
Lick that crack, lick that crack.
Swirl your tongue into A-hole,
Deep then shallow, fast then slow.
It's bitter? It should be—it's a shitter.
(Te-hee!)
Oh, don't worry, you handsome dope,
I washed it good with lady soap.
Because of course I know,
You want me obscene,
But nice and clean.

Pleasant Diversion from Threatened Insertion:
Whoa, boy! Not so fast! Move on south,
No cock yet (—that comes last!) I want your mouth.
Pussy wants you too, little mouse,
But descend, rappel down my meatscape,
(Clean my skin-windows with your tongue,
One by one.)
Pleasure my entire sexual house,
You randy overeager spouse.

Thighs:
Peel off my tights,
With your teeth so white—
Paler than my silky skin,
Harder than your throbbing johnson.
Yes, rip my pantyhose up, pup,
Tear them to shreds, you lusty mutt.
Lick my bared thighs,
(I sigh . . .
The feeling makes my anus clench!)
Their muscles tremble within, against your chin,
As you taste my sweat,

Sweet—salty and wet.
Some dirt too,
But I'm a dirty girl,
Don't look surprised,
I thought you knew.
I got smutty plans to execute with you.

Down, down, down—everyone knows how the journey goes,
You're traveling from my head to my toes.

Knees:
Ignore them please.
They're best in combination with hands for a doggy-style stance.
Honey, I told you I got dirty plans.

Feet:
I am not a fetishist,
Hell no, I'm not.
Or maybe I am, going by the number of pumice stones I've got,
And the hours I spend on pedicures,
So my feet look super-hot.
So keep licking, honey,
And suck those sexy toes.
I need you to appreciate where the money goes!
Suck them like nipples, like their white polish is milk.
What? I didn't wash them? I smell of shoes?
Oh, I forgot—That's why you're sucking them clean, dude!
Pay those dues! My vagina will shortly make it up to you!
Your labor wont be a waste.
Does my nail paint have any taste?
Okay, now lick and chew my soles.
Oooh . . . that tickles.
Do it again . . . and again . . . and again,
And AGAIN!
Shit! Stop! I almost pissed myself just then!
Stop! Fucking stop doing that, you rat!
YOU WIN! I GIVE IN!
YES, YES, YES—SLIDE BACK UP AND SLIP JOHN THOMAS IN!

Ocean of Come:
Spurt it and fill me,
Like you want to drown me,

In a semen sea,
And make a baby.
(With brown eyes like yours or blue like mine.)
Pour it, like milk on coffee,
Delight me with your gush,
I like to feel you rush,
Into me, while you stare,
Into my eyes like you're dying,
Eyes full of tears though you're not crying,
Shrieking out my name.
30 million sperm swim in me,
Tadpoles traverse vagina sea.
Cervix loves them, cervix sucks them in,
Drinks them in like vitamins,
Pumps them into baby hole,
But the egg's not waiting.
Disappointed sperm give up hope,
And die,
But their brothers in your balls prepare for another try.

CHAPTER 21

6 a.m.

The sun was coming up. The rising white orb illuminated cream and black cloud-streaks across the sky—pale-blue higher up set over a bright orange lower portion that in turn rested on the thick black crayon smear of the horizon.

***

Money Rich sat on her father's corpse staring out through the demolished wall. The dust had now settled, the fire was extinguished, the smoke dispersed by the cold breezes of dawn.

Money was naked, her dollar-sign-tattooed body a model of the flawlessness only money could buy—perfect face; sculpted breasts, belly, and buttocks; exquisitely-toned arms and legs. (The Kate Rose necklace hung around her neck, its emeralds blending perfectly with the green of her tattoos.)

Money had told Dillinger and the other robogoons to excuse her. "I want . . . no need . . . quality time alone with Dad's corpse."

Mr. Rich's head had been retrieved from the safe and arranged in position atop his neck. He lay on his back in a bloody patch of the bed, limbs stiff in rigor mortis. Money sat on his belly. His skin was cold against hers.

Money was masturbating as she sat on the corpse staring out through the demolished wall. She rubbed a hundred dollar bill over her vagina, gripping the corpse's legs to steady herself.

She wept as she masturbated, hot tears streaming down her white cheeks. Her primary intent wasn't pleasure, but to relieve her current tension. She felt that was normal enough. That she was loving herself while sitting on a beheaded body (and her father's at that!) felt surreal for sure, but no less so than the past night had been.

While her body climbed the ladder of pleasure toward orgasm, Money coldly ran what she knew through her mind.

"There were two attackers," the goons had said. "Ashley Status and a brunette woman with weird bulletproof hair."

That meant Raye, the woman who'd also killed Bug. Money's heart thrilled with hatred. *Stupid dumb bitch. To think I actually wanted to employ you as my bodyguard.*

While the hundred dollar bill skimmed over her sex, Money regarded the destroyed wall. (The penthouse corridor outside the bedroom now looked like a war zone too.) *The pair shot up everywhere and escaped in a combat helicopter? Where the hell did that come from?*

She looked down at the decapitated body she sat on. Father's head had been ripped off, pulled off his neck. *What a horrible way to die. I'm going to get you good for this, Raye. You're really going to pay big time!*

She reached orgasm then, rubbing the now sticky C-note hard and fast over her clitoris. She grimaced with the force of the climax, her muscles tightening, her breath coming faster and faster, her heart pumping like she was in a race against herself. All the while, her eyes remained fixed outside the penthouse, far away in the sky, where a solitary bird swooped beneath morning clouds.

The sexual moment passed. The tension of ultimate release fled her. Her muscles unlocked again and she collapsed back down on her father's body.

She lay limp, dead to the world, her dollar-marked breasts rising and falling with her breathing.

The pleasure departed, temporarily taking her pain along with it. Lying on Mr. Rich's corpse, Money thought about what she'd do to both Ash and Raye when she caught them. The images in her mind were all bloodstained and extremely horrible. She found them almost satisfactory.

She sat up, legs astride the corpse, and addressed the hole in the wall. "Time to set the machine in motion after the two women who've just made me head of the syndicate." She frowned. "Unfortunately, girls, I'm not grateful. And even if I was, there's appearances to be maintained: Wouldn't look good, would it, if I let you get away with killing Daddy?"

She got off the bed, walked naked out onto the helipad and stretched in the orange dawn light. "So I'm going to find both you idiots and make an example of you. You don't mess with the Richs', bitches."

Realizing she'd forgotten to do something, Money walked back into Mr. Rich's bedroom. There, she picked the C-Note she'd masturbated with off the corpse. After wetting the money again between her legs and winking at Daddy, she glued it on the wall besides the other semen-adhered ones.

She nodded at the results. Definitely a family tradition she intended keeping up.

PART 2: THE CITY THAT NEVER SLEEPS

Women should be seen . . . and obscene! – Femina.

CHAPTER 22

Ash had been raped once. Three years ago. In the stables out on Mr. Rich's Arlington racetracks long before they'd met.

It happened just after she'd begun work there, before she'd been issued with a gun. Her thigh muscle-purse had just been fitted and was still healing into her flesh.

The incident was culmination to an already bad day.

Ash had been given a horrible time by a drunken couple—a skinny brunette and her aging boyfriend—who were vilely upset at losing the fifty thousand dollars they'd staked on a surefire winner. Their horse, Firesturm, had been overtaken right at the death, losing by half a length.

Ash couldn't believe the way the couple had hounded her—*like they held me personally responsible for their stupid bet.*

"We want our damn money back!" the man yelled as security grabbed him. "Damn cheats!"

"Yeah!" his girlfriend seconded. "You rigged the races. Give us back our money!"

"Serves you both right," Ash told the intoxicated brunette after security grabbed her also. "You spendthrifts should have donated that money to breast cancer research!" Then she'd stamped off.

***

Ash was in the stables to give a message to a jockey friend. Unknown to her, the friend had left early to meet her boyfriend.

89

"Marie? Marie, are you here?" Ash quickly questioned the wisdom of her coming out here alone. The stable was empty and dimly lit. Menace seemingly lurked in each unoccupied stall she passed. She felt like the shadows were watching her.

The horses were restless over an approaching thunderstorm.

Ash smelt female perfume, then heard footsteps behind her. She first thought it was her friend, and turned around. "Marie? Is that you?"

But then the female smell was replaced by an intense stink like a fishmonger's dumpster. Then she heard squelching sounds behind her, rapidly getting closer.

Panic gripped Ash. Before she could either turn back again to look, or run away, a slimy hand covered her mouth from behind. A mass of tentacles draped over her shoulders. Something sharp pressed against her throat.

"Don't make a fuss and you'll live, bitch!"

The voice was guttural, corrupted, like that of a man with half his face melted so he was forced to talk out of one side of his mouth.

Ash hadn't made a fuss. All she could think of was surviving, staying alive. She was terrified—she quickly realized that her assailant wasn't human, the tentacles flailing around her testified to that.

And the stink . . . like all the oxygen in the air had been replaced with fish. It took an effort to breathe—her lungs rejected the smell like she was inhaling poison. And yet, amidst the fish stink, she still caught traces of female perfume. Jasmine? The warm floral fragrance was unmistakable.

"Down on the ground."

She dallied. Her unseen assailant pushed her down flat, her face in the mud. She felt the mass of tentacles slop on top on her.

She waited; dreading what would happen next.

It was worse than she'd expected. He jerked her skirt up, ripped her panties off, then with a grunt, forced his penis inside her. Ash screamed. Her vagina felt like he was shoving a knife in it.

At first, it was the worse experience of her life, bar none. The cold penis felt alive inside her. It was slimy and squirmed independent of him, like a fish.

Like a fish? She'd heard of fish fingers, never fish dick.

Surprised by the simile, she looked sideways over her shoulders. Amidst the mass of tentacles almost smothering her, she saw fish. Plaice and cod. Disbelieving, she twisted her neck farther around, saw that the fish amidst the tentacles had no tails—they were parts of the monster raping her. (The monster seemingly also had no head or face.)

Ash gaped at the fish. Mouths working silently, the plaice and cod gaped back at her with dark eyes.

Meanwhile the creature they were part of was fucking Ash hard.

The creature assaulted her, its smell assaulted her. Slime dripped over her, seeping through her shirt, befouling her back like the mud dirtied her front. Fish mouths chewed and bit her hair, her neck, her buttocks and thighs.

She was nauseated, but couldn't puke. Each breath simply brought with it more of the horrendous fish stink.

The penis in her body, the unpermitted hated intrusion, was trauma. She'd read numerous accounts of rape—of the victims' feelings of being destroyed. The fiction was harrowing enough, but to experience it first-hand . . .

Ash had a feeling of her life being ripped from her, of being damaged beyond repair, soiled beyond the cleansing power of any psychic soap.

But then, with that feeling of ultimate dirtiness, came another. To her horror, Ash found that she was aroused.

And not just a little. Every fiber in her body was suddenly screaming to be fucked.

She had no idea of how, no mental record of when, her body had betrayed her. But it was undeniable: even as the monster slid its malformed organ in and out of her vagina, she felt a flood of wetness between her legs that wasn't its viscid slime.

Disgusted with herself, she began forcing her buttocks up into the tentacles. The fish-penis (she assumed it was) hurt her. She imagined she was bleeding a river between her legs, but she couldn't stop. She kept pushing her body back against the tentacle mass that lay on her.

The monster's legs strained against hers. His knees, themselves trunks of tentacles, spread her legs wider for deeper penetration.

She was pumped HARD. She felt like she was being flattened, forced through the stable straw into the concrete below.

And overlaying the fuck was the reeking of a million rotting fish with the delicate thread of jasmine in it. Like a single beautiful flower left untrampled among a hundred thousand corpses on a battlefield.

While she was being violated, the storm broke. Sheets of water came down fast and heavy, the turbulent heavens reflecting her ravaged emotions.

The horses neighed loud in their stalls, pacing restively back and forth.

Ash came. Her orgasm was dirty, incredibly dirty, like she'd been showered with sewage, filth that somehow glorified her. Her disgust mingled with her pleasure—neither knew any limits. "Oh, Gaawwddd!" she moaned, biting down on the mud and straw. Her breasts felt like exploding fireworks. She pulsed and sizzled with sensation, reaching back and grabbing the fish amongst the tentacles, squeezing them till they pulped in her hands and their bones and broken fins cut her fingers.

Her sensations plateaued. She shut her eyes, lay limp on her belly jerking soundlessly, till the monster came inside her.

It felt like he'd turned on a hot water faucet in her vagina. Her sex passage swelled with scalding ejaculate that felt like it was cooking her from within. Ash moaned in her pain (and incredibly undiminished pleasure), helpless as the fish and tentacles bit and whipped her.

Then, suddenly, it was over. The fish-cock slurped loudly out of her. The monster's tentacles dragged across her back as he got up.

"Keep your face in the mud, slut! Don't you dare fucking look back!"

Ash kept her face in the muddy straw. She kept her eyes closed long after she'd heard his slurpy footsteps leaving. Until the nauseating fish smell wasn't even a memory.

Her orgasm faded, her disgust remained. It intensified. She sat, then stood up. A mass of transparent slime like frog spawn emptied out of her sex, dribbling down her legs to the floor. Jelly with black dots in it.

Ash dully noted that she wasn't bleeding. Not a speck of red anywhere.

She felt completely traumatized.

She'd looked dully around at the horses, then left the stables. Walked through the pouring rain. The water washed her clean, physically if not spiritually.

She'd never told anyone her experience. Not the police, not her friends. She'd gone straight home, had a bath, and sat watching TV. Feeling like a zombie.

Her biggest worry had been that she'd caught a disease.

For a long time it bothered her that she'd not reported what had happened. *How many other women like me*—she wondered—*has this happened to, with exactly the same consequences? Nothing ever said. The club of silence—the abused collaborators.*

She doubted anyone would have believed her anyway.

***

Ash's disgust that she'd orgasmed while being raped—like she'd conspired with her attacker—hadn't gone away.

Two days later, she'd been issued her gun. For the next fortnight, she stalked the stables after dark, cocked weapon in hand, praying to smell that same disgusting fish stink again. She'd kill that mutant mass of fish and tentacles so dead . . .

But she'd never smelled it again, not once in the two-and-a-half years she'd worked at the racetrack. Finally, she'd given up her quest for revenge, chalking her experience down to bad luck. She realized that she, like a lot of other women who'd suffered a similar fate, had simply been in the wrong place at the wrong time.

But still sometimes, the stink hunted her dreams. And that floral smell, like a pristine yellow ribbon floating atop sewage . . .

CHAPTER 23

Femina – One Black Eye

One black eye,
Is too many,
One purple bruise,
Is one too much.
How I wish we were back at the beginning,
When you loved me so much.

It's fucking over,
I feel like dead meat while you fuck me,
While you groan,
And moan like my body's your own,
(Property purchased,
In some emotional marketplace.)
And like this sex is the best we've ever had.
Can't you sense the hatred in my heart?
Can't you see the disgust on my face?
No you can't,
I forgot,
I'm hiding it,
So you don't slap me around again.
Fuck—you're hurting me!
My feeling deserting me,
I flee into a safe place,

Imagine I'm slicing off your penis,
And hairy testicles,
Castrating you,
Making a woman out of you,
So you'll know how spousal battery feels.

Are you done yet?
Hell no, you raise my feet onto your shoulders,
Or even turn me over,
My position makes no real difference,
I'm under you either way,
Getting fucked so I don't get beat up again.
I hate, I hurt,
I hurt, I hate.
Too late,
I should have read the vital signs in our early days,
My friends all now say.
But there were none,
Or maybe that was courting conceit,
(You were so good-looking and rich!)
Or self-deceit,
Fuck what it was,
You're not supposed to hit me.

One black eye,
Is too many,
One fat lip,
Is one too much.
How I wish we were back at the beginning,
When I craved your touch.

You keep fucking me forever.
(I'm in total agony,
As you thrust into me,
Your penis feels like a skewer,
And my vagina like raw meat.)
Slobbering spit,
You lean forward and kiss my bloody lips,
The lips you just split,
With a punch!
Kissing the blood you spilled with your macho fists.
(You're a real man, aren't you, you shit?)
Hurry up and come,

You asshole,
Then I'll pack my bags and run,
Far away. But you're too clever,
By morning you'll be on your knees,
Begging me,
Pleading, "Never again, Never!"
Promising me that things will get better,
And I'll believe you again,
'Cos I love you.
But why?
My heart betrays me, my heart always betrays me.
Even now, I know if I don't hold onto my anger,
I'm gonna come,
And then I'll feel so dumb,
A retard enjoying my degradation,
Oh fuck, your cock's so nice,
(I bite my tongue to refresh my pain!
No! I won't be fooled again!)
Fuck you—I'm taking my own advice,
You're getting . . . no . . .
I'm getting well out of *your* life,
As long as I survive tonight.
You might just kill me before daybreak in another fight.

You keep fucking me,
With your eyes closed.
I want to slit your throat,
I really do.
I want to gut you,
Pull your intestines out,
And stuff them in your mouth.
Feed them to you,
You beast in the human zoo.

And now you come.
You REALLY come.
Does beating me really turn you on?
(Abusing your wife isn't an aphrodisiac, you moron!)
You groan and moan,
And I feel you throbbing,
Pumping me with unwelcome come.
And when you collapse on me and sob,
Gasping how you really truly love my big ass so much,

I moan and kiss you back,
And profess equally synthetic love.
But I don't tell you my real thoughts,
No I'll never tell you my real thoughts,
(You slob,)
I'd love to chop your penis and testicles up,
And feed them to our dog.

One black eye,
Is too many,
One rough shove,
Is one too much.
How I wish we were back at the beginning,
When you loved me so much.

CHAPTER 24

660 Park Avenue,
Upper East Side, Manhattan.

Fred Matthews was currently in an extremely embarrassing position.

Fred, a handsome young man with dark hair and smiling grey eyes, was bent over with his head and hands clamped in a set of medieval stocks in Big Tony Marconi's library. He was also stripped naked from the waist down and his legs chained apart. Between his legs sat Bitch, Big Tony's junkie Doberman. The dog sniffed Fred's crotch and ass. Fred tensed each time her whiskers brushed his thighs.

Big Tony Marconi—fat, dark, bandit-mustached, middle-aged, in a blue business suit—reclined in a chair on Fred's left. Big Tony was a TV producer with CBS.

His girlfriend Lana Petrova—a tall sexy Russian émigré, her long legs and knockout body sheathed in a red dress, blonde hair pulled back in a tight bun, red lipstick smear of a mouth—stood on Fred's right. Lana carried the briefcase-load of cocaine Fred had just delivered.

"Spread his hairy ass wider," Big Tony instructed. "Spread those cheeks so Bitch has easy access."

Lana nodded. Her eyes glimmered with pleasure—she was enjoying this. With a delicate hand, she operated a winch that shortened the chains clamped to Fred's legs, pulling them farther apart.

"This okay, Tony?"

Big Tony nodded. "Yeah."

Fred felt the dog's hot breath on his balls and cock. But no licking or biting. Not yet. The anticipation was killing him however. *Why the hell do I have to keep delivering Uncle Luigi's snow to this jerk?* He knew the answer: *Because Tony Marconi buys more cocaine than some Harlem and Bronx neighborhoods combined. Big Tony isn't just buying snow for himself, but for half the showbiz exec in the Big Apple.*

But dealing with Tony Marconi was a pain in the butt. He and this damn dog of his. He paid absolute top dollar, but you had to go through this stupid ritual first. And Uncle Luigi thought it was all a joke. "So make sure you don't attempt to water down the quality," he'd responded to Fred's complaint, adding a hearty belly-laugh. "Bitch never makes a mistake. As long as you play it straight, you'll come back whole."

"It's humiliating."

"So? Look, son—Tony's an asshole, sure. But he's safe. Like unprotected anal with your new girl after you've both just got your HIV-free clearance. He's tight with Mayor Presley; we keep *him* happy, *we're* happy. The city tones down the heat on our operation; the cops don't bug—"

"I'm *not* happy. I swear one of these days, that dog will—"

"Stop grouching; I'll give you a raise."

That had been the end of the discussion.

"Look," Fred grumbled now in his best tough-guy voice, "Can we get this crap over with? I gotta hot date waiting."

Big Tony scowled. "Shut up, or I'll keep you in the stocks all night." He checked his gold watch, then nodded to Lana. "Okay, pour the coke out, baby. We can't be late for *Phantom of the Opera*, I hear Lloyd-Webber's in town."

"Sure thing, Tony." The Russian beauty placed a metal tray in front of Bitch and emptied one of Fred's transparent coke bags into it.

The dog bent its head and snorted up the cocaine.

Lana's sexy voice mingled with the sound of the snorting Doberman. "Now, Freddie, remember the rules: Okay coke, Bitch will lick your asshole; great coke, Bitch will suck or lick your hairy balls . . . crap coke . . . no need to remind you what happens then."

Yeah, no frigging need. Fred could do without the woman explaining how he'd lose a chunk—possibly a large chunk—of his gluteal muscle if Tony's freak dog felt his coke delivery was cut too thin. Hearing Bitch sniffing behind him, his butt clenched in fear; a cold feeling swirled around his gut. *Shit! I hate this damn dog. Uncle Luigi's coke is good, right? I know it's good. He didn't try to screw Tony, right? If this dog bites me, I'll . . .*

His thoughts froze when he felt the dog's breath hot on his backside again. *Nice doggie, lick my anus or balls please! Please, don't bite me!*

Bitch's tongue dipped into Fred's ass crack. With relief, he felt the dog lick his anus, then her muzzle slipped lower. The dog sucked Fred's scrotum into her mouth.

Fred relaxed. He looked at Big Tony. "Okay, you've had your fun; let me go."

Big Tony shook his head, a grin on his fat face. "Bitch ain't done yet."

"What?" But to Fred's horror, Big Tony was right. His black-and-tan dog, her muzzle white with cocaine, had now abandoned sucking Fred's balls and switched to performing full-blown fellatio on him. Worst still, he was getting an erection. Bitch's mouth was hot and wet and Fred hadn't had sex in a week.

Big Tony laughed unsympathetically. "Ha ha, Freddie. Looks like you just found a new girlfriend."

Lana's eyes spread wide with surprise. "I have never seen this reaction before, Tony."

"Dogs need loving too, baby."

Lana giggled. Ignoring the dog lustily sucking on Fred's penis, she slapped Fred heartily on the buttocks. "This must be wonderful cocaine you brought over today."

Fred cringed. He could feel pressure building up in his balls. It would be horrible if he ejaculated in Bitch's mouth. *Big Tony is a lousy loudmouth. I'll never live it down, might even have to leave New York.*

He looked at the TV mogul with pleading eyes. "Please, Tony, let me go."

Big Tony stared back at him, eyes pitiless and hard. "No. Not till you give my little bitch what she wants."

The feeling became too much for Fred. Cursing himself, he came in Bitch's mouth.

The Doberman sucked and sucked while Fred ejaculated, wolfing down his week's buildup of semen. Fred trembled with the pleasure of orgasm, shivering through the debasement, while Lana and Big Tony hooted with laugher.

When Fred stopped coming, Bitch licked his penis pristine clean, then trotted back to sit by her master's side.

Fred looked over at Big Tony. The man was laughing so hard, tears were streaming down his fat face.

Lana let Fred out of the stocks. She was similarly laughing hard, gripping her sides like they'd split if she didn't. "Damn, Freddie—you are a born porno star. Next time you are coming over, I will set up my VCR. I saw nothing like this in Mother Russia."

Fred pulled on his pants.

"Alright, you can go," Tony said. "Tell Luigi the blow's high grade as usual."

"Ah, Tony," Lana said, heading for the stairs. "I have laughed too much. I need to repair my makeup before we leave."

"Woof!" Bitch barked at Fred. "Woof! Woof!"

Fred left, vowing revenge. *Somehow, some day, I'm going to teach this fat slob a lesson he'll never forget.*

CHAPTER 25

Post-dinner, Ash and Raye strode hand-in-hand down the front steps of Frank and Johnnie's Steakhouse sharing a relaxed laugh.

Both women looked different now.

Raye had bleached and dyed her brown hair platinum blonde. She'd also, in the month spent in bed recuperating from her gunshot wounds, put on a lot of weight. In the past this would have bothered her. Now, however—as Ash quickly pointed out—it was great camouflage.

"You look older too," Ash had said. "Like my mother."

Raye had looked at her coldly. "Repeat that one more time, darling, and I'll tan your ass."

Ash had smiled sweetly back. "And have to bleach your hair again?"

That was the other thing—Raye doing anything with her hair instantly wiped out the platinum-blonde treatment.

Ash was now a redhead. She'd also lost some weight, weighed a hundred-thirty pounds to Raye's two hundred and ten.

"Who the hell's going to see it?" Raye had demanded on seeing Ash had crimsoned her pubic hair as well.

Ash had given an embarrassed grin. "Maybe the cops; you know how they're always sticking their hands up people's asses."

Raye's burgeoning rage had deflated into an anguished sigh: Ash's red pubic bush meant only one thing—more boyfriend 'infidelity' was around the corner.

Romantic tension aside, however, both women felt they'd done a good job of, if not exactly vanishing into thin air, blending indistinguishably with NYC's masses.

***

Here in the Theatre District, the darkness was completely banished by streetlights and neon. Raye wondered if night had fallen in this part of town in a hundred years. The sky seen over the rooftops looked like outer space, a distant realm connecting to the other parts of America, just not here.

And just like it was daylight, people were everywhere, going to shows, leaving shows, laughing on the steps of theatres, walking the streets. If anything, there seemed more cars on the roads that during daytime.

The city, even at night, was much cleaner than Chicago with its grime and gangs.

However, a sense of barely-concealed despair hovering about the inhabitants linked both population centers. In Chicago, the source of the gloominess was feeling one was stuck in a lifetime rut, unable to claw one's way above mundane everyday existence into a life like one saw on TV. Here, the despair was one of being stuck on a treadmill, of having to keep endlessly moving just to remain in the same spot; of being constantly jostled forward, backwards, and sideways, unable to rest from the pressure of everyone else hustling for pole position on the nebulous human grid that was The Big Apple.

"Too much fucking traffic," Raye said as they joined the mob milling along West 45th Street. "You'd have thought the city would have found a workaround by now."

Ash smiled. "Not the mayor's fault everyone wants to watch a hit show." She understood Raye's beef. A traffic jam had forced them to park half a mile away, in an alley off West 46th Street—not a walk one wanted to make with a nice hot dinner in one's belly.

They turned the corner onto 9th Avenue. People were still everywhere.

"Neon lights, neon nights," Raye said.

"Everyone seems plastic," Ash mused. "Like the same people endlessly duplicated."

"Yeah," Raye agreed. "No robogoons here though."

"But they've got webcops; those are by far worse."

"Only if you're a violent crook."

"*We are* violent crooks."

"Were. *Were.* And that was an accident of bad circumstances. Don't you forget that. We're making a clean start here."

They turned the corner onto West 46th, walked up past the 10th Avenue intersection.

"A lot less people here," Raye said thankfully as they approached the old Salvation Army building. "Less cars too."

Ash nodded. "Like the mob just evapora—Hey!"

Hailing a yellow taxicab, a man had come leaping down the flight of steps they were approaching and knocked Raye sprawling.

Wincing, he rushed to help Raye up. The taxi pulled away from the curb.

The man got Raye to her feet. He was young and handsome with honey-brown hair. "Damn, I'm really sorry I bumped into you."

"You should watch where you're going," Raye replied testily.

"I couldn't help myself. I'm late for Femina's performance at the Hotel Bizarre. My wife's waiting for me."

Preempting Raye's acid retort, Ash smiled at the man: "Femina's in New York?"

He nodded. "She's playing for a week at the Hotel Bizarre."

"Hotel Bizarre? What's that?"

The man fiddled about in his coat and brandished two tickets.

"Femina's 'Foreplay Sex Orgasm Afterglow Tour'" Ash read off, followed by: "Live all this week at the Hotel Bizarre, 230 Riverside Drive."

"It's right at the West 95th Street intersection, by the Hudson."

"I don't get it," Raye said while patting down her clothes, "Femina sells out concert venues nationwide; what's she doing playing in a hotel here, and for a whole week?"

"Yeah, and not even on Broadway?"

He smiled. "From what I gather, the Bizarre belongs to her uncle; she's doing it as a family favor. The concert's not even being publicized in the media—officially, Femina's currently holidaying in Acapulco." His cellphone began ringing. He pulled it out, glanced at the screen and grimaced, then nodded to Raye and Ash, "It's my wife Kim. Gotta run. Sorry again I knocked you over."

Ash handed the concert tickets back to him. He jogged off, hailing another yellow cab. It slewed to the sidewalk. He leapt in, was gone.

"Nice guy," Ash said.

Raye stiffened at the wistful note in her voice. "Don't you think of anything but sex?"

Ash turned to her. "Uh? What are you talking about? Oh, that? I was just thinking how nice it must be to be happily married."

Raye sighed. "So let's get married."

They stepped out of the way of an arm-in-arm middle-aged couple. Ash seemed to consider Raye's request. Gripping Raye's hand, she shook her head. "That would mean our open relationship would be closed; wouldn't it?"

Raye scowled. "Is penis more important to you than I am?"

Ash shook her head. "It's not." She looked deeply into Raye's eyes. "I'm sorry, honey; I just can't explain it. Committing to just you would be like killing half of myself. I can't ever promise you that it'll be just you and me and no guys. Trust me, if we get married, we'd get divorced even faster. I can't help being bisexual, just like you can't help being fully gay. This way at least I'm not cheating on you every moment. And it's not one-sided—you can have other women too, as many as you want."

Raye had no reply to that. It was true: she *could* play the field too, take a different girl to bed every night if she wanted. *But I don't want to. I just want you to myself.*

"And," Ash added. "You know I've not had any other female lovers in the year we've been together. Not even one—"

Raye bit down on that. It was true, but it wasn't enough. Nowhere near enough.

"—Meaning you satisfy me as much as any woman in the world can. It's just the male part which—"

"Okay," Raye said tiredly. "I get the point. You love me too; just not as much as I love you."

CHAPTER 26

Fifty yards from the 11th Avenue junction, they turned into the alley where their Pink Nissan Altima was parked.

Raye nodded at the car. "How long till it breaks up?"

Ash did a quick mental calculation. "Three hours." She grinned. "Why? Wanna go joyriding?"

Raye grinned back. "How 'bout we go to Central Park and do it in the back seat?"

Ash's eyes widened. "And I thought *I'm* the one with sex on the brain."

Raye squeezed her butt. "You're infectious. I got you well under my skin now."

Ash kissed her cheek. "Your pussy's wish is my command. Central Park it is then." She tapped her right thigh. "Got a rabbit vibrator in the old muscle-purse."

She was about skipping around to open the driver's door, when Raye jerked her sharply back. "Ssh!" She pulled her down behind the car, then pointed down the alley.

Ash followed her finger. Halfway to the alley's far exit, a large man held a woman at gunpoint against the wall. The pair were dimly illuminated by light from a window, with view of them from the farther road blocked off by a stack of crates.

Ash and Raye listened hard as voices blew across to them like bats.

"Please don't hurt me!"

"Lower your fucking voice, bitch. Just hand over the purse and you won't get hurt."

"Okay, take it, take it!"

Loud sound of a slap, then another. "I said keep the fucking noise down!"

An accompanying whimper, followed by terrified weeping. Ash made out dark blood streaming down from the woman's nose over her mouth and chin.

"Please don't hit me." More tears.

The mugger laughed softly. "You know what? Your crying's got my Little Richard all hard. Get on your knees, give me a blowjob to seal the deal."

He pushed the woman down to her knees. The sound of him unzipping his fly reached them.

"I'm stopping this shit right now," Ash whispered, unzipping her left thigh and retrieving her Beretta. She flicked off the safety. "I'm killing this son-of-a-bitch!"

Raye restrained her. "Don't worry, he's already fucked up." She nodded up at the alley wall above rapist and victim.

Ash saw what Raye had noticed. "Webcops?" She smirked. "I almost feel sorry for the schmuck—he looks a definite third-striker."

A shudder of fear went through her as she put her gun away. Best the webcops didn't see she was packing.

***

The man groaned as the woman fellated him. Saliva shone on his penis as her lips slid back and forth over it. Gun pressed to her temple, he urged her on.

"Yeah, bitch, work that mouth. No fucking teeth." He pulled her head back, spat down in her face. "Look here, you stupid cunt—you bite me one more time and I'll knock your teeth down your fucking throat."

He shoved her mouth back down on his erection. "Get back to work!"

The two webcops dropped beside rapist and victim like cats, quiet as falling feathers. Two tall male shadows in skintight black; NYPD emblazoned across their chests in blood red. Spider people. Long untidy hair; faces and hands withered like those of concentration camp survivors. Dark slits for eyes.

The web strands the gene-cops had swung down on disconnected from them and blew away on the breeze, gossamer threads seemingly too frail to bear their weight.

The webcops made no attempt to halt the forced sexual congress.

"David James Newman," one said softly, "Aged thirty-six; last place of residence, 1564 Taylor Avenue, Bronx—"

Rapist and victim finally realized they weren't alone. He spun around, unceremoniously jerking his penis from the woman's mouth. She fell back on her knees, spitting.

"—Twice convicted of rape. One conviction for armed robbery—"

Neither webcop had yet moved. On recognizing the spider people, David Newman yelped 'Shit!', then broke into a sprint for the alley's opposite entrance.

"—Six dismissed charges of spousal battery—"

"He didn't even bother holstering his gun," Ash said as the man charged toward them.

"You mean his dick, don't you?" Raye retorted, regarding the onrushing man's pink erection with interest. "It's still hard, if you want a turn."

Gun in hand, David Newman dashed past Ash and Raye. His expression was of the most abject terror, his pale eyes were hopeless in his unshaven face. His dirty hair flailed in a wind of his own making.

"Nice penis," Ash said. "Too bad he's such a douchebag. Two rapes?"

"This makes three."

"Can't say he doesn't deserve what he's about getting."

The fleeing man almost made it around the corner. Then four gossamer liquid streams hit him in the back and jerked taut, halting his flight as effectively as if he'd run into a brick wall.

Then his motion was reversed. From finding himself running on the spot, the unkempt David Newman found himself doing the impossible— running in reverse.

"No! Please!" he screamed as he was reeled backward like a fish.

Ash looked down the alley. Both webcops still stood beside David's recent victim, pulling on the web material just ejected from their finger spinnerets like they were competing in a tug-of-war.

David was hauled past Ash and Raye, his hands desperately grasping for their car's rearview mirror to stop his reversal. He noticed both women, gestured at them with his gun. "Help me!"

Ash shook her head. "We can't—that'd be aiding and abetting your escape."

David's face contorted with rage. "You stupid bitches!" He swung his gun towards them.

Raye and Ash ducked before he fired. The bullets hit the alley wall behind them, one shattering a window.

The webcops yanked hard on their cords. His eyes desperate pools, David Newman flew toward them. He reached the spider policemen. They instantly disarmed him, then glued him to the wall with web spat from their mouths. He hung there a foot off the ground, feet kicking helplessly.

"Get the pussy wagon," one webcop told the other. A replying nod. The second spider-cop strode out of the alley, disappearing to the left.

"No please! Not the pussy wagon!"

"Shut up, asshole!" The raped woman yelled up from her wet patch of alley floor.

"She still looks frigging dazed," Ash said, helping Raye up, "like he squirted come up into her brain."

"She wants to watch, but doesn't want it to look like she's gloating."

Ash and Raye were suddenly aware of a hissing noise beside them.

"Oops," Ash said when they'd turned. "Ricochet hit the car." She turned back and glared at the man glued to the wall. "Asshole."

"Looks like we're taking the bus to Central Park," Raye said. She calmly watched their pink Nissan Altima deflate like a balloon, silver-colored 'air' squirting from a hole in the front passenger window. To the sound of the escaping gas, the car crumpled like a carton being stamped on. It flattened to cardboard thinness, then dissolved to dust.

"Good thing the police are too occupied to notice how odd this just was," Ash remarked.

Raye nodded her agreement, then returned her attention to David Newman. The second webcop had now returned, pushing a metal cart covered with glittering surgical instruments ahead of him. Behind him, a female webcop pushed a second cart laden with specimen bottles and large trays. Behind her, a large white van with a black cat logo beneath the legend 'Big Apple Cannery' now blocked the alley entrance.

"David James Newman," the webcop who'd remained behind said in tones of judicial neutrality, "being caught for the third time in the commission of an unlawful act of sexual assault, the State of New York has no alternative but to label you a serial sex offender, and sentence you to be converted to cat food."

"Offences against pussy will be punished by being fed to pussy," the female webcop said. (The policewoman's face was wizened like she was seventy years old, but a horrible ageless vitality reflected from her deeply recessed eyes. [Ash and Raye knew that in reality, the webcop would be in her thirties, twenties even.] Her every motion gave the impression of immense strength. Frail and shriveled as she looked, her genetically enhanced frame could lift a yellow school bus without showing even the ghost of a sweat.)

The man stuck to the wall stared at her aghast.

"Do you have any last words before your sentence is carried out?" the third spider person asked.

David suddenly grinned. A smug look settled over his face. "I got you on that one. I appeal the sentence. You can't kill me till my appeals run their course."

"Shit!" the raped woman yelped, leaping up from the floor in her rage. "You're saying this son-of-a-bitch is going to get away with this?"

The webcop shook his head. "He's not getting off. He's a third-striker and it's gone down to the wire this time." He turned to David. "You can't appeal, sir."

"The hell I can't. This is NYC, due legal process has—"

"No, David James Newman, you can't. Due legal process has been observed and completed. You waived your rights to file an appeal by the commission of two clear acts of attempted murder while being apprehended. The law clearly states this as being an indication/acceptance of being guilty as charged, or else you wouldn't have tried to murder the witnesses."

The sudden burst of confidence left David Newman's face. He managed to blurt: "What attempted murder?"

The webcop pointed towards Ash and Raye. "You just shot at those two women, with clear intent to kill them both."

David stared horrified at Ash and Raye, then back at the webcops.

"But . . . but . . ."

One of the webcops spat a wad of webbing over David Newman's mouth, gluing it shut.

"Sir, now please pay attention. While the law is unequivocal that those of your organs not used for cat food must be used for transplants, it humanely gives you the option of choosing where and who to donate them to. You may, for instance, legally decide you don't want someone of Latino, Chinese, or Jewish descent using your liver. You may also decide no vegans can have your stomach, or vice versa. You may also veto us implanting your heart into women or Republicans—"

"Mmmph!" David growled behind his web gag. "Mmmpph!"

"I'm afraid we *can't* let you go, sir." The webcop accepted a clipboard from the female officer with the specimen bottles. "Now to the business at hand: First of all, sir, are you a Jehovah's Witness?"

Eyes agoggle, David shook his head.

The webcop made a tick on his clipboard. "No reservations about donating your blood then." He scanned the clipboard. "So we proceed to organs: Do you have any specific race, age, or gender you would prefer to receive any particular organ? Your eyes for instance?"

"MMMpppph, mmmPPPPHH!"

"I'll take that as a no, sir. So, just to confirm this: On your demise, the State automatically requisitions your skin, blood, eyes, heart, lungs, liver, stomach, kidneys, and prostate for humanitarian organ transplants. Your brain and penis will be preserved and donated to the Gloria Steinem Museum on Prospect Avenue. Do you understand this, sir?"

"Mmmmppphhh!"

"Thank you, sir. New York City appreciates your care for its sick." The webcop handed the clipboard back to his female companion.

Raye, now seated beside Ash on two trash cans closer to David, his erstwhile victim, and the cops, shuddered. "This is too odd to be happening."

"It's the read deal, babe."

Raye pulled Ash's hand. "I've seen enough. Let's go."

Ash tapped the side of her head. "Not yet. I'm recording it into my chip."

Raye looked outraged.

Ash shrugged. "We need the money. There's a huge market for black vid warez like this—feminist collectors who jerk off to it, guys who—"

"Suit yourself. I'll be out in the street when you're done."

"Keep your ass warm for me, honey. I'm earning this money for us both."

Raye stalked off in a huff. Ash made herself comfortable, sitting cross-legged on the trashcan.

The raped woman walked over and sat beside Ash.

"Rough night you're having," Ash said. "You sure you want to watch this shit?"

The woman smirked. She was small, dark and pretty. Her mouth and chin were coated with dried blood. "I wouldn't miss this show for the world. You've no idea what the bastard's cock tasted like. He could at least have washed it first."

Ash raised an eyebrow, but said nothing. Instead,—

"Mmmphh!"

—She pointed to David Newman and the webcops. "Show's starting."

"About fucking time. I've several hungry cats at home."

CHAPTER 27

The webcops slid two thick needles connected to transparent tubes into David Newman's neck. While David trembled in pain, one activated a pump. Both neck tubes immediately filled with blood that ran into a large bottle on the female webcop's cart.

David jerked piteously, his eyes open and staring.

While he emptied of blood, a webcop cut his clothes off with scissors, gluing him back against the wall with web.

After a while, the blood tubes began pumping air.

A webcop slit David's torso open. David jerked one last time, then slumped over, dead.

"They really should use anesthetic," Ash said. "That looked to really hurt."

"The fuck why?" the raped woman retorted. "It's *supposed* to hurt."

Ash shrugged.

The female spider-cop hauled out David's organs, cut them free of him, and stuffed them into refrigerated jars and trays. Stomach, liver, kidneys . . . each vanished into plastic casing. Two snips with surgical shears, a bracing with a separator, and David's chest yawned open. His lungs were pulled out and frozen, as was his heart. His eyes were dug out of his face and boxed.

Ash watched/recorded the webcops' eviscerating David Newman. The spider people's motions were smooth and precise, like watching a morbid ballet. The procedure was clearly well-rehearsed—there was practically no blood spilled on the ground.

Now Ash wished she'd followed Raye back out to the street. Watching a man being killed, even legally, was unpleasant to say the least. She'd thought she'd feel empowered watching what was, after all, the ridding of the planet of one more chunk of male vermin, but she didn't. She felt queasy and sick. She'd have left if they didn't need the money the recording would fetch.

"I know I'm supposed to feel safer watching this," she said. "But I don't. What happens if they make a mistake? Arrest an innocent guy? There's no undo."

"What do you care?" the other woman said angrily. "You don't have a penis—you can't rape anyone."

"That's my point. So far we women find the webcops' actions acceptable because they're mainly directed towards violent and sexual crimes against us, and the offenders are practically always men. However, Governor Coulter's just pushed through new legislation increasing the number of 'cannable' offences."

The raped woman turned to Ash, her expression an angry scowl. "So don't screw around with people who're simply going about their own business. All I was doing was out buying food for my cats when he grabbed me." She pointed to the gutted human husk suspended from the wall, one of the cops now extracting its prostate gland. "I don't get you: what do you want? Me to feel guilty that he raped me?"

"There's no excuse for what he did, but—"

"At least we both agree on that."

"Hear me out. At the moment a felon gets canned only if, having a history of previous such offences, he's caught in the actual commission of a third violent crime. No one cares when one more scumbag becomes pussy food. But . . . mark my words—it's too convenient a fix. It's going to turn out badly. Remember I just mentioned Ann Coulter's expanded her range of 'catfood offences?' Soon there won't be any more jails left in the Empire State, just Big Apple Canneries."

The raped woman humphed angrily. "Try thinking that when someone's slamming your throat with his unwashed dick."

Finally, the corpse was unstuck from the wall and flayed. The skin was dropped in a large bucket. One of the webcops slung the remaining mass of meat and bone over his shoulder and walked out of alley with it toward the white van blocking off the alley.

"Fresh flesh for the meat grinder in the pussy wagon," Ash said as the two other webcops wheeled David James Newman's salvaged, surgically useful remains from the alley after the first.

CHAPTER 28

The raped woman's name was Felicia Johnston. ("Just call me Felix—all my friends do.") Ash and Raye saw her home. It wasn't entirely by choice.

The webcops had given Felix three free cartons of cat food as part compensation for the indignity suffered. Standard practice was one carton, but . . .

"Can I please have five more?" the little woman had asked sweetly. "My cats just adore your product and I've loads of them."

The webcop with the first carton—a tall shadow whose 'NYPD' chest logo and sergeant's stripes did nothing to dispel the fear that filled Ash and Raye on seeing his inhumanly shriveled face—shook his head. "No can do, ma'am. You know the rules."

Felix batted her eyes at him, which Ash found ridiculous. (Who the hell flirted with a spider person?) "Pretty pretty please, Officer? I've a lot of cats, so many like you wouldn't believe. My house is a virtual meow-circus. Please, Officer? Just another five?"

The female webcop peered hard and cold at Felix. "Tell me this, citizen: are you certain you didn't get yourself raped just to get free cat food?"

"What sort of question is that?" Raye (who'd now joined the others) demanded. "How can you even suspect an abuse victim of that?"

Neither webcop paid Raye any attention. The male officer, however, suddenly grinned at Felix, who was still staring at him pleadingly. He rapped on the side of the 'pussy wagon.' "Hey, Mick. Two more cartons for the other two ladies; they look traumatized as hell by what they've just witnessed."

The third cop peered around the van's rear. "Regulations say only the victim, Sarge. How're we supposed to—?"

114

"They're victims too," the female cop interrupted. "The bastard shot at them."

"That's what you said yesterday as well. We keep this philanthropy up and soon half the women in New York are going to be claiming sexual assault just to get free cat food. We won't have enough offenders to meet the demand."

"Just do it, Mick," the female webcop pleaded.

Mick disappeared back into the van. He reappeared a moment later with two more cartons.

"That's all you get," the sergeant said as Mick handed the cardboard boxes to Ash and Raye. "Now git."

"Thank you, Officer."

***

"I live just around the corner on 48th," Felix told Ash and Raye as they left the webcop's 'pussy wagon' behind. Loaded up with cartons, the pair realized they'd no choice but to see her home. Felix's place was fortunately on their way.

"How many cats do you have?" Ash asked, grunting under her burden.

"Yeah. What the hell do you need three cartons of pussy food for?"

Felix shrugged. "Oh, I've *a lot* of the little darlings. My apartment's practically wallpapered with them."

"Yeah, for real," Raye grunted.

Felix took no offence. "For real," she replied sweetly.

On West 48th Street, they turned into another alley. This one was dark. No windows illuminated it, and, even though the moon was visible overhead, its light somehow seemed to end above the alley, truncated like an invisible ceiling blocked it off.

"Can't this woman find anywhere normal to hang out?" Ash whispered to Raye. "I don't get it—she lives here?"

Raye didn't reply. She found the alley creepy. The air was still around them, not the slightest breeze tickled their faces or moved their hair. In the little light they had, they saw the back street was totally empty, vacant of trash and dumpsters and boxes and seemingly vermin too. Its floor shone black like it had just been polished.

The alley's very unclutteredness created worry in Raye. "At least we've seen her safely home," she said. "We'll just drop these boxes and leave."

Ash leaned in close and licked her ear. "We still going to Central Park? I've a Harley Davidson we can ride."

"Screw Central Park. I'm too creeped out now for exhibitionist sex. Let's just go home."

"Aw, shucks. I was really looking forward to eating you amidst the trees and squirrels again."

"Eat me at home in the morning to a Nat Geo Wild broadcast."

Ash giggled. "Ooh yeah, purr for me, tigress."

"We're here," Felix called back to them. She was lowering her carton by a door at the top of four steps with a metal railing.

Ash and Raye had unknowingly fallen well behind Felix. They quickened their pace to meet her.

"I'd never have believed cat food could be this much trouble to lug somewhere," Ash sputtered. "And you wanted six boxes?"

"You get used to it," Felix replied.

Raye said nothing. Now they'd arrived, she felt just as winded as Ash. She waited impatiently while Felix turned the key in the lock. *Just get that damn door open so we can drop these boxes inside and leave.* She was also angered that they'd have to call off their Central Park fuck. There was just something about having your vagina licked by a hot tongue while cool breezes chilled your body . . .

There was also the alley's strange ambience to contend with. The more Raye's eyes adjusted to the semi-darkness, the more disturbing the alleyway looked. For one thing, she'd just realized that there should be a building facing them opposite Felix's front door, not a broke-down fence bordering a yard overgrown with grass. Also, the street beyond the alley exit now looked different . . .

She looked to Ash for confirmation that she was right. Ash was exaggeratedly huffing and puffing, giving no indication she'd noticed anything amiss.

A muffled click. "And we're open," Felix said, pushing the door inward. She picked up her box of cat food then looked at them, her face somehow glowing bright gray in the dark. "Okay, remember what I said—I've a lot of cats. Don't freak out when you see 'em."

"Yeah, yeah, whatever," Raye said, shouldering her box. She peered up into the darkness. "Hey, put the light on, willya?"

"Not till we're all inside. I don't want you freaking out and running off."

Raye looked at Ash, sensed a return 'she's a kook . . . okay, a raped, traumatized, kook . . . let's just get this over with' shrug.

They three entered the apartment.

CHAPTER 29

Felix switched on the light.

Ash and Raye stared around them in shock that turned to horror and dread.

"She really meant it that her apartment is wallpapered with cats," Ash finally whispered.

Every inch of wall and ceiling was covered with living, breathing, mewling felines. Of a hundred different types, shapes, sizes, and colors. From mongrel tabbies to shaggy gold Persians to hairless Sphinxes, from white Siamese to grey British Shorthairs, to leopard-spotted Bengals, to Thai Korats, Russian Bobtails . . . Manx . . . Norwegian Forest Cats . . . Ginger fur was mixed with gunmetal gray, with white and black, spiky brown . . .

"Ha . . . ha . . . how?"

"They're glued to the wall," Felix said. She shook her head at their horrified expressions. "Not my doing. I inherited this place from my grandmother."

The cat patchwork on the walls was quiet. Ranks of calm white, hazel, gold, green, pink, copper, and blue eyes watched the women with curiosity. The cats' breathing was synchronized, rippling in waves across their massed bodies, waves that met and bounced off each other. It was extremely disconcerting to stand amidst such a living tapestry. The cats' heady smell filled the air.

It finally occurred to Ash and Raye to put down their cartons. Both did so, and discovered the floor wasn't the plush gray carpet they'd initially thought. It was covered with thick bristly fur. Like they were standing on the back of an immense cat.

Both immediately looked back up at Felix. "What——?"

Their joint question had frozen because Felix herself now looked different. She looked much older, her face well-lined by age, her dark hair well-streaked with gray. Her clothes too . . . she was now robed in a fur cloak that seemed continuous with the cat-pelt floor. The front of her robe was open; she was nude beneath it. Droopy breasts, saggy skin, and grayed pubic hair confirmed her increased age. There was something else too: maybe it was just a trick of the light, but Felix's face now seemed oddly familiar to both Ash and Raye.

Felix smiled at the confused women. "I can't exactly go shopping looking like this, can I?"

Both nodded back. They avoided looking down at the rippling, bristling, carpet of cat fur they stood on.

"Okay now, time to feed my darlings." Felix opened one of the cartons of cat food, then got out a can opener from a pocket in her robe. "And I think it's time you girls went home." She grinned pearlescent teeth at them. "Or would you prefer Central Park?"

Ash found her voice. "Home." Then: "Park? How'd you know about us wanting to go to the park?"

Felix frowned. "I know lots of things. It's an almost migraine pain in the brain."

"Yes, home'll be best," Raye agreed. "But where'd the door go? There's nothing but cats everywhere now."

Felix didn't immediately respond. She spooned cat food into the mouth of a huge tiger-striped tabby. The remaining cats began mewling expectantly.

"Don't worry about entrances and exits," she said, feeding another cat. She turned to face them again. "The entire world is merely a step away from here." Her face creased in a sudden frown, the expression in her eyes like she'd heard something. "Unfortunately, you can't go home just yet."

Raye's face turned ugly. "What? Are you kidnapping us?"

Felix shook her head. Her eyes met theirs evenly. "Really. Sleep in the park tonight."

"It's almost midnight—"

"I'll send your things after you."

"What things?"

"Bye, girls. I'd love to chat some more, but like you see, I've a roomful of pets to feed."

And with that Felix and the room of cats vanished, leaving Ash and Raye . . .

"What just happened?" Ash asked, looking around at the grass and trees surrounding them. A short distance from them, a newspaper-covered tramp snored on a bench, an empty Jack Daniels bottle beside him. Overhead, grey clouds floated under a half moon. The splash of birds fishing on a pond reached them through the trees.

Raye walked over to sit on a steel bench. "She sent us to Central Park like she said."

Ash sat beside her. "How the hell did she do that?" Then she grinned. "Guess 'how' doesn't matter. Well, we're here now. Make love or go home?"

Raye got up again. She looked around. Behind them, in the tall grass, a wino woman was passed out, clutching a half-emptied bottle of cheap wine to her chest like a baby. "Let's go home, girl. This isn't somewhere I want to—"

Like in a CGI animation advert, objects began popping up all around them. Two suitcases with clothes stacked on top of them, a shoe rack, blankets, a pile of purses and handbags . . .

"This is our stuff from our apartment!" Ash gasped. She looked at Raye in horror. "What the . . . ?"

Raye yawned. "I guess the old kook is serious about us spending the night out here in the cold."

Ash surveyed the mass of newly-arrived clothes and personal effects. "She even sent over my laptop and the groceries we bought yesterday! I mean, how ungrateful can you get?" She unzipped her right arm, began feeling inside its muscle-purse. "I've got a van in here somewhere."

Raye yawned again. "Look, forget going home tonight. Let's just do like the old witch says."

Ash looked hard at her. Raye nodded. "She seems insistent on it. We go home now; we might just wind up back here again." She pointed: "At least Felix was kind enough to send the bedclothes too, it isn't like were gonna freeze to death out here under the moon and stars."

Ash zipped her arm up again. "I just don't get why anyone would be so—"

"The world is full of assholes, and they aren't all men. Just make the bed, honey, then come give me some head."

Ash grinned. "Now that's a pool I want to dive into tonight." She quickly laid out a duvet on a clear patch of grass. Raye came over to her. They sank down in each other arms. Covered themselves over with a blanket. Stripped off.

Raye pushed the blanket off her head. While Ash performed cunnilingus on her, she studied the moon. The satellite seemed sad and lonely. *It has to be*, she mused, *separated as it is from all the stars by those inconceivable distances. Like Facebook friends.*

Then Ash's lips locked around her clitoris in a particularly delicious arrangement and she shut her eyes, moon and night forgotten as she ran delighted fingers through her girlfriend's hair.

A cold fall breeze blew over their warm cocoon. A pattering of dislodged leaves fluttered down on them unnoticed as they squirmed in pleasure. An owl hooted in a nearby elm.

Hands on her breasts, fingers teasing her erected nipples, Raye opened her eyes again. She looked sideways, her eyes settling on the withered wino woman asleep beyond the bench.

She instantly regretted the glance. The woman's mouth was open, showing black teeth. Her poverty-lined face with its framing of dirty blonde hair looked like a hag's—evil like death. Raye imagined she could smell the woman's covering of rags. From the farther-off bench, the paper-covered tramp's snores came loud and clear. Sounded like really bad lungs the man had.

Raye shuddered. The pair of down-and-outs were too much a reminder of she and Ash's own mortality. *Even now we're both just mere steps from being trapped like rats and killed.*

She forced her mind from such glum imaginings back onto her physical sensations, stiffening as Ash dug two fingers into her vagina and rolled them slowly over a point on its front wall. She bit her lip—her sensations had instantly upped a notch. *Yeah, that has to be my G-spot! Go, girl, go!*

"I want to eat you too, honey," she moaned, both bums now as forgotten as if they weren't there.

Ash got into sixty-nine position, her cunt hanging over Raye's face. Her tongue and fingers continued their explorations in Raye's sex—spreading, teasing, licking, flicking . . . penetrating, stroking both shallow and deep. Raye's hips began thrusting up to meet her mouth, the soft pubic hair tickling her chin.

Wriggling like a worm from the pleasure, Raye spread Ash's labia and sank her tongue deep into the dripping vagina. She licked the translucent secretion. It had an hint of iron in it. *Period's close,* she thought, then forgot everything except the musky scent of woman that threatened to drown her in its naturalness.

Surrounded by the oddly misplaced assortment of their belongings, it was hard for both women not to scream out loud as they orgasmed within seconds of each other, protected from the cold night by their warm welling of love.

CHAPTER 30

Vola was there as always. Waiting for him.

Except for her human head and breasts, Vola was a woman-sized skinless bird. An avian version of the Egyptian sphinx.

In place of feathers, her body—wings, bird-feet and all—was covered with snakeskin mottled gold and brown like a rattlesnake's.

Her face was beautiful, though un-humanly elongated, with tilted eyes, a Roman nose, and a full-lipped mouth.

Her tongue was long and forked.

Vola said nothing while Fred undressed. He looked too upset for words. Instead, she lay back on the floor and spread her legs wide, displaying her sex for his appraisal. He always liked her doing that.

Her foot-claws scratched the ground restlessly with her need for him.

Fred dropped his shirt on top of the rest of his clothes. His cock was erect and throbbing. Vola's golden eyes brightened on seeing how turgid it was, how much he desired her too.

Fred's body was transformed in this place. Here, his skin had the same rattlesnake decoration as Vola's. His penis too was altered—a forked tongue poked from its tip. The penis-tongue tasted the air left and right of Fred, then pointed itself at Vola's cunt.

Eyes impatient, Vola gestured to Fred with her wings.

He went to her, taking great pleasure in the knowledge that she loved him. His embarrassment at Tony Marconi's—the damned coke-dog fellating him—dropped off his soul like shed weights as he reached Vola and knelt between her spread thighs, poising his erection at the blood-swollen purple lips of her sex.

He penetrated the birdlike woman (womanlike bird?). She sheathed him like a sword in her moist yielding flesh, wrapped her leathern wings around him, held him to her massive breasts, clasped him tight around the buttocks with her bird feet. Her talons dug into his skin. He thrust into her with abandon, like he knew she liked. She pumped her crotch up to meet his thrusts, granting him more depth inside her body—she knew he loved that.

The sex was familiar, yet very strange. The tongue protruding from Fred's penis licked deep inside Vola's womb. It licked slow, then faster, lengthening in and out of Fred's penis as he thrust. The feel of it sliding in and out of his penis was like someone was fucking him as he fucked her.

Their sensations rose higher and higher. Both exploded—Fred flooding Vola with semen, she gripping him so tight in her wings he imagined his bones breaking.

He lay atop her afterward, both of them feeling the tongue in his penis languidly lick her come-slick interior. She trembled as he rested on her massive breasts.

They kissed, dueling tongues, milking the last threads of erotic sensation from each other.

"You're sad," she said when they sat up.

"Other than you, I've little to be happy about," Fred agreed.

"I've told you to stay here with me."

"I can't."

"You don't want too," the bird woman said with a hint of pique. "I'm not attractive enough for you because I don't look like one of your own women."

"Not true. I stayed a week once."

She stroked his face with her wingtip hooks. "And then left in a hurry." Her expression turned sad. "No one forced you to leave, Freddie darling. You just seemed to tire of being happy. Sometimes I think you actually enjoy your misery, relish your melancholy, prefer your sad place."

He scowled. "I'm not a masochist, if that's what you mean."

She leaned in close and kissed him on the lips, then pulled back to regard him coolly. "So why don't you come see me more often? By your own admission you have no other female. We're always happy together." She giggled coyly. "And the sex is—like you say—dynamite."

Fred's face clouded as he thought up an answer. What Vola said was right. She did make him happy—more happy than anyone he'd ever met. But . . . she wasn't human.

He considered her body. *She looks like someone plucked the feathers and head off Big Bird from Sesame Street and put a lovely face and huge breasts on it instead.* He instantly regretted the comparison. *No, that's condescending and inaccurate—Big Bird is cumbersome and awkward, Vola has style and grace and a delightful naturalness to her body. She's a real-life harpy without the bad intentions. Oh yes, she truly is desirable, but that's only because I'm also transformed. I'm far from human when I'm here.*

He regarded his snakeskin-covered body—his rattlesnake-patterned arms and legs, his hands and feet each now with only three fingers/toes, his limp penis with the long snake tongue dangling from its tip.

How he looked filled him with revulsion. That was the problem: He was and could be permanently happy here, and Vola truly loved him, and he really liked . . . maybe *loved* her. But he didn't love himself.

Fred cringed whenever he saw his transformed face. His eyes were slanted, yellow and bulging. He had no hair, nose, or ears. No lips—just a beaklike protrusion of a mouth with blunt teeth and another forked tongue . . .

His reflection always terrified him. It was viewing a forgotten childhood fear—the bogeyman—come to life. *Here I'm a fucking monster—I disgust myself. For all the love in the universe, I can't live my life looking the way I do now.*

Vola saw that Fred was unable to express himself, was getting angry. "Okay," she said quickly, "tell me your problem. I may be able to help." She grinned at him and stroked his detumesced penis. "And afterwards we'll fuck again. I want some of that thing you say human women love. Cunnilingus, yes?"

He forced a grin. "Okay."

She pushed herself up close to him. The feeling of her large breasts against his body instantly relaxed him. The prodding massive nipples—brown huts in an aureole yard. He stroked her snakeskin wings, running fingers across their thick throbbing veins.

"Tell me," she said, looking into his eyes, her own eyes intent with desire, both for him, and to please him.

Fred explained about Big Tony and Lana Petrova. "And it's getting worse," he finished. "Each time I deliver a shipment there, Big Tony can't wait to humiliate me, put me in the stocks and have Bitch sniff me. And last time, Lana spoke of getting a camera—"

"What is a cam'ra?"

"A recording device for pictures. Then you can play them back and see what happened over and over again." He groaned. "I'm scared stiff that he'll record something and put it up on YouTube—"

"What is yutoob?"

Fred grinned. "It's a place where people post their indiscretions for public approval." He smiled sadly at Vola. "I really shouldn't bother you with all this." He dipped a hand between her legs. "How 'bout I just eat you—"

She pulled back from him, gaping in shocked anger. "Eat? How dare you want to cook me?"

Fred laughed out loud. "Eating is just another name for cunnilingus. Damn, girl, you've a whole lot to learn."

Vola laughed too. "I'm sorry I misunderstood you. She hooked his dislodged hand and pulled it back to her crotch. "Please rub me some more. I like it." She sighed as he did so. "I was wrong, I can't help you with your problem. Cam'ras and yutoob, are too much for me—"

"See what I mean?"

"But I know a woman who *can* help you. Her name is Felix. She lives in the cathouse."

"She's a prostitute?"

"What is a prostitute?"

"Someone who sells sex for money."

"What is money?"

Fred shrugged. "Well at least you know what sex is."

She gasped, amber eyes widening, as he dug fingers deep into her cunt, then pulled him down to the floor. "Quick do the vagina-eating thing to me! I feel like there is fire in my love hole."

"What about Felix the prostitute?"

"Forget her—I'll explain later! She'll still be there after the cunnilingus!"

Fred obliged her, bending between her splayed scaly bird legs and licking and fingering her vagina deep.

Vola moaned and groaned and spasmed, then she pulled Fred up on top of her again, once more burying his penis in her hungry wet sex, wrapping him in her wings, smothering him with her breasts.

He sexed her slow and hard, his penis's tongue again licking at her womb.

They rose like birds, exploded like the big bang, and it was perfect.

CHAPTER 31

Raye creamed deliciously as the dildo slid in deeper.

"Oh shit! Give it to me!"

Jodie Foster grinned. Bracing herself on hands and knees, she thrust the strap-on in farther. Raye moaned. Jodie bent, took Raye's left nipple between her lips. She sucked the turgid pink flesh, swirling her tongue over it, not once missing a stroke of the dildo.

It was cold in the soft bed; autumn wind blew in through an unlatched window. Raye ignored the chill. Jodie's warm breath on her breasts warmed her. She felt herself melting like butter into orgasm.

"I'm gonna come, Edie!"

The croaky old voice, sharp like a razor, hit Raye like a slap to the face.

She jerked awake, Jodie Foster fading regretfully away into haze.

"Oh shit!"

She was naked and uncovered on the blanket on the park floor. Dawn sunbeams poked fingers through the trees at her.

Ash was nowhere in sight, but she wasn't alone.

She looked down between her legs in disbelief.

The withered tramp woman of the night before knelt between Raye's spread and bent legs, sliding an object in and out of her vagina. Raye gasped when she saw what the woman was dildoing her with.

A wine bottle? A fucking wine bottle?

The bottle's thin neck slid smoothly in and out of Raye, a cold intrusion that felt worse than an unwarmed speculum.

While abusing Raye with the bottle, the dirty woman was simultaneously masturbating, a grimy hand working deep within the voluminous folds of the rags cloaking her.

She grinned black teeth at Raye. "Oh, my sleeping beauty's awake now, is she?"

Raye sat up in a rush. "What the fuck? Take that thing out of—!"

"Oh fuck yes, Edie!" A male voice growled to Raye's right.

In her shock, Raye had forgotten the other person in the picture, an old male tramp. She turned toward him.

A huge mistake. The man's semen splattered her in the face. Raye was so confused by the screwed-up turn everything had taken that she just sat back on her elbows, and let the bum splash her with come.

The tramp was so old he looked in the running to be God if the current Almighty tired of the job. His eyes were rheumy gray. Raye had no idea if their gray color was natural or eye disease. The lines in his unwashed face seemed carved like into a wooden mask. Spittle dribbled from his mouth between his few remaining teeth as he pumped his penis, the dirty organ pale as a plucked chicken.

"Squirt that jism all over the bitch, Joe!"

Raye sat paralyzed as the semen covered her face, viscid and smelly as cod liver oil. The combination—tramp fucking her with a bottle plus tramp ejaculating in her face—was too odd to permit her any other action. (The bottle Edie was using as a dildo wasn't even empty—red wine sloshed inside it with each stroke.) Drowsiness also chained her in inaction—how had her delicious wet dream of sex with Jody Foster become this? All she could think during the come-drenching was: *You old son-of-a-bitch! How dare you use me as a jerk off fantasy?* Then: *And where in a rubber duck's butthole is Ash?*

Dirty Edie slid the bottle deep up Raye's vagina and began shuddering through her own climax. She went rigid as one of the nearby trees. She finally relaxed, a dreamy smile on her face. "Yeah, Joe, that was a good one—can't remember when I had me some pussy last!" Like nothing had happened, she slid the bottle out of Raye's cunt, unscrewed the top and took a long pull of wine. She wiped her mouth, offered Raye the bottle. "You want some, dearie?"

Raye managed to shake her head. She was utterly repelled; her skin felt like a million bugs were crawling on it.

The old tramp shook the last drops of semen from his cock, then packed it away in his ragged trousers. Raye was relieved to see the last of the white organ—it looked sick. *Thank goodness he didn't rape me with it!*

Thank goodness? For what? I've just been raped with a bottle! Rage bubbled up inside her. *I'll kill you bastards!* But it was an impotent anger. She was tempted as hell—oh God yes she was tempted!—to beat old Joe to death with her hair, smash him till he was a wet pulp of indistinguishable organs, his bones red pebbles, his brains . . . Edie she'd squash like she'd done Bug, squeeze her till blood squirted from her nose and ears, till her dirty head popped off her neck, then she'd—

"Hey," Edie said, rooting through Ash and Raye's stash of grocery bags. "You don't mind if we join you for breakfast, do you?"

The anger drained out of Raye. The memory of her killing Bug quashed her enthusiasm for a fight. The last thing she and Ash needed now was to draw any attention to themselves. They'd been successfully anonymous so far. Nothing must screw that up. *Dammit!* she thought, *I can't even scream for the webcops.*

She shook her head at Edie. "No, help yourselves." She didn't recognize her own voice. *I sound like a ghost speaking, and where is Ash? These bums didn't kill her did they? No, I'm sure they didn't.*

She watched Edie make sandwiches with hands that stank of her vagina—Raye winced at the intensity of the smell.

Old Joe was swigging from Edie's bottle, looking around at Ash and Raye's belongings. He bent and picked up a pair of panties and sniffed them. "You girls planning on moving in with us here?"

Raye grabbed the panties from him. "Shut the fuck up, douchebag. Leave our stuff alone."

"Hey, I don't mean no harm. Just an honest question."

Raye ignored him. She cleaned his ejaculate off her face with the retrieved panties, then examined her vagina to make sure the bottle hadn't ripped her open.

She wasn't even sore. She *hated* that. Pain would have justified her shame. She hated even more that she couldn't make a scene.

Edie offered Joe a sandwich. He took it from her; bit into it.

"Want one, dearie?"

Raye shook her head at the sandwich Edie was offering her. It was smeared with dirt. Looked like it had been picked fresh from a dumpster.

Edie shrugged off Raye's refusal, bit into the sandwich herself, chewed and swallowed with relish. She took the bottle of wine from Joe, drank up.

Raye got up, found her clothes, and pulled them on. She'd now begun worrying about Ash. Where the hell was she?

It was fully light now. A melee of car horns blew in through the trees obscuring the highways. From the clearing's opposite side, through the woods beyond the benches, came a responsive cackle of water bird noises and loud splashing. Somewhere to the south, sea lions barked boisterously.

On a branch overhead, two squirrels fought over a nut. The nut finally rolled off the branch, leaving both rodents staring confusedly at themselves.

Central Park, its trees painted in fall shades of yellow, red, purple, and brown, was beautiful in the warming sun. Its glory was lost on Raye.

Ashley Status, where are you?

CHAPTER 32

Ash walked out from behind a thicket.

"Where the hell have you been!?" Raye yelled.

"I love you too. I had to take a dump and next thing I know my belly hurts and my period's begun and I've got no tampons with me, and . . ."

Raye nodded dully, turned away. Ash misinterpreted her depressed look. She rushed to her, grabbed her arm. "I'm sorry. You looked so lovely sleeping—like a Disney princess—that I didn't want to wake you." She gestured at the tramps. "You been making friends?

"You could call it that," Raye said disinterestedly. "I just got raped by this pair. Looking at them you'd never think they had it in them."

Ash's face turned six shades of enraged. "Did you just say . . . raped?"

"With that wine bottle."

Ash looked confused at the bottle pressed to Edie lips. It took a moment for the meaning of Raye's words to register fully with her.

Then:

She charged across to Joe and grabbed him by the neck, began walking him backwards while shaking him. "You did fucking what to her, you son-of-a-bitch?"

Joe batted at her with feeble old hands. "Let me go, girl! I ain't done no harm to her. Been ages since I saw a pretty young girl naked. All I did's was wank! Nothing more."

"The bottle?"

"Was Edie used the bottle. I'se having trouble getting it up and Edie thought a porno pose—"

"Let him go!" Raye snapped.

"No! We're handing them over to the webcops! Cat food is all these shits are good for."

Edie's drunken calm instantly collapsed. "Oh no, not the webcops," she moaned piteously.

"Oh *yes*—the webcops. And it doesn't matter if you two run away, I've a chip in my head that's already recorded both your faces."

"Please," Joe moaned, as she tightened her grip on his throat. "We didn't hurt her."

Ash kept walking him backwards and shaking him. He felt ridiculously light in her grip, like he was really nothing but the rags he had on. It was an intoxicating feeling, being stronger that a guy, even a withered stinky one. "And if the bottle had broken inside her? What then?"

"We didn't mean any harm!" Edie yelped. "Honest!" She hurriedly downed the rest of the wine, stared at them in alarm mixed with drunken stupor.

Raye watched Ash's reaction to her abuse with a mixture of pleasure that her girlfriend cared so much, and anger that they really couldn't teach the stupid pair a lesson.

She shook her head at Ash. "That's enough. Forget them, let's just go back home."

"No. Call the spider police on your phone."

Raye rolled her eyes. "Oh, yeah? Why bother to phone? There's one over there. Just yell—damsel-in-distress style." She pointed up between a clump of trees. Across the foliage-concealed street, a black human shadow swung between two high-rises, suspended on an invisible strand of thread. She walked over and whispered in Ash's ear. "They'll likely be very pleased Mr. Rich's killers turned themselves in."

"Oh fuck!" Ash said, remembering the trouble they were in. Furious, she pushed Joe away savagely.

Joe stumbled back two steps, then stepped on an empty Scotch bottle which squirted out from under his foot, upending him. He fell backward, cracking his head hard on the park bench behind him, then slumped to the ground. He lay there on the grass, his head twisted sharply to one side, not moving.

Edie glared at Ash and Raye. "Now look what you've done." She shuffled over to Joe. "Joe, Joe, wake up. Wake up, they're not going to call the cops."

Raye stared at the motionless man in disbelief. Joe clearly wasn't breathing. "Tell me he hasn't just broken his neck," she whispered to Ash.

The color bled out of Ash's face. "Hell no. Not again."

(Both women had been horrified to discover, after arriving in New York, that Money Rich was still alive. It was soul-destroying, knowing that had they bothered to check Money's body that night, they wouldn't currently be on the run.)

Ash rushed to Joe's side. Pushing Edie out of the way, she grabbed his wrist and felt for his pulse, then unwrapped his dirty wool scarf from his neck. Noting the sharp angle of dislodged bone jutting from the back of Joe's neck, she quickly wrapped the scarf round it again

"He's okay," she told Edie, "just unconscious. Here, give me a hand getting him up on the bench."

They lifted Joe into a sleeping position on the bench, Ash once again marveling over how light he was. "I'll get a blanket," she told Edie.

She strode back to Raye. "He's deader than a dodo," she whispered. "We gotta leave right now, before morning folk start coming through here. We're just fortunate to be off one of the jogging courses."

"Dead?" Utterly horrified, Raye gaped at the dirty old man on the bench. "I don't get it. How *can* he be dead?"

"Worry about it later," Ash said, walking past with a blanket in her hand.

She covered Joe up to his neck, then pulled Edie aside. "We need aspirin. He's going to have the mother-of-all-headaches when he wakes up, and he'll also need some balm for his neck."

"We ain't got no money," Edie sniveled.

"We'll lend you some." Ash handed Edie two hundred dollars she'd brought back along with the blanket. "We all need some booze too to take the chill off. Where's the nearest store?"

She felt sickened by the happy gleam that came into the down-and-out woman's eyes as she snapped up the cash in her claw-like fingers. And the smell of the woman! "I'll go get us some bottles," Edie said. "You two watch Joe for me."

She left them, humming happily. Ash recognized the tune—Femina's *Tummy Troubles*:

"Fuck me gently,
Fuck me gently,
I've got dysentery,
So fuck me gently.

If you pump my cunt too hard,
I'll squirt shit out my ass,
I'll really make a mess,
But we won't stop having sex.
No, I won't let you out of bed,
I'll make you give me head instead,
'Cos . . .
I really need to come,

Though I'm suffering from the runs.
Oh, there's fire in my bum,
(My poor hurting ass . . .
Feels packed with broken glass!)
So do it soft and slow,
Or else poop is gonna flow!

Fuck me gently,
Fuck me gently,
I've got dysentery . . ."

Once Edie had shambled out of sight, Ash rushed over to Raye, who was still staring dazedly. She grabbed her shoulders, shook her viciously. "Snap out of it! Grieving won't bring him back to life!"

Raye looked at her, her eyes teary. "It's not *him* I'm thinking of. It's *us*. We're getting deeper and deeper into a mess. Things are just going from bad to worse."

Ash looked from Raye's teary face to Joe's corpse. "Fine. Right. And they'll be a lot worse still if we get discovered here with his corpse." She fiddled about in her left thigh, finally coming out with a little plastic van. She looked pointedly at Raye, then gestured around at their belongings. "Start packing stuff up; pile our clothes in the blankets. I'll look for a stretch of road to inflate the van."

Raye nodded dully. "What happens if Edie comes back?"

"She won't. You saw the look in her eyes when I gave her the money. She'll drink a full bottle herself before she remembers the rest of us."

Raye nodded. Ash kissed her tenderly on the lips, then loped off toward the horns blaring through the trees. When she was gone, Raye started piling their clothes on the blankets. She worked with her back to Joe, scared to even look at the dead tramp.

After a while Ash returned. "Van's inflated and waiting on 5th Avenue."

They tied the blankets into bundles and began lugging their belongings to the van.

Around them, New York City woke up fully. Birds began singing in the trees. A pigeon landed on Joe's nose and took a shit on it.

CHAPTER 33

"I don't believe it," Ash gasped.

"At least now we know why Felix insisted on our not going home last night."

"She could have explained."

"I'm grateful either way. She's a real friend, not the cunt I thought."

Seated in their parked van (a pink Chevrolet Express), they kept staring. 70 Prince Street—their Nolita apartment building—was burnt down. The previously pleasant brick frontage was black. Smoke still billowed from windows as a fire truck sprayed water into them. One side of the building had collapsed. The ground-floor Back Forty West Restaurant seemed to have imploded. Firemen were rooting amongst the rubble for survivors. One emerged with a feebly jerking dog.

This might work in our favor," Raye said, pointing at the building.

"How?"

"When Joe's body is discovered and Edie gives our description, the cops'll trace us here. They'll think we're dead."

Ash shook her head. "You're forgetting the timeline. We were in the park last night at the same time as the building burnt down."

Raye scowled. "Yeah. Which likely means they'll think *we* burnt it down."

"Why'd you have to think so negative about everything?"

"Show me one positive in our current situation."

Ash thought a moment. Then she grinned. "Our being rendered homeless has resolved one major issue for us."

"Yeah? what?"

"You never liked this place anyway; I was the one insisting we live here." She gestured at the smoking brick husk, a kiln swarming with fireproof ants. "Now we *have* to find somewhere else."

Raye nodded slowly. "I think I know just the place to move to."

"Where?"

"The Hotel Bizarre. Remember that guy last night? The one who knocked me over?" She grinned for the first time since waking. "I always wanted to see Femina in concert." She scowled. "What was the address again?" She looked at Ash helplessly. "Can't remember."

Ash smiled. "Just like you. I'll check Google Maps." She was silent for a moment, then said, "It's at 230 Riverside Drive."

"Thanks, darling. Occasionally you're a real help."

"I just hope they have vacant rooms."

"Now who's being pessimistic?"

Ash made a face, then swung the van out of parking, joining the flow of traffic heading north.

CHAPTER 34

[Chicago]

"Deeper!"

It was late evening. Money Rich was having sex with Donald Oates, one of the syndicate's accountants. David was young and handsome, meaningless qualities now he was dressed in one of Miss Rich's money suits.

Money lay on her back beneath the dollar-clad accountant, squeezing her breasts and grunting. Her green eyes were glazed with pleasure as she stared out her new bedroom window—the massive glass square that now replaced the portion of penthouse wall destroyed during Ash and Raye's getaway.

Money gasped and bit her upper lip. "Yeah, that's better, baby. Like that—push a little more to the left."

Unlike with Mr. Rich's money suits for women, Donald's had eye-slits. He'd have preferred it didn't. Not because of his partner—Money's cash-tattooed physical perfection was an incredible turn-on—but because of the corpse in the room that seemed to watch them both with its dead eyes.

Money Rich had refused to bury her father. This despite all her brother Cash's protests. (Cassius Rich had finally been so disgusted with her adamance that he'd returned to Vegas and hadn't spoken to his elder sister since.) She'd instead embalmed him, afterwards propping him upright a corner of her (formerly *his*) bedroom. Mr. Rich's corpse—decapitated head stitched back in proper place—was currently half-plastered over with hundred dollar bills. So far the money reached up to his waist, each fresh plating of notes a testimony to strenuous sexual intercourse.

(During the sex, Donald didn't think about [or look at] Mr. Rich's unburied remains. Mindless as a piston, hot, sweaty and uncomfortable as hell in the money suit, he just fucked his boss and let biology run its relentless course. In his experience, few women could separate diligent effort from emotional involvement on a lover's part. Money Rich clearly assumed both were the same—*if you don't desire me, there's no way you'll fuck me like you do!* For her, a hard cock was a hard cock; it didn't matter *why* the guy wanted to fuck you, so long as you wanted it too, and he did it the right way. In the two month's since Mr. Rich's death, Donald had become expert at 'doing it the right way.')

"Oh, fuck!" Money gasped—and came. The glorious sensation flushed through her.

She lay limp and elated under Donald, loving the feeling of his organ in hers as he as he slid towards his orgasm.

"I'm gonna come!" he gasped.

"Don't you dare squirt it inside me!" She pushed the cash-coated man off her, up to a kneeling position, then quickly spread a handful of bills like a Chinese fan under his penis glans. With her other hand she began masturbating Donald.

Money enjoyed the swollen cock's anguished throbbing as she expertly escorted it into orgasm. Equally expertly, she caught his spurting semen in her handful of hundred dollar bills.

David finished ejaculating. Money let go of his penis; he collapsed sideways onto the bed. He watched her walk over to her father's corpse and plaster the money on it, spreading the fresh notes over Mr. Rich's petrified abs.

***

After Donald left, the robogoons Dillinger, Al Capone, and Bugsy Malone called on Money.

"Have a good screw, Boss?" Al asked.

She grunted. "So, so." She sat up against the headboard, dollar-sign-tattooed body naked, looking from metal face to metal face. No need to get dressed; they were machines—male gender identity or not, human pussy didn't appeal to them. "You metalmen got anything for me on our two runaways?"

Al nodded, his neck making a whirring sound. "We might."

Money cocked an 'interested' eyebrow. "Shoot—I'm listening."

"New York," Al said, thick plastic eyebrows scrunching together. "Two mornings ago, an old tramp died during a fight with a redhead in Central

Park. His niece says there were *two* women there, the other was a plump platinum-blonde."

"Could be anyone. The Big Apple's full of down and outs. Fights are usual. Bum entertainment after drinking—it's their substitute for TV."

Dillinger waved a metal finger at Money. "Uh uh, Boss, these chicks were special. First, they *weren't* real down-and-outs, just *slumming* in the park for the night. And *why* the police alerted us? During the fight, the redhead mentioned that she was recording the tramps' actions with a chip in her head."

Money sat bolt upright. She thought quickly. Two women, one with a mind-chip? Too much coincidence. Their current hair color didn't matter—dyes were all over the place. "Have the cops arrested them?"

"Nah. Edie—that's the tramp's niece—thought her uncle was just knocked unconscious. The girls sent her off to get them some booze. In classic wino M.O., she of course gets blind drunk first before remembering the others. When she arrives back four hours later, the women are gone, along with all their belongings."

He grinned, showing metal teeth. "The cops did a fingerprint search on the bench the dead bum was lying on. The women had wiped it clean. Edie also mentioned they'd covered her uncle with a blanket. That was gone too. That alerted the cops that these broads were special—most people in that situation wouldn't remember the cops can get DNA samples off fabric. With no prints, however . . ."

"They've no proof," Bugsy said, adjusting his porkpie hat.

"They might have some," Al contradicted him.

Money frowned. *Stupid goons.* "Make up your minds, willya? Is there proof or isn't there any?"

Dillinger nodded. "Not our fault, Boss. The New York fuzz aren't yet sure. But . . . when they pressured Edie over the cause of the fight between her uncle and the redhead, she said it was sexual assault. Apparently the old guy raped the blonde with a wine bottle and the redhead took exception to it."

Money gasped. "A *wine* bottle? *I'd* take exception to that. Any guy does that to me, I'll kill his ass deader that last night's steak." Her expression turned quizzical. "I don't get it . . . how does that help *us?*"

"Since the bottle was inside the blonde's snatch, it's got her DNA on it. The NYPD have already checked their databanks—no match. That means she's either not local or just moved to the Apple. She's also not listed in the FBI's databanks either. No criminal record then. The Chicago police are however currently getting Raye's DNA profile from personal effects left in her old apartment when she fled. They've also faxed over photos of both women so Edie can confirm it's them."

Money nodded. She suddenly felt tense. "How soon will we know?"

"Likely by tomorrow evening," Dillinger replied. "We prepare to travel?"

She shook her head. "Not yet. Let the cops find them first—if it is them."

"They might get away again," the goon said, his metal voice pissed-off.

Money scowled. Her face scrunched up in thought. "We've no choice but risk that. This had to be done right. Remember, the only reason the NYPD are helping us is because Big Tony Marconi is tight with Mayor Presley, and she knows he and Dad both got shot up in Syria while protecting our freedoms. She knows nada about their drug dealing. Same deal with Uncle Luigi Rossi. So her administration will turn a blind eye: If they find Raye and Ash, rather than make an arrest, they'll alert Uncle Luigi as to where they are, so he catches them for us. Better than you goons going in and shooting up the whole town."

"Aw, Boss. I was looking forward to the trip. Got an old girlfriend there I ain't seen in years."

Money scowled at Dillinger. She found robot sex too odd to contemplate—'robofuck' was the term used—adjustable-length-and-thickness metal penises sliding in and out of machine-oiled vaginas, the pleasure of both machines coming from spring-loaded electrodes on the surfaces of their sex organs. Also, 'Dill' was quite the mechanical playboy, with an 'old girlfriend' in every town anyone mentioned.

"Forget it," she snapped. "Uncle Luigi's got a firm hold on New York. Nothing extra we can do there." She smiled coldly. "Ash and Raye are going to be delivered to us here in Chicago. Then you goons can show them how angry you are that they killed father."

The robots gave a trio of grotesque metal grins. Dillinger stroked his metal mustache. Bugsy waved his Tommy gun. Al Capone swung his baseball bat.

"Yeah, Boss," Dillinger said. "Breaking their legs, that ain't bad compensation for not seeing Bronzie again."

Money stared coldly past the goons at her father's money-coated corpse. She got out of bed and walked over to it, passing her closet full of money-tailored dresses and evening gowns, greenback trouser suits, and racks of embroidered cash-shoes.

She stroked the corpse's shrunken face with delicate manicured fingers. *Don't worry*, Daddy, she thought, fingers resting on his desiccated brow, *I'll have vengeance for you on those two whores.*

The thought and the whole discussion had her stressed out. She looked back at the three goons. "You guys can leave. Keep me posted on developments."

The robogoons got to their feet and tramped off. Dillinger stepped heavily—he still wasn't a hundred percent fixed after his fall from Bug's apartment.

"Hey, Dill!"

Dillinger paused in the doorway. "Yeah, Boss?"

Money frowned. "Send Donald back up." She indicated Mr. Rich's corpse. "I must get Daddy ready for the big day when we catch his murderers." She thought a moment. "Nah, I think I completely drained Donald's balls. Send up Josh instead."

The robot nodded. "Sure thing, Boss. Have a nice screw."

CHAPTER 35

Femina – Now The Fuck Is Over (One-Night-Standard)

You're softening in my vagina now.
I really liked it, guess I'll be leaving now.
What's your name and number, baby?
What do you do?
Are you worth meeting again,
Or just another random screw?
Someone I one-night knew?

I'm pulling up my panties now.
Wow!
Your condom's *full* of come.
Sorry, hon, it was fun,
But this working girl's gotta run.
But . . . leave your phone on,
When tomorrow's work is done.
Just in case,
I ask you back over to my place.

CHAPTER 36

"Weird name for an ordinary place," Raye said.

"You mean 'grandiose' for 'mundane' or 'nondescript.'"

"Is that you speaking or your Wikipedia brain-chip?"

Her sarcasm was lost on Ash. "Sometimes I'm not sure. Once I've a chip in my head, it's like I'm the smartest woman in the world, and still I'm not."

The pair of them stood by their pink van, peering up at 230 Riverside Drive.

The 'Hotel Bizarre' was a large four-story brick building with a sidewalk overhang (propped up by a metal framework) running the entire length of its frontage. Potted plants decorated both sides of its front door.

The hotel stood at the corner of Riverside and West 95th Street, the latter route running in across Broadway and Amsterdam Avenue to Central Park.

Two hundred yards opposite the Hotel Bizarre, the Hudson River flowed on its languid way. The river was clearly discernable through broken arrangements of trees, its surface a rippling gray waterscape across which the occasional vessel passed.

"I'm not really liking this place," Ash said, drumming fingers on the van's hood. "Central Park's just over there. What if—"

"Edie recognizes us? That's why it's so perfect, darling—the fuzz are never going to expect two killers to be just around the corner. They'll expect us to flee town."

"Fleeing still looks to be our best option." She looked intently at her girlfriend. "I'm worried, Raye. All it takes is us accidentally entering the same drugstore as Edie—"

140

"Rest your mind, we won't be going anywhere. We'll lay low in our room all day and make love."

"Why do I get the impression this is just a ploy to keep me all to yourself?"

Raye sighed. "That'll be a nice first if I succeed in it." She pushed silver hair out of her eyes. "Romance aside, I've a good feeling about this hotel."

"Hmmph. You just want to get as close to Femina as possible, slut."

"Okay, that too. But . . ." she gestured at the ordinary-looking building, "it has an anonymous vibe I like."

"Oh, alright. Let's see if they've rooms to let."

***

The hotel interior was as ordinary as its exterior.

A fat oily man in a brown suit sat behind the receptionist's desk in the otherwise deserted foyer. His black hair and mustache were stiff with grease.

"There sits a born swindler," Ash whispered to Raye as the front door swung shut behind them. "I've never seen anyone so greedy-looking in my life."

The receptionist adjusted thick glasses on his nose while replying their inquiry. "Yes, of course, ladies; we've always vacancies here at the Hotel Bizarre." He gave a little bow. "My name is Edmond Flourish. I'm delighted to serve you both." He looked them over quizzically. "Now what type of room would you like? One double, or two single?"

"Double."

Edmond nodded. "No trouble at all. We've a nice room on the third floor that looks out over the river. I'm certain you'll both love the view. Sometimes in the evening—"

"How much is it?" Raye interrupted.

"Two hundred dollars a night."

"We'll take it for two weeks for a start."

Ash got out money from her handbag and paid Edmond Flourish. ("Stop unzipping your arm in public," Raye had cautioned her. "It's a dead giveaway that you're not some ordinary chick.")

Edmond slid the receipt form over to them to sign. Ash put pen to paper.

"We heard a rumor about this place," Raye said.

Edmond smiled. "What would that be, madam?"

"That Femina's here for a week, playing concerts."

Edmond's expression didn't change. "It's true, madam."

Ash and Raye looked at him. "It's true?"

"Why yes, of course. Ms. Femina is goddaughter to Mr. Luigi Rossi, the owner of this establishment. She's giving private performances to entertain a few of his friends—mostly New York's elite." He bent conspiratorially forward. "Please keep this information secret, ladies."

Ash pushed the signed receipt back to him. "Can *we* get tickets for the show?"

Edmond Flourish nodded. "Why yes, of course. Hotel guests are automatically permitted to attend. He reached under his desk and produced two tickets, identical to the ones Ash and Raye had seen with the young man of the previous night, for Femina's 'Foreplay Sex Orgasm Afterglow Tour.' "Three hundred dollars each."

"Three hundred?"

He grinned slyly. "Except you'd rather prefer to fly to Texas and catch her on tour there." He winked. "I hear the ticket scalpers down south are making a killing."

"It's still exorbitant."

"It's not just for one night. Because you're hotel guests, you'll be permitted to attend all her performances this week. Of course, this doesn't cover the cost of refreshments."

"We'll take them!" both women said simultaneously, then broke into laughter. Ash got out another six hundred dollars from her handbag and paid Edmond. The portly receptionist expressed no surprise at being handed so much cash with a credit card terminal right in front of him on the desk.

He handed them the tickets. "Please hold on, I'll get the bellboy to take you to your room."

***

The first inkling either Ash or Raye had that the Hotel Bizarre might live up to its name was in the elevator.

"Okay this is creepy," Ash said with a shudder. "This building only has four floors, why does the elevator have *twenty* floor buttons?"

"Uh?" Raye looked first at the elevator controls, confirming Ash's observation, then at the bellboy, who nodded toward the elevator's fourth occupant, a handsome young man who'd stepped in just before the doors closed.

"Oh, it's nothing really," the young man said. "Just a prop in keeping with the hotel's name. You'll find lots of little things like that here—mirrors that seem to reflect rooms other than the one you're in, doors that open on brick walls, and suggestions of secret passages. It's just manufacturing a fake mystique."

"Oh, that makes sense," Ash said, with clear relief.

The young man was still speaking: "If you care for creepy stories though, there's a legend that when this building was originally built, it was much taller than it now is, but that one night during a storm, most of it vanished. Those who believe the story say that's the real reason the elevator has more stops than the building."

Raye burst into laughter. "That's the most ridiculous thing I've ever heard."

The elevator chimed for the third floor. "Well it's been nice meeting you both," the young man said. He smiled. "If you're staying a while, we'll likely meet again." He held out his hand. "I'm Fred Matthews, the manager."

"Ash and Raye." They shook hands.

They stepped out of the elevator along with the bellboy. Fred waved at them as it shut.

"What a totally nice guy," Raye whispered to Ash. "I just know you're dying to get his penis into your mouth."

Not to be outdone, Ash laid her head on Raye's shoulder. "Oh, you know me so well, darling. Gosh, he's so dreamy!"

"I was being sarcastic," Raye retorted angrily.

"You were?"

CHAPTER 37

The room was fantastic, with a large blue bed. Its view of the Hudson River as wonderful as Edmond had promised.

"I feel like I'm in paradise," Raye said as the bellboy wheeled their luggage cart in. Raising her arms, she flopped exaggeratedly back on the huge bed.

"Do you think Edmond will find it suspicious that we paid cash rather than by credit card?" Raye asked when the bellboy had left.

Ash mused over the question. "It's possible, but unlikely. He didn't seem to care though." She gestured around. "Despite how great this room looks, I don't think they do great business." She frowned. "If he asks—we lost 'em. Remember what I told you—we slot just one of our cards into an ATM or POS terminal, next thing you know, we'll be back in Chicago with Money Rich."

"This sucks."

"Yeah, but it's safer. This way we're not letting anyone know where we are." She laughed. "Don't know what's bothering you anyway. It's not like either of us have any money left in the bank to withdraw. We drained both our accounts back in New Buffalo."

Raye walked over to stare out of the window. "We've only ten grand left. What happens when that runs out?"

Ash crossed to the window and held her, stroking her pearly hair. "We'll have to find more before then."

Raye turned to stare at her. "Another robbery?"

Ash nodded. "We've no choice." She regarded Raye's upset expression with surprise. "What? You've cold feet now over helping yourself to stuff that doesn't belong to you? You, a professional thief?"

Raye didn't break the stare. "Yes, I do." She gripped Ash's shoulders. "People keep dying around us. Sooner or later our number's gonna come up too and we'll be finished."

Ash pointed out over the gray Hudson waters. "One more strike, honey. That's all it takes. One big score and we're free. We'll take a boat down to Cuba. South America—Brazil, Costa Rica . . . somewhere where we can laze in the hot sun all day. Fade off the grid for good." She hugged Raye tight. "We'll make it, you'll see."

Raye shivered. "I wish I could believe like you that everything will end happily."

"I've enough faith for both of us. We'll make a huge score and we'll split . . . alive and well." Her brow furrowed. "Only thing is—where is there enough money to make risking our necks worthwhile? Anything less than a million dollars isn't worth it."

"Remind me—where have I heard that statement about a million dollars before?"

Ash scowled. "Damn, girl, you are in the pits." She pulled Raye towards the bed, undoing her buttons as they went.

"Ash, what do you think you're doing?"

"What does it look like?"

"I'm so not in the mood."

"Oh, don't play hard to get. I simply have to eat your pussy before the Femina concert."

"Okay, but I'm not eating *you*—not with your period on."

Ash sighed. "But I've a tampon in! Just lick around it. C'mon, darling, be a sport—not a spoilsport." She fluttered her lashes at Raye. "You know I've gotta have it at this time of month—it helps with the pain."

"No. Use Midol."

Ash pushed her down on the bed and pulled her jeans off. "Whatever you say, Prudence Stingy-Pussy-Tightwad. I'll jerk off with the vibrator after you come." She spread Raye's thighs wide, revealing the unbleached brunette bush, the moist pink sexual slit. "Right now, I want to lick you silly."

CHAPTER 38

The Femina concert held in the hotel basement, a large space with a smoky ambience like a jazz club in 1930s Chicago. It had a semicircular stage for the band, two wine bars and space for forty tables.

"Lots of people in attendance," Raye said.

"Everyone looks rich except us."

"Definitely no cops here tonight." She gestured at the table to their left, where a bony woman was bent over several white lines with a straw up her nose. The thin woman wasn't the only one using drugs. The smell of pot was thick in the air. Ash imagined clouds of marijuana smoke floating around, dispensing passive-smoking highs to everyone.

There was excited chatter all around, Ash caught snippets of gossip: "She ran off with him?" "He's gay? But he's Hollywood's top action hero!" "Yeah, she's had her nose fixed—her boyfriend said she looked like Julius Caesar."

Ladies in Disguise, Femina's all-male backing band, were getting ready. The two keyboard players swapped languid jazz chords while the guitarists tuned up. The sax player joked with the drummer while the latter changed a tom-tom skin. The two female backing vocalists sat perched on monitor speakers, laughing and looking pretty.

"Hey! There's the guy who bumped into us yesterday."

Raye followed her finger. "Nice wife."

"If you like small mousy women."

"You sound jealous. Look, there's Fred."

Ash turned to see. Fred Mathews was sitting with three others—two thickset middle-aged men and a statuesque blond in a low-cut red dress.

Raye wolf-whistled. "Now I wouldn't mind getting into *her* pants."

"He looks upset," Ash said.

"Huh? Who?"

"Fred. He's definitely pissed-off 'bout something." She waved to him.

An instant, unmistakable look of relief took over Fred's features when he saw them. He excused himself from his companions and came over.

"Glad to see you two here," he told them. "You don't mind if I join your table?"

"Please do. You didn't seem happy where you were."

He sighed. "Was it that obvious? He sat on Raye's left, then nodded back at his previous companions. "The man on the left's my uncle Luigi. He's cool, if old-fashioned. The pair with him are his business partners."

"Who're they?" Raye asked, now interested.

"The man's Tony Marconi—Big Tony. He's a TV exec. Asshole to the core. He's more obnoxious than he looks. The woman's Lana Petrova, she's sort of like his Russian mail-order bride."

"You don't like her?" Raye probed.

"She's worse than he is. With her beauty *is* only skin deep." He sighed again, much deeper. "Both of them take pleasure in annoying me. Their damn pet is even worse. I dread having to go back and join them."

"Life's full of people like that," Ash said. "People too powerful to get rid of who think they've a divine right to mess with you."

Fred nodded. "I couldn't have put it better my—"

"I think the concert's about starting," Raye interrupted.

They looked to the stage. Edmond Flourish was up there now. The musicians stood posed in readiness with their instruments, both backing singers were by their microphones.

The lights dimmed, overlapping cones of light framed the fat man. An expectant hush came over the room.

Edmond Flourish gave an exaggerated stage bow. "Welcome to the Hotel Bizarre, everyone! Without any ado at all, I present to you: The sexy siren who sings our deepest fantasies . . . Femina!"

The band broke into a soft funky rhythm. Edmond did a jig, then shuffled off stage-left. Femina emerged from the backstage curtains on the right.

The room filled with deafening applause.

Femina—blonde, blue-eyed and pretty; full-bodied and totally naked except for pink satin panties—strode to center stage, picking up a wireless microphone on the way.

The applause died down as she began singing/chanting *Pussy Talk*:

"One vagina touching another,
Two slit sisters,
Slippery with saliva,

And desire,
Sliding across . . .
Cunt to cunt,
Speaking of love:
First, of hard things like money and men,
Cock . . . erection . . . penetration,
Lovemaking like sexual war between nations.
Then again, of soft things . . .
Women . . . lipstick, shoes, and pantyhose.
Finally, discussing pussy—our glorious vaginas!
How do we begin?
I touch you,
You touch me,
We kiss . . . blissfully.
Oh, fuck! You slide down between my legs,
Tease me, make me beg.
I taste sweet, don't I?
What? You're sweeter?
I giggle (glad the ice is really broken). That's a fucking lie,
Get your kit off, honey,
It's vagina-comparison time.

A look across a crowded room,
A date . . . a secret rendezvous.
Two hot bodies on the floor
Each one gasping, "Give me more!"
Four breasts in a bed,
Tongues between our legs.
Who could ask for more?
But scared someone might knock on the door.

Squishing together,
Pleasure building in a forbidden bed.
"Are we lesbian?"
"I don't know? I like this, and I love cock too!"
"Me too, but John and Dave must never know."
"Oh, I love you, but . . ."
"You don't love me, you horny slut,
You'll fuck anyone."
"No! Only you and John!"
"I'm sorry I said that, please don't cry.
Come, let me kiss the tears from your eyes."

Femina fell silent. Her guitarist began a gentle solo.

"She's utterly fantastic," Raye whispered over the soft music.

"It's a 'funny' fantastic though," Fred whispered back.

Raye gave him a defensive look. "How'd you mean?"

"Well, what's so special about her? I mean in an objective sense."

"She sings about love and relationships. The heart's pain . . ."

"And SEX," Ash added gleefully. "Lots of sex."

"Trust *you* to notice that bit."

"Other people sing about relationships too," Fred said. "And they've better voices, and they actually sing, not pseudo-rap, like she does."

"You sound like you asked her on a date and she turned you down," Raye said. "Personally I find her just divine," she added dreamily. "I wouldn't mind having her warm my bed sometime."

Fred raised an eyebrow at her statement, then shrugged. "Lots of women would. Most of the guys here too. What I'm trying to say is—she's far from the best singer, or the most good-looking one—"

Femina's sultry voice cut him off with the song's final verse:

"Vaginas in conversation,
With so much to say to each other,
Most of it wordless.
Telepathy of moist cunt,
What more can you want?"

The song ended, the audience applauded wildly. The tempo of the music changed upward. Femina began belting out the next song, the loud *Officially Fucked!*:

"I'm fucked. I'm a mess (not hot).
Just lost my darn job,
And now I'm obsessed,
With seeking well-deserved redress.
I feel like hell today,
Got a million bills to pay,
But instead I got sent away,
'Cos I didn't let you have me on a tray,
During lunch break.
But hey, asshole, we'll see.
I'll be back with my legal team.

You're fucked, start signing checks,
You douchebag employer,
Offices aren't for sex,

Or for abusing your female staff.
Now it's my turn to laugh,
How does it feel to get shafted up the ass,
Without KY?
Does the payout hurt?
I hope you feel like crying,
Your damn fault for denying,
Me my female dignity,
In the workplace,
Last bastion of your patriarchy.

Sorry, what was that you just said?
It was just biology?
You don't actually hate us chicks,
You just 'love' us too much,
And you listened to your dick?
Just listen to yourself,
You slick son-of-a-bitch.
You can both kiss my ass and eat my shit.
And thanks so very much for making me rich."

The song ended. Fred got up. "I've got to get back to my table. My uncle's staring knives at me." He sighed. "No one wants to be alone with Lana and Big Tony."

"Okay, see you later," Ash said.

He left.

The next song was *Ballad of A Raped Girl*. Femina sang this alone with just an acoustic guitar as accompaniment:

"You fucked me without my consent, asshole.
Without my consent, though I screamed 'NO!'
And begged you to let me go.
You knocked me down and spread me wide,
Left me open to all eyes,
To the world.
To the news, to a whirlwind of truth and lies.
You exposed my secret life,
I was innocent, but had to pay the price.

You pumped garbage where I wanted someone special,
Poured trash in me like I was a disposal,
Fucked me without regard for love or truth,
It made no difference—I was just meat to you.

You left me a bloody, semi-conscious mess,
Wishing I could die, wishing I was dead.

But I'm not dead, I'm not dead,
You never lit my funeral pyre,
I rise up from the fire,
Stronger and with desire to live and love again,
Not ruled or enslaved by the pain,
No longer the disaster you made of me yesterday,
But twice as strong, immunized by the flame.

You fucked me till I bled,
Then you gave me head, and said,
I never needed to consent.
You left me wrecked,
My pussy and self-esteem in shreds,
My dignity dead,
Buried in the grave you left between my legs.

My womb is flushed out for convenience's sake.
No one *really* cherishes the child of a rape."

As Femina sung *Raped Girl*, the eyes of female listeners turned misty.
Many women wept outright, angry tears ruining their makeup. The majority
felt themselves as the violated victim.

Men sat confused, unsure how to react to the stifling vibe of female
sorrow and anger. Several tried comforting their weeping partners and were
savagely rebuffed. Others were gripped tight like they'd never be let go. The
latter—sensing animosity in the vise-like embraces—wished they were
somewhere else.

A lot of men simply excused themselves and went to have a piss.

As Ash listened to the song, memories flooded her like she was the Red
River Valley. Like a hitherto concealed emotional dam had shattered deep
in her soul, gushing torrents of forgotten feeling rushed over her in waves
that submerged her in their murk. Images flashed before her eyes—the dark
stable, the horses, the coming storm, the hint of perfume, the smell of fish,
the . . the . . tentacles . . . the rape . . . THE RAPE . . . THE RAPE . . .
THE RAPE . . .

The memory squeezed her brain like it would pulp it. She felt like she
was carrying the sky on her head. A female Atlas. And then, in the middle
of the horrible recollection, resurfaced the portion of her ordeal she hated
most . . . her shame. That she'd been incredibly turned on by the ravishing,

that she'd orgasmed from it, had one of the most violent climaxes of her life.

But how the hell could I? I hated every moment of it . . . *NO I DIDN'T. WHAT THE FUCK IS WRONG WITH ME!?*

Worse . . . the memory of the experience had her aroused again now—her groin raged to be serviced.

Femina sang on :

"Time heals, stitches heal, bruises fade,
I yank away the blinds hiding my mind from being redefined.
The pills end, the body mends,
The reasons 'Why?' are not easy to comprehend.
Is there any reason other than 'Men?'

The pain it fades, the memory remains,
But memory is fuel to the brain,
Motivation to remain sane.
And I determine, such will never, ever, happen again,
I'm stronger . . .
Stronger than you,
Some days I'm blue, but I'm always true.

I stare into my glass,
The wine is red just like you left my ass,
In it I see 'me' reflected.
I look good, not your 'piece of trash.'

I've stashed you away in my anus, asshole,
So I can I shit on you, yesterday, today, and tomorrow.
And in your fertilizer my new life grows,
A tree planted on your grave.

NO! I'm not dead, I'm not dead!
You never lit my funeral pyre.
I rise up in recovery,
(In empowering personal rediscovery,)
Strong! . . . and with desire,
To live and lust again.
Unweakened, laughing at the pain.
No longer the disaster you left behind yesterday,
But twice as strong, immunized to your reign.

I don't care who you are, your face is unimportant.

Your erection only changed one moment.
I cannot bother to hate you, that would make you significant.
And even if you're caught and jailed, you're simply once more irrelevant,
A statistic of an unpleasant circumstance.
It took me a while to learn,
That you're miles beneath my concern.

And best of all, I can still have sex;
My vagina still gets warm and wet.
I give and take my share of my lover's happiness.
The pleasure is always sublime and sometimes it's the best.

Nobody determines what I am, but I.
And the day I lay that down, I die.
All you destroyed was my memory of a perfect yesterday,
But I'm still perfect today."

Ash touched Raye's hand, seeking comfort. Raye shrugged her off. Ash gaped at her—that had never happened before. Then she relaxed—Raye was stuck in the song. Her face was cold—her eyes frigidly fixed on the nude blonde chanteuse onstage, her ears locked on Femina's seductive voice, on the distressing yet empowering words. Trapped in a private universe so grim no one else could be granted admission.

Raye, come out! Ash wanted to scream. *Please! I really need you here now!* But Raye, like most other women present, was too far gone in her private remembered/imagined torment.

The thought occurred to Ash then: *Has Raye ever been raped? Is that why men don't do it for her?*

She looked around. The same tortured, harried, horrified look marked three-quarters of the faces in the room. One of the few exceptions was the Russian woman, Lana Petrova. Lana's expression was unreadable. She had a smile on her face as she sipped her wine, but was it a smile of amusement or of disdain? Did she enjoy the other women's horror or was she faking to appear tough?

The men present were all clearly very uncomfortable now. There was a desperate atmosphere in the room . . . a fear—Ash sensed it strongly—that like rubber bands stretched too far, the women might all simultaneously snap and turn on their lovers.

Ash's anger at her memories dissolved away now, but her arousal remained.

Sheepishly, she snuck away to the ladies' room. Once there, with tears of shame streaming down her cheeks, she masturbated furiously.

Oh, I fucking want to meet the bastard who did this to me, she thought, tapping the gun hidden in her thigh. *And payback's going to be a total bitch.*

Her first orgasm only took the barest edge off her arousal. Utterly disgusted with herself, she pleasured herself two more times, both times biting her tongue hard to keep from screaming from the intensity of the sexual release that hit her at climax.

After her second orgasm, Ash found a satisfactory rationalization for her masturbation: *Fuck guilt. I'm getting some benefit out of this—orgasm works much better than painkillers to ease my menstrual cramps.*

She could practically feel her womb lining sloughing off each time she came.

CHAPTER 39

"Fuck me with your Patriarchic Prick!
Come here, Let me suck your rapist dick!
You chauvinistic piece of shit!
Man, you really make me sick,
But for the duration of this tryst,
I'll put up with your domination shit!
You abusive son-of-a-bitch!"

Ash gaped. Gone (like a bad memory) was the somber death mood of *Raped Girl*. The room was now in pandemonium as the women all shouted the lyrics of *Pigs!* at their escorts. The music was loud and hard—Rap Metal.

"I know you want to fuck me!
You *always* want to fuck me!
I need love so I'll let you!
I'm horny so I'll let you!
Need money, so I'll let you!
I need sexual validation too!
Oh, yes . . . you'll have your screw!
Else you might beat me black and blue!
Like you sometimes do!
But fuck you and your rape culture too!

Fuck me with your patriarchic prick!
Eat my cunt, lick my ass, and suck my tits,
You've convinced me that I like this,

155

O shit, I really do like this!
How great your erection is!
Nature's most wonderful piece of meat!

Pig, Pig, Pig, Pig, Pig!
Pig, Pig, Pig, Pig, Pig!"

I wish I had a penis too,
Then I'd be a prick like you!
And fuck up women's lives too.
Oh, I'm so jealous of you!
It must be so great to abuse,
To rape young girls and rule!
And not have to learn 'Female Inferiority 101' in school.
Stop grinning, I'm being sarcastic, you muscular tool!
You need me *a lot* more than I need you.
Shit . . . did I just confess that I *need* you,
Slip of tongue . . . it was the booze.
Oh, shit, but you fuck me so good!

Fuck me with your patriarchic prick,
Come here, let me suck your rapist dick!
Just make sure I have my orgasm!
Yeah, do me so hard I come screaming!

Yes, darling, you're lovely unkilled pork,
A swine, a disgusting swill-guzzling hog!
But you're the pig I love!

Pig, Pig, Pig, Pig, Pig!
Pig, Pig, Pig, Pig, Pig!"

Watching the yelling women (Lana Petrova included) leaping on chairs and jabbing fingers down at their boyfriends/husbands (even Raye was up on her chair screaming at any man within distance), Ash was forced to reconsider Fred's comments about Femina's popularity.

She looked at the singer. Femina was as animated as the women she led in the chant, her background singers too.

Damn, she really does tap into something primal in us chicks!

The men all still looked confused, but were at least certain they were in less danger than before, when the basement had the atmosphere of being full of female psychopaths.

156

The 'Pig' chant crescendoed, then slowly got softer. The song ended. Sweaty disheveled women climbed down off tables and chairs, leaping on their men and kissing them passionately. Several aggressively grabbed their partners crotches and squeezed their penises through their pants. Four women, faces flushed, headed for the door, impatiently dragging boyfriends behind them.

Ash grinned. *Parking lot sex ahoy!*

She crossed to her table. Raye leapt down from her chair, and grabbed her. She kissed Ash deep, dueling tongues till they both came up for air. Raye's face was flushed, her pupils dilated. Her nipples were hard against Ash's, her breath hot on Ash's face. "I feel like a major fuck already! How the hell does she do it?"

Ash felt her arousal return in spades. It was suddenly all she could do not to rip Raye's clothes off there and then and fuck her on the table, spreading her crotch wide open, spreading her vulva lips, eating her pussy and finger-fucking her for all to see. She realized it was just a reaction to the song—all the other women present clearly felt the same way. Lana was kissing Big Tony like she was trying to eat him.

The only free man was Fred, who clearly didn't have a date. Fred's Uncle Luigi was in the clutches of a Junoesque blonde who was rubbing herself so hard against him it looked like she was trying to rub her white dress off.

Ash controlled herself. "Later, darling," she told Raye. "The show's not even half done yet."

Raye winked. "Okay, but you're my bitch tonight. I'm getting the strap-on out."

Ash sighed. "I wish. Knowing you, sweetheart, it'll definitely be the other way around."

CHAPTER 40

[Chicago]

The kneeling man in the money suit sprayed semen like a champ. His come thickly splattered the bills Money held fanned out in front of him. His orgasm momentarily paused. She smacked his dollar-covered buttocks. "Give me more!"

The man (Money neither knew his name, nor cared) obliged her with two more spurts of semen, adding a second creamy-white layer atop the first. Then with a loud groan, he sagged down onto the bed.

Money smiled coolly down at him. (He got her so hot! He looked incredibly tasty—like a chicken with cash feathers—smothered in dollar bills like this.) She got out of bed and walked over to her father's corpse, which stood propped in its corner like an idol.

On a sudden compulsion, Money Rich had been having sex for the past five hours, through evening into night. Her first ever fuck-a-thon.

She'd flung the money suit at Dillinger with simple instructions: "Dress a naked guy in it and bring him up to me. I don't want to know who it is. When that one staggers out, put it on another guy, and then another."

The man currently breathing hard on her bed was number twenty-four. After the first fifteen—eight in the vagina, four blowjobs, three in the anus—Money had simply ordered each new bedroom entrant to masturbate and come on the money laid out on her breasts. "Just wank and splooge for me, darling—the more come the better."

Now, standing in front of her father's corpse, she surveyed her night's work with satisfaction. The corpse's only uncovered portion now was the left half of its face.

She frowned at the embalmed half-visage, its erstwhile handsome dignity vanquished by death. For a moment, deep fear gripped her; fear at what death had done to her father—the leathered skin, the once regal nose that now looked less dignified that a turkey's plucked rump, the toothbrush mustache, the shrunken lips, the discolored teeth like shaped shards of marble . . .

Damn, she thought, *once the spirit leaves, we're not even worth the cost of the sand we're buried in.*

Her morbid thoughts shook her. She shook them off, then quickly pasted the semen-soiled dollar bills over the clear portion of cheek, nose, and eye, completing Mr. Rich's money coating.

"There, Daddy," she said, stepping back. "You look great now. Just how you've always wanted to. This is so much cooler than some crap burial."

She turned at a sound behind her. Soft penis swinging left and right, the man in the money suit was sneaking toward the door.

"Hey!"

The dollar-obliterated man froze. Money saw he was shivering with fear. She burst out laughing. "Despite what you think—I'm not nuts."

"I don't think you're—"

She silenced him with a gesture.

"It doesn't matter. Your opinion will likely be as poor as you are—*whoever you are.*" She nodded at the door. "Leave. Tell the robots I said that'll be enough—my art is finished."

The man in the money suit slunk off. The door clicked shut behind him.

Fingers delicately tracing the Kate Rose necklace's curving descent between her perfect breasts, Money returned her attention to the dollar-covered corpse.

She was delighted at how perfect the effect was. Daddy's body was totally coated with greenbacks. *Oh, he looks just beautiful.*

"Now, Daddy, I've a surprise for you; something you're sure to like."

Money traipsed over to the safe, opened it, and got out a strap-on harness with a solid-gold dildo already attached.

She held the golden dildo up in front of the corpse's face. "Say hello to your new penis, Daddy!"

She carried the corpse over to the bed, laid it down and strapped the gold penis between its legs. "Okay, Daddy, I'm a bit sore from all the fucking, but I think I can still manage one more bout of sex tonight."

She squatted over the corpse, lubed the metal cock with spit, and slid down on it. "Ooh, Daddy, that feels so great," she moaned as it entered her vagina. "I've never worn gold like this before."

Money began sliding up and down on the metal penis. While fucking her father's corpse she delightedly roved her eyes over his fifty thousand dollar coating. He was a truly glorious sight—much better than a mere money suit.

At one point she forced his arms up, so his cash-wrapped fingers held her breasts. (Have a feel, Daddy!) "Have to fix this," she grunted aloud when they dropped back to his sides. "Locking hinges in his joints should do the trick."

Her orgasm, one of her most intense ever, rushed up to meet her. She sank down hard on the cold gold penis, accepting the accompanying stab of pain as it jabbed her cervix, feeling like she was being deflowered by her father.

"Oh, Daddy!" she moaned. "Why'd you have to go away and leave me all alone?"

Shuddering, Money collapsed onto 'Daddy's' cash-plastered chest. Her vagina clenched and spasmed around the golden penis. It was an exquisite indescribable feeling, having that most wonderful—most precious of metals—deep inside her. She almost didn't want to get off the corpse.

She did finally. The dildo was slick with her sexual fluids. Trembling with subsiding pleasure, she considered its wet length. It seemed a shame to waste the abundant lubrication, so she inserted the gold penis into her anus instead.

"Oh, Daddy, you're the best. How in the hell didn't we do this when you were alive?"

CHAPTER 41

"I don't know what came over me," Lana said. "Me? Leaping about on a tabletop like a frog? I'd never believe it in a million years."

"Mass hysteria," Uncle Luigi retorted. "All you girls having a go at your men at once? Good thing none of you have guns."

"Nah, it's all the pot in the air," Big Tony said.

"It's primal instinct," Fred said quietly. "Femina speaks to something basic in women. She speaks to them as biology—nature—made them, not to the product of modern civilization." He fell silent.

Karen Lewinsky (Uncle Luigi's blonde girlfriend who'd joined their table during *Pigs!*) looked at Fred with interest. Her face was still flushed with lust. "Go on," she urged.

"It's simple . . . kind of. Today's heterosexual woman is in a constant state of flux where men are concerned. You're told so many things—both truth and lies. Religion, politics, philosophy, dubious sexual 'research'—the conclusion of which varies depending on who interprets it—economics, everything tells you something different about how to relate to men."

Big Tony was looking at Fred, eyes confused. Uncle Luigi watched the stage. Femina was sipping from a glass of wine while her guitarist played a solo. The previous song's exertions seemed to have drained her. She was breathing hard. Her blue eyes, however, were enigmatic, playful even. They roved about the room, occasionally locking with someone else's gaze then demurely looking away. She was clearly delighted with the audience's reaction to her music.

"So how *do* we want to relate to you men?" Lana asked with a cold smirk.

161

"However you want to. You're women . . . emotional . . . fluid as water; more solid—more reliable—that a rock until you change your minds—"

Uncle Luigi laughed. "That's sexist talk, kid."

Fred shook his head. "No it's not. And that's the whole point. And the problem. Everyone keeps telling women how they're supposed to feel till they're all as bottled up as—

"You are correct there," Lana said, with a wink at Big Tony. "I'm definitely bottled up."

Karen laughed. "Me too. I'm just dying for the concert to be over so Luigi can release my pressure." She sighed, turned to Fred. "Sorry we interrupted. Please go on . . ." she gestured at the stage, "before she starts the next song."

"Okay. What I'm trying to say is: Femina speaks directly to women's hearts. She doesn't burden you with gender identity or sexual identity issues. What she does is simply lay out your current . . . excuse the phrase . . . 'identity crisis' as it is. Like this last song. "It's a celebration of hatred of how men have forced women into a subservient role in society . . . but it's also an understanding that the sexes are interlinked—totally dependent on each other—never more so than in the arena of physical intercourse."

Lana scowled. "Oh, I'm dependent on Big Tony for sex alright." Her frown deepened. "But why doesn't she sing of anything else?"

"She does," Karen said. "She sings of womanhood. Of my fight to just be a woman, to simply be able to laugh, to cry, to *be*, without anyone judging me. I like that about her."

Fred nodded. "It's complicated, but I've never thought women were easy to understand. For instance: you want a man who's totally dedicated to you, but he also has to be attractive to lots of other women, none of whose attentions he's permitted to reciprocate."

"Same thing for guys there," Uncle Luigi interjected.

"I never said it wasn't. Also, you ladies want to be strong and competent, able to take on the world and be recognized as a 'strong' woman, while at the same time being 'weak,' drawing strength from your man, wanting . . . needing him to be stronger than you . . . if only to prove you've got the alpha of the pack. You want to be taken . . . conquered . . . but tenderly and with respect. Call it modern-day chivalry."

Karen nodded. "That's sort of true."

"I only want to be weak in bed," Lana said. "Anywhere else and men take advantage of you. But bed is a good place to be powerless, because then you enjoy a man more. He feels harder when you are soft. A knife penetrates deeper into butter than stone."

"Bed alone is fine with me," Big Tony said. "You can carry your own luggage, change your own flat tires . . ."

"Don't you dare try that ungentlemanly un-American nonsense with me!"

Fred grinned. "The point is: women want to be dependent on men, but also don't want to be. Nature designed men to be the protector and provider—we're generally larger than our female partners. A smaller person should naturally be defended by a larger, and—"

"I can protect myself," Lana said. "But Tony has bodyguards. Which of us is stronger?"

"Protection has its limits," Karen added. "Most guys seem to want to protect us women from ourselves. Like we're children. Patriarchy. I reject that shit."

"Pendulum swings both ways," Uncle Luigi said. "You're always trying to mother me—telling me what clothes to wear, how my shoes are too old. How I need better table manners."

Fred nodded sagely: "The *real* problem is—in the modern world, strength has now become overrated. Twenty men's work can now be done with a push of a button, and both male and female fingers can make that push equally well."

"So, my car has power-steering," Karen agreed. "And I make my own money, honey. But . . ." She seemed stuck for her next sentence.

"But you *still* like Uncle Luigi opening doors for you right? Pulling out chairs in restaurants? Treating you with consideration, like royalty."

"Yes, yes, yes! Of course I want that! It shows he respects me. But that doesn't mean I'm weaker than you."

"That's why you . . ." he gestured around, "all of you ladies like Femina so much. She expresses that confusion—how you want what you now have, and how dissatisfied you are now you've got it. It's like some personal form of suffering's being wrenched away from you each time we—men—agree with your new presentation of yourself as the modern woman." He sighed. "I'm sorry I can't explain better than this."

"Easy to understand why not," Lana said, aquamarine eyes peering intently into his. "You are a penis. A massive one. And that is not a compliment."

Big Tony snorted loudly. "It's now clear why only my dog wants you as a boyfriend."

Fred winced at the insults. He stared at the stage. Femina was shaking to a guitar solo, hair down over her face, her bare breasts pogoing up and down.

He looked across at Ash and Raye, saw the pair kissing passionately. Aw . . . and he thought Raye looked cute. Plump and pretty. *Damn, more disappointment. When am I going to find a nice girl for myself?*

"Fred, you sound misogynistic as shit," Uncle Luigi said, bumping into his thoughts. "How the hell can you suggest that women want to be free to be *weak?*"

"At least you didn't suggest they want to be *months*," Big Tony said.

Lana laughed loud, as did Uncle Luigi. Even Karen managed a grin.

Fred now regretted beginning his explanation. Some knowledge was better kept to oneself. Like he'd earlier told Ash and Raye, Femina's popularity had made no sense to him. But suddenly, during the '*Pigs!*' chant—of all things—his and the singer's eyes had met and EVERYTHING about her appeal to the female masses had made sense. And still did. In Fred's head the explanation was simplicity itself. Sharing what he understood with others, however, was a pain in the rhetorical ass.

Still, he'd made his philosophical bed. Lying in it was proving immensely difficult, but he'd soldier on. If only to discomfort Big Tony. He had no idea what was upsetting the TV producer so much. *Maybe Uncle Luigi gave the scumbag bad cocaine.* Then it hit him: *He's got a fucking inferiority complex! That's the problem—my showing signs of smarts threatens him; makes him feel like the brute his is.*

It was slight payback, but Fred took it. He gave Big Tony a superior smile and continued:

"I don't mean it like that, Uncle Luigi. Women want to be free to be who *they* think they are—to do whatever they want, to feel however they want about whatever they want, whenever they want. The confusing point is—there's no fixed standard; it's based on individual choice: Karen for instance, wants the freedom be weak and clingy—pathetically clingy if she wants—and feel that you're in charge even though she knows she's your equal; without you or anyone else judging her. That includes other 'liberated' women." He shrugged. "If she chooses to be 'barefoot and pregnant' she doesn't want you or anyone telling her she ought be out competing with men; if she's a 'career woman,' she doesn't want to be told she's supposed to be a breeder. And if she switches her preferences halfway through life, or keeps changing her view and inclinations on how she wants her relationships to work, she doesn't want to be thought inconsistent."

"Bullshit. I'm your dad's older brother, and even *I* don't believe women secretly want to be dominated."

"No we don't," Lana agreed.

"We do," Karen giggled. "Sometimes."

"No! We *don't*," Lana repeated. "It is we who must do the dominating! Whips, handcuffs, hot leather pants . . . steel Madonna bras . . . high-heeled boots . . . your big hairy man on his hands and knees groveling like the dog he is . . ."

Big Tony gave Fred a look of pure hatred. "See what you've started with your nonsense talk?"

Fred smiled at Big Tony. "View it this way—it's called the war of the sexes. Sometimes you win, sometimes you don't."

Lana nodded. "You are making some sense. Love is war between men and women. A pleasant, satisfying war, sometimes as enjoyable to lose as to win. An emotional give and take, in which our hearts pledge allegiance to the man we love and also hate. But Femina sings only of SEX. Vagina and fucking, not the emancipation that you claim. She sings of how we must sex the patriarchy to our own advantage. Destroy the evil overlord we cannot live without with our vaginas. How does sex enter into this?"

"It's a metaphor for your unevolved evolution."

Lana snorted. "Now you're simply talking like Rubik's Cube. And I never understood Hungarian."

Karen looked thoughtful for a moment. "Okay, a question for you, Fred: Femina sings about how powerful our vaginas are right?"

He nodded.

"So tell me: "If vaginas are indeed the fountain of universal energy she claims, why the hell are the guys in charge everywhere?"

"They are not!" Lana retorted before Fred could reply. "We only let them think so." She glared at Karen, her eyes predatory as a wolf's, like she'd rip out Karen's throat for daring make the suggestion. "Every real woman controls her man. True, we aren't always as big as them, but there are many other ways to make them do what we want. The important thing is to be in charge. It's not a matter of size, but force of personality."

"Strength in weakness," Karen said. "I've heard that before."

"She stoops to conquer," Uncle Luigi said. Lana looked at him sharply. He raised his hands in a peace gesture. "Blame Karen."

"Actually," Fred began, "I'm not sure if I agree with—"

Big Tony grimaced. "Aw, shut up, Fred! You're a clueless jerk! I wish Bitch was here to teach you a lesson."

Fred shut up, a smug look on his face.

***

The guitar solo faded to a few delayed notes. Femina strode forward to the microphone. "Our next song is called *War of the Sexes, Parts One and Two.*"

Big Tony stifled a loud groan.

A loud cheer went up as the song began:

Part One: Desperate Housewife.

"My life feels hard as your cock,
And, darling, you're like a rock.

165

Fuck this penis . . . man addiction,
My most secret, degrading congenital affliction.
I love the person I hate the most.
War of the sexes,
The biology perplexes.
Sex is complex,
My desires are a fire leaving no room for denial,
You are my betrayal of my beliefs,
My rejection of the very equality I seek.
For these moments when I am one with you, with you in me,
(And me all around you,)
Correctness, feminism, equality—none of these things matter:
I'm a hungry body, not a brain,
All I want now is penis and semen splatter,
To be a sacrifice on your patriarchal altar.
Yes! Fill me with cock and come in me.
Equal rights tomorrow,
None of the girls will know.
But if you're bad at cunnilingus tonight,
If you don't worship my body right,
If you don't grant my vagina her bragging rights,
Making me wheeze and grip your head tight,
I won't overlook the grievous slight.
Oh, yes—I'll have my equal rights tonight!

Understand that I'm your goddess,
I'm the religion of which you are high priest.
My pussy smell is the air that you breathe,
The atmosphere in which you exist.
And when I push you away, you must grieve and plead,
Yes, that's the way it is.
Beg, man, beg,
Vagina is my power,
This is my war of flowers.

I'm your princess, you're my pauper.
I like your gun, so I'll grant you favors,
And punish misdemeanors.
So fuck me good, like you know you should.
Be the man I don't really need,
'Cos I'm a fish.
Occasionally I bike under the sea,
And only then may you 'own' me.

I'm a fucking queen, dearie,
I do what the hell I please,
Back down on your knees.
Worship my hole! I said—worship my fucking hole,
Even when it smells like fish and cheese.

I win this war of the sexes. Like it or not,
And if you've a problem with that,
You'd better be able to hit my G-spot.
'Cos if not . . .

My comprehension is you and I, under each other in turn,
Man on top, Woman on top,
And if you're kinky (or liberated), I got my strap-on.
Fucking—sex—is war,
I will destroy you,
You will destroy me.
Our empires both rise between our thighs,
They thrive, peak like the skies, then die with anguished sighs.
A death so sweet, so sweet.

I rise to conquer you,
My breasts—sweaty meat tanks—point at you,
My nipples, barrels to blow you away,
My sex ready to go again,
Ready for you now now now, already!
Oh the bliss,
Of this,
Your dick in my throat.
No I don't permit you to explode,
I want you in my lower hole,
There I will kill you.
I love you, though I hate you more,
It's part of the deal when you score.
Spread me wide, part my thighs,
Enter me, *please,*
Make me moan with my eyes wide.
But even as I dissolve in creamy unfaked sighs,
And feed your ego and pride,
Please realize,
I must kill you, even as I fulfill you.
And I *will* fulfill you,
You will desire only me for the rest of your days,

Or until I say, "Get lost, go away."
But for now let's play,
And pray, to deity, that you serve and obey.
My vagina is your law, your job, your country,
If my wetness is ever scorned, you'll have hell to pay.
Now . . . rise and fuck me!
Do your duty by biology,
I will, I must conquer you yet again,
My love!

Ejaculation so sweet, throbbing so deep,
Fuck you, darling, you son-of-a-bitch.
Why the hell must I need you,
You piece of well-concealed chauvinistic shit?

I look your way,
But you're already dead—
Vanquished by my magnificent cunt,
Reduced to limpness by my stupendous ass,
Unable to overcome my glorious body,
Shattered like fortress walls.
You lost the war of the sexes again.
We fucked; you're dead,
Asleep in our matrimonial bed.
The war nonetheless rages on in my head."

Part Two: Come and Overcome.

"You will come,
I will fucking overcome.

My vibrators assure me victory is certain,
Close on the horizon,
Nearer than my current milky electronic orgasm even,
Then why do I go weak-kneed when I see you?

In bed,
You give me head,
Lick me like I'm a queen,
Like my vagina is the greatest thing you've ever seen.
You tongue my anus; did I wipe front-to-back that last time?
Who gives a shit? You never notice my crime.
You get me wet and hot,

(My breasts feel like batteries of electricity!)
My cunt is like a boiling pot.
So I permit you entry, I allow you to have me again.
Yes, fuck me, just like that,
In and out, in and out.
Feed on my breasts,
I wonder what you fantasize about?
Oh, yeeeeeeesssssss, fuck! I love you!

A slip of tongue . . .

I don't trust you one bit,
But it doesn't matter at the moment.
You will come, honey,
But I, will fucking overcome.

My vibrators are jealous,
Pointy like ICBMs, they disapprove from their shelves,
I'm letting down the cause,
(Refusing once again to ask for my divorce.)
Refusing once again,
To be my own best friend.

"Better than flesh!" they scream.
"We're better than flesh!"
(Sorry, toys, that's incorrect.
Well maybe . . . in your dreams.)

"Maybe tomorrow," I plead with the vibrators.
Because tonight . . .
(You get me arranged just right on my hands and knees,)
Because tonight . . .
(Spit on your hot meat and slide it in,
Deep into my wet, dripping quim,
The juice of sweet defeat running down my thighs,
Like a mudslide.)
Because tonight . . .
Honestly, you toys, doggy style is most definitely what I need to feel
alive.
Shut the fuck up,
You mechanical lot!

But, still, I'll never forget their freedom song:

You will come, darling,
But I . . . I will fucking overcome!"

***

Fred nodded after the song. "See what I mean?" He grinned at Lana and Karen. "It's simple: Men treat you badly, violently even; yet you still violently want them. Biology dictates the rules, not reason. It's woman's real curse from the fall—the chain called love."

CHAPTER 42

[Chicago]

Oh, Daddy!

Money Rich moaned with joy as she surveyed her work. This was just great!

Mr. Rich's corpse lay beside her in bed, gold penis stiffly erect in its crotch.

The corpse's belly was slit wide open from waist to ribcage. Its extracted organs—the withered heart, lungs, liver, intestines, and kidneys—lay on the bed to its left. On its right sat an open attaché case.

Money, seated cross-legged, was transferring handfuls of dollar bills from the attaché case into the corpse.

(The idea had come suddenly to her—*why not stuff Daddy? Do him up like the ultimate pillow.* She'd considered filling him with quarters, then changed her mind. *Nah, he'll weigh too much, and be hard in the wrong places!*)

She began sweating from excitement and exertion. She got up and quickly stripped, hanging her money-dress up beside the others in the walk-in closet. She removed her cash-bra also, its 'Benjamins' all soaked through with her perspiration. She binned the bra; plenty more where it came from. She kept her panties on—she had to have some cash against her flesh, and where better than protecting her sex?

Her cellphone rang. She rolled her eyes at the intrusion into this most private of times, then picked it up.

"Hello, Mia. . . . Calm down Mia, I can't understand you. . . . Rosita? She's been kidnapped!? (She cast a regretful glance back over at the corpse

171

she'd been stuffing.) Are you sure? . . . Antonio's down at the station filling out forms? . . . Okay, take a deep breath. Now, tell me everything—when and how it happened. . . . Three days ago? Why the hell are you just calling me now?"

She listened, growing more angry by the moment. "Okay, I'm on it. I'll have the goons ask around. Tell Antonio to call me once he gets back. . . . No, no, don't worry about that: *I'll* call *you* once I find out anything."

She disconnected the call, then instantly redialed.

Dillinger's metal voice came over the line. "Yes, Boss? You need a new dildo or something?"

"Al Capone and Bugsy with you there?"

"Yeah, sure. What's up?"

"Someone's kidnapped Rosita Diaz."

"Your goddaughter?" A puzzled pause. "Who'd be that dumb?"

"I'd like to know that, Dill. I really would."

"Okay, Boss, what do you want us to do?"

"You three get your metal asses outside. I don't care what time of night it is. Start leaning on people. Break down doors and break jaws till someone says something. I want this resolved fast. *Nothing* must happen to that little girl. Nothing. You got that?"

"Sure thing, Boss," the metal voice said. "We'll get started right away."

That taken care of, Money relaxed somewhat. After taking a few deep breaths to calm herself, she resumed stuffing her dead father with money.

CHAPTER 43

Femina screamed: "Ladies—I love my cunt, and it's that time of month!"

The respondent screams rolled around the basement like pitch-shifted thunder.

"I said—do you love your vagina as much as I love mine!"

"Yeeeeaaaahhhhh!"

The band started up with a hard-rocking groove.

"It's that time, girls. What time is it, girls?

"Lottery time!"

She cupped a hand behind her ear. "What time, ladies!?"

"Lottery time!"

Femina pranced across the stage. "Well, girls, I know you all know the words to this one! Come on, sing it with me! It's time for *The Bleeder's Report*—don't sell me short!"

All the women in the room turned and began chanting at their partners:

"My monthly curse,
Is yours, hubby dearest, for better or worse.
(Our contract's signed on the dotted line,
It's yours for as long as you're legally mine.)
And you'd better love my PMS,
As much as you love my ass and breasts,
Or else . . .
Now help me get that tampon in,
It's like a little penis with a string.
Oh, I really hate original sin.

But I digress . . ."

Heavy guitar chords; a staccato drum roll. Femina yelled: "Sing the chorus, girls! Oh yeah! Oh, hell yeah!"

The response was spine-chillingly thunderous:

"Sex on the rag, sex on the red,
C'mon, honey handsome, give me some head.
My bleeding cunt's spread wide open in bed,
My little pussy's having her monthly distress,
Gorgeous as a brand new crimson dress.
So what, if it's a little bit red,
Like a lion's mouth that's just been fed?
Hey! Why's your cock suddenly gone soft?
Don't tell me you now want a divorce,
When all *I* want is a good long fuck.
Menstrual sex rocks!"

While the song went on, Poppy-Z, one of Femina's keyboard players went round with a little box, handing out white cards with numbers on them to all the men in the audience.

"We really, really, need to keep meeting like this,
All I want tonight is a drawn-out kiss,
Downstairs, baby—pucker up those lips.
Stay a while down there,
(Don't be scared!)
While I grind my hips.
Okay, now come up for air.
Wow, you look like you're wearing glossy red lipstick.

My period is punctuation to my monthly sentence.
(Screw my monthly sentence!)
Every thirty-odd days,
My body takes stock,
(In its blood bank vaults!)
And prints out the results,
For each time we fucked.
(And we fuck a lot!)
Oh boy, you shot blanks again,
Your account's in the red,
Your fault, darling, you didn't give me a kid.
(You know, you really need to spill some fertile come in there.)

Now my womb's pronounced judgment,
On your negligence.
Yippee! I'm not pregnant!
Thank God, I'm not pregnant!
Aren't you pleased I'm not pregnant?

Sex on the rag, sex on the red,
Lick my pussy or I'm gonna kick you out of bed.
Now don't go yet, Joe, I feel a brand new flow,
Rushing down to meet you.
(It really wants to meet you!
My crimson tide,
Like a horny bride!)
Hot new blood, coming like a flood.
C'mon lap it up, lap it up, lap it up.

Hey! Why's your cock suddenly gone soft?
Don't tell me you now want a divorce,
When all *I* want is a good hard fuck.
Menstrual sex rocks!
Baby, menstrual sex rocks!"

The song ended to thunderous applause and a crescendo of female shrieks.

Femina spun a roulette wheel fixed atop a monitor speaker. She looked around the room. The room was raptly silent.

She smiled. "The winner is number thirty-two."

CHAPTER 44

Fred smiled smugly. His number was twenty-six, the card safe in a jacket pocket. No way did he want to be the winner of this lottery. Femina was hot, true, and the lottery prize included a night with her, but, it was what went *before* that he dreaded. *How could she? How did she think that up?*

He smiled at his companions at table. Uncle Luigi smiled back. Big Tony grimaced angrily at Fred, apparently still pissed-off over their discussion about women's wants.

Fred shrugged. *An asshole can't help but be itself—it must shit. He returned his attention to the stage.*

"Number thirty-two," Femina repeated in a sing-song voice. "C'mon, baby, where are you!?"

Lana poked Fred. "Thirty-two—That's you."

He turned to her. "Nah, I'm twenty-six."

"She shook her head. "Uh uh. You're thirty-two—check your card again."

With a sudden feeling of horror, Fred got it out of his pocket and did so. His previously '26' card now had a massive damning '32' printed on it. He looked at Lana in horror, grey eyes perplexed. *But how?*

Then he saw Big Tony grinning broadly at him. "Looks like you're gonna drink some tea, son—better you than me!"

The blood drained from Fred's face. He went white. "Let me see *your* card," he said quietly.

Big Tony scowled.

"Please."

Big Tony showed him. '26.'

Fred's eyes widened.

Lana leaned near and whispered in Fred's ear. "Before Tony imported me from Mother Russia, I used to be a pickpocket. Very good. Also, I am very jealous—I'm not shamed to admit. Remember the winner will sleep with sexy Femina afterwards. The only vagina Tony is licking is mine."

"Number thirty-two?" Femina repeated. She laughed. "Okay, ladies, looks like we have another scaredy-cat in our midst. Flush him out, girls!"

Lionesses on the hunt, the women surged out of their seats. Laughing gleefully, Lana leapt to her feet, yanking Fred up after her. "He's here!"

The women instantly rushed at Fred. In the interlude before they reached him, he stared at Uncle Luigi. The man was laughing like he'd split his sides. Karen too was giggling like mad. Fred stared hopelessly at the pair. Then a hundred female arms grabbed him and bore him relentlessly towards the stage.

The women deposited Fred onstage and returned to their seats. The musicians had left the stage. An electric kettle—steam pouring from its spout—was now set up at the front of the stage, along with several large mugs on a metal tray balanced on a tripod.

Femina draped an arm around Fred's waist and pulled him close to her. "Freddie darling," she said into the microphone, "long time no see. Say, hon, why didn't you return all my calls?" The room burst into laughter.

She grinned at Fred. "Now, you know the rules of the lottery. *You* get to spend tonight with *me*. But first . . ." she pointed to the tray and kettle, "you have to drink my special monthly brew—tampon tea."

All the women in the room immediately took up the chant: "Tampon tea! Tampon tea!"

Fred nodded weakly, then physically sagged against her. He looked across the room at Big Tony and Lana. Lana licked her luscious lips. Big Tony gave him the finger. The staring eyes across the room were like bullets penetrating Fred, he wished the floor would open up and swallow him.

***

Ash and Raye, who'd been amongst the women who'd borne Fred to the stage, were now laughing their heads off.

"Damn, look at the look on his face."

They watched as Femina did a short striptease, sliding her satin panties down her legs and back up again, finally slipping them off completely while bent over with her buttocks to the audience. Appreciative female yells filled the air.

"You notice it's us making all the noise?" Raye asked. "The men all look stunned."

Ash laughed. "They're all relieved they're not tonight's 'victim.' Fred's taking one for the team."

Femina now squatted like she was going to take a pee, and in full view of all, pinched the white string dangling between the lips of her vagina and slowly pulled the tampon out.

It was BIG and swollen red with blood. Fred gaped at it. Femina held it up proudly. "Behold my essence!"

The women burst into laughter. The men remained silent.

"The real reason men don't like sex during our periods is because they're scared of blood," Femina said with a grin, her blue eyes twinkling like stars. She pointed to Fred. "Damn cowards. Tonight I'm gonna cure me one of 'em!"

"Men *aren't* scared of blood," Ash whispered. "They love war, don't they?"

Raye smirked. "I think that's because *they* make the blood then. Women are miles scarier to most men than a battlefront. Bleeding's no big deal to us."

Ash giggled. "You may be right. Most guys I know have deflowering a virgin top of their list of no nos."

Femina waved her massive bloody tampon at the audience. "Okay, here's the first teabag!"

The women laughed louder.

She dropped the tampon into the largest mug on the tea tray and poured boiling water over it. She dabbed the tampon in the water. Steam billowed as the blood percolated out of it.

She turned back to the audience.

Okay, ladies, the tea's brewing!" She looked around, laughed. "Now, y'all know me—I'm not one to monopolize the fun. In my opinion, this tea's still a little thin. Not enough bloody vitamins for little Freddie! Any of you sisters got additional teabags available?"

Ash leapt to her feet. "Yeah! Right here!"

"Bring 'em to the stage, girls!"

"Hey, sit down!" Raye yelped.

Ash grinned back. "Darlin', you must be kiddin'. My own Femina moment? I'm not missing this for the world."

She rushed off to climb the stage and carefully extract her tampon and hand it over to the blond singer. Two other women did the same.

Femina added the three new tampons to the mug and added more hot water.

A fourth, bony dark-haired woman handed in a sanitary towel so blood-soaked it seemed she'd bled half her womb into it.

Fred cringed in horror when Femina dunked the sanitary pad into the mug. *Hell no!* The pad's ends poked out like the head and tail of an obscene white fish in a bowl of soup. Fred gawped. He'd never seen anything so gross in his life.

Strutting to loud applause, the four women returned to their seats.

"Yeah, looks nice and red now. Too red—I'm forgetting something, aren't I?"

"Milk!" came the thunderous reply. "Breast milk!"

"Yeah, you're right! We can't have tea without milk!" Beside her, Fred wilted like a young plant in hot sun, like he was literally fading into a shadow of himself.

"Okay, ladies, who's just had a baby!?"

A fat woman in a frilly blue dress shook off her boyfriend's attempts to restrain her, finally knocking him back over his seat. With a snarl-like grin, she strode fiercely to the stage. Femina welcomed her, then held out a cup. The woman exposed her breasts (they were HUGE) and squirted milk into the cup. She bowed to the audience and returned to her table, to help her dazed lover up off the floor.

Femina poured the breast milk into Fred's tea. She smiled sweetly at him. "Would you like sugar with it, darling?"

***

Fred shook his head in response to Femina's question. Watching the naked singer stir up the strawberry-colored mix of menses and breast milk, he felt frozen, like his disgust had petrified him. The world had ended, he was alone in the universe. *How on Earth can she legally be allowed to do this?*

She removed first the tampons, then the submerged sanitary pad from the mug, squeezed their contents into the rest, then offered him the brimming mug.

"Drink it up, don't spill a drop; this menstrual tea, is the truth of me."

Fred gaped at what he was being offered. Large dark clots floated on the pink surface in mince-like chunks. And the *smell* of the witches' brew? In addition to a nauseating stale-blood odor, at least one 'teabag' provider had recently taken a generous pee—a smell of 'clean' urine (like what one smelt/tasted during oral sex if one's woman hadn't washed after urinating) was mingled with the others.

Fred glared angrily at the skinny brunette who'd handed over her sanitary pad; she had to be the offender. The woman in question was looking intently at the stage. Fred hoped she'd remembered to pad herself again. (In the front row, he could see Ash surreptitiously slipping a blue applicator tube up herself.)

The watching women wolf-whistled and screamed, "Drink it up! Drink it up! Tampon tea! One two three! Tampon tea! A B C! Tampon tea! Do re mi! Menstrual Tea! Menstrual Tea! Menstrual Tea!" Loud table-banging accompanied their lusty chant.

Fred accepted the cup in a daze.

"Drink it up! Empty the cup!"

Fred looked at the screamers. Their eyes were wide and staring, spit flecked their lips. *These aren't women*, he thought in desperation, *they're ani*—

"They're everyday women having fun," Femina whispered sternly into his ear, off the mic. "Wives and girlfriends and mothers and daughters; lovers and friends. Now drink the fucking blood up. Let's get the concert over with and go fuck. I'm horny."

Fred stared at her stubbornly. His resistance was futile; she glared just as stubbornly back. "Do it—pussy power compels you to!" Fred gave up. He lifted the cup to his lips.

To loud female applause and male grimaces, Fred drank the tampon tea. It was a nauseating mix. He imagined he felt a million germs flooding him as it filled his mouth, slipped down his throat. It had cooled now to tepidity. He drank it down in one endless gulp, one ceaseless swallow, knowing that if he stopped for any reason he'd be unable to start again. He stoutly resisted his natural instinct to chew the meaty chunks of blood clot and womb lining as they swept over his tongue.

Finally it was over, the bloody cup empty. Fred faced everyone with an inane smile plastered across his face. To keep from puking the menstrual tea back up, he concentrated hard on the female noise in the room, the raucous whistles and screams. He looked from one rapt female face to the next, trying to understand from their glowing eyes why they felt so elated. It was an exercise in futility.

A pretty redhead bared her breasts at him; her friend wrote a telephone number and 'Sheila, CALL ME' across them in green magic marker. Several women threw panties on stage. Most of the panties had wet crotch discolorations.

Fred was aware of the men in the audience pretending not to notice his embarrassment. (Several were doing lines of coke or smoking pot, and offering same to their cheering lady companions, most of whom, already tripping out on natural euphoria, ignored the proffered chemical high. Other men seemed to be conversing about nothing in particular.) He was vaguely aware of Femina raising his hand like he'd won some competition. He heard her whisper, "See you later, stud," then she led him to the side of the stage. Existentially dazed, he descended the steps and trudged back to his seat.

"You are a real man," Lana whispered huskily once he was seated. "If not that I love Tony so much, I will fuck you silly tonight! So hard you die and go to Heaven!"

Fred, dumb smile still in place, nodded at her. Then he jerked back in alarm. Lana's red mouth looked like a menstruating vagina. Shocked, he looked around. All the women had mouths like vaginas, vaginas laughing at his humiliation. He blinked; the vision cleared up. Everyone had normal mouths again. Several blew him kisses.

Big Tony and Uncle Luigi said nothing. Uncle Luigi was clearly lost for words; Big Tony wore a smug 'I put one over on you, sucker' smirk.

Karen giggled, then pushed a plastic baggie at Fred. "Here, do some lines to clear your head."

Femina began singing again. Fred spilled the cocaine on the tabletop and began cutting it up with a credit card.

***

The concert ramped up a notch. The next song, *Abandoned Kat Rock,* had a balalaika-driven East-European feel to it:

"I've not been fucked in four months,
Ain't had no cock in four months.
Jacking-off for a hundred-twenty days,
Makes Jill a dull girl all the way.
Fingers and vibrators, just ain't the same.
(I don't feel no shame,
It just ain't the same).

You were the worst partner in history,
Caused me endless tears and misery,
Kept messing me about,
So I booted your punk ass out.
But now I miss your kiss,
And your hard penis,
Oh, yesssss! That bedroom bliss!
Do I regret letting you go?
Yes . . . and NO!
It's the best decision I ever took,
But life don't play by the Feminist rulebook.
Sometimes I want to feel you on top of me,
Folding back my legs,
Till my knees touch my breasts,
Your hardness inside of me,
Pressing me down into the bed,
Love's hard sensual caress,
Squashing my buttocks into the mattress,
With each thrust,
Of your pure, unbridled lust.

I've not been fucked in four months,
Ain't had my nipples sucked in four months.
Eating chocolate for a hundred-twenty days,
(No Jack for a hundred-twenty days.)
Has really helped me put on weight.
(Ooh, Jill, you've really put on weight!)
I'm amazed that I'm still sane,
And yes, you really are to blame.

Oh yes, you called me yesterday,
Asking if you could come and play,
(With me,)
And I warned you to stay far away,
(From me.)
If need be,
Emigrate across the fucking sea,
Find some vulnerable girl in France,
And lead her on your merry dance.
If you dare show up in my yard,
I'll have the cops hard on your ass.

My vagina is Nobel Prize intelligent.
It has a mind of its own.
It likes MAN!
It refuses to understand,
That I have to use my hand.

My friends all tell me,
A series of one-night-stands,
Will flush you out of my system.
But I don't want no drunken encounters.
(Worries about condoms, faked orgasms,
Regrets the morning after?)
I want a loving non-violent man,
Whose penis stands to attention at my command,
Who I can rustle out of bed at 2 a.m.,
Who'll dash halfway across town,
To unquestioningly fulfill my pussy's demands.

See you later, masturbator,
I just bought two new vibrators.
They'll do,
To replace you,

Till I find some one new.
So get screwed!

Ain't had no luck in four months.
Ain't had no luck in four months.
All work and no fuck, makes Jill a dork!
All work and no cock, makes Jill a dork!

PART 3: ENDLESS STREET

Unfortunately, an Orgasm isn't something you can package and keep for reuse. The memory quickly fades and you need the next one, then the next, and the one after that – Femina.

CHAPTER 45

11 p.m.

Fred was in Femina's luxurious bedroom, on the Hotel Bizarre's second floor. Situated almost directly under Ash and Raye's suite, the room also had a fantastic view of the Hudson.

Cloaked in a white robe, Femina sat at her dresser, removing her makeup. Her expression intent, she swabbed off her eyeshadow with a wedge of foam. Fred silently regarded her with appreciation. She was really lovely, superlatively female; and yet there was a charming quality of the everyday woman, a 'girl next door' aura, about her too.

He remembered his epiphany when their eyes met, how he'd suddenly understood her appeal.

He pulled his gaze from contemplating her, looked out the bedroom window at the mirror-like river. He wondered what she'd think if she knew the Hotel Bizarre's real secret—something he'd never confided even to Uncle Luigi.

Femina dropped the used wedges into a bin, then spun round to face Fred. "How'd you find the concert?" She grinned. "I mean the tea?"

Fred shook his head. "No words exist to express that horrible experience."

Femina tossed her blonde head and laughed. "It was fun."

"For you, maybe."

"For the women in the audience."

"But was it really necessary?"

"Show business. Giving the people what they want."

"That sounds like a pat, rehearsed answer; something you regularly throw to placate adamant paparazzi. Answer me honestly—why'd you humiliate me like that?"

She got up and flung off her robe, letting him revel in her glorious body afresh—the almost hemispherical breasts with their large roseate aureole, the delicately muscled belly, the deep navel, the dip then spread of waist and hips, her blond pubic furring . . . "Okay, but get undressed while I explain."

Fred thought her breasts looked like chewing gum bubbles. He began undoing his shirt.

Femina sat down on the bed beside him, playing lazy fingers in his groin. "Like all men, you misunderstand the 'tampon tea' ritual."

"What's there to understand?"

She laughed. "You can't deny the female reaction to your drinking the blood, can you?"

He shook his head. "They *loved* me."

"Damn straight, they did. Most of them wanted to fuck you there and then. Of course they wouldn't actually do it—that's simply the concert atmosphere. Now here's the thing: Like pregnancy and childbirth, menstruation is a *totally* female experience. But for all its exclusivity, few, if any, women actually enjoy the process. In addition to the mess and constant need to change pads and tampons, there's the cramps, which can be really horrible. There's also that premenstrual emotional crap—hormone mood shifts, and there's also the fact that you retain water and put on weight. All-in-all a lousy time of month."

Fred began unlacing his shoes. "So? What's that to do with us?"

"*That is* what's to do with you. Most of you guys simply pretend women don't menstruate. It's dirty, it's the curse, it makes us unreasonable . . ."

Fred pulled his shoes off, undid his belt. "So, the ritual's to punish our lack of understanding?"

She shook her head as he shrugged out of his trousers. "Nope. The ritual is to show you men that menstruation is a natural thing."

Fred thought on that and decided that . . .

"It's female logic, which of course makes no sense," Femina said.

"What?"

"That's what you were about thinking."

"How'd you know that?"

She grinned, but said nothing.

Fred rolled his underpants off. He sat naked, his penis erect. Femina grabbed the hard rod and stroked it. Fred leaned back. She bent over in his lap and took him into her mouth, slid up and down on him while he groaned.

Then a sudden wave of fear hit him. *Fuck, I forgot! She's—*

Femina lifted her mouth off his erection. "Having her period. I hope she doesn't want me to give her head in return?" she finished for him.

He sat bolt upright again. "You can read my mind?"

She shook her head. "I'm only moderately psychic, but you come through very strong." Then she grinned. "And the answer to your first, unspoken question, is—yes, I do want some cunnilingus."

She stood up and pulled out her tampon. A tiny trail of blood streamed down her leg after it. She dropped the tampon, climbed onto the bed. "Lie on your back, we'll do it sixty-nine. And yes, don't even bother to think it— the reason I want to be on top is so my menses drops straight into your mouth."

Fred made to get up. "Hell no!"

She pushed him back down firmly, then rearranged herself with her crotch over his face. "Fucking do it, Freddie! Accept the totality of my womanhood."

He stared up at the proffered vagina. Now, in a reversal of his concert 'vision/hallucination,' the vagina looked like a garishly lipsticked mouth.

Femina was meanwhile back hard at work in Fred crotch. His penis felt like it had died and gone to Heaven.

Then she stopped sucking him.

"Please don't stop."

"Then do me too. Ignore the blood for fuck's sake. I've just explained that it's totally natural."

"Okay."

"What are you waiting for?"

He looked at the vagina. Blonde-furred pink folds stained like her sex had been stabbed.

She laughed. "Look, stop stalling—it isn't going to bite you. I'm not sucking you again until you start licking me too."

Fred winced. His penis felt like a lost soul seeking salvation. He lifted his head off the bed, locked his lips to the overhead vagina, and began slurping at its bloody opening.

Femina moaned deeply, an almost leonine growl, then once again smothered Fred's penis in her mouth.

They brought each other to climax like that.

Femina laughed. "That wasn't so difficult now, was it?"

Fred kept quiet. He had no thoughts, not because he was scared she'd 'hear' them, but because he didn't know what to think. The experience of sucking, imbibing her genital blood was disgusting, but beyond that, it seemed almost . . . *holy?* Was that the right word? He wasn't sure. But there'd been something religious about it—like he was performing a sacrament. Of course, he had no intention of ever doing this again (*except it's with a woman I really love*), but once was okay. It seemed his lot tonight.

Femina grinned knowingly but said nothing.

***

They made love again.

Her sex fit around his just right—neither too loose nor too tight. A total delight. The sex was nothing exceptional, but yet perfect. Not mind-blowing, but yet . . .

Fred was lost for words. Femina was all he'd hoped for.

In a sense, he was disappointed that she wasn't more exciting (more inventive?), but that was it—what she was . . . was enough. *But then, her name is Latin for 'woman.' Is that the idea? That she's every woman in one?*

They were doing it doggy-style—Femina on hands and knees in the perfumed bed, Fred thrusting between her buttocks. Their bodies rocked back and forth together, their hips slamming into each other then separating to collide again and again. He regarded his penis as it penetrated her—her clear genital secretion had fat worms of blood in it.

He wondered how many other men had experienced this same, felt this overwhelming perfection that was really pure normalcy; had understood (at least for a moment) that nothing was sexually better or greater than the ordinary, simple pleasures of a woman's body. Had understood that the female vagina couldn't be improved on—it was an already-perfect gift of God.

And the way her cunt felt on him?

She moaned. "Every man I go to bed with thinks that."

"Fuck. I forgot you can hear my thoughts."

"Don't worry about it. They're very flattering—get me hotter than hell." She looked back at him, her eyes slits of lust. "It's my talent—I *satisfy* men—*all* men. Doesn't matter who you are. I'm like a combination of wife, mother, sister, the teen daughter you secretly want to fuck, girl-next-door, dominatrix and pony-girl, porno actress, mother superior, runaway teenage tramp, your favorite high-school teacher/crush, sexy movie actress, strung-out junkie hooker and high-class whore all rolled into one."

He thrust deep, vanishing completely into her wet tunnel. "That's incredibly egotistical."

She fluttered eyelashes at him. "A pussy-whipped fat guy thought that while flooding me with semen. Before we had sex he'd been impotent for six years—even Viagra hadn't worked. You can't have better recommendations than that."

Fred gripped her hips, squeezing the sweaty white skin. "Do you have sex at other times of the month too?"

She made a face. "Shut up and fuck me."

They came together two more times. The second time it felt to Fred like he was ejaculating all along his penis, like the organ was exploding inside her.

Afterwards, totally drained, Fred collapsed beside her and fell asleep.

CHAPTER 46

1 a.m.

"Oh fuck, yes," Ash moaned. She went limp, sexual tension flooding out of her as if she'd been punctured.

Raye gave Ash's clitoris a final lick—well above the reddened vaginal slit—then looked up from dildoing her. Ash pulled her up for a long passionate kiss. Their tongues entwined, dueled like snakes. Their breasts squashed together, tingling nipples pricking.

Afterwards, she made love to Raye also, first tonguing her till she came, then fucking her in the ass with a strap-on while Raye held a blue vibrator over her clitoris.

When Raye had fallen asleep, Ash went to the bathroom. She removed the shitty condom from the strap-on and flushed it down the toilet.

She felt blood drip down her vagina. *Oops, I forgot to get a new pack of Tampax. And Raye's all out of sanitary pads.*

She wadded some tissue paper into her crotch as a stopgap. Definitely temporary—tissue shredded messily once soaked. *Screw the rituals of womanhood,* she thought angrily. There was a drugstore opposite the hotel, across the intersection. She remembered its sign reading 'Open All Night.' It might have tampons in stock. She walked back into the bedroom, pulled panties on to hold the wadded tissue in place.

Raye was snoring softly. Her disheveled hair spread like tentacles over the pillow. The sight put a thought in Ash's mind. *It's been ages since Raye's used her hair for anything—I hope it doesn't have an expiry date. It'll be a total bitch to find ourselves in a bad spot and discover she's lost her powers.*

She frowned, tapped her left bicep muscle purse. *No problem. I've still got some rocket launchers.*

Cool air swirling over her nakedness, she leaned out of the window. She made out the drugstore. Its lights were on; a woman pushed open the sign-plastered door and exited. It looked like Femina—same blonde hair, hot bod—but Ash wasn't sure. She watched the woman light up a cigarette, then straightened up back into the room.

Raye was turned over onto her belly now. Staring at her girlfriend's pale plump buttocks, Ash felt a hot rush of warmth in her cunt. She was tempted to climb back into bed and give Raye head again, licking the wet pink slit from behind, tonguing the fresh-fucked anus, squeezing her ass—kneading each soft gluteal mound like dough, then . . .

Her gaze shifted left, to the dresser. Her mind-chips—like plastic matchbooks—were stacked on it. The bulky red/black military Warpedia chip topped the pile, king of the hill. (Ash tried not to use the chips during her menses—they sometimes triggered migraines.)

Everything's been moving so fast these past two days, she realized. *I need to sit down and edit the footage I got of that rapist prick being killed, then search online for buyers and—*

A cramp hit her like a punch to the gut. *Fuck!—that hurt.* She felt a squirt of blood begin the short descent to her crotch. *I have to get to the store—the pain . . . I'm also out of Midol.*

She crossed into the bathroom, doubled the tissue pad in her crotch, then returned to the bedroom and dressed in a blouse and skirt.

She examined her reflection in the wall mirror. Her face had that rosy glow to it that accompanied good sex. She grinned; her skirt was hooker-short, but who the hell was awake to see it this time of night?

Another menstrual cramp hit. *Shit! It's like they've been postponing themselves to catch me at my time of greatest inconvenience!* Picking up her purse, she rushed for the door.

CHAPTER 47

1:45 a.m.

As Ash switched off the lights, she heard a sharp click above and behind her.

She spun around. A trapdoor had dropped open in the ceiling over the bed. A swinging concrete flap hung down into the room.

Confused, Ash gaped up into the rectangular opening. Daylight flooded down from it, brightening the room again.

This is impossible, she thought. *There's both another floor of rooms above us, and this is the middle of the night.*

She glanced at Raye, now outlined in a bright rectangle of light. Raye snored on regardless, adjusting her body so her vagina was vaguely visible between her buttocks.

Ash peered up into the odd opening. She saw it wasn't a trapdoor, but an actual door set in the ceiling, one opening on a world/realm/somewhere set perpendicular to hers.

Beneath an azure sky streaked with fragmented gray/white clouds, a woman was walking toward her in the ceiling.

The image stretched Ash's mind. It was so odd, she forgot to feel frightened.

On a sudden impulse, she lay down on the floor and stared straight up. This way (as long as Ash didn't look sideways) the approaching woman was correctly oriented.

The woman was a skinny brunette, thin as a rail. Ash quickly recognized her as the woman from Femina's concert, the one who'd handed in a massive bloody sanitary towel during the 'tampon tea' slot.

A quick peek around the woman showed a more or less normal street and people. But . . . *does that man really have three eyes?*

Ash pulled her mind from background to foreground again.

The brunette had reached the door. A wash of floral scent announced her arrival. She stood framed in the opening, peering through with cool dark eyes set off by long lashes. Close up, her face was classy, like she'd once been rich, but those glory days were long past, memories swallowed up in whatever addiction had reduced her to almost-penury.

"Shit," she said. "Not again."

She looked at Ash. "Hi, this wouldn't be the Hotel Bizarre, would it?"

Ash managed to nod.

"Thank heavens for that. I'm always getting the directions wrong. And it's a straight walk too, with just one turn. But sometimes the road bends . . ." She squinted at Ash. "Hey, I remember you from the concert. You also handed in a tampon." She made a face: "Why are you lying on the floor?"

"All the better to see you, my dear."

In a maneuver Ash considered impossible, the brunette stepped (down) through the ceiling opening onto the wall beside the bed, then walked down the wall to the floor. Now, she was both standing on the wall beside Ash, and lying on the floor.

"Let's both just sit up," Ash said.

The woman looked at Ash, then laughed with understanding. She removed her legs from the wall, placed them on the floor, then sat up.

Ash followed suit. "This is so much better."

The brunette stretched out a bony hand. "Sorry for alarming you. My name's Skunk."

Ash shook the offered hand. *What kind of name is 'Skunk?'* she wondered.

She was prevented from asking. Skunk was staring at the slumbering Raye with telltale lust in her eyes.

Oh hell, gaydar strikes again, Ash thought.

"She has a fantastic ass," Skunk said with an evil grin. "I saw you girls kissing in the club earlier, so I know you're a couple."

She got off the floor, strode over to the bed and ran an appreciative hand over Raye's rump. "I like plump girls too, more to hold on to seeing as I'm so thin." She laughed. "I'm bi—I actually prefer men. I love muscles, facial hair, and hard cock, but . . . women are like nature's pillows—for lush unmatched physical comfort, we rule: nothing compares to us in the whole wide world." Another laugh. "Not me, of course—I'm more like a bed lacking a mattress—but . . ." she spread Raye's buttocks wide, "hot mamas like ladyfriend here."

She stroked Raye's anus, grinning when her finger sank easily through the sphincter. She rubbed her fingers together. "Vaseline? Ooh, you just fucked her ass, honey." She licked her thumb, then plugged Raye's anus with it, slowly thumb-fucking the opening. "Yeah, that's right—it's got that lovely post-coital slackness to it."

Raye moaned appreciatively. She shifted in bed, squeezed her pillow tight and snored louder, a happy smile on her face.

Ash gaped where she sat. It wasn't just the intruder's brazenness—this was practically rape, goddammit! And . . . *Rachel Emily Risk, how can you possibly sleep through everything that's going on? No wonder the tramps fucked you with a bottle!*

Ash was angry—her hands were bunched into fists—but memory of that horrible Central Park encounter with the hobos prevented her from attacking the brunette thumb-screwing her lover. What had Raye said? 'Bodies seemed to be stacking up?' Ash had a sudden vision of her beating the shit out of Skunk and the woman dying on her. *She looks thin enough to expire from even modest violence.*

And I definitely know this woman from somewhere else besides the concert. But where? It has to be long ago, but she definitely . . . ouch! A menstrual cramp truncated her thoughts. She groaned with the pain. *C'mon, uterus! Go easy on me! I just had sex! You normally like that!*

Skunk removed her thumb from Raye's anus and sucked it clean. "Delicious." Raye made a series of very loud snores like she'd just come in her sleep. Her buttocks twitched.

Skunk grinned at Ash. "Maybe we can threesome sometime if you're up for it. As for now? I gotta go."

Ash nodded at the brunette.

Skunk reached down, gave her a hand up off the floor. She looked Ash over casually. "You're not thinking of going out like that, are you?"

"My clothes? What's wrong with them?"

"That skirt's so short, I can see your cameltoe. You walk down the street looking like that, you're practically a fuck-me invitation."

Ash smirked, then struck a pose. "I *like* being a fuck-me invitation—gets me hot having guys lusting for what I've got. But if you really mean 'rape invitation,' don't bother your cute little ass about it, I can *definitely* look after myself." She shrugged. "Beside, I'm just crossing the street to the drugstore."

Skunk nodded back coolly. "That's where I'm expecting you to get screwed. Mack, the guy who runs the drugstore, likes trashy chicks, and you, honey, look like you *invented* sleazy." She pointed to the door. "I have to leave. See you around."

"Hold on a minute."

Skunk paused in mid-step. "Yes?"

Ash pointed up at the door still dangling open in the ceiling, with, beyond its rectangular aperture, the world lying on its side—the sky on the left and ground on the right. "What do you intend doing about that? More important: *where is that?* How come that place is tilted at ninety degrees to this one?"

Skunk's cool expression suddenly became tired. "It'd take way too long to explain. Just forget you saw it."

"Forget it?"

A nod. "Safer for all concerned." She nodded toward the slumbering Raye. "Don't tell sexy there."

Ash shrugged. Skunk climbed onto the bed and pushed the ceiling door shut. The ceiling smoothed out into uninterrupted plaster again. The room darkened, its only light now leeched from the streetlights outside the window.

"How do you intend getting back home?"

"No problem, I'll just take the . . ." She shut up and regarded Ash slyly.

"The *what?*"

"Forget it, willya? Forget you saw me—forget tonight every happened. Go to the drugstore, buy whatever you want to, get fucked or not, come back here . . ." she stroked Raye's buttocks, "give sweet cheeks here another strap-on session. Just forget what you've seen. You'll be miles happier if you do."

Before Ash could retort, the bony brunette opened the door and exited. Her perfume hung in the air behind her—a memory ghost.

***

Ash didn't immediately leave for the drugstore. She couldn't. She was suddenly gripped by a myriad of cold chills, like she had a fever. *That didn't just happen. That woman didn't just step through the ceiling.*

Now Skunk had left, it was very easy to agree with the woman's suggestion—*This is all just a hallucination. Yeah, just a dream. I'm asleep. I'll wake up in a short bit and everything will be normal.*

A belly cramp hit her. *Ouch! But if I'm dreaming, how come I'm having period pain?*

With regret, she glanced at the mind-chip stack on the dresser—*I really should have kept one in—in this case a recording would have been worth a million words. But it's not my fault they . . . and anyway, how the hell was I supposed to predict this happening?*

She looked over at Raye. *One thing's for sure, 'sweet cheeks,' you ain't hearing nothing about this.*

She left the room. Now in addition to tampons, she needed booze. Otherwise, there was no way she'd ever get to sleep tonight.

CHAPTER 48

1: 55 a.m.

Karen Lewinsky rode the elevator to the fourth floor. Unable to sleep, she wanted some valium—Uncle Luigi kept a spare pack in his office.

Karen was totally wired. There'd been a massive after-concert party in Uncle Luigi's suite, with loads and loads of TV bigwigs and their hangers-on in attendance. Drugs and Dom Pérignon, cocaine and caviar. In one en-suite-bathroom several skanky chicks with meth works had spent the whole party getting wasted. Other drug underground celebrities had also been there: Dr. Crack Soul had been in one corner . . . hash brownies and a large marijuana cake . . . The famed amphetamine guru, Dr. Robbie Roberts, had attended with his entourage of sexcretaries.

Karen, never one to waste a party, had immersed herself in the debauchery, reveling in it.

The drawback? Luigi had used too much cocaine at the party, meaning he'd been unable to get it up in bed afterward and fuck her to sleep. So now she needed chemical help to neutralize all the 'up stuff' she'd drunk, swallowed, and snorted.

The elevator hummed between floors. Karen chortled at a memory—Lana Petrova claiming Big Tony's junkie mutt Bitch had the coke hots for Fred. The dog gave Fred head? Lana, drunker than a skunk philosopher, insisted it was true. A coke-white-nosed Big Tony had seconded her. Fred wasn't available to comment. Big Tony had even promised a demonstration—he was coming personally to the hotel to collect his next shipment of blow, and bringing the Doberman over with him.

The elevator stopped.

Karen stepped out of it and froze.

Fifteen yards ahead, light spilled into the dark corridor from beneath the door of Uncle Luigi's office. A soft diffuse illumination that reached the opposite wall. Karen considered: *Luigi's downstairs snoring . . . Fred's busy balling with Femina, so who? Robbers? Or did Luigi just forget to turn the lights off?*

The sudden loud sound of shifting furniture nixed the 'forgotten lights' theory.

Behind her, the elevator shut and left, answering a downstairs call. Karen now realized that the intruder must have heard the elevator arrive on the floor.

Already wired on the after-tendrils of her drug binge, Karen's curiosity quickly became fear, just a step down from full-blown panic. In an unconscious defensive gesture, she undid, then re-secured the sash of her dressing gown tighter about her.

She pressed the elevator's 'call' button. *Prince Valium Charming can remain in his plastic castle—I'll just head back downstairs right now and jerk off to sleep after I alert Luigi that there's an intruder in his office.*

The elevator's direction indicator kept blinking 'down' however. *Hurry up, godammit! This building only has four floors!* There were stairs ahead, past Luigi's office, but Karen didn't feel up to making a mad dash down the corridor. *With my luck, I'll likely trip over my own feet halfway.*

Eyes fixed on the blinking indicator, she suddenly became aware somebody was watching her. The scary thing was . . . she'd heard no sound of motion announcing that person's arrival in the corridor. And there was also now an almost overpowering stink of fish. *Fish?*

She spun round, prepared to scream her lungs out if it was a man in a ski mask with a gun.

Her scream died unborn in her throat. *What in the . . . ?*

The oddest creature she'd ever seen stood in the corridor in a spreading puddle of water. 'A bear covered with green tentacles,' was the best her drugged mind could make of it. She gaped at it, totally confused at its sudden appearance. "What . . . ?"

The bear-like creature exploded into a profusion of tentacles that flailed toward her.

Karen's confusion fled her. She opened her mouth to scream. A thick tentacle hit her in the mouth, blocking it, completely muffling the sound. Karen gagged and retched as the disgusting wet appendage forced its way down her throat.

She grabbed hold of it to pull it out, but other tentacles—slimy like seaweed—wrapped around her arms and legs. They jerked taut, halting her action, preventing her from running away.

The monster's fishy smell intensified.

The tentacles pulled Karen towards the creature. She screamed silently. Her gray eyes widened in horror—a mouth had spread wide open in the monster's middle, a mouth filled with a sea (A SEA?) in which sharks and giant lobsters swam.

She began flailing wildly to get free. To no avail. The waiting sea thrashed with waves, pincers, and teeth. Saltwater smell filled the corridor. The monster's tentacle feet squelched messily on the floor.

Karen's brain raged with thoughts: *This is impossible! Sharks in a sea inside a 'bear' made of tentacles!? And what can this monster possibly be doing in Luigi's office!? Oh God! Someone must have slipped acid into my drinks!!!*

The thought that she was having a bad trip was no consolation. Nor did she really believe it. Her eyes bugged with her effort to breathe. The fishmonger's atmosphere and the puke fighting to bypass the tentacle blocking her throat were a lethally asphyxiating combination. Nevertheless, she kept fighting the tentacles pulling her to the opening in the monster.

The tentacles slid her through the hole in the creature—into the turbulent water beyond. She splashed, trod water, got her bearings, looked about in confusion.

Panicking, she tried to swim away, but to where? She had no idea where she was. And the sea creatures . . .

(The sharks and giant shellfish instantly sped at her, churning the already turbulent water like paddle boat wheels.)

The sky was black as death's cape, the sun purple. In the distance, Karen made out massive black cliffs topped with oddly fluorescent trees.

She looked behind her. The hole she'd been pushed through was a tentacle-fringed opening in the sky four feet overhead. Near, but oh so far—too far to reach from the water. Through it she saw the corridor. At its end the lift—the lift she'd summoned—now slid open and waited. "Who the fuck are you waiting for now, you piece of mechanical crap!?" she screamed at it.

Then the sharks and giant shellfish reached her.

As the first sharks ripped into her with their horrible jagged teeth, Karen Lewinsky had the clear impression that she heard heels clicking above her, past the opening in the creature, and also that she smelt perfume—jasmine.

Then she was too busy screaming and dying to think of anything else.

The sea foamed and thrashed like it was angry. Karen's blood sprayed everywhere.

CHAPTER 49

Femina – Vagina's Revenge

I'm infected, and I intend to spread it.
Fuck ethics, I've more than enough,
And, darling, I'm generous,
I'll make sure you have a good share of my tainted love.
Not my fault that I'm a bad hole now,
My brain was too trusting,
Now I'm permanently adjusting,
To living with what I've got,
Whether I like it or not.
What have I got?
It doesn't matter.
What's important is that you hurt like I hurt.
And when you've got over the shock,
Then you'll go to the doctor too and be met with disapproval,
Like I was,
And be praying that they've shots to cure your cock.

I'm infected.
It's not as bad as I expected.
I itch and bitch and often feel a little sick,
But most of the time I'm on top of it.
I take my medicine,
But I don't think it's working.

Well, there really is no cure,
For my health,
But the hurt to my self-esteem is much worse,
Than a well-publicized divorce,
And having my dirty sexual laundry aired in court.
I'm not sure how I got this curse,
Was it Ray, or John, or Tim?
(Or someone else?)
But all three guys looked so clean.
One face hid the secret mine does now,
But the sex! WOW!
Was oh so incredible,
Only now I'm stained indelible.
But I'm not done yet,
I'm far from done, you bet.

Hell has no fury like a pussy burned.
I, a pure vagina turned into a cesspool of worms,
And publicly scorned,
Will have my revenge.
Guys, lessons will be learned,
Payment made for vengeance earned.
I RISE AND FUCK AGAIN,
You all will share my shame,
And my pain.

So I'm infected, but I'm not going down alone.
Every night I take a new baby-faced guy home,
And let him feed my rotting dog his sexual bone.
He suggests we use protection;
I decline: "I'm trying to spread an infection."
He laughs; he thinks I'm joking.
I assure him that I am. We sit awhile, eyes smoking,
Then I spread my legs, so my cunt is on display,
Waxed like in his favorite DVD,
And ask him to taste me.
He does so gladly,
Kneeling and drinking from my fountain of poisoned waters.
As I orgasm, I feel a little guilty leading lambs to such delicious
slaughter.
But not enough to cease,
Spreading my venereal disease.

CHAPTER 50

2: a.m.

When Fred awoke, he was somehow back in his own room. Still naked, but in his own bed.

How? he had no idea. He had little time however to consider the incongruity of his current location. His penis was itching.

He reached down and scratched it, then froze. It felt like . . .

He looked at it. *Oh, fuck, hell no!*

His penis was covered with hair.

Totally confused, he held the organ. It felt normal, except for its new grayish-white covering, which felt like an animal's pelt—like a puppy's back. The hair was bristly and thick. When he parted it, there were dandruff-like white specks at its base. The lush hair covered his entire penis including his glans. His urethra was a tiny hole at its tip.

Thoughts tumbled through his head like clothes in a dryer. *This is the result of the blood I drank. No . . . it's the blood I licked. No! Shit—I knew there had to be a reason why no one likes menstrual sex. It's—!*

"Meow."

It took a moment for Fred to realize that the sound had come from his penis. He stared down at it in dismay.

"Meow!" the organ yelped again.

Fred didn't attempt to reason out how his manhood could be 'meowing.' He leapt out of bed and hastily pulled on his clothes, which were draped over a chair.

He charged out of the room. *Femina, you stupid bitch—where the fuck are you!?*

***

Femina wasn't in her room. Her door was open but she wasn't there. Fred checked her bathroom and balcony, then rushed off. *Where the hell can she be at two in the morning? The drugstore?*

His penis itched in his trousers as he rode the elevator downstairs. He ignored the sensation. He also ignored the stream of meows that blurted from his crotch.

"Yes, Mr. Matthews," Edmond Flourish replied Fred's inquiry at the reception desk, "Ms. Femina did go out a short while ago. She crossed the street to buy cigarettes. She's however since returned to her room."

"Her room? Edmond, I'm just *coming* from her room. She's not there!"

The receptionist's fat face instantly creased with worry. "She rode the elevator up just before you came down, sir. Maybe she got off on the wrong floor."

Fred's face fell. "A distinct possibility." Crotch obscured from view by the reception desk, Fred was pinching his penis through his trousers. He had firm grip on his furry glans, which was twitching furiously, trying to meow again.

"Do you want me to look for her, sir?" Edmond asked.

"No, don't bother. I'll go myself." He turned and dashed back to the elevator.

***

Fred rode the elevator up and down twice, stopping on each floor. Femina wasn't in any of the corridors. She wasn't in the basement either (he checked there as an afterthought).

He got out on her floor. She still wasn't in her room. Still gripping his crotch to keep it quiet, Fred rushed over to his room—*Maybe she's gone looking for me.* She wasn't there either.

He sat on his bed for five minutes considering his dilemma. *If I keep going up and down, I soon wake everyone up and . . .*

He unzipped his pants and sprung out his hairy penis. "Meow!" it yelped instantly. *Hell no! No way am I showing this off!*

Only one place to go now, Fred decided. He once more zipped his cock away, then dashed out the door for the elevator again.

***

Fred pushed the twentieth-floor button on the elevator control panel and kept it held down. The elevator didn't move, but the entire panel suddenly altered, its silvery surface turning an obsidian black, with its buttons now fluorescent green ringed with neon purple. Frowning grimly, he pushed the button for the nineteenth floor. The elevator began rising. Fred waited impatiently as it traveled up past the limits of the hotel, to the realm called Bizarro.

CHAPTER 51

2:30 a.m.

Ash waited patiently for the elevator, her mind elsewhere.

(She'd forgotten her purse in the room, but decided against going back for it. She had more than enough money in her arm; she'd get some out before crossing the road.)

Ash was too preoccupied with thoughts of Skunk's impossible appearance in her life to realize that the elevator's floor indicator now signaled that it was on the nineteenth floor.

CHAPTER 52

2:31 a.m.

The elevator stopped, slid open. Fred stepped out of it onto a desert landscape in blazing mid-afternoon sun. He instinctively looked around for danger. There was none in sight; even the mindless meats—carnivorous hills of flesh—were far off.

Behind him, the elevator was now an old ramshackle wooden hut in the middle of nowhere. An equally ancient piebald horse stood tethered to a pole by the front door. Behind the derelict shack, sand extended far back to where the Beer River cut its path of turbulent rapids through the landscape.

***

Fred untied and saddled the old horse, then swung himself up onto its back. His itching meowing penis fuelling his sense of urgency, he rode off across the desert, heading left.

The old horse was much stronger than its raddled frame suggested. Its hooves clopped furiously across the barren landscape, like it sensed Fred's urgency.

Fred looked back. The old hut was now a distant nipple-shape crowning a sand-dune breast. *Should be any moment now,* he thought.

As always, it happened without him realizing it had. From galloping in a saddle, Fred suddenly found himself behind the wheel of a blue Aston Martin convertible with the sunroof down. How his horse had become a car he had no idea. It just had.

The only vehicle in sight, he now drove on a sixteen-lane freeway in the middle of the desert with lots of cacti on either side of it.

The biggest difference, however, was the sky overhead.

The sky was now split into three vertical parts. Its left sector was black with a purple sun (or was it a moon? Fred could never tell the difference—the orbs never brightened or dimmed). The middle swath (beneath which Fred currently drove) was red with a similar yellow sun. The right sector was pink with a green sun.

In the far distance, beneath the pink right sector of sky, were mountains. Straight ahead led to the literally unnavigable conglomeration of concrete roadways called Bypass Station. Fred had been there once—the disorder was beyond impressive—seemingly every road in the universe converged there.

Fred shifted gears up, pumped the gas. He swung the Aston Martin left, to the far edge of the freeway, so he was driving beneath the black sky and purple sun. He was headed for a cliff overlooking a dark sea filled with sharks and giant lobsters.

After a while, the final transformation occurred. Fred's body began altering, taking on the monster aspect he so loathed. His skin thickened to snakeskin-patterned leather, his hair all shrunk into his scalp, his tongue lengthened . . . He felt the auxiliary love-tongue slither out through the tip of his penis. *Am I cured?* he wondered. He felt inside his pants. No, his manhood was still as hairy as before.

He cursed and sped on. *I need to get to Vola, already. She'll have an idea what to do.*

The freeway had now contracted to just two lanes, the sky to just black with the purple sun/moon. The light of day/night was fluorescent.

Fred reached the turnoff to Vola's house. He drove down it awhile, then parked the car under a tall vaguely human-shaped plant with rainbow-hued tentacle leaves.

He got out of the car, stripped off his clothes, winced at his reflection in the rearview mirror. *Hell, you sure do look ugly, motherfucker.*

His penis was so hairy now it looked like a fox's tail. *I sure hope Vola doesn't freak out when she sees what I'm bringing her,* he thought miserably.

***

Vola lived in a small white cottage on the cliff top. Before knocking on her front door, Fred walked to the cliff edge and peered down into the dark sea. *The sharks and lobsters seem particularly agitated today, like they're fighting over food.*

He walked back to Vola's house, musing on their odd relationship. How they'd met? Fortuitous happenstance. He'd been exploring and stumbled on this place. The rest was a bedroom story.

***

Once Vola saw Fred's hairy penis, she backed away from him in horror. Fred was surprised at the amount of fear and disgust in the bird woman's eyes. She waved her wings at him. "No, no, stay away from me, darling. You have a sexual disease."

"I know. That's why I'm here. I need your help."

She looked at him fearfully. "You're not here to infect me with it?"

Fred rolled his eyes. "Why the hell would I want to—"

"Meow!" his penis yelped loudly.

Vola leapt up so high in her alarm, wings flapping, that she banged her head against the ceiling. She crashed down stunned. Fred rushed over to help her. She instantly backed away across the floor, scuttling on her buttocks. "No, no, no! Don't come near me!"

Fred sighed and sat in a chair. He couldn't actually blame her. But . . . her posture . . . She was sitting on the floor with her bird-legs parted, her vulva splayed wide. Staring at the pink opening, Fred got an instant erection.

"Meow! Meow!" his penis yelped. "Meow!"

"You want to fuck me!" Vola yelped. "Your man thing is hard! Horrible, like a brush!"

"Of course it's hard. I can't help it that you're so beautiful. But I'm not going to attack you."

She smiled at the compliment, relaxing somewhat for the first time since his arrival. "Okay, just stay over there where you are." She frowned. "What disease have you caught?"

"I don't know."

"How did you catch it?"

"Sex."

Her frown deepened. "So you lied. You do have a human woman you sleep with. You men are all untrustable. I don't know why—"

"Meow!"

"Tell your man thing to stop making cat noises. I don't want to hear its excuses for your behavior."

Fred winced. "Vola, I have no idea how to." He smiled seductively. "Honey, trust me, I have no other woman. You know I only love you."

The bird woman smiled and spread her legs wider, letting her sex gape open for his inspection. "Do you mean that honestly? You really like me best?"

Fred nodded.

Vola grinned. "Then I think I know someone who can help you."

Fred nodded again, eagerly. "Yes? Who?"

"Felix, the woman I told you about last time."

"The cathouse woman? I thought you were joking."

Vola laughed.

"What's funny?"

"Last time you could choose. I said: 'go and see Felix in the cathouse,' and you refused. Now, you have no choice. Your man thing's karma has come full circle."

"I didn't refuse. I just thought—"

"Meow! Meow! Meow!!!"

Fred wondered how his furry erection could make the sound with the tongue in it. Then he understood: *Tongues are the universal organ of speech, having one in my dick actually helps it meow easier.*

"Okay, I'll go. Just tell me how to get there?"

"No choice now, right?"

"No choice."

"I won't tell you."

He gaped at her. "Vola, please. I already told you I'm sorry, and I honestly don't have another woman."

She giggled, in command of the situation. "I mean: I won't tell you until *after.*"

"After what?" He saw the lust-filled glaze in her aureate eyes. "Sex? Vola, you just called it an infection."

"It isn't man thing I want now. I want tongue—the cunnilingus." She got up off the floor and arranged herself on her sofa, splaying her rattler-patterned thighs wide, pushing her buttocks out over the seat's edge. "No .. . no sick meowing man thing today, only tongue. A lot of tongue. Yes, come over quickly. Get down on your hands and knees. Lick my woman place. Lick it very, very good. Outside and inside . . . *deep* inside. Ah, yes, Freddie baby, lick it like that, and like that . . . and *like that* . . . oooohhh!"

***

Afterwards, Vola escorted Fred away from her cottage back to his car. She staggered dreamily against him, steadying her trembling legs with a wing around his shoulders. Her vagina still tingled from her multiple orgasms.

Fred put his clothes back on, got into the blue Aston Martin.

Leaning on the car door, Vola kissed him. "You're sure you understand the directions?"

He nodded. "I first drive back the way I came. Once the road spreads out again to sixteen lanes, I cross over to the farthest right one and head back this way."

She smiled, stroked his snakeskin-patterned face with wingtip claws. "That will put you under the pink sky with the green sun."

He nodded again. "I follow that until the road shrinks to two lanes, and keep going till I get to the crossroads, where I turn left, and—"

"You turn *right* at the crossroads. Left leads to Hell—a hot roasting place."

Fred gulped. *Hell? That's hard to believe.* "Okay, I turn *right* at the crossroads. And then, Felix's house is straight ahead?"

"You can't miss it. It's under the skin sky."

She kissed him again under the fluorescent purple light that was neither day nor night, then staggered off towards home, flapping her wings to lift herself off the ground—her legs were *that* weak from the cunnilingus.

What marvelous sex lives human women must have, she imagined.

Fred watched Vola go for a while, then he reversed the car and set off for Felix's house.

It was only half an hour later, while zooming through a landscape that seemed a melding of human skeletons, that Fred realized he'd been too preoccupied on his arrival in Bizarro to deactivate the elevator's special controls in case someone else wanted to use it.

He stared ahead in horror for a moment, then shrugged. *Back at the hotel, it's three-thirty in the morning. Who the hell wants to use an elevator at that time?*

CHAPTER 53

2:36 a.m.

Ash was so preoccupied with her own thoughts that she didn't realize there was anything wrong with the elevator till it reached the floor *below* the basement.

It was only then, after it had opened onto a street that was anywhere but Riverside Drive outside the Hotel Bizarre, that she looked at the controls properly, noticing for the first time their black/green/purple transformation, and also, that the lowest button (which she'd absently pressed instead of the one for the ground floor), was in fact one that previously hadn't been on the controls.

This new one read simply: 'Endless Street.' The original basement button was immediately above it.

That in itself wasn't as unsettling as Ash's recognizing the street outside the elevator.

Except that it was now correctly inclined, Endless Street looked exactly the same as Ash remembered it from her brief spell spent on her bedroom floor looking up at Skunk walking down it towards her in the ceiling.

For a moment she stood confused as to her next action. Her first impulse was to simply press the ground-floor button and get the hell out of there. But then she realized that none of the passers-by were looking at her askance.

Why? She peered out of the elevator. Here, it was set in the rear inner wall of a motor garage, left and right of which the road continued. *But if I'm on one side of the road, how come I can see down it?*

The puzzle boggled her. She remembered Skunk saying something about 'losing her way because the route bent.' That explanation would have to do.

Ash's curiosity was now pricked. She *had* to investigate this odd place, this 'Endless Street' that by all rights shouldn't be here.

Okay, I need to record this . . . oops. She remembered the mind-chip socket in her head was empty, her collection of chips neatly stacked on the bedroom dresser upstairs. She quickly checked through her muscle-purses for a spare, then winced. *Damn! They're all upstairs?'*

She scowled on realizing she had no way to record what she saw.

Her period cramps had subsided for the meantime. *And anyway, this is a street and it's midday, there are people and open shops. I'll definitely find some tampons here.* She tapped her left thigh-purse. *And I've got my gun—any muggers are in for the surprise of their lives.*

There was one final thing to resolve however before she set out. How to get back up—how the elevator worked. Ash had no intent of being stranded down here.

She examined the elevator. The garage itself was empty of people. The few cars it contained were dust-coated like the workshop had been abandoned a long time. Ash suspected no one came in here except they knew about the elevator.

Okay, that's cool. But just how does it work?

It took her fifteen minutes before she worked out how to turn the 'special functions' (as she thought of them) off and on. Simplicity itself— just press-and-hold '20.' Once deactivated, the steel cell transformed into a small office with two desks and a chair, with the elevator controls replacing the light switch.

After a trip back up to the ground floor, and a peep out to see Edmond Flourish at his reception desk (didn't he ever sleep?), she descended back down to Endless Street and confidently set out on her adventure.

CHAPTER 54

As far as Ash could tell, Endless Street went on forever ahead and behind her.

The garage with the elevator was called 'Lloyd's.' It was sandwiched between a rooming house and an old folks home, and was a block down from a Taco Bell. Once sure where to return to, Ash headed up past the eatery.

The street was largely deserted, with the occasional person entering or leaving a store. Ash kept walking. This place seemed normal enough. Bright midday sun, clear sky.

Then, some distance ahead, like someone had poured paint over the heavens, the sky momentarily 'flashed' black, then instantly normalized again. *Yeah, this is an odd place alright.*

Next, a parcel-laden pregnant woman exiting a clothing store looked Ash's way, and smiled. Ash shuddered—the woman had only one eye. The cyclopean woman dropped her load of hatboxes and shoeboxes in the rear of a grey Lexus, got in and drove off.

Ash looked after her for a moment then walked on.

She passed a few more people, then reached a group of six early teens sniffing glue on the front steps of a dilapidated brownstone with the mailbox number 2m2006. One of the teens was a cyclops like the pregnant woman. The others were normal. All had bright blue hair and eyebrows.

"Hey, lady! Give us some money, willya?" one of the blue-haired girls said as Ash walked past.

"Yeah," a young male voice gruffly added. "This is our turf. Pay the toll!"

Ash unzipped her arm and gave the girl fifty dollars. The teens goggled at her muscle purse.

"Wow. Thanks, lady," the girl said. She indicated the zipper in Ash's arm. "Where can I get one like that?"

"At the races, hon. But you need to be like eight years older."

She stepped on quickly, forgetting the adolescents faster than she left them behind. She'd now realized there was something strange about Endless Street. The next two houses were numbered 2m2008 and 2m2010.

2m . . . can't possibly mean two million can it? House number two million, two thousand and ten? Does this street actually literally go on forever? But that's impossible!

Impossible or not, the next few buildings maintained the same numbering scheme. A long block of apartments was 2m2016–2m2034, and so on . . .

Ash peered into the next alleyway she reached. The connection was clean and empty, the street beyond nice and quaintly suburban. She decided to cross over and take a look. *At least it won't have numbering up to two million.*

Once on the next street she quickly realized her mistake. The first house she looked at was numbered 6m534,228, the one opposite it, 6m534,235.

Ash gave the pleasant suburban vista the once-over. She calmly noted a winged couple having sex in a tree two houses down.

Grinning stupidly, she stepped back through the alley to the first street. She sat on the front steps of the first house she reached to think. Her confusion now gushed like water: *It's all the same street! House number six million!? Winged people?*

She calmed herself. *Nothing bad has happened. I only discovered this place. I don't live here. I can leave when I like, thank God.*

Figuring she'd so far walked half a mile, she decided to explore some more before returning home.

Then, ahead of her, the sky abruptly transitioned into darkness. The darkness became suddenly apparent, like it had previously been obscured by an invisible fog.

Ash stopped dead in her tracks, her breath coming in startled gasps.

The darkness was contained, nightfall walled off in its own separate room. Here, Ash stood in full daylight that rose all the way up to fluffy white clouds, while a hundred yards ahead of her, night similarly rose skyward like black liquid in a bottle. There was a sickle moon, too, hanging over the rooftops.

She collected her wits about her again, remembering the fleeting darkening of the sky she'd noticed a short while before. *Okay, this must be what that was.*

She walked closer. The area beneath the dark sky was a red-light district. Garish signs proclaimed 'Girls! Girls! Girls!' 'Hardcore Peepshow!' 'Sadie's

Sensual Massage!' 'Foxy Delight's Adult Theater.' A bevy of prostitutes frolicked beneath blazing streetlights.

Ash shrugged—*Just one more surprise in pseudo-paradise*—then boldly walked into the dark zone, into city nightlife in full swing.

***

She was immediately hustled by two men.

The first was a seedy-looking slob. "Wanna buy some blow? Also, I got the best crystal meth on Endless."

"Hot-looking bitch like you was born to make porn," the second man said. He was middle-aged and better dressed. He was also severely drunk.

Ash was disgusted. "Fuck off!"

The drug man took her advice. The porn man was more insistent. He grabbed Ash's arm, dragged her across the street into a dark doorway. "You're gonna make porn with me and like it, you redhead slut!"

Ash looked the man over. He was handsome and clean-shaven, with dark eyes and thinning dark hair. His suit, though well-tailored, was faded. He looked down on his luck, really down. The smell of booze on his breath had obliterated his perfume.

She looked beyond him, out at the street, for help. A crew-cut blonde prostitute winked and gave her the thumbs up. *Okay, no help there. She clearly thinks I've scored a hot one.* She looked helplessly back to her drunk assailant. He was unbuttoning her top.

"Get your damn hands off me!" She tried to push him away, but he was very strong. His strength gave her a momentary thrill. The image of both of them naked on satin sheets flittered through her mind . . .

"I want to see the goods I'm filming." The clumsy way he was fumbling to undo each button, Ash almost wanted to help him.

"Look," she said evenly, "I don't want to be in your porn movie. Stop pawing me."

"With a body like yours? You'll fuck on camera and like it."

Ash couldn't believe the audacity of the statement. *And where's my choice in the matter, dickhead?* She swatted at his hands. "I said, let me . . . !" then she calmed and smiled. "What's your name, porno man?"

"Eddie . . . Eddie Fiddle."

Ash was taken aback. Eddie Fiddle, the world's greatest porno maker, here? Holly Wood's husband? Then she rolled her eyes at the lie. *Total bullshit. Dude, you look like you fell on hard times and broke them instead of the other way around.* She smiled sweetly "Now, Eddie, I've a question for you."

Eddie had loosened her top two buttons, spread her top. "Nice tits . . . good! I'll make a *massive*, superlative, ultimate bukake special with you!" His voice was fever-toned, his eyes someplace else. "Much bigger than I ever did with Holly. Just imagine it: Two hundred fucking guys spattering your milk factories with jism. And then—"

"Eddie, you asshole, you're not listening to me!" She slapped him hard. "Look at me, man!"

Eddie finally looked at her face. "What!? What is it, you stupid redhead slut!? You dared hit me? I'm gonna fuck you so good on camera—"

Ash grimaced; the insults/threats were becoming too much. "Look down, Eddie—not at my breasts—between your legs."

He looked. Then looked back up at her. "What the . . . ?"

Ash smiled sweetly. "I see you've now realized I've a gun in your crotch. My question is: Are you going to let me go, and find someone else to make your stupid porn, you damn wannabe, or do I have to shoot your balls off first?"

(People were walking past them like nothing unusual was going on. The blonde prostitute who'd given Ash the thumbs up was nonchalantly feeling up a potential client between the legs. "Wow, darling, your pork sausage feels like it's been in the freezer for a week. But the oven I got between my legs will sizzle it right up. Oh yes it will. Now whadda ya say? Three hundred bucks for an hour of companionship.")

Eddie gaped at Ash in confusion. "But I just wanna make you a star! You should be fucking grateful to me. I'm Eddie Fiddle, the world's greatest porno maker. Hook up with me and you'll be bigger than Holly Wood! Bigger than Jenna Jameson, bigger than Georgina Spelvin, bigger than—"

"Your dick. Go sober up, Eddie—your celluloid delusions have gotten the better of you." She dug the Beretta painfully into his crotch. He winced. "Get going; your unborn kids will be thankful to you later."

Eddie instantly let go of her and backed off. From a safe distance, he glared at her angrily. "How ungrateful can you bitches be? All I wanna do is make a movie with you."

"And I don't wanna star in it." She waved the gun at him. "Get your punk ass in motion, man. Go chug some coffee." As he turned away, she added: "And for fuck's sake, stop calling yourself Eddie Fiddle. You don't look like you could shoot a movie if someone else held the camera for you."

The insult punched through the drunken man's alcoholic haze. He turned back to face her. "*I am* Eddie Fiddle," he said with cold sober dignity. "The reason I'm in hiding here is because some thieving bitch with tentacle hair stole my Kate Rose necklace." Looking about to cry, he gestured around him at Endless Street. "Why the motherfuck else would I be down-and-out here with these losers?"

Ash just kept staring at Eddie. *Oh no. You really are the famous porno director? Super-oops. Raye . . . this man thinks you've got his necklace.*

Speech done, Eddie flipped Ash the bird and shambled off. He took two steps, then collapsed, ending up face-down in a puddle of water. He didn't move. Air bubbles began popping out of the water. None of the prostitutes or johns paid him any notice.

"Screw you too," Ash said with relief. She didn't zip the gun away again, instead, she stuck in her waistband, under her top. *Endless Street may be a realm apart from Earth, but there's clearly no shortage of crazies here either.*

Her meeting the movie director here had really shaken her. He was an unwelcome reminder that she and Raye were still fugitives.

She looked back the way she'd come. Like she expected, the street outside this dark zone was in bright daylight, with the sun overhead and white clouds in a clear blue sky.

Oh, yeah. This sure is one crazy place.

She left the nook. Walking past the blond prostitute (who instantly pulled the john she'd been chatting up into the doorway in Ash's place, pulled down his pants, and began licking his penis vigorously so he could 'sample' her fellatio technique), Ash realized with shock that the woman had two tongues.

She froze for a moment, shaking her head to clear it.

Eddie Fiddle still lay out cold in the puddle of water, which no longer foamed with air bubbles. Ash realized he'd drown if she left him there like everyone else was doing.

Ah, my fucking heart of gold, she scowled, bending down and rolling the unconscious director over so he didn't asphyxiate in two inches of water.

Then, walking with confident swagger, Ash strolled on down Endless Street, taking in the nightlife.

CHAPTER 55

Femina – Cunt for Rent

I'll sell myself to you,
Rent myself to you,
'Cos I need the cash,
And you need some ass.
But don't think I'm trash,
Fuck you if you think I'm trash.
Okay, fuck me anyway, just pay me first.

I'm an ordinary girl,
And in this horrible world,
I find myself,
Wanting more than I'm allotted,
To possess.
And, yes, I'm quite impatient,
And I like beds.
A job on my back fits me like . . .
Like your cock fits in me.
Neither hurt a lot.
Oh, you ask why?
Well, why not?
I really tried, but couldn't hold down a steady job,
My attention tends to wander,
When faced with a computer screen,

And stacks of reports.
But men say I'm pretty,
So I thought:
What the fuck?
Why not . . .
Just help you all get off?
All you want is cunt?
Alright, I can do that . . .
Just give me what I want,
In return.

You come to me, hon,
For some fun,
And leave afterwards,
Drained of your come,
With your wallet empty,
And my purse full.
A monetary transfer,
Of which the state doesn't approve.
Yes, certainly,
I do MasterCard and Visa too.

I'm selling what you're buying,
Whatever it is you're buying,
I've got,
More than enough of.
(Once it concerns down-payment love!)
Everything your penis wants.
Don't walk past,
Let's have a blast,
Wine and dine and a real good time.
In bed,
My head between your legs,
Sucking your cock till you beg,
To fuck me.
Cover you up with a condom,
(Love protection!)
Now let's get it on,
Get our nasty on!
Ooh, baby,
You're so sweet,
Stuck in me deep,
Like a fork in tenderloin meat.

And even sweeter, honey,
Is the money you're paying me.

When your lady love's having her monthly distress,
(Her pussycat stuck up in the baby tree again!)
Come visit me, honey, I'll relieve your testicular stress.
(I mean 'blue balls'—I'm sure you've already guessed!)
It'll be money well spent,
This cunt for rent.
Yes, it seems indecent,
But it's worth every cent.
FDA-approved cunt for rent.

What did you say?
You never lose with *her*,
You've got a season ticket?
Permanent admittance to her vagina games,
Whenever you need it?
Okay, but when she's having a slump,
No need to languish in the sexual dumps,
I'll tide you over her existential pain,
(Or it might just be bedroom-strain,
Vaginas need to recuperate every now and then.)
Fuck you till her kitty's back on its feet again.

The one real difference,
Between *me* and *she*, honey?
I never kiss on the lips.
And it's not 'cos I'm scared of herpes.
I need to keep my distance from my feelings,
And that would just be too intimate.

In my business there are no cheaters.
(I'm not a home-breaking deceiver!)
Your state of incarceration,
In the marriage institution,
Doesn't matter.
You're aren't renting my vagina,
With emotional commitment,
A promise to love and cherish me alone,
Forever.
Nah, I'm a lot cheaper,
Just two hundred dollars per the hour.

And then I'll send you . . .
Safe and sound back to *her.*
This is a financial bedroom dance,
(A casual erotic happenstance,
Where you pay, and we both drop our pants!)
Not some fairy tale romance.
No happily ever after,
Just temporary lust-induced trance.
I'm 'fucking,' not 'sleeping' beauty,'
You're always Prince Charming when you screw me.
(See? The perfect fantasy.)
Nothing's lost,
In this transaction,
This rented relationship,
Of mutual satisfaction.
It ends,
Once you spend,
(Your cash and come,)
Then to 'Darling' you return home.

Oh, you ask me why?
Well, girl, why not?
I know I'm hot!
(And I'm even better fucking in a hot tub!)
This sweet ass and tits are what guys want.
I'd be a fool, not to sell,
My tight little cunt.
Which every other girl does as well.
Oh, no—I'm not fooled that your price is wedding bells.

My vagina for rent,
Is your hard-earned money well spent.
Guaranteed to be worth every cent.
You can even fuck and pay in instalments.

I'm selling pussy to you,
Renting myself to you,
'Cos I need the cash,
(I want a fast car, and a room in a five-star!)
And you need some ass.
But don't you dare think I'm trash,
Screw you, if you think I'm trash.
Well, screw me anyway, just pay me afterwards.

CHAPTER 56

Shop signs informed Ash that this dark section of Endless Street was called the Nighttime Zone.

The tissue padding Ash's panties felt soggy. Quickly, before blood began running down her legs, she bought a box of 'Kotex Super Plus' from a shop. She looked around for somewhere to use them—an alley, a dark corner. *I'm definitely not doing it in the middle of the road.* Worse, the damn cramps had resumed. "Ouch!"

Then she sighted a space, a break in the row of houses a short distance ahead. She headed for it.

Passing a porno theatre playing *Anna Andrew's All-Accommodating Asshole: Astounding Andalusian Acrobatic Anal Adventures!*, Ash was suddenly aware of a thick smell of exotic floral perfume.

She looked back. The only person behind her was a thin woman in a wine-colored dress, blonde wig, and huge yellow sunglasses, peering at the racked display of gaudy dildos in a sex-toy emporium.

Ash shrugged. *Just another weirdo.* She resumed walking.

The space she'd spotted was a playground/park of sorts. A cracked concrete expanse bounded by a green picket fence, with a makeshift children's swing (two tires hung from a frame), two bent slides, and four benches set amidst straggly clumps of grass.

Ash heaved a sigh of relief. The dilapidated park was devoid of people, it afforded her privacy. The strip—lights, prostitutes, and all—resumed full-blown action again a short distance away.

She hurried over to the most shadowed bench, sat and pulled down her panties. She was just in time—the tissue was soaked through.

A noise startled her. She leapt up in alarm, then relaxed on seeing a large black rat scurrying off.

She sat back down, noting that the thin woman who'd been inspecting the sex store display had also wandered into the park. Her thick perfume hung over the park, an invisible cloud Ash sensed if not saw. The woman sat two benches away from Ash, spread her legs, and inserted a purple vibrator (which she'd apparently just bought) up inside herself.

Ash winced. *Damn, lady, couldn't you just wait till you got home?* She looked away from the masturbating woman, who'd begun moaning, back to her own business.

Bent over, about sliding the blue tampon applicator in, Ash froze. An overwhelming stink of fish had suddenly filled the air.

Ash instantly felt the return of a three-year-buried dread. Mingled in with the intensely pungent fish stink was the smell of the woman's perfume. (In isolation, the perfume—she'd immediately identified it as jasmine from its fruity undertones—had held neither significance nor menace. Now, mixed with the fish smell, it instantly reminded her of her rape in the Arlington Park stable back in Chicago).

Oh fuck! she thought in horror, scared to look up. *No!*

She heard footsteps squelching towards her.

"Hey, bitch! Did you miss me?" an inhuman voice growled.

With rapidly multiplying horror, Ash did look up. And wished she hadn't.

Shit! The approaching monster defied belief. It was HUGE, seven feet tall, and vaguely human in form. It was a writing mass of tentacles and fish. Large fish—white cod, orange-spotted brown plaice, silver mackerel—were stuck into its body between its feelers, along with several massive lobsters.

Ash felt paralyzed, utterly nerveless. Such was her shock and dread, she was totally unaware of dropping the tampon applicator, of its bright plastic clatter on the concrete.

She puked; a totally unconscious reflex. Her disgust exited her mouth in a single bitter projectile stream, spattering the approaching monster. *This obscenity—this is what raped me!?*

She had no time to think anything else. The monster grabbed her with its tentacles. It forced her back on the bench, restraining her arms, spreading her legs. From its crotch, it aimed a black-striped Atlantic mackerel at her bleeding vagina. "Yeah, girl. Great of you to stop by here. I've really missed your hole!" It had neither face nor mouth; its voice seemed to come from its lobsters.

"Help!" Ash yelled toward the street. "Help me!!!"

But like before, when Eddie Fiddle was fiddling with her, no one paid the slightest heed to her. While the monster pushed its mackerel-penis at her sex, she stared in disbelief at the people milling just yards away on either side of her, who apparently saw nothing amiss with what was going on.

And Ash now had another problem to contend with—herself. Her legs suddenly felt weak, like they'd dissolved into water. Her crotch was warm, her vagina wet. She wanted to be fucked, wanted the monster to take her like it had three years ago, wanted to drown in the smell of it, to orgasm violently as it simultaneously spurted goo inside her.

She fought to clear her head. *What the hell is wrong with me!? I don't want this bloody thing to rape me!*

But her body was conspiring against her. The monster stroked her with its tentacles, covering her with slime. Ash's skin crawled with disgust at its touch, her eyes widened with the extent of her revulsion; she fought against vomiting. But like it were part of a separate her, her vagina flooded with pleasure moisture. Her crotch trembled with desire for penetration. Her thighs shone wet with sex secretion and menstrual blood.

She got a grip on herself again. *Hell fucking no! This is oh so not happening!*

Clearly, no help was coming from Endless Street. She remembered she wasn't alone in the park, turned her plea closer to home:

"Hey! You lady jerking off! Help me!"

No response.

Ash couldn't see around the monster; its bulk dominated her vision. Either side of its massive body, waving tentacles blocked off her sight. (Its legs too were immense, like living tree trunks, a plaiting of trembling tentacles and seaweed over which crabs scuttled. Sardines and starfish plopped out of the mesh, desperately flopping between its wet root-like toes.)

No, Ash couldn't see the masturbating woman. But surely the woman could see *her* . . . her plight.

Then she understood: The mingling of fish scent and perfume (both back then and now) made sense. *It's the woman! She's the one who turned into this monster!*

The monster yanked Ash's legs farther apart. The mackerel began nosing into her vagina.

"Oh, fucking yeah!" the monster moaned in guttural bursts. It lashed her with its tentacles, ripped her top open. Its fish nibbled on her nipples.

Oh, yeah! Ash moaned in response, as the fish head between her legs spread her vaginal lips like she was being fisted. *Take me, make me yours!*

With a wrenching effort, she cleared her mind again of lust fog. *OH, NO!* she thought savagely. *I WILL NOT BE RAPED!* She looked up at the creature's head, flailing lobsters planted amidst tentacles.

She yanked her buttocks back. The fish's head plopped out of her cunt. It was now striped with her blood. She twisted her hips sideways so it couldn't reenter her.

"Stop playing around, bitch!" The monster growled. "Let me in—you want this as much as I do!"

"Fuck you," Ash said coldly. "I didn't agree to this." It was taking all her self-control to not give in to the lust ravaging her, to not submit to the horrible mass of tentacles, to not let it fuck her senseless.

"Who cares what you agreed to?"

"I do." She freed her left hand from the coils restraining it enough to reach the gun in her waistband. In seconds, the Beretta was in her hand.

She cocked it, then stuck it into the midst of the tentacles. A huge lobster snipped her shoulder so she winced with pain. "Let me go!"

The mackerel-penis was once again nosing at her vagina. A tentacle was wrapped around it, steering it into the bleeding opening.

"Let me go," Ash repeated quietly. Her heart was beating like it would burst. Sensation and desire flared in her like exploding fireworks. *But no, I'm not giving in to this crap. Sex will be on my terms or not at all. But, holy shit, I feel like I'm the world's largest, most horny vagina. I want to come! NO! STOP THINKING THAT SHIT! I DO NOT WANT THIS!!!*

The monster laughed. "I'm gonna fuck you super-good, girl, like you want me to. Remember last time?"

"You talk too much." She pulled the trigger, emptying the gun in a loud sequence: Boom! Boom! Boom! Boom! Boom!"

The monster let go of Ash and staggered back. "What the hell did you go and do that for, girl?"

Water spurted out of it, pouring from between its tentacles. It expanded like it would burst, portions of it erupting outward then shrinking back toward what Ash now saw was a transparent watery core. *No, Ashley Status, you dimwit, that is not a sea—there are no sharks swimming in the midst of this creature! The stink is addling your mind, that's all! Don't be a dumb blonde—Get it together!*

Whatever her reservations about the monster's contents, she understood now that it was really just water—water with sea-creatures embedded in it.

And bullets couldn't harm water.

The creature was still fighting to pull itself together. Her vision of the park clearer now, Ash looked around.

She saw something that scared her almost shitless.

The masturbating woman hadn't become the tentacle monster. She still lay across the metal bench, rubbing the purple dildo over her clitoris with slow strokes.

A long green mist extended like a cord out of the woman's vagina to the tentacle monster. Ash gaped. The green mist *became* the tentacle monster. *This beastie is coming from her cunt?* How is that possible?

The smell made sense now, but . . .

Like she could read Ash's thoughts, the masturbating woman, face shrouded by her blonde wig and massive yellow glasses, gave Ash a thumbs up.

Ash was suddenly more confused than anything else. Everything made no sense. Stinky tentacle monsters don't come out of vaginas. She decided to leave, get lost . . . *figure this insane shit out later.*

She'd left it too long, however; made her decision too late. The tentacle monster had repaired itself. It stepped towards her, once again blocking off view of the woman behind it.

"You little tramp. This time I'm gonna fuck your ass!"

Ash gaped at its mackerel fish-penis, which now dripped a clear black-dotted jelly like frog spawn from its chewing mouth. *Damn! If that thing goes inside me, it'll force my rectum up into my throat! I'll never shit again!*

She still felt erotically charged, but was now too perplexed to want to take advantage of it.

One thing she didn't feel was fear. She now knew the creature could be hurt. And, oh yes, she planned to hurt it.

"Okay," it said, gesturing tentacles at her, "turn around. Hands and knees on the bench, doggy-style. I got a load of a beluga caviar about to hit your stomach the wrong way."

"Wait a minute," Ash said. Now she'd definitely seen its lobsters moving their mouth parts as it spoke. *But who's doing the actual talking? This creature or the woman it's coming from?*

"Wait for what?"

It reared back, tentacles flailing like whips around it. Several huge cod spilled out of it and thrashed wildly on the floor. Two king crabs as well. *Are they falling out of its body or from the sea beyond? Stop thinking this crap! There's no sea beyond this thing—it's just an illusion coming from that bitch's vagina!*

She however realized the creature was wary of her shooting it again. "Just hold it. I wanna get some condoms. Extra Large. You don't want poop on your dong, do you?"

Before it worked out how dumb the question was, she quickly unzipped her right thigh and rummaged inside it, cursing herself for being so untidy. *But then a purse is a fucking purse, isn't it? You don't arrange its contents, even if it's in your leg. Now where the hell is this damn thing?"*

She found what she was looking for, held it up for the monster's inspection.

It slung tentacles over her. "Look, forget the damn condoms—fish don't mind eating a little poop, it's vitamins. Okay, okay. Turn around, hands and knees. Gonna hump you extra hard now, but you asked for it."

Ash turned round. She grimaced as the monster spread her legs wide, and placed the fish-penis in her ass-crack. It began pushing. The pain was like . . .

Ash wasn't waiting to find out how deep the mackerel could get into her rectum before she began ripping up. And its fins would tear her up even worse. *Oh shit! Gotta end this right now!* She put the tiny tube taken from her muscle purse to her lips and blew into its inflation straw.

In five seconds flat, the RPG-7 grenade launcher was fully inflated.

Ash hefted it, taking satisfaction in its weight. It was pre-loaded with a massive green oblong warhead and also pre-cocked. She flicked the safety off, reversed her grip on it, and pointed it back over her shoulder. Angled it down.

The monster was slobbering all over her back now, wrapping its appendages around her. Her clothes were soaked with its wetness. Pincers snipped at her hair, fish bit her ears. "Oh yeah, girl, this ass of yours is super-tight. But don't worry, I'm widening it just right. After tonight, you'll be able to take on dicks of any size. A great career in porn lies on your horizon."

It gave a deep thrust into her anus. The mackerel's head felt like a switchblade slicing her open. Ash stifled a scream. *No matter—I'm already bleeding from one hole, I'll just tampon them both.*

Along with the pain, a burst of sexual pleasure surged through her body, almost making her knees buckle with its intensity. *Oh, please fuck me!* She fought off her desire to drop the weapon and masturbate. *NO! NO!! NO!!! CUT OUT THAT CRAP!!!!*

Ash pushed the RPG-7's muzzle/warhead back through the tentacles smothering her, deep between their roots. "Just what the doctor ordered for safe sex. For me, that is."

She pulled the trigger with grim satisfaction.

Her ravaged anus was instantly unplugged. She was yanked backwards off the bench as the shell blew the monster off her. She landed in a patch of grass.

Then there was the sound of the creature exploding.

She dropped the rocket launcher, got up and looked around.

Bits of the tentacle monster were strewn everywhere—piles of diverse fish, lobsters, and crabs in a flooding of moonlit water. Several fish were impaled on the green pickets of the surrounding fence. There were tentacles in the midst of it all, a hundred fat meat-whips futilely lashing the ground like they were frustrated sadists. Heaps of seaweed with clams in them. An upside-down turtle. Above everything floated a dispersing green mist.

(Incredibly, the people in Endless Street were still going about their business like nothing odd was happening in the park.)

Ash sneered at the carnage. "Let's see you put yourself back together again now, Humpty."

She remembered the woman who'd birthed the monster. She turned. The woman was gone. "Why didn't you hang around?" she growled. "I'd have kicked your ass so good!"

All that remained where the woman had lain was her purple vibrator and floating above that, fading words in frozen green smoke: "Ouch, that fucking hurt, bitch!"

The dispersing words reminded Ash of her backside. *Ouch, the pain. That damned mackerel . . .*

She staggered back to where she'd dropped her tampons and picked up the pack. (Her uneven walk wasn't just caused by pain—she was sickened to find herself still aroused from the creature's assault. It was all she could do not to masturbate here and now, not to lie down amidst the dying tentacles and give into her body's demands for satiation.) She considered still inserting the tampons here in the park, then shook her head. *Too dangerous—no time to waste in getting lost. For all I know that monster-making slut may return.* She looked around at the sea creatures scattered everywhere, the flopping fish and tentacles. Oh, the smell! *And if there are others like her . . .*

She got out another inflatable from her leg, blew it up. Ten seconds later, she climbed on the red Harley Davidson Superlow and turned the key in the ignition.

While rolling out of the park, she grabbed the purple vibrator off its bench.

Then, blood dripping from her anus and vagina and staining the motorbike's leather seat, Ash zoomed through Endless Street, from the Nighttime Zone back into daylight, back to the garage with the Hotel Bizarre's elevator.

CHAPTER 57

Beneath the Skin Sky

The skin sky was just that—a Caucasian-toned pink overhead expanse. Blonde hair-clouds floated across it. The landscape beneath it was also skin-colored—a vaguely-sloping treeless expanse that transitioned from flesh-pink by the roadside to inland purple ridges.

The sun was a massive human vagina.

Fred almost drove off the road on first sighting the vagina-sun. Then he steadied the car and gaped at the huge radiant sex organ. Its folds shook slowly like it was speaking to him. They separated then came together again, revealing a dark cavern—a literal black hole. Golden moisture dripped from the vagina, seemingly raining on weird trees and mountains far, far away.

***

In his sojourns across Bizarro, Fred had learnt to use the sky's variegated colorings to determine his location. He'd never gotten lost yet, but there was always a first time.

Heading back from his current location—going left at the turnoff instead of right—led beneath another black sky, this one with a burning sun. This was no exaggeration—the sun was on fire. The clouds were a bright yellow, and the city in the distance—a hulking black obsidian skyline delineated from the sky falling on it by flame like the entire city was afire— gave off the chilling vibe of also being a living, sentient being.

'Welcome to NYC' read the massive green signboard crossing the left road just after the turnoff. Fred had shuddered on seeing it. That NYC definitely wasn't the one he knew. Vola had said the road left literally led to Hell. Fred believed her now.

***

Felix's house was on the left. Vola had been right: the building was unmissable. It was the only one he'd seen since making the turnoff under this sky.

He parked the Aston Martin ten yards from it and got out.

The house (or rather hut) was small and lacked windows, didn't look to be more than a single room. An existential restroom. It stood right by the roadside like it was expecting him.

He scowled. *A ridiculous impression, but . . . a damn convincing one.* As was normal in this part of Bizarro, Fred hadn't encountered anyone on his drive over. *So what's a single hut doing here, of all places?*

"Meow!" his penis yelped.

Fred patted his crotch and sighed. Other than for his mutated manhood, his body was normal again.

His penis cat-yelped again. Grimacing, he set off for Felix's front door.

***

"Come in!" a voice called before he could knock.

Somewhat startled by being so anticipated, Fred pushed the front door open, stepped inside.

He immediately understood why Vola had call it a 'cat house.' *She stuck cats on the wall? And ceiling? There's thousands of 'em!*

He looked over the impossible décor—the tapestry of feline fur, the thousand pink tongues, bared claws, and curling tails. The cats looked him over in return. Their endless duplication of slit-pupiled eyes felt like the universe itself watching him.

Damn, lady—the thought leapt into his mind—*you must have a massive hairball problem.*

He was aware of a human figure facing him . . . female . . . smiling . . . but . . .

"Meow!!!" the stacked cats thundered.

"Meow!!!" Fred's penis thundered back. His pants unzipped themselves. His briefs split, baring the furry organ.

Dizziness swirled in Fred's head. He staggered, reached out to steady himself. The furry floor bristled, its hair rolling in waves. He felt stranded at sea, swimming in cat piss, or in a desert with different-colored dunes everywhere, a billion eyes watching . . .

There was a hole in the wall directly opposite Fred. He focused his gaze on it to clear his mind. *No, something's wrong here—it was daytime outside just now, not night!* He peered through the hole at the impossible dark sky beyond. Black punctuated with glittering stars.

He felt his mind sucked toward the dark opening amidst the cats. Alarmed, he tried to stop the extraction . . .

Fred suddenly felt like he was one of the cats on the wall. He was staring into the room at himself . . . Yes, he could see himself clearly . . . staring bewildered at the hole in the wall that he occupied . . . that his befuddled mind occupied . . .

His eyes, part of the cat-slit ovals staring at him, *saw.*

The eyes saw as one unit, like a compound mammalian eye.

They saw *all* of him—his bones, his flesh, his beating heart and pumping blood, his very cells as each formed and died.

The eyes saw *through* him, they saw his motivations, his questions, his justifications.

Finally, the eyes saw *beyond* him—far out into the universe, to the birthplace and graveyards of stars, to where black holes were simply period marks on celestial writing paper, to the outer limits of the most inestimable distances ever conceived. To the point where a thousand light years were in proportion less than a human centimeter. To feet striding across those impossible distances.

The eyes saw to a face they couldn't see.

The cat eyes saw God. Fred too knew he saw divinity, but like the cats, the sheer glory of the vision blinded him to its true awesomeness—his mind simply could not process what the eyes fed it.

(He was conscious that the cats were intensely angry with God for some reason—and that it wasn't because they were spending their lives stuck on walls.)

"You finally got here."

The voice shrunk the universe back to a pinpoint. The sense of overwhelming immenseness, of monumental purposes on a scale no human could conceive, dispersed like gas leaking from Fred's ears and nose. He ceased being a window on the universe, part of the compound feline eye. Fred became himself again. He now remembered the woman in the room, the woman he'd come to see.

Felix.

He looked her over. Mid to late sixties. Graying hair, dark eyes. Body concealed beneath her robe of cat fur. A fading beauty. No, that was wrong, she was a woman trading the beauty of youth for wisdom, the beauty of age.

The room reeked of musk like the scent was oxygen. The smell was her, and also the cats on the wall.

"This place is overwhelming," Fred said. "And I'm not even mentioning the vagina-sun shining outside."

She nodded. "That's partly because you're connected to it."

That voice. Fred looked at the fur-clad woman in confusion. Confused at her words, but also because he suddenly *knew* her. His brain crunched with the impossibility of what he was seeing. *This woman is older, at least thirty-five years older, and her hair's darker, but . . . but . . . she looks, . . . no, more than just her looks . . . it has to be . . .*

"You look like you've seen me before, Fred," Felix said.

Her voice had altered. The slight adjustment in pitch and timbre confirmed Fred's suspicions. He gaped at the old woman.

"How . . . what the hell? Femina? You . . . you . . . you're Felix?"

She nodded serenely at him, her lips framing a mischievous smile. "Sort of."

"But how? How? How?"

"Stop repeating yourself." She stroked his cheek with old fingers. The cats mewled. "And stop staring at me like your eyes are hungry."

"How? Just explain *how?*" Fred shook his head. "I mean: What? Or is that even the right question? As at this moment I have no idea what's going on."

"Meow!" his penis said.

He pointed down at the exposed furry organ. "And what is this thing? Do something, please. It's driving me out of my mind."

She grinned. "Thanks for bringing it over. One of my cats died. I needed a replacement from the human world."

"What are you talking about?" His eyes beseeched her. "Can you cure this infection?"

Felix chuckled. "No need to—it's not an STD." She grabbed hold of Fred's penis, taking firm grip behind his glans. With her other hand she gripped his testicles.

"Hey, don't squeeze those so hard. I don't yet have any children."

A cool, amused smile. "Hold on." She pulled slowly on the furry organ. The hairy covering slid off it.

Fred gaped. She was pulling a cat off his penis.

The cat plopped free. Fred stared at the gray/white feline in horror.

It bared its teeth at him and hissed, hair standing up straight on its back. It looked at him like his penis had been plugging its intestines.

"Yeah, furball, I'm glad to be free of you too." He regarded his normal-again member with deep relief, then looked at Felix. "Thank you *very* much. Okay, now so—"

She silenced him with a gesture. "Hold on a moment."

Carrying the cat with her, she walked out through the front door of her house, which (he somehow wasn't surprised to see) was now a large storeroom full of shelves covered with odds and ends.

She was back in a moment, carrying a syringe of Loctite superglue.

Fred winced. "Oh no, you're not going to . . ."

Felix was already busy squirting the superglue all over the cat's right side. (The cat was now looking at Fred like he was salvation, like it would pay any price to be back on his penis.) Once done, she looked at Fred. "I need your help." She pointed to the hole in the wall through which the stars were visible. "I'm too short to reach that."

Fred took the glue-smeared cat from her. (He was glad it seemed resigned to its fate, didn't attempt to bite or scratch him.) He didn't wonder how you could glue an object into empty space. He placed the cat over the hole, it stuck. He refused to dwell on it.

He looked back at Felix. "Okay like this?"

"Thanks. Just hold it in place till the glue sets."

Fred kept a hand on the superglued cat. Eternity flickered through his mind in nova flashes. He felt the cat resist becoming one of a matrix, then its acquiescence.

Two minutes later, Felix grinned. "It's okay now. Pack your cock back into your pants, zip 'em up, and come sit down. We've a lot to talk about."

CHAPTER 58

Fred had no intention of sitting on the bristling jungle of cat fur that formed Felix's floor. He had no idea if cats had lice or fleas, and considering the size of the creature that had provided its pelt to carpet Felix's house, he had no intention of finding out firsthand.

"There aren't any bugs."

"You've no chairs."

"I forgot."

A pair of lions suddenly appeared in the middle of the room. The lions roared. Fred leapt away from them to hug a wall of cats. "Hey!"

Felix giggled. "Sorry." She snapped her fingers. The lions both froze into immobility. She gestured to Fred. "They're safe to sit on now."

Fred nodded. He extricated himself from the cats (who'd begun licking him) and walked back over to examine the frozen lions. "What did you just do?"

"I stuffed them—instant taxidermy."

He nodded again. After prodding the nearer lion to confirm its death, he climbed atop it. Felix got on the other. They faced each other across two feet of unmown-lawn cat hair.

This is crazy. How the hell do you stuff two living lions in half a second? "I'm so-oo confused," he said. "What is going on?"

"Stop repeating yourself," the old woman said, pulling her fur robe tighter around her. "It's boring except when making love."

He scowled. *Damn, lady, do you have to be such a smartass? Cut me some slack here, you stupid—?*

"Stupid old cow?"

He shook his head quickly.

Felix smiled coldly. "Remember, I can read your mind. Keep your thoughts to yourself—I liked the sexy ones when you were fucking me much better."

He rolled his eyes. "Shit."

"Exactly. At least you said that out loud." Her expression warmed somewhat. "You're on my turf now—in my realm. Behave yourself, okay?"

He nodded. "I still don't—" He saw her forming grin and shut up. *Yeah, that'll be repeating myself again, won't it?*

He realized Felix was toying with him. "Okay," he said carefully. "You clearly know a lot more about stuff than I do. You talk. I'll just listen."

She smiled sweetly, stroked the tawny pelt of the lion she sat on. "Now you're being humble. The right attitude in my presence."

Something about the way she said it, had Fred instantly worried. "Who are you? Are you Felix, or Femina, or—?"

"The vagina singer is one of my incarnations," she interrupted him, frowning. "Definitely my favorite version of myself. However, I am many other people, some you wouldn't believe."

The air around Fred shimmered, then slit open. He was suddenly staring into an office at . . .

The air normalized around him again. "You've got to be kidding me. You're also Priscilla Presley—the New York mayor?" Then, a helpless: "How?"

She shrugged back. "I'm studying to be God. Women deserve one of their own. A divine Matriarch as opposed to the current tyrannical regime."

"And?"

"It's so much harder than it looks. I'm doing fine so far with Omnipresence—at the moment I'm in six different places, including a suite at the New Orleans Riverside Hilton, having my pussy eaten by the most gorgeous young man you ever did see." She trembled momentarily as if from sexual pleasure, then shrugged again. "Omniscience however . . ." she raised pleading, exasperated eyes skyward, "I don't know how the Old Guy in the sky does it."

"Knowing everything must be hard."

"No. That's the *easy* part. The info's in the air for the taking—you just tap into it."

Fred frowned. "So what's the problem?"

"There's a world, no, a universe of difference between knowing everything, and KNOWING EVERYTHING. The first is like I just explained—I just tune into whatever information I need. The second . . . ?" She scowled. "The human brain has a definite limit to how much information it can hold or remember. I once managed to cram all the data about New York—major and minor details about people's lives . . . all the transport system routes, number of cars and their individual fuel consumption, animals . . . you get the picture?—into my head. Almost drove me insane. I had a nervous breakdown, lay here for two weeks without food or water. When I finally got my brain together again, I was covered with cat shit . . . several meows had died too. And that's just for one city."

"You did good though—largest population center in the USA."

"Whatever. It's still just *one* city. So what I want to know is how does HE do it?"

She looked extremely piqued by her lack of success. (Now the cats' anger while viewing the actual Almighty made sense to Fred—it was jealousy on Felix's behalf.)

"How 'bout omnipotence?" Fred asked.

"Don't die. I can't bring you back to life." She shrugged. "Well I can, but you wouldn't enjoy coming back." She frowned. "Similar trouble as with the previous. I resurrect birds and rodents okay, but then they start rotting."

"Zombies?"

She nodded. "The stink was disgusting and the bastards kept trying to eat my brains. So I stopped . . . *for now.*"

She fell silent, squeezing the head of her lion seat. The cats also went quiet. Even the floor was quiescent, like it sensed Felix's moodiness.

"What I came to see about . . ." Fred ventured softly when he felt they'd been quiet too long.

Felix looked at him. She looked older. "Don't worry about it."

"I don't mean my penis."

"I know. The original reason the bird woman sent you here was Big Tony and Lana always screwing with you, right?"

Fred nodded. "I'm sick of it. "You know Big Tony won the tampon tea lottery and they switched cards on me?"

Her face lost its somberness. "Trust me, I . . . Femina . . . was grateful they did. You're much more fun in bed. Big Tony is the Russian girl's sort of man—muscular and uninventive. She likes it hard and fast. I, however, like to take my time . . . okay, sometimes that is."

Her grin faded. "Now back to those two: Don't sweat yourself about them. They'll soon stop bothering you."

"They will? Thank God. Felix, they're major pains in my—"

"I know. Don't worry." She frowned. "You need to take care of their dog though."

"Bitch?" Fred's face fell. "Look after that stupid cokehead Doberman mutt? Why?"

"Nice dog. Promise me you'll look after her." She stared at him coldly. "No faking. Remember, I can read your mind."

There was a loaded pause. Then: "Okay, I'll look after her. But she stays away from my ass. She goes after my dick one more time and I'll blow her canine brains out, deal?"

Felix nodded. "Deal. She'll behave."

He didn't ask how she intended to ensure that. He scratched his hair with a finger. "What is this about?"

"Be patient. You'll find out. I'll however tell you this: That dog is fantastic karma for you."

Before Fred could enquire further, she opened her fur robe and let it fall and drape over the stuffed lion.

"What are you doing?" Her body was well-preserved, though there was no hiding the cellulite and droop of age. Her breasts sagged, but her waist was thin and her hips wide.

She spread her legs. Her vagina glared at him amidst its forest of gray-striped brunette hair.

"I don't understand."

"That's because there's nothing *to* understand. I'm about giving you a blowjob."

Fred jumped down off the lion's back. "I need to get back to the hotel before I'm missed."

She leapt down off her own lion and blocked his path. "No one will miss you." He made to push past her. She grabbed him. He found she was unnaturally strong. She forced him back down onto the cat-back rug, grinned down at his distressed face.

"I told you I'm training to be God, didn't I? No way under Heaven are you stronger than me, boy, so just relax and enjoy the suck."

She undid his trousers, dropped her mouth over his penis. He breathed in sharply, instantly came erect.

She sucked him hard. Fred, floating on the hair-rug, disbelieved the feeling of her mouth on him. He stroked her shoulders and back.

He came in under a minute, which had never happened before. "Oh, fuck!"

Then he realized she was no longer sucking him as he came. Instead, she'd locked her lips around his glans and was stroking his shaft rapidly with her fingers, milking him into her mouth. And the amount of semen he was ejaculating? Was impossible, considering he'd already had sex thrice with Femina that evening.

Felix also wasn't swallowing. He felt himself spurting onto her tongue, but no suction.

And the feeling . . . was endless. Like eternity? It flashed through his mind that this orgasm was Felix making a point, stamping her divinity on his consciousness.

Fred finished ejaculating. His penis plopped out of Felix's mouth. Lying back drained, he was suddenly worried. Her cheeks bulged with his copious ejaculate, like she was a chipmunk hoarding liquid seeds.

Oh no. She's not going to spit it on me, is she?

Felix winked at him, then spat the semen out into her cupped hands. Then, while he goggled at her in disbelief, she smeared it all over her face.

"What are you doing?"

She grinned back, her face youthfully smooth, her wrinkles completely buried—coated over in a double layer of his come. "Semen makes a great facial peel. I'll just leave it on overnight." She licked her hands clean. "And it's full of vitamins too."

Unable to find appropriate words, Fred nodded dully. He zipped up his fly again, then looked around the room of cats. All were now asleep, bodies swelling and deflating with their breathing. He was suddenly conscious of how long he'd been here. Time to go.

"Would you like a trip back to the Hotel Bizarre?" he asked Felix.

"No need. I'm still there." She looked eerie, like she wore another face over hers.

"Still there? So where were you when I was looking for you?"

"Lying in bed, watching you."

"Your bed was empty."

"Nope, I was in it. I just didn't let you see me. If I had, you wouldn't have brought me my spare pussy."

He glanced at the cat he'd stuck on her wall, then back at her. "That's a joke, right?"

She grinned coquettishly. "What else? Thanks for the come too, I'll look ten years younger come dawn."

"I'll pretend I didn't hear that."

"Don't be boring. We're bedroom buddies now." She spread her aged vulva folds with V'd fingers. "You know you're totally hot, right? Feel free to come see me anytime you're in the neighborhood . . ." she gave a throaty giggle, "or in the mood."

Fred gulped at the old woman with his semen coating her face. "Please, let me go. I've just slept with two different versions of you. What else do you want from me?"

Felix patted his cheek, then kissed it. "Whatever you've got left. You're intensely satisfying—vulnerable. Most men aren't. They fuck us and get us off, but don't really care about us. You *do* care. You want to satisfy each woman you're with. With me at least, that counts for a lot."

She linked her arm in his. "Come on, I'll walk you to your car."

They stepped through the front door back into the desert beneath the pink sky.

Fred gestured up at the skin-toned expanse, the massive puffs of blonde-hair clouds floating across it. The humongous vagina sun. "This is your doing?"

"Yeah. It's impressive, right? Used to be a boring red, green, and blue."

Fred shuddered. "Did you *have* to?" The vagina sun's orifice brimmed with golden moisture. Light visibly spurted from it in urine-like showers.

"I'm a woman—it's a fantastic sun to have. A Sunt—that's a combo of sun and cunt, obviously."

"It's intimidating."

"Patriarchy reservations. You'll get used to it. How'd you think women feel surrounded by phallic symbols everywhere? It's like an endless symbolic rape."

"It looks like it wants to eat me."

"It does. *I* just ate you, I don't hear you complaining."

"I just don't like having a vagina watching over me."

"Big Mother? Ha ha ha!"

"It's not funny. That thing is scary."

"It's a trap. I'm hoping God will come and fuck it. Then I'll take him captive."

"What?" Fred looked from the massive vagina-sun to the woman—or goddess, his brain hurt from the complications Felix represented—who'd made it. He was suddenly very bothered. It occurred to him that Felix wasn't actually mad or deluded, that given enough time and patience, she actually might capture God, overthrow/dethrone him . . . And then what?

"Better times for everyone," Felix said. "Ladies especially." She pulled him towards his car. "I'll sing you a song about *my* universe—the Pussyverse."

Fred listened to her sing, all the while unable to take his eyes off the glowing Sunt.

CHAPTER 59

Femina – The Pussyverse

Deep inside the Pussyverse,
In my cavern of exotic delights,
Your personal Arabian nights,
(Your tour-guided magic carpet ride,)
Starts tonight.

Drive your train into my tunnel,
Travel down me, oil swirling in a funnel.
Come inside,
On the sensual roller-coaster ride,
Of your motherfucking life.

I'm all charged up,
A fiercely sparking vagina.
Pubic hair static electric,
Electrons in live wire!
I'll shock you,
With hidden, forbidden desire!

Insert your key in my ignition,
Quicken me to transition;
Warp speed accelerate,
Into vaginal hyperspace.
I want to orgasm on planets far away.

Drill me for crude,
Sink your rig through my crust,
(Be rude, I'm not a prude, dude!)
Mine out my reservations,
Replace my suspicions with lust,
My superstitions with trust,
In science . . .
In the Space Age of Free Womanity.
Then you can fuck off,
If you want.
Or you can fuck me instead,
Till I'm half-dead . . .
(From pleasure, not violence!)
Blast my cunt light years away from Earth,
Here deep in the Pussyverse.

The universe is in my cunt,
This boundless space that pleasure haunts.

The universe,
Is I.
Everything resolves around SHE!
I expand as you fill me,
Then contract . . .
To trap you within.
(Contract! Like when we signed
The dotted line.)

Pilot your starship across my internal skies,
Through caverns abysmal wide,
Across rivers deep, over mountains high.
Glide . . .
With rolled-back eyes and trembling thighs,
Moaning . . .
In pussy paradise.
My universe beckons,
Traverse light years in sex seconds,
Of excruciatingly pleasant penetration.
Your love-rocket,
Pins me to the floor,
Give me more!
I want more fucking more fucking more!

VAGINA MUNDI

Here inside the Pussyverse,
Where daylight is pitch-black night,
Your penis navigates just fine.
(My vagina grants it second sight.)
As we rise to Paradise,
The sensation is divine.

My breasts, your silky Milky Way,
Sexual chocolate,
Slip a Mars Bar,
Up my gap.
My vaginal galaxy,
Is packed with wondrous sights to see.

In the Pussyverse,
Man and woman are one,
Daughter the same as son,
Penis and vagina simply inversions,
Of a single intimate, ultimate ONE!!!
Such Feminist revelation!
Flesh reversions,
The organ inside, the organ outside,
Are exactly the same.
Day becomes night,
And back again.
To fuck is being fucked,
Delicious cock versus scrumptious cunt,
Ooh, sensations sweet and soft.
Everything's a pleasure game!
To penetrate is to incubate,
To enclose is to dilate.
My orifice is the eclipse of your sun.
So . . . accompany me, everyone,
Into my world of fun,
The Vaginal Renaissance has begun.

The stars at night,
Are nowhere near as bright,
As the shine in my eyes,
When you . . .

Fly your starship into my nova,
(I am your nirvana, your dharma,

Your ass-tronaut karma!)
Melt and explode,
Overloaded by me,
(Overloaded with me!)
Your generators detonate.
You asphyxiate,
In deep space,
No one can hear you pray,
(In alien tongues!)
Or see the fear on your face,
Your ecstatic dismay . . . as you drift away . . .
As you . . . as you come . . .
Your ejaculation . . .
Liquid meteorites on my tongue.

Glow, falling stars,
Dissolve into ash in me.
Blow apart, into newborn worlds,
Riven by chlorine seas.
Fill my womb with young Venus and Mars,
My heart with glee.
You have found me,
Reborn young and sweet.
My lovely sweet tight-but-spacious pussy—
A new cosmos for erotic discovery!

Here inside the Pussyverse,
We float far above Mother Earth,
Yet lie deeper than the ocean depths.
No worries, all is peace and love.
(Now you're trapped by my gravity!)
Freefall into me, honey!
I will set you free.

CHAPTER 60

Next Morning

"You were drunk, darling," Raye said. "Just admit it."

Ash shook her head aggressively. "I was stone cold sober."

Raye shrugged. "Either that, or you dropped some acid."

"I didn't."

Raye sat up in bed. "Ash, darling, our ceiling *didn't* fall open. A woman *didn't* fall through it. You *didn't* travel to Never Never Land in a magic elevator. No tentacle monster tried to rape you there." She looked pointedly at Ash. "Okay, say you really did see all you're claiming . . ." she tapped her right eye, "why didn't you eye-cam it?"

Ash pointed to the dresser with its pile of mind-chips. "I haven't been wearing them for the past two days. You know how they——"

"Sometimes give you menstrual migraines?" Raye glanced dismissively at the stacked chips. "How convenient."

Ash scowled. "I don't frigging believe this. Okay, I'll take you there."

"There's nowhere to go to." Raye's plump face contracted with thought. "I'm not saying *you* don't believe you left the room, but someone must have slipped you some acid during the concert."

"And it took four hours to kick in? Be realistic."

"I'm trying to—you must have dreamt all that stuff."

Ash grimaced. "No need to try—really. I'll take you there tonight."

"Ash, I'm not go——"

The phone rang. Ash answered it. "Edmond Flourish," she mouthed to Raye. She listened, replied, "Yes, we'll be right down," then hung up.

243

"He said our van's been stolen. Start thinking up a good excuse."

"You didn't re-park the inflatable?"

"I didn't remember. Don't blame me—neither did you, you were too busy coming while I rimmed your ass. Just get dressed; we're lucky he didn't see it deflate and dissolve. Then we'd really have a problem."

***

"We'll need to call in the police," the portly receptionist said.

The blood drained from Ash's face. "For a van? Just forget it, okay?"

Edmond was surprised. "Don't you want it back?"

"It was older than the Statue of Liberty," Raye said, patting down her platinum hair. "Let it go. We'll buy another one."

"Yes, we will," Ash quickly seconded.

Edmond considered for a moment, then stroked his impresario mustache. "This is highly irregular. If word of the theft gets out, it'll hurt the hotel's reputation for safety. And the police might also later wonder—"

"Don't worry your mustache over it," Ash said, slipping Edmond a hundred dollars.

He grinned broadly, revealing large white teeth. "Of course, of course. You ladies make a valid point about the vehicle's age."

Ash grinned back. "Surely there a car rental around here somewhere?"

"Yes, ma'am, several. What model—"

The elevator opened. Fred and Uncle Luigi rushed out looking extremely bothered. The pair hurried across the lobby to reception.

Edmond gave Ash and Raye an apologetic look and turned to serve them.

"Yes, sirs, is there a problem?"

"Karen's missing," Uncle Luigi said. "I can't find her anywhere. Also, my office was broken into last night, and some money stolen."

Fred nodded to Ash and Raye. Both women smiled back. Ash fluttered flirty fingers at him.

"I'll call the police immediately," Edmond said.

"No, don't!" Uncle Luigi looked pained. (Ash and Raye looked at each other in simultaneous worry, then relief.)

"But, sir, you said Miss Karen—"

"Don't be a dork, Ed. It's not Karen I'm worried about." He rubbed his lined forehead with meaty fingers. "I'm sorry, I don't mean it like that. Of course, I'm concerned about Karen. What I mean is . . ." He bent forward and whispered into the receptionist's ear.

Edmond's eyes widened as he listened. At one point he mouthed: "Water . . . on the floor?"

Ash pulled Raye aside. "They don't want us hearing about the drugs. I think they're dealing big out of this place."

"Good for us; means the NYPD won't be buzzing around our flowers."

Uncle Luigi had finished whispering and straightened up.

"Twenty grand?" Edmond asked.

Fred nodded. "Yeah, and Karen's nowhere to be found either. Looks like she's been kidnapped."

Edmond shook his head. "Not kidnapped. I think she's skipped town, sir."

Uncle Luigi's lips tightened. His expression became deadly. "What makes you think that, Ed?"

Edmond pointed to Ash and Raye. "These two ladies just had their van stolen."

Fred and his uncle looked at the two women. "Stolen?"

They nodded back.

***

The elevator opened. Femina and her background singers walked out. The singer was dressed a blue 'Free My Kitten!' t-shirt over ripped denim trousers and ankle boots with pirate buckles.

Raye sighed as the blonde strode towards them. "Damn, she's hot. And she's not wearing a bra—check out those jugs."

"Just keep your own kitty in captivity," Ash whispered. "I can practically hear your pussy 'meowing' at her."

"Look who's jealous now."

"I'm not jealous. I just don't want to see you get embarrassed. She's not into chicks."

Femina reached them. "Hi, Uncle Luigi. Is everything cool? You look super-pissed."

He grunted. "Just some mixed-up bookings. Nothing to give me another coronary." He smiled at her background singers, "Hi, girls," then turned back to his goddaughter. "I thought hedonists never got out of bed before lunch. Where you headed?"

"Gotta get to the studio. Just wrote a new song I wanna record."

"New song?" Fred asked softly. "What's it about?"

She smiled at him coyly. "I call it *The Pussyverse.*"

Fred turned three shades of embarrassed.

"Hi," Raye said shyly to Femina. "That was a great concert yesterday."

Femina smiled at her. "Glad you enjoyed it." Her blue eyes flowed from Raye's to meet Ash's. "Thanks for the teabag, sister."

Ash regarded her blankly for a moment. "Oh?" Then she blushed. "It was my pleasure." She grinned at Fred. "The senate should make tampon tea a legal requirement for all men."

Chortling, Femina turned to Fred. "See, Freddie darling? You've started a trend."

The elevator doors opened again. Femina's backing band Ladies in Disguise stepped out.

Femina sighed affectedly, nodded to her singers. "Okay, everyone, gotta run, the boys are here."

Ash watched her sashay away, buttocks set off in the tight jeans. "I just know *you're* also thinking what *I'm* thinking about her ass, right?" she whispered to Raye.

Raye colored in a fierce blush.

***

Femina disappeared through the front door. Uncle Luigi turned from watching her to stare coolly at Fred. "What's she like? In bed, I mean?"

Fred looked scandalized. "Uncle Luigi!"

"Don't 'Uncle Luigi' me, Frederick! Sure, she's my goddaughter, but she performs naked, and we were both in attendance at the concert." He scowled. "And don't you dare claim that these two fine ladies . . ." he indicated Ash and Raye, "would be embarrassed by the intimate details." He looked at Ash and Raye, "Would you be embarrassed, girls?"

Both vigorously shook their heads. "Of course not," Raye confirmed.

"Neither will I, sir," Edmond Flourish added.

Uncle Luigi nodded. "So what was the vagina singer like in bed? Was she all talk and no fuck? Or was she worth drinking that bloody tea for? Simply put—is she a good lay?"

Ash and Raye nodded fiercely, ears alert as cable TV antennas.

Fred sighed. "She was much better than good, Uncle Luigi. You have no idea." He looked shrewdly at his uncle. "Hey! You're not planning to try and win the lottery tonight, are you?"

Uncle Luigi shook his head. "Heavens, no! I'd never be able to face her parents if I bedded her. Besides, you know Karen; she'd never—" His face turned angry with memory. "Karen!" He looked at Ash and Raye, Femina now totally forgotten. "You were saying your van got stolen?"

Ash nodded nervously. "Mr. Flourish called to say it was gone. He was going to call the cops, but—"

"Forget the damn cops!" Uncle Luigi snapped. He glared coldly at his fat receptionist. "Sometimes Ed takes things too seriously." He turned back the women. "Now you both need to understand something: We don't want to get the police involved in this."

246

"We don't?" Raye asked, a shrewd glimmer in her eye.

"No we don't," Fred said with finality. "Karen stole certain property of my uncle's which—" He fell silent while two fat women with Chihuahuas dropped their keys at reception. When they'd gone he resumed: "Karen stole some of Uncle Luigi's property which—"

"Put it this way," Uncle Luigi interrupted. "I love Karen, and I don't want her getting into any trouble with the cops."

"Not even if she stole twenty grand from you?" Ash blurted out. "You must really love her ass."

Uncle Luigi looked pained. "We're still assuming. She might have been kidnapped."

"And then again, she might not have been," Edmond, pissed-off at being reprimanded, added.

"So," Fred concluded, "it's in all our best interests to not summon the fuzz."

"So what about our van?" Raye asked after a surreptitious wink to Edmond.

Uncle Luigi considered. "What make was it?"

"A Chevrolet Express. Less than a hundred thousand miles on the dash. If we don't make the police report, the insurance company won't pay up."

"Forget the police," Uncle Luigi said. "We'll buy you another van."

"You will?" Both women fought to conceal their surprise.

"Yeah, sure," Uncle Luigi said distractedly. "It's the only thing to do. Give Fred an account number and we'll pay four grand into it." He looked at Fred. "That'll be enough, right?"

Fred nodded.

Edmond sniffed unctuously. "I think five thousand would be more in the range of the van's value, sir."

Uncle Luigi looked at him sharply.

"It looked quite new, sir. And we do have to consider maintaining the hotel's good name."

Uncle Luigi rolled his eyes, then nodded to Fred. "Get on it." He turned a piercing gaze on Edmond. "Call Riley at 26th Precinct. Have him send over some boys with forensic equipment. I want to get to the bottom of this."

"At once, sir."

"I thought you didn't want the cops involved," Ash said.

"This is unofficial," Fred replied. "Lt. Riley owes Uncle Luigi several favors. They'll check the office for odd fingerprints."

Uncle Luigi scowled at Fred. "Come with me. We'll look around one more time before Riley's goons arrive. I don't think Karen could have done this alone. Maybe whoever hit us left some clues."

Fred looked suddenly baffled. "They did. Water, crabs, and seaweed."

"Like I told someone I wanted an indoor beach."

The pair left for the elevator.

Edmond Flourish coughed politely. "Ahem, ladies,"

They turned to him. Phone in hand, he regarded them with an oily smile. "The extra thousand the boss is paying you is mine, of course. Four grand is more than sufficient to replace a bus you didn't want anyway."

Raye smiled coolly back. "You'll get it." Her face creased in thought. "Did Fred just say there were water and crabs in the corridor outside Mr. Rossi's office?"

"That's what I heard too," Ash replied her. "Seaweed also."

"Don't worry about it," Edmond Flourish said. "Maybe Karen *was* trying to build him an indoor beach." He pointed out the door. "The Hudson's walking distance. Easy enough to get water and crabs." He turned from them to attend to a middle-aged man who'd just entered from the street.

Ash pulled Raye after her across the lobby to the elevator, walking in a hurry.

"What's your bug?" her girlfriend asked once the elevator was rising.

"Seaweed."

"What about seaweed?"

"I don't think Karen was kidnapped. Seaweed has to come from the coast, and we're a long way from the coast."

"We're near enough. I've heard some seaweed grows in brackish water too." She saw Ash didn't look convinced. "C'mon, girl. Don't tell me you think your monster got her?"

CHAPTER 61

[Chicago]

Money Rich crossed her legs. "You'd better talk, Ned. Where is she?"
"Please!" Ned yelled.

"*Please* doesn't answer my question, Ned. Where is Rosita Diaz?"

"I don't know. I didn't kidnap her!"

Ned Thomas was a dark stocky man with a badly pockmarked face and pale shifty eyes. The robogoon Dillinger currently held him upright in front of Money's office desk, his fly open.

Ned's penis lay on the desk, forcibly stretched out by a weight attached to its glans and dangled over the desk's opposite edge. Ned had a Prince Albert piercing—there'd been no need to cut him to insert the hook for the weight.

The weight swung like a pendulum in front of Money, who sat behind the desk facing Ned.

The fourth person in the room was Al Capone. Dressed in a new pinstriped suit, the robogoon stood on Money's right, slapping a baseball bat against his metal palm.

Ned kept glancing anxiously at Al and the bat.

Money uncrossed her legs and leaned forward. She carelessly flicked the penis-weight (making Ned shudder), then got up and walked over to her office window.

She stood there, resplendent in a sleeveless money-dress tailored from hundreds, with fifty-dollar breast pockets (Ulysses S. Grant's head situated perfectly over each nipple) and a gold-clasped belt sewn from twenties. The dollar signs tattooed on her pale arms made them seem an extension of the dress.

Stroking the Kate Rose necklace (now her favorite piece of jewelry), she looked out over downtown Chicago. The dull fall morning, the smog-infected gray clouds. She suddenly felt depressed.

She turned to face Ned again. "Don't waste my time! Where's the little girl? Your friend Mo Barnes said you fessed up to pinching her, planned on squeezing her folks for two million bucks."

Ned momentarily forgot his state of restraint. "That asshole snitch; once I get out of here, I'll—"

"Ned, you're wasting my time. If you don't tell me what I want to know soon, you'll never see Mo again. You'll be going to Lake Michigan to sleep with the fishes. Let me explain: Rosita's mum Mia and I went to Chicago State University together—same sorority house. It's imperative I get the kid back."

"Honest, Miss Rich, I don't know anything."

Money nodded to Al. "Give him a little tap to refresh his memory. Just a little one."

"Sure thing, Boss."

"No, no!" Ned yelled. Then he screamed "YEOOOOOW!" as the robogoon smacked his baseball bat down 'Thwack!' on Ned's penis.

Money noted the fat purple swelling just behind the cockhead with satisfaction. She smiled at Ned, who, held in an iron grip by Dillinger, was shivering like he had a fever from the pain and looked about to faint. He gaped at her in horror.

"Please!"

She laughed. "You're not damaged goods yet. It'll just hurt you to pee for a bit." Her gaze became steely. "Now where the fuck is the little girl?" She turned to Al Capone. "Next time I tell you to hit his cock, whack it like you're Babe Ruth making a home run."

The robot grinned metal teeth. "Gotcha, Boss."

"You better tell the boss the truth," Dillinger said, his bronze face gleaming. "Your dick has only one life to live."

Money looked at Ned pointedly. "Okay, I'm asking you this last time: Where is Rosita?"

"I don't know."

She shrugged, then turned to Al. "Whack the fucker."

Al raised the baseball bat again. High . . . higher . . .

Ned's eyes gaped wide. "No . . no . . I'll talk, I'll talk!"

Money stayed Al Capone with a hand. "Okay, I'm listening."

"She's down in the basement of the old Marvin's Cannery on South Wood Street."

Money nodded. "Alive or dead?"

Ned gulped, but didn't reply.

"For your sake, she'd better be alive." She picked up the desk telephone and dialed. "Hey Bugsy, it's Money. . . . You still over in Greektown? . . . Good. Now listen: Take the goons with you over to Marvin's Cannery on South Wood. . . . What? . . . Yeah, the abandoned one near the United Center. Rosita Diaz should be in the basement. . . . Yeah, the missing kid. Call me back once you confirm she's okay."

She hung up, returned her attention to Ned again. "Now we wait."

The phone rang again almost immediately. "That's fast, Boss," Dillinger said.

Money picked it up. "Bugsy is that you? . . . Oh hello, Lt. Jenkins. . . . You do? . . . Positive? . . . Yes, yes, that'll be great, I'll expect the files. Thanks so much for your help. . . . Your wedding anniversary's next week isn't it? . . . Please stop by the office anytime tomorrow—my accountant will have a little something to help you get Mrs. Jenkins a lovely present, maybe even that cruise she's been dreaming of. . . . Have a great day, Lieutenant."

She hung up again, looked at Dillinger and Al Capone. "NYPD have confirmed our two fugitives as the ones who killed the old tramp in Central Park. The DNA on the wine bottle was a perfect match for Rachel Risk."

Dillinger, still holding Ned Thomas firmly in place in front of the desk, nodded. "So we forward the descriptions to Uncle Luigi and wait?"

"Yeah, once the mug shots from Jenkins come in."

"Shouldn't be a long wait," Al Capone said. "Uncle Luigi's darned efficient."

Money smiled coldly at the captive Ned Thomas, her green eyes gemlike. "You really don't want to be either of those two women when I catch up with them." She pointed to his extended penis, its bruise purpler than a black eye. "And you really need an icepack for that."

Ned stared back mutely.

The phone rang again. "Ah, this will be Bugsy," Money said, plucking it from the cradle.

"Hello, Bugsy, you find her? . . . What? . . . Fucking what!!!? . . . Shoot, I'm listening. . . . Don't spare me the details, you damn metalhead—tell me everything!"

An uneasy quiet developed in the room. Money listened in silence, phone pressed to her ear. Suddenly she began crying, tears streaming from her eyes and down her cheeks. Finally she dropped the phone. She wiped the tears from her eyes, fixed them in a steely gaze on Ned.

When she spoke next her voice was deadly soft. "You've been a very bad boy, Neddy, haven't you?"

"I . . . I . . . didn't mean it, Miss Rich," he stuttered. He couldn't look her in the eye.

"They find the kid, Boss?"

"They found *parts* of her." Money sat on the edge of the desk, and stared at Ned. She reached out a hand and stroked his face. He flinched at her touch, still not meeting her gaze. "People like you make me sick, Ned. Okay, so we're crooks. But I don't get it. Rosita Diaz was seven years old— a total innocent. Okay, so you kidnap her. *Do it the right way!* Feed her loads of candy and let her watch Cartoon Network and the Disney Channel till late at night and eat all the pizza she wants. Pig out on ice-cream too. Her scared father pays the ransom—you let her go. Nothing's hurt except Daddy's bank account. The girl returns home like she's been on holiday and tells the cops and all her friends about these cool kidnappers, and how they should all aspire to get snatched too."

She paused, sighed. "But, Ned, what do you do?" Her tears had begun flowing again. "I'll count them out. First, you rape the little girl both vaginally and anally, and what's more you film yourself doing so—"

"That wasn't me!"

Money turned to Al. "Hit him once in the mouth. Hard, to shut him up. Break all his teeth."

"No! Please, it wasn't—!"

"Thwap!"

Money regarded the results of her instruction. Al Capone had slammed the baseball bat so hard into Ned's mouth that it remained wedged in it. Broken teeth were stuck into the wood, over which blood spurted. Ned's watery eyes gazed pleadingly at her over the ruin his mouth had become.

She nodded with satisfaction, eyes still full of tears. "It *was* you, Ned. Everyone knows the fat-abuser-wearing-a-hood ruse now." She wiped her eyes dry again. "Let's continue. Next, you sell the movies online. Then, like that's not bad enough, you film yourself killing little Rosita with an axe, then you *grind her up,* and can her—as fake Big Apple Cannery cat food imported from New York. And you *sell* the cat food."

Green eyes malevolent with bad intent, she leapt down off the desk. Her money-dress caught on something; she ignored the dollars ripping along her thigh. She smiled coldly at the now violently shivering man. The baseball bat jammed in his ruined mouth prevented him from doing more than mumble incoherencies which she interpreted as him professing his innocence.

"And, Neddie, don't forget the icing on the fucking cake. There were sixteen other kiddie-porn-snuff videos in your basement computer. Bugsy checked out the victims—each was a young boy or girl between the ages of four and eight, abducted in Chicago within the last two years."

Ned visibly slumped in Dillinger's grip. Money got out a tissue from her purse and dabbed her face. "Shitheads like you make me ashamed to be a criminal," she said. She looked at Ned in disbelief. "What the hell is wrong with you? Bugsy says that in one of the videos you were fucking a kid in the ass with the handle of a tennis racquet!"

Al Capone peered glowing eyes at Ned. "You sure are one sick human being, man. You make me glad to be a machine." He turned to Money. "What do we do with him, Boss? Want me to batter his dick to mince? His balls too?"

Money shook her head. "Too ordinary, been done so many times it's lost its punch. I need something original. Hey, take the bat out of his mouth."

Al jerked the baseball bat out of Ned's mouth. It came free in a shower of blood and enamel splinters. Ned's mouth was totally demolished now, merely a wound with a throat behind it. Teeth were embedded deep in his tongue and his lips were ripped off in strips that flailed about his mouth.

"So how *do* we do him, Boss?"

She waved dismissively. "Take his ass back over to his basement of horror and grind him up . . . alive. Then can *him* as cat food."

Ned's eyes widened in terror. "Noooo!" he sputtered, spewing blood everywhere.

Money considered a moment. "Okay, guys, now you gotta do this right."

"How d'you mean, Boss?"

"First, hang a large white sign reading 'I'm the pedophile bastard who molested and murdered your child' round Ned's neck. Then stick him in the meat grinder feet-first, so he stays alive as long as possible. Tourniquet both his thighs close to his dick so he doesn't bleed to death on you before the grinder reaches his crotch. Film *everything*—make sure you get the pain on his face—then take a copy of the video to Rosita's mum." She grimaced. "Shit! How the fuck am I supposed to explain this to Mia?" Then she smiled coldly, wagged a finger at the robots. "No, not just Mia . . . take copies to each of the victims' parents with my condolences. Take them each some of the cat food you make from him too."

She watched dispassionately as Ned, bloodied, jerking, and gibbering like crazy, was carried off by the robots.

"Asshole," she gasped as the door shut behind them. "Fucking pathetic waste of human skin." Then she began weeping again.

Outside, in the distance, tower-high factory smokestacks pumped out smoke to taint the sky. The black billows formed clouds. Random spaces in them looked like demon eyes.

CHAPTER 62

Femina – War of the Sexes Part Three: Love me, LOVE ME!!

What do you love about me?
I mean—what *do you* fucking love about me?
Do you even fucking love me?
By me, I don't mean my super-tight ass,
My daddy's cash,
Or my polished high-society class.
I mean ME!
I don't mean the 'I LOVE YOU,'
When your semen's spurting from you,
And I'm gushing endearments too.
You can help yourself then. You HAVE to love me,
Your penis compels you to.
Hell no, then I'm as guilty as you,
Guilty for even fucking you,
With your narrow-minded 18th century point of view.

What do you love, honey?
Am I a 'something' or a person?
All, or nothing at all?
I've got your back against the wall,
And I'll have my pound of emotional flesh from you before the curtain
call.
Speak, I'm listening:

Tell me—what is it?
My mind? My business savvy?
The way I never fart in public?
The sweet texture of my slit?
Or was it that time I fellated you in the toilet while I was taking a shit?
You want a sleazy bitch?
Yeah, honey, I'm it.

I know you love,
How much I conform to the image of the me I should be,
That you see on TV.
(Another victory for your patriarchy.)
How I—the working trophy wife—
Make you look fantastic in polite society,
With the right tits, lips, nails, hair, and teeth.
How I'm so curvy, yet still slim,
My Botox for Christmas, and the collagen . . .
I mean . . .
Those injections I got so my mouth now looks like a pink donut
wrapped around your prick . . .
My endless tummy tucks,
And best of all, how I feel when we fuck.
(I know you like that A LOT.)
I mean . . .
How I got my cunt tightened for your fortieth birthday,
So it felt like I was fourteen.
Oh, you pervy old thing.
Statutory rape, I rest my case;
You're imprisoned in my vagina till old age.

Now I'm confusing myself.
Is that me?
I look in the mirror,
And I like what I see.
Oh fuckin' yes, I fuckin' *love* what I see,
(You're welcome to objectify me!)
I'm the hottest thing on two legs in this vicinity,
Desperate Housewives has nothing on me,
And you know it.
I'm your personal Sex in the City.
Screw your revolving door secretaries,
Honey, you ain't leaving me.
I'm the perfect hook,

You, beloved, are just a fish I reel in now as I please.

Oh! Fuck these insecurities!

But . . . did I do it, I mean, do I look perfect now,
For you or for me?
Just background nonsense mental chatter,
It doesn't matter.
The really worrying question is:
Is this me I see in the mirror the real me?
And If I like it,
What's wrong with *you* liking it?
But *it is* wrong,
I'm more than what I see,
More than what you see,
More than my own perfect creation.

Come on, fuck me harder; suck my nipples too.
My mind wanders as you pump,
Silk bed sheets caress my rump.
I'm in bliss, pleasure as I rub my clitoris;
But I need to resolve this question,
My orgasm depends on it.
My mind tizzies then calms again,
In my vagina,
Your sliding cock is the pleasure that is almost pain,
That frazzles my brain.

Do you love the real *she*?
The *she* you can't see, only known to me?
You say you love *she*, but you're lying, honey,
You don't know *she*, only *I* do,
And I'm not revealing her to you.
Your sexiest impressions of *her* are untrue.
My lie is sweeter than verity,
'Cos some things about *she* are unlovable,
Trust me, I ain't telling you, beau.
What you love is the image I present to you,
You're only seeing what I want you to,
And, honey, I assure you,
I'm working extra-hard to make what you view,
Extra-perfect.
I must conform to the accepted,

Politically-correct norm.
Fuck imperfection, fuck individuality,
Just fucking fuck me with your patriarchy.
You wouldn't . . . no, couldn't . . . love me any other way.
So I'll play your little game today,
And maybe tomorrow too.
Oh, anyway, whenever I need a good screw.
And in between, I'll emasculate you.

You're comparing me with that girl on TV,
My pussy with a porno magazine,
My buttocks with Kylie Minogue's,
My attempts at talent with J-Lo.

So what the fuck do you fucking love about me?
Is it how well I do the birds and bees?
I mean: how well I fuck?
Trade secret: I study sex manuals during lunch break at work,
Like 'How to Suck Cock' by Anonymous.
Sorry, darling, I know it's not ladylike to swear,
But do you really care?
When I suck your balls hard, and jack you off and squeeze,
And set your painful erection at ease?
You love the fact that I never tease,
And in bed, let you do whatever you please,
(Anal's quite okay, just use the Vaseline.)
How I lap dance for you, then get down on my knees,
Sucking your penis so delicately . . .
Then swallow your come like it's Chinese sweet tea.
Is *this* what you really love about me?

You love your impression of me,
Not my reality.
I'm making do with second best,
But then, so are all the rest.
There, girls, I've gotten the truth off my chest,
I mean, off my 36FF implant breasts.

'I love your breasts, honey,' you confess,
They're the absolute sucking, tit-fucking best.
Oh no, you didn't complain at my augment,
And now I look like Dolly Parton running for President.
Honey, what the fuck do you love about me?

If I took of all my skin,
So you could slip another woman in,
Would you notice the difference?
Am I anything more than who I seem,
Still life as a physical dream?

My emotions, my estrogen shifts,
How I can't really cook, or mind the kids,
How I don't like any of your relatives,
(You're the sole clean turd from a family of shits!)
I know you hate all this.
And we're still faking marital bliss?
I must be dynamite between the bed sheets.

All our truths are lies,
I read it in your eyes,
In romance we both compromise,
Enemies in lovers' disguise,
Double-agents of lust, spies and allies,
With whispered erotic alibis that trivialize.
You bury your disappointment with me between my thighs,
Ejaculating your skimmed milk deep inside,
Then cannibalize a version of me from many different sources,
You make ME, an individual assembled to your personal choices.

13 types or orgasm, Cosmo says,
Two for each day,
The last to make me watch and pray,
On Sundays,
For salvation from the lie that I am,
The lie you've made of me,
The lie I've made of myself,
The lie everyone—both friends and enemies—demand that I be.

And suddenly . . .
(O glorious fuckness!)
Suddenly . . .
(I see angels dancing on a pinhead.
Am I still living or dead?
Heaven is my vagina in this waterbed.)
What you love about me doesn't even matter.

Oh, Holy Fuck, I'm coming. And it's a good looooonnng one!

PART 4: FIST IN MEAT GLOVE

The truth is an easy corpse to bury – Big Tony Marconi

CHAPTER 63

The two fat female hotel guests with Chihuahua's stepped out of the elevator. Raye made to follow them. Ash pulled her back. "Wait, I forgot something."

"Go get it alone. I'll grab us good seats before everyone else arrives."

Ash held on to her. "No. We're going together."

The elevator shut. Before Raye could protest, Ash long-pressed '20' to activate its special functions.

The panel glowed black, green, and purple. Raye's mouth dropped open. "Okay, you weren't hallucinating."

Ash laughed. "You ain't seen nothing yet, darlin'." She pressed the sub-basement button for Endless Street.

***

They reached the garage.

"I don't believe this! Someone stole the Harley."

"Forget it," Raye said distractedly, entranced by their surroundings. "Can't be more than a few hours usage left on it."

Ash scowled. "Yeah, you're right. C'mon, let's walk—it's not that far. No point inflating another bike except we've an emergency."

***

Raye goggle-eyed, they walked the same route Ash had the first time.

"Number two million, two thousand and four?"

"Six million's just an alley away. Okay, remember, we're looking for—"

"Hey, ladies, pay the toll!"

It was the glue-sniffing teens again.

Ash waved to the blue-haired kids sitting on the front steps of No. 2m2006. "Hi, guys."

Raye gaped at the cyclopean boy amongst them, then ducked out of the way, to a chorus of giggles, of a similarly one-eyed woman pushing a pram.

"Hi, Mrs. Johnson," the teens chorused.

Mrs. Johnson waved back, nodding to Ash and Raye. Raye's stunned glance into the passing perambulator confirmed that the happily gurgling infant in it also had just a single eye.

While Raye gaped after the departing pram, Ash handed the kids another fifty dollars. A cute curly-haired chemically-cross-eyed cheerleader-type took the note from her.

"Thanks, lady," the girl said. "I'm Liz." From her seat on the left of the first row of teens (who were seated in two rows of threes on the third and fourth steps), Liz introduced clockwise around the group. "This is Mandy and Joey, my older brothers Jim and Tim—they're twins—and Lucy."

Joey, the cyclops boy, looked at Ash. "What're you ladies looking for here?" he asked. Then he stuck his face into the brown paper bag he held, took a long draught of glue fumes, and sat back looking stoned.

Mandy took the bag from him and stuck her nose into it.

Joey's question threw Ash. "What do you mean: what are we looking for?" Then: "Do we stick out *that* much?"

"Worse than sore thumbs," Liz said. "You confirmed it by giving us money. People from the hood would simply flip us off."

"Aw, Liz!" one of the twins yelped from the back row. "You shouldn't have told her that! Now she won't give us any more."

Liz smiled at Ash. "She's nice."

Joey revived, groggily blinked his single eye. "Don't worry, Timmy, we'll raid the woodshop again tomorrow."

Liz grinned broadly at Ash. "So what are you two looking for around here?"

(Ash smiled uneasily back at the teen, who looked about fourteen. Surely this wasn't the YA version of gaydar? *Damn, kid, does your mother even know you're out? And why are all the gay chicks always hitting on me anyway, and not on Raye, who actually is gay?*)

"Thanks," Ash said carefully, "but it's adult business." She pointed down the street. As if responding to a mental cue, the sunny sky ahead momentarily 'flashed' black. "We're looking for someone in the Nighttime Zone."

"Oh, Nighttime Zone's no big deal," Joey said.

Liz nodded. "Yeah, we go there occasionally. Our high school's on the other side of it."

"What sort of asshole town planning's that?" Raye asked angrily. "You have to wade through a sea of hookers and pushers to get to class?"

Ash shuddered, remembering how Eddie Fiddle had tried to recruit her into the porn industry last night. If he got his hands on cute crush-struck Liz here, with her curly pubescent cheerleader charm . . . Creampies!

Liz gave Ash a coy glance, then giggled. "No, the school bus route runs through six-million sector, but it's more fun to dash through the adult areas. No one ever bothers us."

"Who are you looking for?" Mandy asked. "We might know them."

Raye looked at Ash, who shrugged back. "Okay. I'm not sure how to explain this, but, it's a woman who can make ghosts—"

"It wasn't a ghost," Ash interrupted. "That thing was as solid as you and me." She took over the narration. "A skinny chick who makes monsters with her vagina—"

"When she masturbates," Raye finished.

She became aware that the seated teens were all staring at her and Ash in shock. Then all simultaneously turned to look at Joey, who now had a smug smile on his face.

"What's the matter?" Raye asked. "I warned you it was gross adult stuff."

"No," Liz replied, "it's not that at all." She pointed to Joey. "He told us about the woman you described a week ago—"

"And they all called me a liar," Joey said. The one-eyed boy blinked several times. "Now who's wrong?"

"Where'd you see her?" Ash asked.

"At the Bourbon Hotel."

The Bourbon Hotel. Ash nodded. "Go on. How'd you meet the woman with the pussy monsters?"

"Joey has a crush on Candy Ample," Liz said, leaping away before he could smack her. "He's hung up on her jugs."

"Who's Candy Ample?"

"She does a burlesque act at the Bourbon," Liz said. She made a grabbing gesture at her chest. "She's very well-endowed. There's a bad slat in the Hotel's side fence and Joey likes peeping in her dressing room."

"And having wet dreams of her," Tim grinned, coming up for air after a huff of glue. "He says each of her boobies is like the universe."

"That's not true!" Joey said, red-faced. He looked pleadingly at Ash and Raye. "I'm not a Peeping Tom!"

Ash waved it off. "Just tell us how you met the woman with the pussy monsters."

"I didn't actually *meet* her. My dad owns a pizzeria. I sometimes work as a delivery boy for him after school. Last Friday, he got this order from the

Bourbon. Both Donny and Rita, who normally deliver to such places were out, so I said I'd do it."

"To catch a glimpse of Candy Ample," Liz said.

Joey shot Liz a black look. "At least she's got more on top than you do!"

Liz was furious. "You're just jealous 'cos I refuse to date you!"

"That's because you're a stuck-up princess snob who's biased against optically-challenged people!" the one-eyed boy shot back.

Liz looked to explode. "You think you're so smart, right?"

"He is," Lucy said from behind her in a trippy voice. "He gets straight A's to your C's."

"Hey, stop bickering, both of you," Ash said. "Joey, what did you see?"

"I made the delivery by the servant's entrance, round the back." He grinned sheepishly. "It *was* for Miss Candy Ample. She paid, tipped me, and told me I was very good-looking, but too young for her. I was leaving when I smelt fish."

Ash tensed. "Go on."

"The smell was coming from a door on my right, which was a little ajar. I was so surprised that I walked over and peeped in.

"Q.E.D. by the professor himself!" Liz yelped gleefully. "You *are* a Peeping Tom!"

Joey summoned some dignity and ignored her. "I was just curious. I've been there before—"

"To peep on Candy Ample!"

Ash was tiring of the girl's heckling. *Crush on me or not, don't be a drag.* She forced a smile. "I'll pay you twenty bucks to not interrupt again."

"Do-one," Liz sing-songed sweetly, and kept silent thenceforth. She picked up a paper bag and began carefully trickling glue into it.

Ash looked back at Joey. "Go on."

Joey continued: "I was going to say that I know from previous visits to the Bourbon that the kitchen is on the other side of the building."

"Okay, we get that," Raye prompted. "What did you see in the room?"

"A thin woman in a chair. She had her eyes closed, her skirt pulled up, and was sticking a vibrator inside . . . herself." He paused. "There was green mist pouring from between her legs and forming into a huge green man. I mean, this dude looked like the Incredible Hulk's twin brother. And he had live lobsters and fish sticking out of him and tentacles for hair."

"That's why we didn't believe him," Mandy said, pulling herself upright from a slumped position with her head on Liz's shoulder. She looked at both women. "That's impossible, right?"

"Oh, it's possible all right. So what happened next?"

Joey gulped. "I was paralyzed with fright, standing there trembling and hoping the masturbating woman didn't open her eyes and see me, when the green man turned to look at me."

"What was his face like?"

The boy shivered with memory. "Freaky. Normal but twisted—like a moron's. But then he opened his mouth, and . . . it was like I was looking into an ocean, and there were fish in the ocean—sharks . . . At that moment the woman opened her eyes and saw me. She didn't stop masturbating or even seem bothered by my being there. She just winked at me. Then the fish-covered man started towards the door, arms outstretched like he wanted to catch me." He shuddered. "I ran for my life. I could hear her laughing loudly as I fled."

"Ha ha!" Jim, who'd been looking stoned all this while, laughed behind him. "Scaredy-cat. No wonder Liz won't date you."

Joey looked around accusingly. "And I came and told my . . . *pals*, and none of them believed me."

"*We* believe you," Raye said with heartfelt sincerity. She turned to Ash, "I'm *sorry* I ever doubted *you*," then back to Joey. "How do we get to this Bourbon Hotel?"

Liz, now glue-eyed herself, raised a hand for permission to break her silence. Ash nodded.

"It's on the other side of Pedophile Park."

"Pedophile Park?"

Liz grinned. "It's just a name. It's supposed to be a children's playground in the middle of the Nighttime Zone. But no one ever uses it."

"I mean," Lucy said groggily, "why would anyone situate a children's park in the middle of a red-light district, if you're not looking to make kiddie porn there?"

"The Bourbon's on the other side of the park," Liz said. "I think the sixth house."

"The seventh," Joey corrected. "Number two million, two-one-six-oh."

"Smartass!"

"Thanks," Ash said. She handed a twenty to Liz, who was staring at her with something akin to hero-worship (or was it pubescent lust?), then turned to Raye. "Come on; I told you about the park."

They left the teenagers huffing and arguing in tripped-out voices about how Liz's twenty dollars was communal property, particularly since she'd ruined their extortion scheme.

"Hey, guys, give it back!" Liz yelped. "I need to buy new undies!"

CHAPTER 64

Femina – The Virgin (The Bloody Flower)

Spreading like wings,
Like water flooding,
It stings!
Virgin new blooding,
Hymen stretched too taut,
Flesh will rip, unzip,
Desired or not.
Tight young pussy,
Nature's balloon, fucked, pricked, burst.
My bloody truth.
I HURT! But . . .
But later . . .
Coming without regret like a new morning,
Orgasm like the day dawning,
Spasm like I'm falling into myself,
Through myself, onto my true love's manhood.
So good!
My sex without regret, without fear,
My tear, my tears.
You tear me, my roseate flower bleeds tears.
You free me, open me,
I'm undone,
Completely undone.

VAGINA MUNDI

Bloody cunt, seal of new womanhood,
Fresh as a battlefield greeting a new year.
Because I am the hole,
The hole truth,
Nothing but the blooming youthful woman.

CHAPTER 65

The Bourbon Hotel was an old three-story brownstone reminiscent of the Hotel Bizarre. A white sign above the front entrance blazed its name. Two green and orange neon uprights proclaimed 'Rooms,' and 'Shows: Girls! Girls! Girls!'

"A nice sleazy place," Ash said.

"Well past its 'best before' date," Raye observed.

The entrance was reached by steps beneath an overhang. People ascended and descended, laughing and trading comments.

"They're quite busy," Ash commented as they climbed, indicating the framed posters on either side of the steps.

"There's Candy Ample," Raye said.

They paused amidsteps. Ash considered the poster Raye was pointing at. "Sweet! She looks like Lolo Ferrari."

"Who?"

"That French hottie with the largest breasts in the world. I mean her cleavage was designed by an aircraft engineer! She's dead. Her husband Eric Vigne was charged with murdering her, then let go."

Raye nodded. "I'll bet he did it too." She considered the woman in the poster some more, then grinned. "Or like Anna Nicole Smith with massive tits. The big-boobed blondes brigade."

"I can't fault young Joey for being smitten. Candy's chest must seem to him like the meaning of life."

Raye pointed to the next poster up. "Hey! Who's this!?"

Both women gaped at it. The poster featured a skinny brunette holding a blue glow-in-the-dark vibrator. She wore no skirt or panties. A green ribbon of gas descended from her crotch, its end splitting into a 'man' and

268

'woman' whose bodies were covered by large orange scales. The pair were hairless, with pale bulging eyes and finlike ears.

"Meet The Goldfish People—Magic Creatures from the Marvelous Marine Vagina of . . . Skunk!" Raye read off. She turned to Ash. "I remember her from Femina's concert. Yeah, that's right—the heavy bleeder who handed in that flooded pad."

"This is the bitch who dropped through our ceiling," Ash said hotly.

"And apparently the same one who assaulted you."

"And you too."

Raye's eyes widened. "What?"

"Nothing serious. She ran commentary on how beautiful you were while sticking her thumb up your butt. Dammit, girl, you'd sleep through the fourth world war."

"I'll kill—"

"You loved it. You were coming in your sleep like Greta Garbo being fucked by Mercedes de Acosta."

Raye looked mortified. "I'll still kill her." She calmed, looked from the poster back at Ash. "What do we do now?"

Ash held up a wad of bills. "We buy tickets and see the show—should be good. There's no rush to confront her."

Raye was still staring angrily at the poster. Ash grabbed her arm, pulled her up the steps to the ticket booth.

***

This time Ash hadn't forgotten to load in a mind-chip before leaving the hotel. Once she and Raye were seated, she switched it to record mode, saving everything she saw to digital memory.

The show was great.

After Candy Ample sang,—Ash wondered how she managed to not topple over with that massive chest; it would have made Pandora Peaks envious—the stage dimmed to a spotlight trained on a red love-seat.

"And now, Ladies and Gentlemen . . . the moment we've all been waiting for . . . Skunk!"

Loud applause exploded all around.

"She looks like a skinny version of Femina," Raye said as Skunk strode onstage. "And Femina's already thin."

"She carries herself very well, and I like how she goes panty-less, and bra-less in that ripped T-shirt."

"And how she's not ashamed to display a lot of pubic hair? That's liberating. Not like all those porno shaved-fish fannies."

"And those pink thigh-length boots are way, way hot."

"We're both sounding like we're here to screw her, not to kick her ass. The stupid skanky rapist bitch."

Skunk sat on the love seat, thighs spread, her sex displayed like a pink snake slithering through her mocha pubic bush. She waved a hand to the audience. "Now, please excuse the smell, I can't help it."

Everyone laughed except Ash.

Skunk leaned back and slid a vibrator into her vagina. She began stroking it in and out in a smooth fast motion. Almost immediately, wisps of green gas spurted from her sex. The smell of fish filled the air.

"She's a real pro," Ash said.

"How so?"

"She's been warming up."

"How'd you know that?"

Ash frowned. "I don't. It's just what I'd do, so the creatures come out fast. You don't want to keep the audience waiting, do you?"

The creatures came out. First, the green gas formed into a man like the one on the poster, then into a woman also. The orange fish-skinned couple fell to the floor and began making love, bodies twining sinuously like they had liquid skeletons in their arms and legs. Light shimmered off their golden plating of scales. Soft music set a faux-romantic scene.

"Okay, this is fucked up."

"What did you notice?"

"They've both got gills."

"I saw that on the poster."

The crowd watched in silence. It wasn't boring. While Skunk sexed herself hard and fast, the orange couple went through a variety of positions in quick succession.

"Someone's been reading the Kama Sutra."

"Quiet, I'm enjoying this!"

The goldfish-man came into the woman, then dissolved into gas again. The crowd applauded. Skunk waved a languid hand at everyone, then resumed masturbating.

The orange woman collapsed down onto the stage. Her belly swelled, its covering of scales expanding like flat balloons. With confused eyes she watched her pregnancy grow. In seconds it was full-term. It burst—she screamed out loud. Two golden babies popped out and hung in mid-air. As their mother dissolved into green gas behind them, the infants floated down to the stage and grew rapidly through childhood, into adolescence—

"Two pretty girls," Ash observed.

—Into adulthood.

"Two utterly breathtaking women," Raye said. "Okay, they would be if their eyes didn't bulge like those of frogs, and they had ears instead of fins. But those breasts—fuck!"

"No nipples though."

"Or navels."

The goldfish-women, bodies like burnished bullion bars, climbed down off the stage and waded into the audience. Their dead-seeming eyes scanned the crowd. A loud wave of expectant 'ahs' and 'oohs' resounded round the hall.

The women pulled a man away from his protesting girlfriend and stripped his pants off. One of them knelt and began fellating him.

"That must feel utterly incredible," Ash said. "She's got no teeth."

The fish-woman's head bobbed up and down in the man's crotch, her ear-fins wagging like Chinese fans.

"Women too!" came a female yell. "No sexist bullshit."

"Right on, girls! I've got me some horny ladies here tonight!" Skunk waved a languid hand. A moment later, the second fish-woman altered into a man.

Raye winced on sighting the goldfish-man's erection. It was segmented like a lobster tail. "Ugh, he's going to stuff that up inside someone?"

The fish-man grabbed the protesting girlfriend of the man being fellated and forcibly laid her out over the couple's table. He ripped her panties off and began performing cunnilingus on her.

The woman scratched at his back with her nails. "Let me go!"

The goldfish-man ignored her.

She grabbed a wineglass that had fallen on her chair, broke it on the edge of the table, and stabbed him in the back. She raked the jagged glass through his scales, opening him up.

Seawater gushed from the rip—fish, crabs, and seaweed poured from his body. The woman gaped in surprise. The audience applauded wildly.

The fish-man knocked the glass from her hand, then spread her legs wide and slid his erection into her cunt. She screamed, then gave in and began moaning loudly. Seawater and fish poured out of him as he fucked her.

The woman's boyfriend (who'd been watching while being fellated) pulled the goldfish-woman's mouth off his penis. He jerked her off the floor, spun her around, and bent her over a chair. Spreading her gold-plated buttocks, he penetrated her from behind. He fucked her hard. She slammed her ass equally hard back against him. Her large eyes gaped ahead, expressionless as a corpse's. Her toothless mouth chewed soundlessly, like a fish's.

"Those two have to be shills," Raye said. "Screwing fish-people on first meeting? It's too disgusting to be believable."

"It's fun!" Ash said flatly. "Stop judging people on appearances."

"Don't support the bitch, remember why we're here. She tried to—"

"I do, but this turning me on!"

"You hussy, you should have been born a man! You seem intent on giving women a bad name."

Ash turned to her angrily. "And you? You sound like the patriarchy you're always railing against."

Raye looked at her incredulous. "What!?"

"I mean it. What gives you the right to dictate my sexual response? I'm sick and tired of you disparaging my sexuality just because I love to fuck. If *you* want to be frigid, fine, but stop pulling *me* down."

Raye looked at her, immense hurt in her brown eyes. "How dare you suggest I'm frigid?" she growled in a harsh whisper.

"You keep calling me a *slut*, endlessly implying I should be content with having less sex."

"I meant it in an empowering way."

"Screw that reverse-psychology bullshit. To women like you, everything's empowering so long as it excuses your actions." She scowled. "Tell me, Raye: Why is it only guys who are entitled to enjoy screwing?"

"I'm sorry, darling. You know I didn't mean it like that! And don't change the subject! *You* brought *me* down here because you were *raped!*"

"Lower your voice! I was *almost* raped. That was yesterday! Right now, I want to enjoy this erotic show without you laying a guilt trip on me."

Raye's eyes turned cold. "Enjoy this nonsense? Fuck you, Ash—you're not worth feeling sorry for."

"I'll tell you *when* to show me sympathy, darling."

"Hey!" a man yelled behind them. "More! More! More!"

The audience took up the chant: "More! More! More!!"

Ash and Raye stopped glaring at each other and turned back to watch the show. Both the orange-scaled man and woman had finished with their first partners and were now 'molesting' a fresh couple.

"More! More! More!!!" The sound became thunder befitting the cloying fish smell in the hall.

Skunk smiled. Four additional tendrils spurted from her vagina. The end of each became a goldfish-person who instantly began having sex with a member of the audience.

(The fish smell in the air felt like a living thing—a creature out to ravish the watchers. A seagull navigating sea-storm clouds, Skunk's jasmine fragrance was a barely noticeable thread running through it.)

Seaweed and shellfish were everywhere now. A goldfish-woman plucked a large crab from her vagina and dropped it on the floor. It scuttled towards Ash and Raye.

Raye scrambled her legs out of the decapod's way. It snapped at her ankles, to the amusement of those seated nearby.

"Screw this crap!" she yelped, kicking it away. She leapt to her feet and glared at Ash. "This is too gross for disbelief even. I'm leaving. See you at home."

Ash watched her stride angrily out of the hall, then rushed after her.

***

She caught up with Raye in the lobby.

Raye shook her hand off. "Fucking let go of me. Go back and let two of those orange fish-freaks sandwich you on a table in public view with their crawdad cocks. See if I care." She peered at her coldly. "I don't get it: If you're so damn horny, why not just enroll for a career in porn?"

Ash gaped at her, tears welling in her eyes. "I can't believe you said just that."

"It's the truth, you little bimbo!"

"Well, fuck you, Rachel Risk! Fuck you!"

With that, Ash, crying fiercely, spun on her heel and stalked off, back toward the concert hall.

Raye rushed after her and grabbed her from behind.

Ash spun around to face her, her eyes blazing. "Let go of me, you controlling bit—"

Raye silenced her with a kiss. Ash sank into her softness for a moment, then pushed her away violently. "I hate you! You do nothing but make me feel like shit."

"I'm sorry," Raye said. "I love you." Tears began pouring from her eyes too. "I really, really mean it. I just can't stand it when you keep making me jealous. Sometimes it's like I should strangle you, kill you so no one else can have you."

Ash kissed her. They stood like that, kissing and weeping on one another until they became aware of the aged doorman regarding them with disapproval.

"Please either go in or out, ladies," he said stiffly. "And if you intend to hold your own sex show here, please go and see the manager for a license."

They broke apart hurriedly. "Yes of course," Ash said. "We were just going back into the show."

The doorman held the door open. "Please do."

Greatly embarrassed, they did so, arm-in-arm.

***

By now, the hall was fully a-fuck. Vagina-spawned fish-people and humans were going at it full-steam-ahead, in all sorts of sexual configurations. Ash goggled: Several women had 'lobster'-penises in both anus and vagina.

Up on stage, a hooded man in leather bondage gear was now fisting Skunk. She moaned rapidly as his hand slid in and out of her. Her voice sounded like detuned birdsong.

"She's still having her period," Raye said.

Ash giggled. "I can't believe how red his hand looks each time he pulls it out of her pussy."

"And she's *still* pumping out the gas that's becoming these freaky fish-people."

"Sixteen of them now; all screwing people in different degrees of undress."

"Sixteen? She should be on America's Got Talent. Hey! You're recording this, aren't you?"

A broad grin was Ash's response.

Raye pointed. "Look! Better not miss those."

To their left, two goldfish-men held a naked woman spread-eagled in midair while a female of their number performed cunnilingus on her. The fish-peoples' bodies glittered like gold jewelry, light rippling in erotic cascades over their scales and fins. Their gaseous umbilici wavered sinuously under them.

"It has to be this stinky green gas making everyone so randy," Raye suggested.

Up on stage, Skunk yelped to a particularly deep fist thrust.

Ash's brow crinkled. "You know, it's like Femina's concert spilled over to here."

"It has. Listen to the music."

Ash paid attention to the tune coming over the hall speakers. "Oops, Not *Fist in Meat Glove?*"

"You'd better believe it, honeybunch."

"Deep and wide,
Slip and slide through my wet insides.
Fist me honey,
I can take it.
(Vagina's not plastic—you won't break it!)
Like childbirth in reverse,
Slot your key into my lock,
Open this lubricious pussy up.
Shit, fuck!
Damn, that hurt!
(It's not supposed to hurt *that much*, you jerk!)
Stretch my pussy,

Stretch me lover,
Like I'm about to be a mother.
I need your hand,
I demand . . .
Feed my cunt your magic wand.
Fist me from pleasure to pleasure,
Till my orgasm commences,
Squirting juice without measure.
(Gosh, this is damn awesome!
I feel like I'm losing my senses.)
My pussy's gonna drench you, sugar.

Twist it as you slide it in,
Bigger than a rolling pin.
Roll me like I'm dough,
Putty in your hands,
Handball me hard and slow.

Caress my cervix with your fingers,
Let them softly linger,
On the mother mouth.
Don't punch,
Just jerk and twist,
Yeah, you get the gist.
Love me with that sexy fist,
You fist-fucking maven wiz."

Up on stage, Skunk was having a massive orgasm. Her hooded male partner was now fisting her vagina with both hands at once—thrusting into her at speed.

"I know you think I'm prudish, but—"

"Don't bother. That is oh, so sickening to look at. His wrists are so red it looks like he's ripping her womb to shreds . . . I can't even conceive what her cervix looks like now—"

"So how the hell is she enjoying it?"

"Maybe she's faking."

"Oh no, she ain't faking! She's creaming like she's in Heaven."

"We seem the only two sane people in here. Everyone else is naked and humping monsters like Armageddon is tomorrow."

"Twist it as you slide it in,
Bigger than a rolling pin.
Roll me like I'm dough,

Putty in your hands,
(Ooh, feel my cunt-lips grip your wrist.)
Handball me hard and slow.

Fist me, honey,
Do it good.
Fill my cunt,
Like an immense log of morning wood.
(Yes, *this is* what I want.)
Your knuckles on my G-spot,
Gets me incredibly hot.
I'm a horny bitch, a sexy beast,
Can't resist,
I gotta stroke Miss Clitoris,
Like I've nympho sex disease.
Fuck me with your hand, man.
(Slow and steady,
Won this race already, Teddy.
C'mon, now pick up the pace.)
You feel large as a bowling pin,
Evil . . . powerful like sexual sin.

Can you fit your other hand in?
You'll try . . .
Oh, shit! Oh my!
Both your fists are deep inside!
I never thought a vagina could stretch so wide.
I feel . . .
I feel faint, like I'll die.
Tears in my eyes,
(It's hard to breathe, hard to see . . .
But I weakly force a grin.)
No, darling, *you're not* hurting me!
I'm not in any agony . . .
(You've no idea,
How I feel down there,
How much I frigging,
Love what you're doing to me!)
It's pleasure making me cry,
Please . . .
Push both hands farther inside!

Damn that feels right,

Nice and snugly tight,
I've been stretched GOOD tonight.
North, South, East, West,
I got tingles in my breasts,
Chills in my spine and trembling legs,
'Cos handymen are the best.
(Please don't call me fist-obsessed, but . . .)
Handymen *are* the best."

Raye shrugged as the tune replayed. "Our table's still vacant. We'd better get back to it before it's commandeered for doggy-style."

Ash shook her head. "Let them have it." She leaned against Raye. "Though watching this does turn me on, I'm happy here with you." She pulled her aside to a quiet dark storage nook, well away from the coupling couples, then down onto the floor. "Quick! Make love to me. I really need you right now."

"Ash, please . . . not here. I'm not in the mood. When we get back home."

"*I am* in the mood, girl. I'm not saying fist me, like that brunette bitch up there is getting . . . just *love me*."

Raye relented and slipped a hand under Ash's skirt, under her panties. She grinned. "I like this approach to revenge. Pleasure before business."

"Shut up and do me," Ash moaned, "before I go ask a pussy-monster-woman to do it."

Raye rubbed fingers over Ash's clitoris. "Oh no. No one shares you with me."

"Whatever. Just keep doing that. I'm yours! I'm definitely yours!"

CHAPTER 66

Ash and Raye waited till all the fans and hangers-on had left Skunk's dressing room before barging in. They didn't knock, just pushed the door open.

Skunk sat at her vanity removing her makeup. Her onstage fisting partner stood beside her, hoodless now, but still wearing his leather bondage gear. His hands were now clean.

Both looked at the intruders in surprise. Skunk's eyes narrowed to pissed-off slits. "It's polite to knock, you know. The fact I perform naked and have sex on stage doesn't mean you can take liberties—"

"Shut up, you freak-vagina slut!" Raye growled. "Why'd you sexually assault my girlfriend?"

Skunk looked her and Ash over, her eyes flickering with recognition. She smiled coldly back. "Non-consensual sex? Me? You have the wrong vagina, darling."

"Don't make a joke—this ain't no mistaken identity case. Hey, Ash, say something!"

Ash, however, wasn't paying the confrontation as much attention as she'd intended. She'd recognized Skunk's male companion.

She gaped at Eddie Fiddle. "You again?"

"He's my boyfriend and manager," Skunk said. "What of it? Don't tell me he *also* assaulted you."

"He did!" Ash protested. "He tried to recruit me to make porno movies!"

Skunk grimaced. "That true, Ed?"

Eddie, however, wasn't paying her or Ash any attention. His eyes were riveted on Raye. "You!" he spat at her. "Thieving bitch!"

Raye, about to verbally assault Skunk again, was taken aback by the man's vitriol and the hatred in his eyes. "Hey! Cool off! Do I know you from somewhere?"

Next thing, Eddie had pulled a gun, was pointing it at Raye. "Where the hell is my fucking necklace?"

"What necklace?"

"Don't play dumb with me! I'm not fooled by your bleaching your hair and getting fat! Where is Kate Rose's fucking necklace!"

The penny dropped. Trembling, her eyes now confused, Raye looked at Ash. "Eddie Fiddle? *This* is Eddie Fiddle?"

Ash nodded glumly.

Eddie swung the gun to cover Ash. "I forgot, fattie," he told Raye, "the necklace makes *you* bulletproof. I'll perforate the dumb redhead instead. Give me my fucking property back!"

"I don't have it." *The hell with camouflage,* Raye thought, *we're about getting murdered here!* Her hair sprouted brown like chocolate tentacles squirting from her scalp, its platinum-blonde tint peeling off like wrapping paper.

For a long moment, Eddie looked about to pull the trigger. He stared at the huge brown fist forming from Raye's hair and smirked. "Yes. I *knew* it was you! Stupid thieving cunt!"

"If you dare repeat that," Raye said. "It'll be the last thing you ever say." She wove a second huge fist from her hair. Both hair-fists floated by her head like clouds of mud. "Just dare me!"

She glared at Eddie, who, gun covering Ash, glared equally angrily back.

The tension was thick in the room, everything poised on the brink of carnage and disaster. Ash stared pleadingly at Skunk, who was regarding Raye's hair-fists with interest.

Skunk saw Ash looking at her and nodded. "Put the gun down, Eddie," she said. "I think the four of us need to get properly acquainted."

Eddie shook his head emphatically. "Screw that. This bitch has my necklace and I want it back. It's her fault the pair of us are living like this— on the run and down-and-out, putting on these disgusting shows—"

"I'll get it back," Skunk said softly. "Trust me, baby."

Eddie released a long breath. "Okay." He lowered the gun, sat on an overstuffed sofa.

Skunk nodded at Raye, pointed to a chair. "You too, plump butt—relax with the hair."

Raye's eyes widened. "You talking to me, bitch? How dare you?"

"Calm down, Raye," Ash said. She glared at Skunk. "Watch it, will you?"

Skunk grinned, her skeletal face humorous as death's. "It's a compliment—I *adore* honeys with fat asses." She looked pointedly at Raye. "Sit yours down, cutie pie."

Raye stared her down, hair-fists hovering menacingly, poised to strike. "Not till you explain why you attempted to rape my girlfriend ."

Skunk indicated the chair again. "Please sit. Everyone in this room has some explaining to do."

"Stop telling me to—"

"Sit your fat ass down!" Ash and Eddie yelled at the same moment.

Raye sat. Fuming with anger, she reeled her hair back in.

CHAPTER 67

The atmosphere in Skunk's dressing room simmered. Of the four present, Skunk was the only calm one. Maybe it was all the sex from earlier. She felt totally sexed out, all she needed now was to go to sleep . . . *but now this turns up.* She smiled coolly at the two glowering women, then stroked her darling Eddie's arm. "Calm down, Eddie."

He bristled some more, but didn't shake her off. That was a good sign.

She turned to stare evenly at Ash and Raye. "First things first. "*Where is* the Kate Rose necklace? It's worth twenty million bucks at the very least."

Raye's face turned glum with memory. "I don't have it. I got totally screwed too. I was set up to be the fall girl. Didn't make a dime." She gestured at Ash. "We were forced to take it on the lam."

"I don't believe her!" Eddie thundered. "She has it!"

Skunk looked at him sharply. "Calm down!" She frowned at Raye. "Let's say you're telling the truth: Who has the necklace now?"

"Money Rich."

Eddie's anger instantly, visibly, drained from him. "*Money Rich?*"

Raye nodded.

"How is that possible?"

Leaving out the details of Mr. Rich's death, Raye explained about Bug's double-crossing her and the fallout of everything. "I don't understand," she finished, "why are you both so surprised that Money Rich has your necklace now?"

"Because Ed owes Money ten million dollars. It's the reason he went to Chicago to sell the necklace in the first place."

Raye frowned. "Okay. Now *you've* got some explaining to do."

***

"It's simple," Skunk explained. "Eddie has . . . I mean *had* . . . a gambling problem. It wasn't a big deal when Holly Wood was alive—she made millions for him—but once she died . . ."

Ash looked at the sullen leather-clad man. "But even so, how much money could he possibly lose? I mean, Eddie Fiddle is America's top porn filmmaker."

"Used to be," Eddie corrected. "Now no one's ready to finance my flicks."

"Because you gamble all their money away, darling," Skunk said acidly. She nodded at Ash and Raye. "It's true. He once blew two million in Vegas in one night. It was like he had a poverty wish or something. And don't even mention the horses, which is what really ruined him. He's never once picked a winner. Would you believe he's blown fortunes on hot tips that never went anywhere?" She regarded Eddie with affected disbelief. "I really don't know why I love you."

"Hey," Ash said. "That reminds me. That night in the stables, what was that about?"

Skunk looked at her blankly. "What night?"

Ash smiled coldly. "Don't act dumb. Three years ago in Chicago at the Arlington horse tracks. I bounced you and your drunk boyfriend here from my teller's window and then—"

Skunk's eyes widened in shock. "It was *you?* That snotty bitch explaining how me and Eddie were both losers? Who told us we should have donated our stake to breast cancer research?"

"Oh, so you *do* remember. Do you make a habit of going round assaulting—I'm assuming you've butt-fucked several guys too during your career as a serial-rapist—people who annoy you?"

Skunk scowled, her expression unapologetic. "I was drunk. You were so snotty I was certain I was doing the world a favor teaching you a lesson."

"Ah, I see. She's raped you before," Raye said coldly. She looked pointedly at Ash. "You never mentioned it."

"It isn't exactly something I want on my romantic C.V." She frowned. "Besides, you didn't believe me when I told you about last night, did you?" She turned back to Skunk. "So you were teaching me a lesson three years ago. What's last night's excuse?"

"We're supposed to be talking about the necklace," Eddie interjected in a pissed-off whiny voice.

Ash smiled sweetly at him. "We are talking about your necklace."

He sank back into moodiness. The women continued their face-off.

"Go, on," Raye said. "We're listening. Why'd you assault her last night? And I heard you were fondling me too."

An embarrassed smile flitted over Skunk's thin lips. She shrugged. "Too much cocaine. Look, I'm sorry." She stared pointedly at Ash. "I did, however, warn you that wearing a skirt that short was asking for trouble."

"From *guys!* Not another chick!"

Raye scowled. "Us women should stick together against the rape-culture establishment, not start preying on each other."

"I'm sorry, okay? You looked super-attractive done up like that, and when I saw you walking past . . ."

"Okay," Eddie said, resurfacing wearily, "if you'll forgive a pun, we've larger fish to fry than your sexual memories. Can we move on back to the real discussion?"

Raye looked at him narrowly. "Hey, Mr. Expired Big Shot! Rape is always the real discussion. *Nothing* is *more important* than my vagina's public safety."

Eddie rolled his eyes. "And you listen too, fattie . . . Oh, whatever!" He fell angrily silent.

Ash kept staring hard at Skunk. Skunk broke their locked gaze. "Eddie's right," she said softly. "We're wasting valuable time crying over spilt creampie. With this new info about Money having the necklace, we've much to discuss." She held out her hand to Ash. "Truce? You can kick my ass later. Or fist it in revenge."

Ash dallied. "That wouldn't be much of a revenge."

"Why not?"

"I just watched you take two fists in the vagina at once without crying for help. Even my foot wouldn't make an impression on such a cast-iron cunt."

Skunk grinned slyly. "Oh, that? It is tight."

"For sure. And both Eddie's hands are the size of my pinkys, right?"

Skunk giggled. "I said fist my ass, honey. Not my pussy. My anus is tight as shit. Eddie hates anal fisting 'cos of the poop stench."

Ash shook her hand. "You're so dirty, it's unbelievable. Okay, truce. You know, for a long time after that night in the stables, I planned on killing you." She scowled. "I still might, but not tonight." (This was a barefaced lie. Even as she spoke, Ash's legs were trembling with remembered arousal. Her face was getting flushed—she hoped everyone interpreted her sudden ruddiness as residue of her anger. She was weak-kneed, vividly imagining herself and Skunk caressing each other in a heavenly fragrant jasmine-scented bed, the air around them a fog of sensual leaf-green olfactory illusions, while last night's vagina-creatures also made passionate love to her—delightful sex on her own terms, not ravishment. She stole a peek at the brunette's sex. It was now sanitary-padded over, with not the slightest reek of fish. Skunk herself looked like an emaciated soccer mom preparing for bed.)

Skunk smiled coolly at Ash. "And I, might yet . . ." She shrugged like what she'd intended saying wasn't that important (or was self-obvious) and turned to Eddie. "Fill them in on the interim, baby."

Eddie lit a cigarette and looked grim. "What Skunk said about my gambling's true. I had good luck while Holly was alive, and then . . . boom . . . everything went bust. Even Holly's dying had the element of a jinx to it. Sure she was stoned, but the cops determined that she originally wasn't even near the swimming pool. She tripped over a turtle—they knew this 'cos her left high-heel was still stuck in its back—skidded five meters and landed in the water. How odd is that? The damn turtle had only found its way into the pool the day before." He sighed. "Holly was dead once she hit the water. The deep end of the pool? Fuck! She couldn't swim. I'd tried teaching her—she refused to learn. She was too stoned to even make splashing noises or scream, not that anyone would have heard."

He blew smoke into the room. "I fucking loved that woman."

"You got the order of the words wrong, Eddie," Skunk retorted. "You *loved fucking* her. Not the other way around. And you frigging adored the money she made you."

"Believe what you like." He sighed. "After Holly died, I went into freefall. I lost interest in making movies, began drinking and partying like crazy—"

"And gambling?" Raye prompted.

"Yeah, and gambling. The rest is exactly like Skunk tells it. I lost immense sums overnight. Sometimes I was too wacked out of my mind to even realize how much I was betting, or on what. I borrowed two million from Money Rich—who wanted in on a slice of the porno action—to set up a new studio, porno on the scale of MGM or Thirtieth Century Fox, and gambled it away. Which is how I come to owe her—"

"That doesn't add up," Ash said. "If you only borrowed two million from Money, how come you owe her ten?"

Skunk sighed. "Because Money's *smart*—the stupid greedy bitch. For ages she'd had her eyes on Holly's necklace. Eddie wasn't selling. It was the only thing he never gambled away, never pawned. Said it reminded him of her. So Money finds another way. First she tells her father's racetrack and casino managers to extend Eddie unlimited betting credit, then, when he's neck-deep in gambling debts, she buys up all his markers. All eight million dollars' worth of them. So now he's only owing her. Then she offers him a deal—she'll write off his debts in exchange for the Kate Rose necklace. Either that, or if he doesn't cough up the ten million in one week, she'll send that asshole robot Al Capone round to break all his bones with its baseball bat."

Eddie mopped sweat from his brow with a dirty hanky, then took over the narrative again: "Skunk and I were dating by then, however. I asked her advice. She suggested we auction the necklace instead. As she put it: 'all rich people are scared to sleep at night.'" He looked gratefully at Skunk. "I've no idea what I'd do without her. She's also tamed my boozing and gambling. Okay, I still like a good wager, but I'm no longer the self-destructive high-roller I used to be." He took a long drag of his cigarette, ground it out in an ashtray, then smiled sadly. "Someone offered us thirty million dollars for the necklace." He winced. "That money would have paid off all our debts and left us well on our feet again."

"And then," Skunk finished, giving Raye a poisonous look, "*You* came along and stole it."

"I already told you two—I stole a fake. The goons guarding the necklace switched it before I got there." She sniggered. "Bug said Eddie here was too cheap to pay them enough; they were *easy* to bribe."

The barb hit home. Eddie scowled back. "That's neither here not there—"

"Okay," Skunk interrupted hastily, sensing the potential renewal of hostilities between the pair, "let's think this through. Money's got the necklace, but . . . she still denies having it. She still insists that Eddie pay her back his gambling debts. That's why we fled town."

"She's just annoyed," Ash said. "Bug sold it to her for twenty-four million. That's fourteen million over what it would have cost if Eddie had just handed it over. If she can squeeze Eddie for ten million, the necklace ends up only costing her fourteen."

Eddie spat. "She's a greedy conniving bitch. It's *my* property."

Skunk patted his arm soothingly. "It's alright, baby." She looked at the other two women again. "The point is—Eddie doesn't have ten million. Neither do I. From what you girls told us, Money is after you too."

"Oh, she's going to be after us forever," Ash said. Shrugging off Raye's warning glances, she explained in gory detail about Mr. Rich's death.

Skunk gasped. "*You two* killed him? Word on the street was he had a heart attack. There were rumors it was actually a bedroom bust-up, but no details ever surfaced."

Ash sighed. "Oh, it was a bedroom bust-up alright. You should have seen the bedroom afterwards."

Eddie looked equally surprised. "You two are *that* good?"

"Good?" Raye smirked. "Our luck held. 1 was bleeding like a pig. Ash was so scared I'd die she almost crashed the helicopter when we landed in New Buffalo. Then the doctor mixed up the antibiotics . . ."

"The point is," Skunk said, "you girls are tough. You took the bull by the horns when you could have run away in fear . . . and for only twenty grand?"

"We didn't know there was all there was in the safe."

Ash and Raye saw Skunk was grinning broadly at them. "What is this leading up to?" Raye asked cautiously.

"A robbery. Worth four million dollars in all." She looked them both dead in the eye. "If you girls come in we'll split equally four ways."

"We're not inter—" Raye began.

"Shut up, darling," Ash interrupted her." She grinned at Skunk. "We're *very* interested. Please go on."

CHAPTER 68

Femina – Raining in my garden of Eden

I grow, I grow,
Nature's most adaptable hole.
You in me, and I around you,
You moan with the pleasure I create.
I am she—woman, flesh Mother Earth,
The motherland that incubates.
The soil you cannot hate.
I accommodate,
You give, I take.
Till me with your rake,
Sow me with seed,
And watch it germinate.
Oh, how my flower aches,
When you penetrate,
(I ache with need,)
For you, for myself,
For this pleasure we both create.
Your massive bee hovers round my nether flower,
Seeking to pollinate,
And as you slowly infiltrate . . .
I feel . . .
Like I'm the queen bee,
Making honey.

Flying outside of myself,
Like an eagle. . .
Leaving feathers in my wake.
Your balls smack my ass,
I vibrate.

It flows, it flows, my honey flows,
Like a white river through fields of ripened gold.
Morning dew forms,
Sweat, cool on my skin,
Calm after fuck's raging storm.
(I hold my barn door open with moist fingers,
Please, drive your tractor in.)
Your body a cloud of love over me,
Your cock a plough within!
The birds and bees,
Fluttering leaves,
Our legs, branches of sexual trees.

You bull, you plow me,
Like a field,
You till me.
I yield,
(Abundant blooms, fruit and seed,)
My crops!
Just don't stop,
Giving me that ever-fertile cock.

My well is deep,
But you fill it with ease,
Watering my emotional sheep,
With kiss and caresses,
Soft finger breezes through hair trees.
Oh, fuck me again, please.

When you crush my farmhouse with yours,
Abundantly filling my front porch,
Deep as you go, needing to know,
(More?)
Me better,
Your sex reading mine like a love letter,
I grow wetter and wetter,
Raining in my garden,

I love the way you increasingly harden,
And how you fuck,
A real rooster stud,
Approaching it like work,
Not mere fun,
But a job that must be done,
(To keep Mother Earth's vagina irrigated,
Her soil soul aerated,
With testicle worms.)
Your face grim as you race to come.

CHAPTER 69

Eddie Fiddle explained:

"There's a massive drug shipment coming through the Hotel Bizarre tomorrow. Big Tony Marconi, who usually buys for the TV guys, is coming over with two million in cash. The drugs are from Chicago—"

"Money Rich?"

Skunk nodded. "She's running the show now big time. And she's ambitious, obsessed with expansion. Normally, the weight of coke coming through here might be thirty, forty keys a month, but Money is upping the scale—she wants to push that much weekly. Word is, she's made a deal with the suppliers down in Philly—undercutting their normal sources. And it's not just blow. Meth and heroin . . . the new hyper-pot too."

"We don't want to get into the drug trade," Raye said.

"Except for occasionally powdering our noses along with our faces in the ladies'," Ash said. "Raye, stop acting so righteous."

"The point is," Eddie continued, "the shipment arrives tomorrow. Big Tony's agreed to mule for the Philly cartel. He'll be there tomorrow with two million in cash—"

"Two million? You said *four.*"

"We intend taking the drugs as well," Skunk said. "Don't worry, we've already got a buyer waiting. Some guy from Philly too."

"So *we* get the cash and *you* get the drugs?"

"No, we share everything equally, money and drugs."

"How the hell are we supposed to dispose of ours?"

"I just told you—we'll do it for you."

"This is getting rather complicated."

"You're coming in as equal partners. There's a risk our buyer might try to double-cross us—you share in that risk too." She frowned. "We're not going to screw you, if that's what you're thinking. We'll share the two million in cash, then the drug money when we get it."

"Hold on a minute."

"Yeah?"

"How'd you know so much about this?"

"We've been casing the Hotel Bizarre for three months now. It's the perfect place to hit. Luigi Rossi has practically no security. That's mainly 'cos no one dares mess with Chicago, but also 'cos it keeps the hotel image clean. Most of their supply comes via a safe route from Brooklyn. If there's a shipment due, or an emergency, Luigi calls in Mark Fennel, an ex-cop who runs a Chinatown security agency. Fennel's guys watch the shipment till it reaches the hotel, then leave. Same thing if there's money to take out. They don't make themselves noticeable, but they're there."

Ash grimaced. "So now we know this isn't a walk in the park. That doesn't explain how you *know* about the incoming shipment."

"Last night, when I dropped into your room, I was actually heading for Luigi's office. I planted a bug there. We'd been considering doing it for a while, but the partying after Femina's concert provided the perfect opportunity."

"You were coming from the street."

Skunk rolled her eyes. "You're inquisitive, aren't you?"

Ash nodded slowly. "I like to cross my T's and dot my I's."

"It's the chip in her head," Raye explained. "Makes her too smart for her ass's good."

Skunk shrugged. "Okay. I forgot the bug. Had to go back for it. But stop interrupting me. So I placed the bug last night, and—"

Raye gaped, then jabbed an accusing finger at Skunk. "It was *you!*"

"Me? What?"

"Karen. Uncle Luigi's girlfriend is missing. You got rid . . ." Raye's eyes widened. "Shit! You . . . *killed* her." She stood up. "C'mon, Ash, we're leaving."

Ash shook her head. "We're not. Sit down, baby."

Raye remained standing. "No way am I getting involved with another set of murders. I've enough crap on my conscience already."

Eddie waved his gun at her. "Plump your ass back down. You know too much to leave. We're not having you run off to Luigi and his nephew and ratting on us."

"I won't rat. I just want out." Her belligerent expression turned pleading; her eyes implored Ash. "C'mon, baby, let's go. This can't end well."

"Look," Eddie explained patiently, "Skunk didn't mean to kill Luigi's girlfriend."

Skunk nodded, skeletal face grim amidst her brunet mane. "There was nothing else I could do. She surprised me—I had to think quick. If I let her live and took the cash in the office, she'd alert everyone, and they'd search the office. If I killed her and left the money, you'd have a similar investigation."

"So you both killed her *and* took the twenty grand," Raye said coldly. "It worked like a charm. Uncle Luigi and Fred think she robbed them and ran off." She looked around the room, then sat down again. "Okay, I'll stay." Her eyes fixed on Eddie Fiddle, frigid like ice. "If you ever point a gun at me again, I'll kill you. For real." For emphasis, she sprouted a hair-fist from her head.

He laughed coldly at her anger. "For someone opposed to murder, you're extremely violent. You know that, right?"

Ash groaned out loud. "Will both of you please stop being assholes? Can we just get on with this?"

Skunk went on, addressing herself directly to Ash like Eddie and Raye weren't in the room. "So there you have it: I set up the bug last night and get out. We do a test-listen this morning, and amidst their talk about Karen's disappearance, they drop the info about tomorrow's shipment arriving. We're both shocked to find we've hit the jackpot so fast. Then Fred calls Big Tony who confirms he'll be over at four in the afternoon with the cash."

Eddie nodded. "And afterwards Fred is pissed-off over some crap about Big Tony bringing over his Doberman to check the quality of the coke, while Uncle Luigi is laughing his head off. Made no fucking sense."

"They're both using too much of their own product," Raye, hair normal again, said with a thin smile. "Okay, so what time tomorrow do we hit them?"

CHAPTER 70

Femina – Masturbation (My Sweet Little Feeling)

Let me touch myself,
I do it much better than anybody else.
Fingers deep in my cunt,
Are what I need and what I want.
Now when I'm angry,
Now when I'm happy,
Lovey dovey, sappy,
Or after watching Julia Roberts falling in love,
(Julie's always getting married to a hunk,
Then getting well-fucked!)
In my favorite chick flick,
And you are either not around, or fast asleep,
With your nice hot prick.
So I flick my little clitoris,
(Flick, flick, flick!)
By myself.
I help myself,
I love myself,
I fuck myself.

Masturbation,
Is a great sensation,
Sisters, do it without hesitation.

I need to do myself again tonight,
You understand this, honey, right?
The sex I had with you was nice and sweet,
Quite fantastic,
Now, darling, please take the hint,
(Or some pills) and fall asleep real quick.
I need another orgasm,
Another set of creamy spasms,
Amidst steamy fantasies,
Just because I can,
Since I'm not a man,
But there is no master plan,
To replace you with my hand.
I really love you, I really need you,
Can't live without you,
But I just have to solo-come tonight.

Masturbation,
Is a great sensation,
Girls do it without hesitation.

Sometimes I use a dildo,
Magic like a rod of willow.
Bum up on a soft pillow,
I slide it in deep,
Imagine I'm Little Bo Peep,
With a horny sheep . . .
Or I'm a James Bond girl,
Getting screwed around the world.

Pussycunt, Pussycunt, where have you been?
I went to a drag show to see the queens,
Then I went to the sex shop to buy a few things,
Toys you don't see in fashion magazines.

Masturbation,
Is a wonderful sensation,
Sisters, DO IT without hesitation.

Ladies, come all you want,
As often as you want,
Jerk off all you want.

VAGINA MUNDI

Masturbate all you want!
(Without guilt or shame!
Play the finger pussy game!)
Remember it's YOUR cunt!
IT'S YOUR CUNT!

CHAPTER 71

Seductive, sultry, smooth, raspy like sandpaper . . . Femina's voice floated around hall. The concert audience were held entranced by her sung poetry.

Fred was the only one in the room not affected. Femina's singing passed through his consciousness like air through cloth.

Fred's mind was fixed on a sudden crisis he had to resolve.

Like most men of his generation, Luigi Rossi was totally lost at sea with modern technology. Edmond Flourish, (assisted by a geek girl named Jody Harris), handled all the hotel's IT stuff. Karen, doubling as Luigi's secretary, had handled his private emails. That included all the drug dealing communications. Fred had been pleased with the arrangement—for one thing it had meant less contact with Big Tony and Lana. But now, with Karen missing, the task had fallen to Fred. Which he currently found very fortunate . . . if not exactly pleasant.

He got out his iPhone, pulled up Yahoo Mail again. He was alone at his table, Uncle Luigi was upstairs, still mourning Karen's disappearance. Big Tony and Lana were out and about, making final arrangements for the cash to cover tomorrow's shipment.

He nodded appreciatively. From all accounts, Money Rich ran a tight ship—money up front or no deal.

He frowned. He'd never met the lady. He'd heard rumors she was a major kook. A drop-dead-gorgeous kook though, if Uncle Luigi was to be believed.

He looked around at the concert attendees. Several nodded to him. He nodded back. A cherry-redhead with piercing green eyes stroked her denimed crotch at him. She turned away, sniffing haughtily, when he pretended not to notice.

His eyes caught Femina's, the singer sipping scotch during a saxophone solo. Tonight she wore a white bikini top and blue hot pants. No shoes. She smiled at him, winked sexily. Clearly, a repeat of yesternight's bedroom activities was on the cards. He winked back. It was on then. *Only I'm not licking any more tomato-juice pussy.*

He grimaced when she frowned at him. *Oops, sorry—I forgot you can read my mind. Okay, I'll lick it.*

She beamed at him, then turned away to discuss something with her backup singers.

He returned his attention to his phone. To Uncle Luigi's drug email account—nasalminers@yahoo.com. A simple message heading: 'Photos of Missing Persons.' The attachments were two clear inline head-and-torso snaps, of two very recognizable women—Ash and Raye, although in these pictures Ash was a blonde not a redhead, and Raye was a brunette not a blonde, and also a lot thinner.

Fred stared at the pictures a moment longer, then closed the email.

He sat quietly, thinking, while Femina's guitarist began playing along with her saxophone player, skillfully converting the latter's solo into the extended intro to *Marriage Made in Hell.*

Ash and Raye? They're the two who whacked Uncle Rich over in Chicago? She-it!

Fred disliked violence. He was in 'the business' purely by family association, had begun managing the Hotel Bizarre because he'd thought that was all it was—a hotel. His brow furrowed. *No way am I letting them ship those women back to Chicago. If Money sets those robot gangsters of hers on them . . .*

The thought of Al Capone, Dillinger, Bugsy, and the others being let loose on Ash and Raye made Fred shudder.

His plan was simple. *I can't delete the pics—Money's already told Uncle Luigi to expect them. So I'll warn Ash and Raye to check out and leave town. Then, tomorrow morning, when they're long gone, I'll tell Uncle Luigi the email's arrived.*

It was a good plan, he felt, with only one flaw. *Where are Ash and Raye? I haven't seen them since Raye gave me her bank details.* He looked around the room again, checking to see if maybe they'd come in late. *No, they still aren't here. I already checked their room twice tonight. Edmond said they might have gone out but he wasn't sure . . . Damn!*

He resigned himself to seeing both women first thing in the morning. *Money's unlikely to call before noon anyway.*

The intro to *Marriage Made in Hell* was concluding.

Femina stepped up to the mic. "This song's dedicated to everyone who's ever been in love with a total douchebag—of either sex."

"When we first met,

The wine was red.
In my glass my reflection was red,
Like I saw my future corpse in my head.
(Me—DOA—stone dead.)
I should have took the hint and fled,
Instead,
I grinned at your physical request,
Smiled when you stroked my legs,
Then we went to bed,
And had mind-blowing sex.
Something I do and don't regret,
As it led direct,
To us getting wed.

On our next date,
I sensed your hate,
As you stared grimly at your dinner plate.
I should had left you and returned,
to my ex-husband.
But, no, I stayed on.
I'd passed the point of no return.
Us girls really do never learn.

Now . . .
You're really generous,
Pummeling me thrice daily with your fists.
Thanks for the beatings,
I've had enough of this shit!
Wonder why I went to court,
The restraining order never worked,
And this time it was my fault:
I found out where you lived,
And visited my favorite jerk.
I HAD TO!
'Cos each time I see you,
I get wet under my skirt,
My pussy wants a fuck,
Even though you make me hurt, afterward.

How do you manage it?
I mean, satisfy me so fully,
You post-schoolyard bully?
You've only a little, teensy weensy prick,

But it fucking DOES the trick.

Black and blue,
Half-dead in a hospital bed,
POP on a baseball-bat-broken leg.
"I don't get it," the nice old doctor said,
"Why'd you keep going back to him?"
I grinned like a pig,
Through split lips and broken teeth:
"He's dynamite in bed,
Gives utterly superlative head."

A handsome cop came a-calling,
And asked: "Tell me what happened, ma'am?"
I said, "I fell down the stairs, and broke my leg and arm."
"And the bruises on your face?"
I said, "Nobody hit me, I did this to myself,
I'm a masochistic bitch and pain is my thrill."
He said, "I don't believe you, ma'am."
I said, "Get lost, Uncle Sam."
Shaking his head in disgust, the cop dragged himself off,
As I coughed up blood,
From rib-punctured lungs,
Then pissed red in my bedpan,
And made plans,
Hell yes, I made plans.

Back home again,
(After my hospital vacation, a blissful occasion.)
And the scene's gotten worse;
Broken leg or not,
You whip me like a racehorse,
Fuck me continually on the cold kitchen floor,
Like a thirty-dollar whore,
But I keep begging for more.
My sanity returns as a matter of course,
I ask for a divorce,
As response . . .
I get four slaps and a curse,
Then your cock slips up my ass once more.

Okay, darling, you've had you're fun,
Way too much fun for anyone.

I've bought myself a gun,
(And I didn't forget the bullets,
Or shooting range practice.)
It's time to even up the score.

But I don't *want* to kill you,
Fuck no, I don't want to kill you,
I fucking LOVE you,
Despite all the sadistic abuse.
(I hate to say it but it's true.)
I LOVE YOU!
But what else can I do?

Nothing else to do.
Honey, I just can't reason with you.
Once you've been guzzling booze,
Your brains are screwed,
Stewed like pot noodles.
See? Now you've picked up a knife,
Dick, I'm not a steak—I'm your friggin' wife,
Asshole.
What happened to love for life,
Or even blissful strife,
Commonsense/common-nonsense arguments,
About kids against careers, or mortgage payments versus rent?
Trouble with mother-in-laws, or where last holiday was spent.
(And . . . rather than beat me up on weekends,
Can't you just go fishing with your friends?)
But, oh no! You're hell bent . . . !
Your eyes bloodshot with murderous intent.
You take another shot of JD, and then . . .

You stab me in the side,
I spurt blood and cry!
Yell and scream,
Hell! This isn't real, it's a bad dream!
(A suburban nightmare transposed from the silver screen.)
It's not happening!
I crash to the carpet,
Crawl across the floor,
Seeking somewhere to hide,
Along the corridor,
To the bedroom door,

Trailing blood.

Footsteps behind me.
Suddenly it's raining,
Raining inside the house?
But the rain smells like . . .
What the fuck?
You're fucking pissing on me, you louse?
Pissing on me?
So I'm your toilet now?
What the hell is wrong with you?

Hell, that's it!
Enough of this shit already!
I stagger to my feet with dignity,
Dripping pee,
Stagger into the bedroom,
Almost swoon,
Clear my head,
Resist the temptation to collapse on the bed,
Get out my gun . . .
I turn,
You're gone,
(Apparently I'm not even worth finishing off—
Not worth your concern.)
To the living room I return.
To the showdown,
Long overdue,
(Unequal odds now stacked in my favor.)
Between me and you.

I reason it like this:
I've tried to break free,
But each time I see you, you kill me,
All over again,
With your kiss,
With your penis,
With your words, fists, and kicks.
With your sarcasm.
With . . . my . . . stupendous Orgasm.
Fuck the memory—
My knees go weak again.

Got massive pressure in my brain,
Headache worse than three migraines.
I fall down on my knees and scream,
And you're the cause of everything.
Nightmarish daydream,
My new fat lip and purple patches of facial skin,
I mean my bruises.
You've no excuses to go on hitting me;
You say I talk too much,
Have no idea when to shut up.
Dick, you're so out of touch.
This ain't the fifties,
(Haven't you heard of gender equality developments,
In the interim,
Between now and then?)
Women's rights and freedom of speech!

Your eyes widen,
Then you smirk:
"Put the gun down, Helen,
And let's go fuck."
Oh, so you think I'm joking, jerk?
What now *really* pisses me off,
Is the stiff outline of your little cock,
Erect in your pants and ready,
To take me to sexual paradise again.
And my body threatens to betray me,
If I fail to jump right in,
And do what I intend.
(Damn, Your tiny willy,
Really makes me act silly.
How can you be so unkind,
Yet send me out of my mind,
When you do me from behind?
Shit, love really is blind.)

I bare my bruised breasts and pretend:
"Come over here, Dicky baby,
We've burnt bridges to mend.
Then you can fuck my tight little pussy again."
I smile until you're in unmissable range,
Grab you by the balls . . .
"Sorry, honey,

It's time for my revenge!"
But don't worry, hunk,
You know how I ADORE your junk,
You're not about having a sex change operation.

So bang boom, asshole!
Thanks for the rape.
I'm gonna shoot you a new navel,
No, you can't escape.
Suck this gun like you make me suck your dick,
You sick prick.
Then I pull the trigger back quick!
Bang, boom, boom!
There go your brains,
Splattered all over the room.
And I'll spread them again.

But soon . . .

Bang, bang . . . Fuck!
The cops are at the door.
I'll get off on self-defense,
Definitely, for sure,
But I don't wanna live no more,
With you dead now, I've nothing to live for.
Though the jury,
Sets me free,
The pain of losing you is a cell,
Can't spend the rest of my life a pining miserable girl.
I place the gun in my mouth,
Look at your corpse,
Fondle you down south,
Then jerk the trigger back with force.

Like I'm yanked down by a spell,
I fall right through the floor.
There's fire down below,
And a Mephistopheles music score.
Beyond the screams from burning cells,
I hear infernal nuptial bells.
Wait for me, honey darling,
We'll continue our marriage made in hell.

CHAPTER 72

We're not doing it," Raye said emphatically as they threaded their way between the hookers and pushers of the Nighttime Zone. "Screw those two wannabe gangsters."

"You agreed."

"Just so we'd leave there alive. That punk porno producer pervert had a pistol."

"We need money."

"We'll get some from somewhere."

"Raye, think: two million dollars!"

"My memory's real bad right now, honey pie, but wasn't that what you said the last time?"

"Can't you forget that?"

"Why should I? It's the reason why we're in this mess."

"So now you're blaming me?"

"Ashley darling, I'm blaming both our asses. *Me* for listening to *you.*"

A fat greasy man sided up to them. "How much for both of you for the night, ladies?" He matched his pace to theirs, stroked Raye's buttocks while speaking. "You, my dear, are incredibly well padded back here. I can't wait to fill your slit with my prick."

"We're not hookers," Raye said stiffly.

He sniggered, squeezed harder. "You're not? You'd have fooled me."

"We're lookers," Ash said, plucking his fat fingers off Raye's ass.

"Lookers?"

"As in 'look but don't touch.'" She stared him down till he grew uncomfortable and left them. "Jerk."

Then she stared at Raye just as intently. "See the kind of crap we'll have to keep putting up with if we don't get rich soon?"

Raye sighed. "Ash, be reasonable. It's not just the robbery. Remember what Eddie said they overheard? How, because of the amount of money he's carrying, Big Tony's having some webcops escort him over? And how he thinks it hilarious the NYPD are unwittingly going to help him break the law?"

Ash mused in thought. "So? I think it's funny too. Webcops in their pussy wagon escorting thirty-five kilos of cocaine back to the Upper East Side."

Raye rolled her eyes. "Ash, you're missing the point."

"Which is?"

"Which is that . . . what the hell?"

They'd reached a group of people surrounding a corpse. A man lying in the middle of the road with his head bust open like a smashed pumpkin. Pieces of brain lay about his upper body in a shining red pool.

"What happened to him?" Ash asked the onlookers while almost gagging at the sight.

"Weirdest thing I ever saw," an old prostitute in a red corset and black fishnet stockings replied her. "He was riding this sparkling new motorbike—a red Harley Davidson—down the street at speed, when all of a sudden it disappeared from under him. He kept going like a bullet, spinning sideways, then shattered his noggin on the ground."

Ash and Raye looked at each other, then at the dead man. The blood from his exploded head was garish paint in the street lighting.

Raye pulled Ash away.

"Look," she said savagely as they strode quickly on. "You saw that corpse? He's dead because he had no idea what he was getting into when he stole your bike." Her voice broke. "Darling, I don't want that to be us."

"Eddie and Skunk—"

Raye hugged Ash tight, her eyes misting with tears. "Baby, Eddie and Skunk are desperate enough to risk suicide if it promises them a better life. They're both already at the bottom of the barrel. Performing live sex shows? Letting yourself be publicly double-fisted while on your period . . . anything's better than that!"

"Okay," Ash said, tentatively. "I'm with you. I don't totally agree with your argument, but . . ."

Arm-in-arm they walked out of the Nighttime Zone.

"You know," Raye said, as they approached the house steps with the glue-sniffing teens, "one thing we forgot to ask Skunk is where she made her accidental detour."

"Which one?"

"The one that opens into our bedroom. It would have saved us all this walking."

CHAPTER 73

Next morning

Raye watched Ash turn the laptop on. "You promised to leave this alone," she said, her eyes narrowing.

Ash frowned at her across the bedroom. "We can't. We've both forgotten that all hell's going to break loose once they rob this place. And don't kid yourself they won't rob it without us. We're simply an insurance policy—their inside players, so to speak."

"We could simply warn Fred."

"We wouldn't be able to explain our knowing Eddie and Skunk." She left the laptop powering up and gave Raye her full attention. "The way I see it—we're stuck with doing this. Damned if we do, more damned if we don't."

"I don't follow you."

She counted off on her fingers.

Little finger: "If we don't join Skunk and Eddie, they'll likely have a vendetta with us. And with four million bucks, they'll be rich enough to smear our remains across half the USA—they could just ask their drug buyer to off us to seal the deal. They'd have good reason too to murder us—we'll likely be the only ones able to link them to the robbery afterwards."

Ring finger: "So we run and keep running, only now our troubles have doubled—we've two groups of crooks after us: Chicago and our porno-fiends. And there's nothing stopping both groups working together to catch us."

Middle finger: "If we *do* join Skunk and Eddie, we'll likely get rich, but we just might die trying. Or afterwards. Money Rich is already mega pissed-off with us, this just ups the ante to thermonuclear level."

A patronizing smirk followed. "She's just *one* chick tho'; no way in Hell is she smarter than *both* of us."

Raye pulled a face. "Ash, Money's got the mob behind her."

"True, but we run to Cuba, or some Third World dump where she's got no pull, and laze in the sun the rest of our lives. Just imagine: going down on each other on a hot beach as the sun sets fierce orange over the horizon."

"Tempting. But, let's stay closer to home for the moment. You're overlooking something."

Ash pulled up MindNet on the laptop. "Talk."

"We're currently wanted criminals in Chicago. We pull this heist, the FBI steps into the mix."

A laugh. "And I thought it was something serious. It's *drug money*, they'll never report it to the feds, they'll get pinched for money laundering."

A deep scowl etched its lines in Raye's plump face. "You've an answer for everything, haven't you?" Her expression of displeasure smoothed out to one of worry. "I'm *really* not liking this, Ash. How many times do I have to point that out?"

Ash fiddled with some settings on the MindNet app. She smiled. "I'm just pointing out, honey dearest, that, as we're certain to end up fucked good and hard by cock or strap-on either way, why not enjoy it?"

"No," Raye said with finality. "And stop the crappy sex metaphors."

Ash looked at her in amusement. "No? You got a mind-control device to make Money stop looking for us?"

"I'm not joking. I just thought of a third option."

"I'm listening."

"We foil the robbery ourselves. If it never occurs, the status quo's maintained."

Ash twirled her hair around a finger while she mused on that.

"Think with me," Raye said. "We're sitting pretty here. Anonymous as ducks. No one knows or cares who we are."

Ash yawned. "This discussion really isn't making sense anymore. It's *Money's* drugs they're dealing here. Surely, sooner or later she'll come visiting?"

"You're forgetting the elevator. We can get lost in Endless Street."

"That's Skunk and Eddie's robbery plan: get lost in Endless Street—with Money's money." She saw Raye had begun scowling again and sighed: "Okay, lay your thoughts on me, thick and heavy like your vaginal butter."

"Stop joking. What I'm thinking is, we knock off Skunk and Eddie."

"Kill them?"

A shrug. "It's the only safe thing to do. They're both dangerous. Eddie was prepared to shoot both of us yesterday, Skunk has already raped you twice, and—"

"Once."

"Twice—it's the attempt that matters. My point is that she wasn't particularly remorseful. And Eddie? He's certain to stab us in the back once we've done his dirty work."

"I begin to agree with you," Ash said slowly. Then: "Hey! I thought you were squeamish about bloodshed?"

"Only when it's my own blood likely to be shed."

"But . . . how about if we kill them, then do the robbery ourselves? A shame to waste that much money."

"No . . . no . . . no!"

"Just kidding." Her expression turned deathly serious. "Okay, that's settled. We off their asses, sit tight here for a bit longer, then vanish into Endless Street ourselves?"

Raye nodded, her face relaxed for the first time. "Question is when and how?"

"Easier done than said. They're both coming here at three-thirty." She pointed up at the ceiling. "Through there."

"I still can't believe it just opened up like a door."

Ash smiled thinly. "Just wait; you'll see." She frowned with concentration. "Killing them will be easy. They won't be expecting any kind of ambush till *after* the robbery."

"How?"

She tapped her left thigh. "Trusty Beretta here'll do the trick." She frowned again. "We'll need to dampen the gunshot noise. Pillows?"

"Potatoes."

"Potatoes?"

Raye nodded. "Regular Irish spuds. One time use only, but they'll kill the gun noise. We'll go grocery shopping."

Ash nodded. "Only thing left then, is how to dispose of the bodies."

"Not a problem." Raye pointed at the ceiling. "We'll simply stuff them back up where they came from, slam the door shut."

"From someone who didn't want blood on her hands yesterday, I'm becoming uncomfortable with how comfortable you are with murder."

"It's not murder—it's self-defense." She gave a forced smile. "Look, I'll brush my teeth, and then we'll go get some breakfast."

"'Kay."

Raye entered the bathroom. Ash clicked a movie camera icon on her laptop. "Okay, now let's have a look at you lot." She sat limp in her chair while video data downloaded across from her head to the laptop, then hissed loudly.

"I can't believe this shit."

Raye peeked worriedly out the bathroom door. "What's wrong, baby?"

"My recording from Endless Street. Everything's messed-up."

"Wiped off?"

"No difference if it was." She pointed to the monitor. "Just four hours' worth of pink static and color bars."

CHAPTER 74

"Sweet and sour cunt,
Sweet and sour cunt,
Flavor of the day,
At my Chinese restaurant.

Breakfast, dinner, brunch,
Have a lick for lunch.
Slurp, slurp, slurp,
At my Chinese restaurant.
Ying-Yang restaurant.

This ain't no ordinary venue,
Vagina's on the menu.
Enter, sit, and then you . . .
Meet dainty Su-Ling Wu,
Who has something to feed you,
Genital recipe to blow you,
Far out of your shoes.

She's a tasty motherfucker,
Tastier than lobster,
Sweeter than apple pie.
(My oh my, oh my!
She spreads her thighs so wide!)
Dive right in and taste her,
Fill your mouth with vagina.

Lick her moon, lick her moon!
Tiǎn yīn, Tiǎn yīn!
Juicy Juicy Pussy!"

The Femina lyrics floated around Fred's psyche as he stared at himself in the mirror. "Oh, yeah," he told his haggard reflection, "we really did get it on last night."

Fred was tense, conscious he needed to see Ash and Raye post-haste.

Shit, but there was no time for that now. It was already eleven.

Fred had overslept big-time. Uncle Luigi had woken him up. Phone playing Queen's *We Will Rock You* and an angry "Where the fuck are you?" Uncle Luigi was understandably tense. The big shipment—the test run— went through today.

Fred splashed water on his face. He still felt drained. *Damn, Femina literally fucked my brains out last night. No other description does it even half justice.*

He winced on remembering how oddly the sex had begun.

They'd ordered burgers and fries from the kitchen, then sat cross-legged in bed with the food.

"They forgot the ketchup," Fred said.

"No, they didn't. I asked them not to send any."

The bright note in her voice warned Fred something was up. He looked up from his tray . . . and groaned. "Hell, no!"

Femina was leaned back, legs spread wide. She'd 'magicked' her hot pants off, and was swirling several French fries around inside her bloody vagina.

"Nicely dipped," she said, brandishing the reddened fries at Fred. "Open up, baby."

That was the part that pissed Fred off. With almost no protest, he'd eaten the blood-smeared potato strips. She'd 'ketchuped' the rest of his fries also and fed those too to him. Fred didn't understand how she'd got him to do that. Goddess avatar or not, he had free will, didn't he?

Okay, I blame myself. I could have left, but didn't. Something about that woman, despite her perversion really . . .

He quit his self-defense. *Exactly what makes you eat a menstruating vagina two nights in a row? It's definitely not the fact that she's good-looking.* He scowled for a moment at a disturbing thought. *Felix? Are you messing with my free-will? What sort of God will you be, if even before any confirmation of divinity you're forcing people to do things they don't want to?*

He shrugged the thought off. *I can't prove it was the cat lady—it could be just a manifestation of my own repressed perversion answering to a kindred spirit.*

It was past anyway. Once he'd licked her clean, they'd fucked, and it had been great. Ordinary, but great; great, but ordinary.

That was the other thing: Other than for her menses fixation, sex with Femina was meat-and-potatoes sex—no frills. Nothing better or worse than he'd ever had with any of his girlfriends. And while deep in Femina's body, sharing the product of his testicles with her, he'd understood. (*I seem to be understanding a lot of stuff these past two days!*) He'd understood that there was good sex, great sex even, but all sex was *fantastic*, once it was consensual. You didn't even have to come for it to be incredible. It was enough to become one with the other person. One came during masturbation, but it lacked something—the dimension of sharing another person's body. Being with a lover felt right, oh so right. Even without penetration, the touching, the kissing, the squeezing, the stroking, were themselves passports to bliss.

"You love my natural taste,
I eat pineapple every day,
And I never ever douche,
So my flavor doesn't waste.
But my pussy's nice and clean,
Just like vagina ice cream.

My scent is ever changing,
My spices are wide-ranging:
Sweaty, pissy, dirty, bloody,
Sweet, sour, stinky, milky.
I'll be whatever taste you please,
After the right activity.
There's a perfect blend of cunt,
At the right time of the day,
On the right day of the month,
At my Chinese restaurant!

My acidic vagina,
Tastes just like cider,
Or like a classic wine.
My alkaline cunt,
Tastes like diet-yoghurt,
Either way, I'm just divine.

(Even after I piss,
You give vagina a kiss!)

Lick my moon, lick my moon!
Tiǎn yīn, Tiǎn yīn!
Juicy Juicy Pussy!"

Fred splashed more water on his face, then groaned. Femina had kept singing 'Chinese Restaurant' all the while he was giving her head. He'd recognized the melody, even though with the way she'd been groaning at the time, she might as well have been singing in Cantonese.

And then they'd made love energetically and with abandon, like new lovers, time and time again, and fallen asleep.

And once again he'd woken up in his own bed, with his clothes draped over a chair. And thankfully, this time—the first thing he'd checked—there was no fur coating his penis.

His phone rang from the bedroom. He dabbed his face dry. *That must be Uncle Luigi again, to remind me to get my ass down to Brooklyn and wait for Manny Rivera with the shipment. Damn, I'm late.* He shambled back into the bedroom. *I need coffee.*

He picked up the phone and froze. *Oh no. Not Money Rich. This has to be about Ash and Raye.*

He considered ignoring the call, then decided against it.

"Hello . . . Miss Rich?"

The voice floated over the connection; Femina's sexiness cranked up to 11, and yet . . . still ruthless, coldly disconnected from any other reality than mob rules.

"Hello . . . Freddie? I'm so glad I got you. Uncle Luigi's line keeps going to voicemail."

"I think he's finalizing arrangements with Big Tony."

"Good . . . we need to show Knox Arnold in Philly that we're reliable. They're used to long delays shipping up through Florida. Also the bikers who moved the stuff along the East Coast have been having some kind of beef for two months now." A recollective pause. "Angels versus Wizards or some such nonsense."

"Hell's Angels versus Warlocks. It's like Israelis versus Arabs—an eternal feud. The Angels had been running coke, skag, and meth up to Philly, but it's traditionally Warlock turf, so the Warlocks want in. They've threatened to knock off every shipment till Knox agrees to play ball. Obviously he can't—it's a loss of face—but in the meantime, till he reaches an agreement with the Warlocks, he's losing money—no one else dares run drugs up the east sideboard and the cops have the port sewn up tight. Word is, the party scene in the City of Brotherly Love is getting desperate for blow."

"Good for us," the soft sexy voice said, "but that's not why I called."

"Yes?" Fred felt a sudden dread, then it passed.

"Did you get the email I sent?"

"Must have arrived, but I haven't opened it yet. My phone isn't letting me log on to Yahoo."

"No?"

"The internet's messed up—I think it's a virus. I can check now on my laptop, but it's not set up and Uncle Luigi's hustling me out the front door already." He kept his voice neutral, hoped she didn't sense anything odd about his response. "Will tomorrow be okay? I have to dash off to Brooklyn to meet Manny."

"Tomorrow's fine," Money said. The sultry voice dripped with sudden menace. "I want the search begun before the bitches suspect we're onto them and skip town."

"Don't worry about it, Miss Rich," Fred said. "If they're here, we'll find them. And ship them back to you . . . dead or alive."

She laughed. "Alive, please. I'd prefer them both hale and hearty. Father and I have so much to discuss with them."

Fred felt a cold chill. *Did she just say 'father?'* "Of course, Miss Rich."

"Okay, then. I won't keep you with idle chit chat. It is after all, my business empire you're working to expand. Ciao."

"Have a nice day, Miss Rich."

She hung up.

Fred stared at the phone. *Father?* Then he grinned. *That worked out okay. Now I've got till tomorrow to alert Ash and Raye that the hounds of injustice are after them.*

His phone rang again. "Yeah, Uncle Luigi, my ass is already halfway out the door as we speak."

He dressed hurriedly. As an afterthought he picked up a pistol. He was a crappy shot, but this was a big day. Protection was likely needed.

CHAPTER 75

Femina – Dinner

We do it on our feet,
Me bent over the kitchen table,
And cutting up raw meat,
For dinner.
Make my pussy simmer.
Heat me up,
While I drop meat in the pot,
(Put your meat into my pot,)
And add spice and salt.
Squeeze my ass all you want,
And my breasts around in front.
Stir me up, stir me up, good,
Oh, baby, I just love your spoon.
I'll soon be serving the food,
But . . .
Damn, my oven feel so hot.
(Fuck, now see what you done,
You've gone and made me come!)
Sorry, darling, dinner's burnt.

Do me on the kitchen table,
Stir me with your lusty ladle!
Love me like delicatessen food.

Imagine I'm thanksgiving turkey,
Stuff me, stuff me, stuff me, stuff me!

Do me hard, but don't be rough.
Rub that steak between my legs,
Glide it slow over my love spot!
Then . . . let's progress . . .
Drip the soup over my butt,
(Let some fall into my anus!)
Then . . .
Lick it off! Lick it off!
How dare you complain of thirst?
There's sweet juice in my puss,
Get it out with your tongue!
Oh, honey, that fruit salad looks so nice,
Dress me in it,
(Like a pretty Food Network bride?)
Smear it all over my tits,
Then eat it, eat it, eat it, eat it!

Oh, yes, darling:

Do me on the dining table,
Put your steak into my grill!
Love me good, like I'm gourmet food.
Imagine I'm thanksgiving turkey,
Stuff me, stuff me, stuff me, stuff me!

And now for the final course,
Of love . . .
Of course . . .

What's this between my legs?
Oh, honey, don't look so scared!
No, I haven't suddenly grown a penis down there.
It's just the salami, dear!
(It is a tight fit in my slit, and I must admit, it hurts a bit.)
Now come here,
Take a bite!
What's the matter, dear?
It's gay . . .
To eat sausage this way?
(Oh no, it's quite alright.

I honestly don't mind at all,
I really wish I could make fake balls!)
Te-hee! Tonight,
You'll find out what eating cock is like!
Don't worry, no one will ever know but me!
Now open up, I know you're hungry!
Oh, c'mon, hon,
Don't spoil my fun,
Give my sausage-dong some tongue!

CHAPTER 76

"We really *would* have been able to do it."

Raye looked across from the bed. "Do what?"

Ash looked up from her laptop. "Well *I can* jam all telephone calls and internet access from the hotel like Skunk wanted."

Raye frowned. "I thought we—"

"Don't worry," Ash interrupted quickly, "I'm just doing this to pass the time. I need something to distract me before Skunk and Eddie get here. If I think too much about us killing them I'll never be able to do it."

Raye nodded. "Me too. Now we've taken the decision, I'm having serious cold feet."

"Mine are colder than yours," Ash replied. "But you're right, we've no choice. Either they die or we do."

"We could go buy our new non-inflatable van. Fred's paid in the money."

"Why didn't you think of that earlier? Not enough time now." She grinned. "Besides, you're just saying that to relax me. You know we can't withdraw the money here."

"We should have asked for cash."

"Five grand in cash? It would have looked suspicious."

"Not if we claimed an income tax dodge. They're crooks—they'd understand that. Darling, what use is the money if we can't spend it?"

"Nest egg for if we need to leave the Apple in a hurry. We withdraw it from here, by the time the transaction is traced we could be in Belgium."

"And Edmond's cut? Damn, you were right, the man *is* a born swindler."

"He probably isn't being paid much here. No problem, we'll settle Ed from the cash with us."

"Okay, but Money's guys could be watching our account credits as well as debits."

"Unlikely. Paying money into our accounts gives no indication of where in the country we are. They'll rather keep an eye on when we try to get it out."

"I hope you're right, darling."

"Don't worry. I am."

The laptop beeped twice. Ash waved at Raye to hold on, then studied the screen. She grinned. "I set an automatic descrambler to work on the email accounts recently accessed from inside the hotel."

"Ash, hacking's looking for trouble."

Ash tapped the mind-chip socket behind her right ear. "Not with this new Warpedia intelligence software I downloaded. It clones the incoming data, diverting the clone to me. Essentially it creates a duplicate account for me to access. No way can the real account owner ever work out that I'm reading their secrets."

Raye sat up, eyes agleam. "Really? I'm intrigued. Any fun dirt?"

Ash shrugged. "So, so. I've so far unscrambled fred_mathews@hotelbizarre.com and lurossi@hotelbizarre.com. Nothing odd in either." She grinned. "Fred gets loads of junk mail asking him to increase the size of his cock, and Uncle Luigi just got a purchase confirmation slip for some Viagra. Karen clearly liked bedroom activity— here's a similar confirmation email from three weeks ago."

The laptop beeped again. "Aha! Nasalmining@yahoo.com is done."

"Nasal mining?" Raye chuckled. "That's unique."

"Clearly an allusion to their drug-dealing shit." She clicked on the top email. This should be good for some laughs. Everything will likely be written in the most outrageous gangster code slang to prevent the cops—"

She froze.

Raye made an amused face. "Quit with the drama, already. What have you found?"

"*Found* is exactly right," Ash stuttered, sounding like each syllable was stuck in her throat and being forcibly yanked out to make the words.

She looked up from the laptop with an utterly horrified expression. "You made the right comparison earlier. *We are* as anonymous as ducks— *sitting* ducks that is."

Seeing how serious she was, Raye leapt off the bed and rushed over to her side. "What are you talking bout?"

Ash pointed.

Raye stared at the inline photos of Ash and herself in Money Rich's email to Uncle Luigi. "Shit!" She gaped at Ash. "They *know* we're here?"

A grim nod. "The email's been opened and read. They definitely know we're here."

"So why haven't they moved in on us? The time on the letter is six p.m. yesterday."

Ash closed the damning email, mentally dissolved the duplicate email account. "Has to be that they're waiting for the deal to go down first. Money must have told them we're dangerous—your hair and all. So they need reinforcements, likely those security guys Eddie mentioned."

Raye began pacing worriedly. "What the hell do we do? They must be watching our every move now."

"We do the only thing we can. Join the foreign legion."

"Speak English, or at least American."

"We cancel our plans to kill Skunk and Eddie. We go along with the robbery instead."

Raye stopped pacing and sat on the bed. For a minute she stared at the floor, then looked up with a resigned expression. "I'm trying to think of a good reason to say you're wrong."

"And?"

"There aren't any. It's like you said. "We're damned if we do, damned if we don't."

"We do then?"

A solitary barge honked out on the Hudson. Raye got off the bed again and strode briskly across the room to watch its progress from the window, a large black shape like a bug crawling across a mirror.

"We need to make up our minds," Ash insisted. "Do we cut and run or join the fun?"

Raye turned from the window to stare coldly at her. "I wouldn't exactly call it fun, but we definitely do join."

Ash nodded. "That's settled then. We need to get prepped." She giggled, pinched her nipples through her top. "Nothing like sex to up a woman's testosterone levels before violent action."

Raye shook her head in wonder. "Don't you ever think of anything else?"

Ash unzipped her skirt, let it fall to the carpet. "Aw, darling, stop playing hard-to-get. It's two o'clock now. Skunk and Eddie don't arrive till half-past-three." She winked. "You have a better way to kill the time than screw?"

Raye's cold visage thawed. "I'm thinking of how we're going to get killed."

Ash peeled off her thong, then undid her blouse. "Everyone dies. Not everyone has the consolation of a last orgasm before meeting the reaper." She turned her back to Raye. "Help me undo my bra?"

Raye grinned, then walked over to unsnap the bra's hooks. She slid the straps over Ash's pale shoulders and down her arms, bending to kiss the freckled skin of her neck.

"Oh, you're giving me goosebumps!"

Ash spun around and kissed Raye. She quickly undid Raye's shirt, sliding her hands up over the soft mounds of her breasts, feeling the nipples stiffen as she stroked them.

"Oh, I love you, darling."

"Nowhere near as much as I love you."

"Let's not argue now."

Raye stepped out of her pants, and backed Ash down onto the bed.

Once they were both on the cool sheets, she spread Ash's legs and licked up her thighs. Ash's skin tasted of salt sweet sweat. Raye felt each excited muscle tremor on her tongue—miniature meat earthquakes.

"Oh yes, darling!" Ash gasped as Raye's mouth roved higher, gripping her head and moaning. "Don't stop!"

Raye licked up to Ash's cunt. She paused momentarily, regarding the sexual crevice with the tampon string dangling from it. The vulva wasn't bloody, but still she dallied. Then she decided 'screw hygiene, this really could be our last time together,' and swirled her tongue up the sexual crack, through the tangy gash, up onto Ash's clitoris. She stroked the white thighs, her fingers roving over them like ants exploring spilled mounds of sugar.

Ash's trembles and shudders doubled. "Come up, let me taste you too."

A quick repositioning on the bed and they commenced soixante-neuf in earnest. Tongue in vagina, lick, lick, lick, tasting each other deep. Hands gripping hips, stroking buttocks and thighs, probing the dark smelly tunnel called asshole.

Pleasure flowed through and between them. The pleasure of love—of being one with each other. The pleasure of contact, of soft friction, of excited nerves, of excited minds, of their breasts rubbing against each other's bellies, stiff nipples delving into navels like explorers descending into caves.

The pleasure of penetration. Ash splaying Raye's dripping orifice, dipping in two fingers, twirling them around. Feeling for the G-spot. Raye tensing, releasing a fresh flood of genital moisture. Ash peeling back her clitoral hood, licking the engorged pink bud, sucking on it, licking up into Raye's vagina to meet her probing fingers. Coming up for air with a happy smile.

Moans and gasps—sharp exhalations as Raye similarly tongued her into ecstasy: "Oh . . . mama! Yes, *I like that!*"

Ash spasmed and came. Raye (fearing a blood deluge despite the tamponic vaginal obstruction) moved her tongue out of the way. But there was nothing. Just a fresh release of sexual secretion inside the orifice, confirmation of the induced hyper-pleasure.

"Looks like your period's running to a standstill."

Ash lowered her head from between Raye's thighs. She smiled dreamily. "About time. You taste like yours is on the way down from wombsville."

She dipped her lips back between Raye's thighs and licked her to orgasm.

They shifted positions, lay side-by-side breathing hard, arms around each other.

"That was fantastic," Raye said, stroking Ash's dark nipples. "No one does it for me like you do. No one ever has."

Ash leered. "I want to do you again. This time with the strap-on."

Raye shook her head. "Not with the strap-on."

Ash's expression was a question: "Why?"

A sad smile: "If I'm gonna die, darling, I want my last sexual memories to be of soft lady-skin against me, of silky legs entwined, of loving female fingers caressing me, blooming my sex like the sun opening a flower, of a woman's soft lips pressed against mine—not of being jabbed with pseudo-male plastic."

A smile, a girly giggle. "We're not gonna die, silly." She kissed Raye again, dipped her tongue in deep, seeking to lick her throat. Raye kissed her back hungrily. Like armies on the march, their hands traversed each other's bodies. Their hair mussed together, blending at its meeting into a cherry-brown that reflected the sun streaming in through the windows.

Ash licked down over Raye's chin, nibbling her neck, chewing on her shoulders, down to her breasts. She sucked each nipple into her mouth in turn. Her hands were busy as well, spreading Raye's sex and caressing her clitoris in a smooth circular motion that raised and lowered the organ's hood in an erotic rhythm.

Raye gasped. Ash looked at her—her eyes were shut, her face taut like she'd had a facelift.

Ash grinned. She dug her fingers into Raye's vagina. Raye stiffened, bit her lower lip. Ash resumed sucking on her nipples, drawing her lips around the soft flesh, compressing it between palate and tongue. She felt Raye's heartbeat speed up, feel her breathe faster. She dug her fingers in deeper, rolling her thumb over Raye's clitoris. Eyes still closed, Raye jerked, screamed silently, and went limp. Ash relaxed against her.

Raye opened her eyes once. She lifted her head slightly, smiled weakly. "That was even better than the first time." She shut her eyes again.

Ash smiled at her lover, who now floated in that afterglow limbo that while not quite sleep, is not awakeness. Sucking Raye's right nipple like a straw, she clamped Raye's right hand between her own secretion-slick thighs and ground her vagina against it. Softly, slowly, deliciously. Using Raye as her sex toy.

From somewhere amidst her fucked trance, Raye found the presence of mind to stroke Ash's cunt with her fingers, the reciprocal action continuing till Ash also shuddered through her second orgasm.

They lay like that, faces wreathed with happy smiles, waiting for when the ceiling would swing open above them and disgorge Skunk and Eddie—the harbingers of strange destiny.

PART 5: BLOWUP SHOWDOWN

War is simply Love inverted – Ashley Roxanne Status

CHAPTER 77

Femina – War Song (Women in Uniform)

Uncle Sam fucked me.
He turned me into his bleeding whore,
Ripped apart my hymen,
Destroyed my sweet virginity,
Rendered me impure,
Then kicked me out the back door,
Sent me off to fight his goddam war.
Now Daddy and Mama don't love me no more,
'Cos I'm dirty for sure.

Uncle Sam fucked me.
He fucked my ass with his cock-and-bullshit reasons,
Gave me a gun, sent me off to kill,
Some people in a distant Hell.
After a while, it wasn't too hard—
They were pointing guns at me as well.
But still . . .
I ain't been home in sixteen seasons,
And if I say 'no' it's desertion or treason.
I'm walking through mud, tramping train tracks,
I've found fame as G.I. Jane, but I want my goddam life back.
My darling fiancé's just married some other childhood sweetheart.

I'm thinking of stepping on a landmine,
Terminate myself to end my existential hurt,
Just to spin me back to time,
To the place I was not.
But freedom's enemies never slumber,
And somehow seem without number,
(Idiot ideologists keep on screwing extremist chicks,
And breeding terrorist kids,)
So I keep on ass-kicking,
Ejecting spent submachine gun clips, sliding full ones in,
And try to grin,
Imagining I'm an empress war queen,
While around me the universe spins.

Uncle Sam fucked me.
Oh, he really fucked me up,
With his stiff howitzer cock.

Once I REALLY tried to leave,
This butcher shop.
I got myself knocked up,
(I mean: got pregnant in the field),
I was about to be shipped off home,
I thought my great escape was sealed.
But then, the base got bombed,
And while running for an anti-aircraft gun,
I slipped in some mud,
Rammed my womb on a log,
And lost the fucking kid.
(Oh, the irony of it!)
Had a miscarriage.
Damn, that made me feel stupid.
And I HATE feeling stupid.

So now I'll see this tour of duty through even if it kills me.
(Oh, God, please don't let it kill me!)
I don't care how 'tough as nails' I seem,
I'm really soft and sexy underneath,
And I've never lost my childhood dreams.
At heart,
I'm just a girl,
Flesh and blood,
Who wants something good from this world.

VAGINA MUNDI

I still want a life and a man to love.

Uncle Sam Fucked me,
Took away my innocence,
Played on my common sense,
Seduced me with promised decadence,
Now I've got a gun, and I'm on the run,
In the land of the rising son,
A prodigal daughter,
Leading my unit across another enemy border.

Your nuclear sub is in my trench.
(Down where it's cold and wet!)
Your nuclear sub is in my trench,
Dispatched by the Department of Defense.
Uncle Sam, I love your confidence,
How, while you're filling me, killing me,
With your 'big dick' rhetoric,
You kiss my lips and whisper softly,
Explaining how you're really fulfilling me.
Just like the patriarchy.

Hey, peace-loving bitches!
I'm a fish with heavy artillery.
Fuck bicycles,
Gimme some anti-tank guns,
Flamethrowers and RPG's.
This fish needs reliable weapons,
Not strap-ons.

We're gonna rock and roll over the overdogs,
Those fat well-fed designer-suited political hogs,
Who look like the frogs and bugs,
I'm endlessly stomping on,
And sometimes even chomping on,
As I trudge,
Through landmined mud,
Enforcing peace and law,
A woman internationally abhorred.

I went away to fight Uncle Sam's fucking war,
I came back home a half-psychotic gore whore.

Uncle Sam fucked me,
Then gave me a gun.
Then he humped me some more,
Just to make sure . . .
I fought the war,
(And no, it wasn't fun!)
But Uncle Sam won.

CHAPTER 78

Raye peeked out into the corridor. "Coast is clear."

The four of them stepped outside the room.

"This way," Skunk said, leading the way left. "One floor up, end of the passage."

Eddie Fiddle walked directly behind Skunk. He carried his pistol. He was stone-cold sober, eyes grim, lips pressed tight together like he'd squash them into nonexistence.

Ash walked behind Eddie, carrying an inflated bazooka balanced on her right shoulder and a pack of shells in her left hand. Her mind-chip socket housed her Warpedia chip.

Raye was on Ash's right.

None of them spoke during the short walk to the stairs.

Skunk was dressed in her performance getup of t-shirt and boots without pants or panties. She had one vibrator stuck in her vagina and duct-taped in place, a second duct-taped over her clitoris. Both sex toys buzzed like bees. Tendrils of green smoke dripped from her sex with her each step, curling like wraiths around her legs and hips. Occasionally she moaned, repressing the sexual sensations rippling her body. Her dousing of jasmine perfume neutralized the cunt-fish smell, becoming itself an offense by the aroma's intensity.

While they silently climbed the stairs, Raye admired Skunk's ass. She was surprised that now, of all times, she was being affected sexually by the bony brunette.

Skunk's buttocks looked like someone had vacuumed out most of their contents, but the overall effect was pleasing. Raye suppressed her sudden fierce desire to stroke the curved white skin with hair-fingers, to fuck the tight anus with a hair-dildo. She smiled. *Okay, maybe, just maybe . . . after this is over, Ash and I will do a threesome with skinny-and-stinky here. Ash loves stuff like that, and I—love-struck sucker that I am—I just want to make her happy.* She stifled a giggle. *Okay, I'm lying—I'd love to vacuum Skunk's carpet.*

Skunk signaled a pause. She peered out around the end of the stairway then ducked back down. "One guard," she whispered. "I'll take care of him."

She stepped to the top of the stairs, a sudden gush of green gas from her vagina wrapping around her hips and legs like a sarong.

***

Joe Smith, the burly guard watching the corridor, spun around on hearing Skunk on the landing. He reached for his pistol, then relaxed. No danger here, just some lady who'd lost her way. She was really thin though, and the way her green skirt swirled about her legs like gas . . .

He walked toward the landing, her dense perfume enveloping him as he reached her.

"Hey, lady," he said, his voice gruff, "you can't come up here right now."

She grinned. "I'm sorry, I've lost my way. I think it should be the lower floor, but I'm certain he said fourth not third." She smiled helplessly. "This always happens to me—I'm utter shite where directions are concerned."

Joe nodded. "Happens to the best of us." In an indefinable way, he was suddenly worried. The woman's skirt was thinning from around her legs, puffing away behind him in gusts like a wind was blowing it. Then there was only a single green thread depending from her crotch, fluttering in invisible wind. And . . .

"Why is there a vibrator taped to your crotch?" Joe asked, bemused.

Skunk moaned. "All the better to eat you with, darling."

Joe stared at her. The first thought through his mind concerned oral sex. "Oh no, lady. I'd love to accommodate you, but . . ." he shrugged helplessly, whispered: "I'm working, see? Maybe later, once—"

That was when he became aware of the heavy stench of fish behind him. He gaped at Skunk in confusion, then spun around.

Joe stared at the monster facing him—a pulsing mass of fish, lobsters, and tentacles—in even more confusion.

"Like I said," Skunk said behind him, "all the better to eat you with."

Joe's confusion faded fast. He went for his gun.

Not fast enough. A tentacle wrapped around his wrist, preventing him from drawing the sidearm.

Next, in lightning-fast sequence, a hole opened in the middle of the monster's body and seemingly a million tentacles flailed at him. The tentacles seized him and pulled him into the opening in the monster, which slurped shut behind him.

Arms flailing wildly like he was trying to fly, Joe opened his mouth and screamed. But like his previous reaction, he'd left it too late. Inside the creature, there was no one to hear his alarm, except the sharks and giant lobsters thrashing on the surface of the black sea he was falling towards.

"Yummy," he heard Skunk whisper far overhead.

***

"Let's do this," Eddie said.

The others nodded grimly. Tentacle-monster plodding ahead of them, they padded down the corridor.

"Okay, Ash," Skunk whispered above her monster's squishy footsteps, "you know what to do."

Ash nodded. The other four (counting the monster), paused outside Uncle Luigi's office; Ash moved quickly past them to the elevator.

One button push and it was on its way up. Good. While waiting for it to arrive, she mentally jammed all the Hotel Bizarre's internet connections and all phone communications within a hundred yards radius. *We'll be long gone before anyone investigates.*

The elevator arrived. As its doors slid open, Ash realized she had nothing to jam them with. Then she grinned. She lowered her rocket launcher off her shoulder and stuck it end-to-end between the doors. An almost perfect fit. The elevator made a futile attempt at shutting, but lost the contest of steel versus steel.

Great. She placed the pack of rockets within easy reach inside the cage.

On a sudden remembrance, she entered the elevator and long-pressed '20,' something Skunk had clearly forgotten. *Best we're prepared to leave in a hurry.*

Raye's words about dying fluttered through her mind like candle-struck moths. Ash no longer considered them melodramatic. A webcop 'pussy wagon' *had* arrived along with Big Tony and Lana. Two spider policepersons were currently walking round the Hotel Bizarre, ostensibly looking for rapists and muggers to process into cat food.

She stepped out of the frozen elevator, unzipped her left arm, and fiddled inside it till she found a tiny shotgun. Blowing air to inflate it and its pack of shells, she strode back towards the others.

Time to rock and roll.

CHAPTER 79

Fred felt totally mortified. No words accurately expressed the depths of his current dismay.

He stood legs spread, pants down around his ankles, bent over Uncle Luigi's office desk. Bitch, her muzzle white with cocaine, was sniffing his ass.

Uncle Luigi leaned against the wall by the door, watching. Big Tony sat behind the office desk. Lana Petrova was snuggled in his lap, grinning at Fred's discomfort.

The consignment of drugs and money, the reason for their meeting, lay ignored in four pigskin cases on the floor.

Bitch licked Fred's buttock crack. Then he felt her tongue, hot, thick, and wet, slither down over his scrotum to his limp cock. Next, the Doberman began fellating him again.

"Damn!" Uncle Luigi said. "I'm seeing it and I still don't believe it!"

To Fred's consternation, he was once again getting an erection. In negation of his disgust and horror, sluggish blood was flowing into his penis, inflating it. "Can I pull up my pants now?" he asked desperately.

Big Tony shook his head. "You know the rules. Give my dog what she wants. She's a good girl."

Fred turned to his uncle, his eyes pleading. "C'mon, Uncle Luigi, gimme a break. I don't deserve to be treated like this."

Uncle Luigi shook his head. He was doing his best not to laugh.

Pushing a pistol aside, Lana leaned forward over the desk. "Is she deep-throating him yet?" She scowled. "She-it, Tony, you were rushing me so much I forgot to bring my new Sony video camera."

Big Tony shrugged nonchalantly. "You'll record it next time, baby. Look, use the one in your phone for now." He patted her ample leather-clad behind, then checked his watch. Then he leaned forward himself and ruffled Fred's hair. "Hey! Hurry up and feed my dog some come—we've business to conduct."

"Yes," Lana said, "today, premature ejaculation has financial benefits."

That did it for Uncle Luigi. He burst out laughing, tears streaming down his cheeks.

Fred's penis was now fully erect. While fighting not to enjoy the velvety canine mouth sucking on him, he ran intricate scenarios through his mind of how he'd murder Big Tony. But the dog's mouth was . . . ah, the hot breath, the warm saliva, the tight clamp between tongue and palate combined with the slipperiness almost perfectly duplicated the feel of a cunt on his penis . . . the steady slithering friction, the whiskers tickling his thighs . . . *Oh, no,* he thought miserably as the sensation shivered down his legs to weaken his knees. *Oh, God, please help me! Please! I don't want to come in this mutt's mouth again!*

Lana had meanwhile taken Big Tony's advice and was fiddling with her cellphone. "Ah, yes!" She pointed the phone at Fred and giggled.

Fred was utterly disgusted now. *She's actually, really, going to film this?*

Then Lana lowered her phone and wrinkled her nose. "Hey, what is that smell of fish?"

"Fish?" Uncle Luigi asked. Then he nodded. "Yeah, I'm smelling it too. Just like when Karen—"

Then the office door was violently wrenched off its hinges.

***

Uncle Luigi instantly recognized the woman who'd pulled the door off its hinges with her hair. *One of the two whose van Karen stole.* A chill went through him, as, still standing outside in the corridor, her hair-hands flung the steel door aside like it was paper. *Damn! This has to be to the lady Money is looking for. And there's her girlfriend too. They've both been here all this while?*

His eyes turned cold. "What the hell do you think you're doing, barging into my office like this?"

"Hey, Luigi, we're here for the dough and drugs!" an unseen man replied from the corridor.

Uncle Luigi turned to the others, "it's a robbery!" then went for his gun.

Even old as he was, his reflexes were great—the pistol leapt into his hand as if by magic. Before he could fire at the woman with the tentacle hair, however, the singular most unimaginable thing in the world happened.

A shark—long and gray and with a mouth full of triangular teeth—floated through the air at him. He gaped at it. Water cascaded like monsoon

335

rain off its torpedo-shaped form. Behind it, he momentarily glimpsed the creature it had come from. *No that isn't poss—*

He never completed the thought. The shark slammed into him. Its jaws snapped together over his head, biting it completely off. Uncle Luigi and the shark both crashed to the floor. The headless body pumped jets of blood into a corner while the fish threshed about in a rage of bloodlust, repositioning itself to eat it.

Big Tony and Lana leapt to their feet, knocking their chair over to get out of the shark's way.

***

Fred, Big Tony, and Lana were still gaping in disbelief at the shark feeding on Luigi Rossi's headless corpse, when, preceded by the tentacle-monster, Raye, Skunk, and Eddie walked into the office.

Fred recovered first. He was unsure which emotion was greater in him—his horror at his uncle's death, or his relief that his ordeal of debasement had abruptly ended. And not a moment too soon—seconds more and he'd have spurted semen down Bitch's thirsty throat.

Covering his penis with his hands, he spun round and gaped at the entrants. *Damn*, he thought, seeing Raye among them. *And I was trying to protect you?*

The monster stood in the middle of the office, Eddie on its left, Raye on its right. Skunk was behind it, just visible through the forest of tentacles studding its mass. Its fish growths nibbled at the air. The room filled with green mist and fish stink.

(Outside, Ash had walked past the others to guard the stairs.)

Eddie leveled his gun to point squarely at Fred's heart. "We're here for the money. "Don't screw with us and you'll all live."

"There's . . . there's no money here," Fred sputtered. Once again, he was mortified. His penis was still hard, and Bitch was still licking at it. He pushed the Doberman away but she leapt back playfully at his erection, like it was a master she'd not seen in ages, slobbering and sucking at the turgid pink meat.

Eddie's eyes widened at the dog's behavior. "Wow, I should have brought a movie camera."

Lana peered out from behind Big Tony's bulk, her beautiful face worried. "I have the same regrets. This is a good movie to film."

"Shut up, Lana!" Big Tony snapped. "This is serious."

The blonde's face creased with displeasure. She ducked back out of sight behind him.

Peering over Fred's shoulder, Big Tony stared from one intruding face to the next, his eyes settling on Eddie. Winds of recognition blew the storm clouds of confusion from his fat face. "Hey, don't I motherfucking know you?" Big Tony's mustache practically leapt off his lip as he yelped, "Eddie . . . Eddie Fiddle?" His face reddened. "Eddie, you lousy son-of-a-bitch! Where the hell is the three hundred grand I loaned you to make *Pterodactyl Pussy Paradise?*"

Skunk, meanwhile, was having an orgasm while keeping her monster creature together. She sensed the room through it, and what *it* saw was Fred fending off the dog sucking his cock. Skunk found the sight incredibly erotic. Bitch evaded Fred's hands and slid her mouth down on his erection. Skunk gasped at the sight—it accelerated her into another orgasm. She staggered back against the wall shuddering.

Raye (previously astounded by Fred's sexual deviancy) was crouched to the tentacle-monster's right, examining the four pigskin cases on the floor beneath the wall safe. She snapped each open, then looked up. "The money and drugs are all here." She stood up, then wove her hair into four pairs of hands that shut the suitcases again and picked them up. She frowned across at the climaxing Skunk. "Ready to go."

CHAPTER 80

Big Tony stared at Raye, his face wobbling like he'd have a heart attack. His gun lay on the desk to Fred's right. He felt paralyzed, impotent. He was confused like he'd never been before, not even during the war with bullets and shrapnel flying everywhere and his unit being sliced apart into ribbons of flesh all around him. *On my right I got a shark eating dead Luigi and simultaneously choking to death; in front of me there's a bear-shaped mass of tentacles with fish and lobsters stuck in it and a hole with an ocean in its belly.*

And now? On my right, a fat brunette, effortlessly lifting four suitcases with hands formed from her hair.

It was the money that triggered Big Tony to act. The two million dollars from Philly. The thought of that much mob money being stolen terrified him. *No way they're not going to think I colluded with the robbers. And Knox Arnold's a certifiable loon . . .*

"Oh, no," he said, "you can't take that money. Knox is gonna freak—"

"Shut the fuck up!" Eddie growled. "Mail him your paunch as replacement."

Big Tony's gaze dropped to the pistol on the desk.

Eddie sneered at him. "You dare reach for the shooter and you're history. Just like the money you lent me."

"Please!" Lana yelped from behind Big Tony. "The Philly mobsters will think we double-crossed them!"

Eddie gestured at Fred to get out of the way. Fred stumbled right, but then got his legs tangled up in the pants around his ankles. While trying to right himself, he was hit by the shark's flailing tail. He toppled over the shark, winding up knocking himself half-senseless on the wall. He slid down on top of the dying elasmobranch, face up, penis out and remarkably still

338

erect. Bitch was on him like white on rice. The dog settled happily atop the shark's twitching gray bulk, gently chewing on Fred's penis like it was a bone.

For a moment both Eddie and Big Tony were distracted, staring at Fred and the dog, then both returned their attention to each other.

"The money stays," Big Tony said. He pointed at dazed Fred. "Take the drugs if you want—Money'll kill you all but it'll be your own funeral, but—"

"Shut up, old man," Raye said. "We're taking everything. And if you don't like it . . ." she gestured at the gun on the desk, "make your move."

Eddie smirked. "Don't bother, Tony. Bluster won't cut it. You're outnumbered four-to-one here. Quit while you're ahead or wind up dead." Lips curled in an evil smile, he jerked his thumb at the tentacle monster. "And afterwards we'll feed your hot blonde to the ocean beyond."

Behind the creature, Skunk moaned in orgasm. Then she gasped, "Or Eddie will use her for his next flick. Your Ruskie has nice big tits."

Lana shivered behind Big Tony. He felt her body trembling. He reconsidered. *Yes, maybe letting the money go will be best. Fred'll corroborate my story with the Philly crew. And then I really do pity Eddie and his cohorts, no one wants Money Rich after their ass. But . . .*

Experienced in reading men's eyes, Big Tony could see Eddie was frightened behind the bravado. He suddenly realized Eddie's gun was for show. *The punk's likely never killed anyone in his life.*

Stifling a laugh, he grabbed the gun off the desk and fired twice at Eddie.

By the wall, Bitch yelped in fright at the noise, then returned her attention to Fred's erection.

Eddie stood shocked. He looked down at his chest, at the two holes in his heart from which blood spurted like the come Fred was now ejaculating into Bitch's mouth.

"You . . . you . . ." he gasped at Big Tony, then slumped to the floor, dead.

Big Tony instantly swung his gun to cover Raye. "Put the cases down, lady."

He was shocked by the sudden brown wall that dropped down in front of her. Thinking it was offensive, not defensive, he fired at the shield of woven hair, ducking behind the desk as the bullet ricocheted back. He yanked Lana down beside him.

Lana looked at him with terrified eyes. "What is going on, Tony? Nothing like this is in Mother Russia."

"Just stay out of sight."

Then Lana pointed under the desk. "Look, the tentacle-monster is a gas leak from the woman's cunt. She is masturbating it out."

Big Tony nodded. "One shot to the head will finish her then," he whispered in a rush. "Then I'll figure out how to deal with the other one."

He picked up Luigi's dropped gun. Covered with blood, the shark weakly chewed meat ripped from the corpse's belly. Strangling in air, but still eating. Stretched out on the fish's tail, Bitch's legs trembled, her tail wagged as she licked Fred's penis clean.

Big Tony winced. "That dog is fucking crazy," he told Lana, "it ain't just the drugs. Okay, keep your head down, baby."

She nodded back fiercely.

A gun in each hand, Big Tony leapt back to his feet.

He was shocked to be instantly snared in a tangle of tentacles and pulled towards the hole in the monster. He was even more shocked to see the shark leaping out of the sea in the creature, its jaws spread wide to clamp on him.

"You killed Eddie, you son-of-a-bitch!" Skunk shrilled. "I'm gonna fuck you up so bad, your mama will think you're tuna spread!"

Big Tony almost pissed himself with fear. Then, wrenching his hands free of the tentacles, he pointed both guns at the onrushing shark and began firing. The bullets blew the exiting shark back into the creature. Big Tony sighed with relief as it sank back to the water, large bloody holes in its head.

His relief was short-lived. The tentacles resumed pulling him toward the hole. Little tentacles squirmed like worms around the opening. Big Tony trained both guns on the creature's body above the hole and began shooting. Water spurted from its wounds, but its grip on him never slackened. Instead the tentacles seemed to get stronger.

"No!" Lana yelled, leaping to her feet and grabbing hold of Big Tony's legs. "You cannot have him! He is mine!" Neck muscles corded with the effort, she strained against the tentacles for control of Big Tony's body.

One of Big Tony's guns clicked empty. He discarded it and stopped shooting. He had no idea how many rounds the other held, but now he had to make every shot count. And the easiest way to do that was to hit the masturbating woman. But she was totally concealed by the creature. *I need one shot, just one fucking shot.* The tentacles wrenched him left and right. He braced himself against the edge of the hole, pushing against the creature as Lana pulled him back. His heart beat triple-time like he was racing to meet a coronary.

He saw that the other woman, the fat one with funny hair, had now lowered her hair shield and was watching the contest. Their eyes met. Hers mocked him, taunted him over his inability to get free. He imagined dislike in them, but dislike over what? *Lady, I don't know you, and you hate me?*

He remembered seeing her at Femina's concert kissing another, thin, girl. *So what if you're gay—that doesn't give you the right to . . .*

He forgot her, turned his thoughts back to resolving his current dilemma.

A faint hope glimmered. *Mark Fennel's guys are downstairs. And the webcops. They'll have heard the gunfire and come storming up. But Eddie said I'm outnumbered four-to-one, not three-to-one, which means there's a fourth member of their team—likely outside in the corridor—waiting to ambush any help.*

"Shit," he gasped.

And the smell! The stink of fish everywhere . . .

Beside him, Bitch was now curled up on Fred, gripping him with her paws like they were lovers. *Oh, yeah, there is something wrong with that dog. Fred—the dumb know-all punk—deserves her!*

He caught a glimpse of bare thigh to his right. Then duct-taped brown pubic hair. The masturbating woman! At last revealed! He knew this was his single chance. His strength was failing fast. He couldn't resist the tentacles—which felt like anaconda coils around his arms and legs—much longer. Behind him, Lana's breathing came loud and fast. He felt her grip on him weakening.

Come on, you freak robber bitch! Big Tony thought. *Just show your face, so I can end your miserable life!*

Like an answer to prayer, Skunk stepped into full view. "Stop resisting," she said in a lust-slurred voice, "the sharks and lobsters are hungry."

"Fuck you!" Lana yelled. "Shoot her, Tony!"

Big Tony swung his gun arm up in a last desperate move. "Die, cunt!"

To his amazement, she laughed at him. With a wrench stronger than he could resist, the tentacles twisted the gun's direction away from her like he weighed nothing.

He pulled the trigger anyway. He was surprised as hell when the bullet ricocheted off a metal plaque hanging by the masturbating woman's head, then zinged left and hit the funny-haired woman in the forehead.

Splat! Raye's brains exploded in messy chunks out the rear of her head. Eyes confused, she slumped to the floor, dead before she hit the carpet. Blood pulsed from her wounds like her head was an opened fire hydrant.

Skunk shrieked in absolute rage. Before Big Tony could fire again, the tentacles gave an almighty yank and jerked him out of Lana's grasp, off his feet, and straight into the creature. His gun fell from his hand and clattered to the carpet, ending up under the desk.

The suddenness of the action knocked Lana completely off balance, she staggered backward, tripped over a leg of the overturned chair, then was upended out of the office window.

As she fell outward, hands futilely clutching at nothing, her terrified eyes saw Big Tony disappear into the tentacle creature, the hole sealing shut over him.

CHAPTER 81

Lana fell seemingly in slow-motion. Like an over-gorged fish swimming through sluggish water. The fact that she was flinging her arms and legs about wildly in a vain effort to halt her descent made no difference to the subjective time she experienced.

Her lifetime was compressed by acceleration due to gravity.

She saw it all as the ground came nearer—her childhood in the city of Dmitrov; teenage love affairs; winning the *Miss Moscow* beauty pageant at age twenty-two; her career as a model; being blacklisted due to unreliability caused by her habitual drug use; her totally down-and-out time when she'd survived by pickpocketing; her shame and attempted suicide; drunkenly entering her profile on an online dating website as a gag; Big Tony's contacting her; burning her bridges and the whirl of packing; the nervous flight to America; the first time they'd made love—tasting his cock as he tasted her cunt, the sweet penetration, the dizzy sensations of her first orgasm on US soil; she and Big Tony's drug-fueled affair . . .

She shut her eyes as the ground grew extra-close.

But now I die on foreign soil, far away from beloved Mother Russia.

Only she didn't.

Two moments before Lana would have shattered her head and half the bones in her body on a concrete abutment, she was snared in a silk-thin web which shot through the air and glued her to the wall.

It took her a moment to understand what had happened. *I live—webcops!*

Breathing with heavy relief, she opened her eyes (she was hanging upside-down), and stared at the two spider people who'd saved her. One male, one female.

The female webcop—NYPD logo bright red across her large breasts, her shriveled facial features ugly deep rifts and ridges, her hair white like an eclipse's corona—pointed up the building's side. "What's going on up there? Who's shooting?" Her voice rasped like the ghost of her leeched youth.

"It's a robbery!" Lana gasped. "They've killed Tony and Luigi!"

The webcops smiled at each other. "New York's cats need food," the spider man said.

"Yes they do," the woman replied. "Let's go get them some."

Even viewed upside down, their smiles chilled Lana.

Before she could ask that they unstick her, both webcops were streaking up the side of the building, moving as effortlessly as if it was a stairway.

CHAPTER 82

Standing on the stairway landing, gazing down the descent, Ashley Status heard the first two gunshots.

Damn! she thought, *Someone in there's decided to play the hero. There goes our hope of a quiet escape—the calvary'll be up here any moment now.*

She listened: Skunk was screaming.

Ash was suddenly frightened. *Eddie must have been hit.* Conscious of the distance between herself and the jammed elevator in case of the need for a fast getaway, she backed quickly away from the landing towards Uncle Luigi's office, keeping her eyes and pump-action shotgun trained on the stairway exit.

Behind her, voices yelled. Skunk's and a male voice she didn't recognize. There were further gunshots. Also, loud noises like furniture being dragged around.

She was almost at the office door when she heard one final gunshot. After a following moment of silence, there was the crash of several objects hitting the floor at once, amongst them something heavy that landed with a dull thud.

Then Skunk screamed again.

A chill instantly went through Ash like she'd been dipped in Arctic water. *Raye!* Forgetting about guarding the corridor, she spun around and ran into the office.

***

Raye lay on the floor with her eyes and mouth open, her tongue frozen midway between her upper and lower lip like she'd been about speaking

344

when the bullet hit her. Blood still dribbled from the small hole in her forehead. Like a swarm of millipedes entering a cracked wall, her hair was shrinking back to normal, seemingly disappearing into her head. In gaps between her hair, chunks of reddened brain could be seen.

Dropping her shotgun, Ash sunk down to her knees besides Raye. She grabbed her shoulders and lifted her up, then put her down again and collapsed on top of her weeping.

The world contracted to just the two of them. She was vaguely aware of Skunk and the monster being present. Of bodies to her left.

Ash wept—violently. Tears poured from her blue eyes like they were waterfalls, like Raye's death had unplugged a reservoir of liquid horror deep in her soul.

"C'mon, wake up, Raye. C'mon, baby, don't leave me alone. I LOVE YOU! Don't leave me here like this!"

She lifted the corpse again and sat hugging it, tears pouring down her cheeks. "Just wake up, Raye! We'll get married and have some kids and I promise I'll never, never, ever look at anyone else again! I promise!!! I'm sorry I made you jealous with all those men, baby." She held Raye out at arm's length, like the corpse was a doll or a dress she was inspecting. "Just wake up! I'm serious! We'll get married and go away, and I'll never go off with a man again in my life."

"Snap out of it!" Skunk said.

Ash didn't. She hung on tight to Raye's corpse, professing her undying love with every endearment she should could think of. "Please, please, please, come back! You're the only one I ever truly loved!"

She kissed the corpse . . .

She felt a sudden sharp pain on the side of her head. The pain came again. And someone was tugging on her. But she wasn't about letting go of Raye. "NO! We'll be together forever, darling! We've got money now. We'll buy an island somewhere and make love—scissor each other while the sun goes down over distant waves!"

Another sharp pain—her cheek felt like a furnace now.

The physical pain broke through her emotional turmoil. She looked dully up. Skunk was staring coldly down at her, hand raised to slap Ash again.

"I said: snap out of it," the brunette repeated. "We've got the money and everyone's dead. Let's get out of here before Fennel's guys arrive!"

"I LOVE RAYE," Ash moaned miserably. "I can't leave her!"

Skunk sighed. "Listen, Ash," she said in a ghostly, equally miserable voice, "I loved Eddie Fiddle more than I thought it possible to love anyone in this horrid world, and now he's dead." She turned to gaze at Eddie's corpse. (Eddie's face, visible beyond the tentacle-monster's legs, was turned toward them, its expression one of dying agony.) Misty-eyed, she looked back at Ash. "Right now, I feel soulless, emptied of emotion—you could grind up a baby in front of me and I wouldn't cry. You know what makes it worse?" She tapped the vibrator taped over her clitoris. "I was having an orgasm when he died." She winced, bit her lower lip. "And I'm having another right now . . . damn!"

She trembled with the unwanted pleasure. Monster tentacles caressed her back.

Ash stood up. Skunk had got through to her. Still, she cast a miserable look down at Raye's corpse. "What good is wealth without love?"

Skunk pulled Ash close and hugged her. "We'll each find love again, girl. No matter how much it seems like the world's over, the pain always passes." She scowled at a sight over Ash's shoulder. "Shit! We've spent way too much time talking, the webcops are here!"

They broke apart in alarm.

Framed in the window, the female webcop yelled, "Freeze, in the name of the law!"

The pain of Raye's death instantly converted to rage in Ash. In a single fluid motion, she grabbed her shotgun off the floor, spun round, and discharged it into the woman's face.

Boom! And again. *Boom!*

The spider woman's head above her lower jaw disappeared behind her in a red gush of flesh and blood. She fell back from the window, dropping into space, blood jetting from her truncated neck.

"Fuck you!" Ash spat after her corpse.

"That's cold," Skunk said. "Okay, let's get out of here, I can hear voices out in the corridor."

Ash turned toward Skunk, who was checking the pigskin cases. Skunk looked up. "The cash is in these two; we'll each carry one." Then her eyes widened again. "Shit, not another one!"

Cocking her shotgun as she turned, Ash spun around again. "Can't you pigs take a simple hint?"

The male webcop had however anticipated her action. As Ash turned, he jetted web from his fingers. The silken material coiled around the smoking shotgun barrel. It sizzled but did not melt. The webcop jerked his hand back, wrenching the shotgun out of Ash's hands. The weapon sailed out of the window and far away.

The man perched on the windowsill, outlined in the frame like a justice-dispensing gargoyle. He spoke, his voice cold and even:

"By the powers invested in me by the State of New York to be both judge and jury in case of the willful, intentional murder of a police officer in the line of duty, when such death is witnessed in its commission by another officer—"

While the webcop spoke, Ash looked desperately around for another weapon. The only gun in sight lay beside dazed Fred. It looked to have fallen out of his pocket. She noted Bitch, lying on the shark and licking Fred's limp cock. *What?* She couldn't fathom what had been going on there. She also realized she couldn't dash for the gun, the tentacle monster blocked her way to it. And there was no time to get a new inflatable from a muscle-purse.

"—I hereby sentence you to death and to be canned as cat food."

Ash straightened up. "I can explain . . ."

"No explanation is acceptable in this case, nor any evidence admissible. By cold-bloodedly murdering policewoman Samantha Jeanette Simmons you have waived all right to legal representation. No appeal will be considered. Your sentence will be carried out immediately, and—"

"Fuck you," Skunk said softly. She gave the webcop the finger. "Bye-bye, spider-guy!"

"In the name of the law, I order you two women to remain—"

The next moment the webcop was blasted off the windowsill and out into open space by the massive great white shark that exited the tentacle creature's body. Outside, in midair, the shark's teeth came together in the webcop's body, splitting him in three—his head and shoulders fell away from its mouth on one side, his legs above the knees on the other.

Ash gaped as the shark fell out of the air toward the ground.

"C'mon, let's go! Fennel's boys are outside waiting!"

Ash spun away from the window. She'd seen the shark crash down in the street. She rounded on Skunk:

"Why the hell did it take you so long? I was practically pissing myself with fear. All I could see was cats eating me and asking for second helpings!"

"Calm down. I like hearing them recite that legal bullshit. Besides, I was looking for a suitably big shark to eat him."

She handed Ash one of the money cases. "Fennel's guys will ambush us the moment we step into the corridor. Remember, those guys are pros—don't shoot to wound—"

"You're not going anywhere!"

Ash and Skunk looked down. Fred was pointing his gun at them. "Put the money down!" he gasped weakly. He was still dazed; his eyes were crossed like he wasn't really seeing them.

Skunk laughed. "Or what, you sick dickhead? You'll fuck us like you did the dog?"

Bitch growled at her. She laughed coldly at the dog, "You liked that, didn't you, you canine slut—human cock in your doggie vagina?" then began groaning in orgasm. "Oh, holy fuck!"

"Put the money down," Fred repeated.

Ash stepped out of his line of fire, then plucked the gun from his weak fingers. She stuck it in her belt. "Ignore him," she told Skunk, "he's harmless."

Skunk nodded. "Okay, here's how we do this: I send the monster out first to attack them. While they're confused, we dash for the elevator." She gaped at Ash. "What are you doing?"

Ash held out the pack of inflated grenades. "Too complicated. How 'bout we simply blow 'em up?" She winked at Skunk. "Don't worry, girl, I got this." She jerked a thumb at the tentacle monster. "Just pack stinky there back into your cooze so it doesn't get in our way. Besides I don't think it'll fit in the elevator."

Before Skunk could retort. Ash had pulled the safety pins from two grenades and flung them out into the corridor, right, towards the stairway landing.

The following explosions rumbled the floor. A scream mingled in with the noise. Nodding grimly, Ash armed two more grenades and flung them after the first pair. More explosions; no more screaming.

She turned back to Skunk, saw the brunette had dispersed the tentacle-monster, and picked up her pigskin case. "Let's go. I doubt anyone will bother us now."

Bitch licking his face, Fred dully watched both women prepare to leave.

CHAPTER 83

They peeked out first. The far end of the corridor was a mess. Two bloody mangled corpses lay by the staircase. The sprinkler system rained down on the bodies amidst clouds of smoke, spreading the blood towards them.

"All clear," Ash said. She'd now compartmentalized her grief. Raye's death hurt her—*fuck! It hasn't even begun hurting me yet!*—but she was soldiering on.

They ran into the elevator, leaping over the rocket launcher wedging it open.

A shadow appeared at the head of the stairs, then two more, then another. The shout of angry male voices followed. Next, gunfire reverberated down the corridor, the muzzle flashes as the shadows fired prophetic indicators of death. Slugs pocked the corridor walls. Two holes appeared in the rear elevator wall.

"Shut the door and let's get out of here!" Skunk yelped. "This was a crap idea of yours! I should have used my fucking monster!"

Ash suddenly felt waves of calm wash over her. Simultaneously, she was possessed by a desire for revenge. Rationally or not, she held the oncoming security men responsible for Raye's death, just like she had the webcops.

Two men rushed down the corridor at her, firing as they came. Ash calmly shot them both with Fred's gun. (With her military mind-chip's targeting abilities there was no way she could miss.) Both men toppled over dead. The others stayed by the stairs, firing intermittently between grunts of conversation.

Ignoring the gunfire, Ash bent and picked up the rocket launcher. The elevator doors began closing, she blocked them open with her foot.

Skunk gaped at her. "What are you doing? "Let's go."

"Get down on the fucking floor," Ash replied in an icy voice. "The backwash from this thing can melt your face off."

Skunk quickly lay down flat. "Some people just can't take a hint," she muttered, her cheek on cold metal.

With grit teeth, Ash swung the rocket launcher up, aiming at the patch of corridor wall directly opposite the stairs. Ignoring the bullets pattering the elevator door (one of them whizzing past her cheek, one zipping through her skirt between her legs), she pulled the trigger.

"Fuck you guys!" she yelled as the shell blew down the corridor.

More slugs hit the doors. One blew through her hair, slamming into the elevator wall behind her. It didn't matter—suddenly Ash felt invulnerable, like Raye's ghost hovered over her, protecting her. *I've survived this far, you gangster sons-of-bitches, no way am I going out now!* She watched the shell explode amidst the smoke and fire, watched three men blown sideways down the stairs as the wall disintegrated.

She quickly reloaded the rocket launcher, keeping the elevator doors from closing by standing in the gap. She raised the weapon and sighted again, mind-chip tracking her vision left and right like she was a robot. Behind her, the elevator cage boiled with exhaust gasses. Ash ignored the heat. She looked down once (to ensure she hadn't cooked Skunk), then focused her mind on the upright rectangle thirty yards away on her left from which more offense was expected.

"Shut the door and let's frigging leave," Skunk said from the floor in an exasperated voice. Then she shut up and grimly moaned and shuddered her way through another orgasm.

Ash ignored her. *Dammit, woman! Turn those vibrators off—even if we are going to run into trouble later!* She waited like a hunter for someone to show their face at the corner of the stairs. A straight dispatch to cocksucker eternity.

No one emerged.

Disappointed, she lowered the rocket launcher, stepped back fully into the elevator cage.

She smirked down at Skunk, the brunette lying angrily on her side, sexual lubrication glistening on her thighs. "You can get up now. The war's over. We won."

The elevator door shut. Ash hit the button for Endless Street.

CHAPTER 84

"No," Skunk said, standing up in a rush and killing the cage's descent, "we go up, not down."

Ash stood back from the controls. "Why?"

"More thugs will be waiting down in the lobby, maybe with heavy artillery. If we drop, the elevator automatically stops there if anyone calls it. We go up, however, and it won't return down till after we get off. Only, by then we'd have deactivated special mode. So they'll get an empty cage back, and will be confused where we got off. Even if they do figure out how to turn on the additional functions, we'll be long vanished."

"What floor?"

Skunk considered the green buttons. "Six." She punched the number then groaned. "Oh, shit, I'm coming."

"Turn those damn vibrators off."

"The pleasure's stopping me from becoming depressed." She sat back down, this time on her money case.

The elevator ascended two floors. Stopped, opened.

Ash looked out and shuddered. The landscape was dark and stark. The sky was black, with a purple sun. The only vegetation was rows of fluorescent trees with hand-shaped leaves. The trees glowed like pale dancers. "Where the hell is this place?"

Skunk stood up, picked her pigskin money case off the floor. "Bizarro. Let's go."

She deactivated the elevator controls. The metal cage instantly altered to the inside of an old wooden hut with a dust-and-cobweb-smothered rocking chair in one corner. Triangular beams of light filtered in through a myriad dislodged slats, spotlighting roaches and centipedes milling in the floor's ancient dirt.

Outside now, a dusty porch extended. Timbers supported its thatched ceiling; wooden stairs descended to the ground.

Skunk stepped out onto the porch, waited for Ash to follow.

Ash didn't move. This landscape looked . . . "Did you call it *Bizarro*?"

Skunk nodded. "It's part of the same place as Endless Street. No, that's wrong—Bizarro *is* the actual place, Endless Street is just one component of it. All the hotel's extra floors open onto different parts of Bizarro." She gestured to Ash. "Come on, hottie, we need to split, and fast. Just in case."

Ash conquered her apprehension and stepped out of the wooden hut. Feet leaving tracks in the ancient dust, they crossed to the porch's edge, stood looking out at the glowing trees.

"Which way?"

Skunk scratched her nose. In this odd light, her face appeared ghoulish, transparent, like her bones were glowing through her skin. "Straight ahead. The Everywhere Freeway's a short distance off—"

"Everywhere Freeway?"

"It leads to Bypass Station, which in turn leads *everywhere*."

It didn't make sense to Ash but she felt questions could wait. Skunk was right—they needed to put some distance between themselves and the elevator.

"The freeway leads off to different zones," Skunk continued. "We'll get lost easily, lay low for a while, then double back down to Endless Street. Or we might find somewhere we like up here. Hey! What are you . . . ?"

Ash looked up from her squat, intense concentration on her face. "I don't feel like walking."

Skunk's eyes spread wide as eggs when Ash pulled the miniature helicopter out of her anus. She winced at the blood on the machine and Ash's fingers. "That hurt, right? And how in Hell's blaze do you poop with that thing inside you?"

Ash wiped the blood off on her skirt. "It's not blocking my ass, if that's what you mean. There's a muscle-purse in my rectum which I use to store really big things that would otherwise bulge out my arms or thighs." She indicated the chopper, which was the size of a man's fist. "Getting them in or out, however, occasionally presents a problem." She cleaned off the model's inflation straw, blew into it, then flung it out across the landscape, well away from the hut. "So we fly. Up in the sky, we'll see better to know where we are."

Skunk goggled again as she watched the UH-60 Black Hawk helicopter inflate. She turned to Ash, pointed to her buttocks. "What else do you have in there?"

Ash shrugged. "There's one more chopper—a Bell AH-1 SuperCobra. Also, a nuclear submarine, two tanks, a B-2 Stealth Bomber . . ." She stopped. "I can't remember everything. I like military shit—big-girl toys—I grabbed everything on display when I had the chance to."

Skunk regarded Ash with new respect. "You're one in a million, woman."

Ash managed a smile she didn't feel. "C'mon," she said, pointing to the waiting helicopter, "you're the one who's been chafing at the bit to leave since we got here."

Depressed and additionally burdened by the weight of the cash they carried, they walked over to the chopper.

It hurts to be rich, Ash thought glumly.

CHAPTER 85

Femina – Death

Episode One: Me.

Your grave is my cunt,
I have buried you,
But not how I want.
Come in me, die in me.
Never leave me,
Alone,
But that's what you've gone and done.

I have entombed you,
But not deep enough.

The world is in my womb,
The future, children unborn.
And now, I think of you,
And all I've lost,
Because I wanted more than 'just us.'
My ravening LUST,
I just wanted to fuck.
(My pussy was an open door—
Many keys turned in my lock,
Not just your lovely cock!)

You're dead,
And in dying you've killed me,
Where once you fulfilled me,
Eating my pussy like it was cake,
Traveling in and out of me,
Penis pleasure almost more than I could take.
But now . . .
Oh . . . the motherfucking pain
Of being bereft again.

Episode Two: The Child.

It died inside me,
Older than us both before it was born.
Slid out of my vagina on its bloody red carpet,
Pussy premiere,
Accolades for a movie never made.
So you fucked me again,
And made another,
A sequel of flesh and blood,
To have and hold as my very own.
The critics all hate it but what do they know?
And what do I care?
This is *my* baby show.

Episode Three: Mad Sexy Grief.

You fucking died.
I'm fucking still alive,
But I might as well have died as well,
'Cos now my life is hell,
With you not here with me,
Without your arms around me,
I can hardly see clearly,
To make it through the day.
Why the fuck'd you go away, honey?
Travelling to that mist-veiled place,
Where I can't just reach out and stroke your face.
At night I long, I pine, for your embrace.

It's not right.
I've visited your grave,
Sat on the cold stones,

Tried to feel you through the Earth,
To make sense of your death,
Of your end that marks no new beginning for me,
No spiritual rebirth.
A dog barked, a crow howled,
The sun stabbed through the trees,
As I guarded your remains,
Remembering how things used to be,
How once we loved, and laughed and were free.
Free as the air,
As the birds and bees,
Kissing, happy, without fear,
Of this future now here.

I walk from your grave,
Slowly, weary and dreary as a slave,
Flogged by a cruel master.
I'm a walking disaster now,
A catastrophe waiting to happen to someone else.

Fuck me, faceless person! Help me remember,
Help me forget.
It doesn't matter, who you are tonight,
Sex is death, every action now I regret.
I orgasm, I come, but you come back too,
Your face . . .
Nothing I do banishes you.
The tears pour as I come,
The pleasure should help, but makes me feel guilty instead,
A one night stand, to mourn the man I can't forget.
Fuck this! I'm going off sex,
What the hell will go wrong next?
My brain?
But how much of that still remains, anyway?
I already feel half-insane,
Like there's sawdust and chipmunks in my head,
And woodpeckers also in there,
Hammering away.

And yet, as the faceless man walks out the door,
(His come in my cunt; feeling great to have scored,)
My epiphany arrives!
I understand—it doesn't matter anymore.

I can be mad as a hatter,
If it helps me survive,
Your death and my subsequent miserable life.
I just need to hide it well in idle chatter,
Postpone my nervous breakdown till I'm all alone,
Safely locked away at home,
And able to enjoy it.
Oh, shit! How fantastic!
I call the faceless man back in and fuck him again,
Moaning: "Thank you, Charlie!" (I hope that's his name?)
He just barely gets it up, (until I give him head),
Then he slides it in and pumps me full-steam-ahead.
And as he's poking me from behind,
A gust of wind blows away the blinds,
And I see you at the window,
Staring in at I, your grieving widow,
With grave disapproval.
"Mourn me!" you plead.
And I, down on hands and knees,
Taking it like a bitch in heat,
Protest:
"But I am, my dead darling, indeed!"
Besides, I no longer care.
I'm mad you see,
And can thus do—screw—who I please.
It's your fault for leaving me.

When I look again, you're gone,
Back to your cold mausoleum.
To your angels or demon girls,
To your mansion in Heaven or torment in Hell.
And I smile back at faceless Charlie,
Who's now fucking me real well,
Breathing hard like he'll soon be deceased himself.

Go for it, Charlie!
I'm fucking my darling, the man I love—out of my mind!
I'm fucking *myself* out of my mind!
I'm fucking . . .

And next day?
I'm now really mad, which is really sad.
But . . . good news!

The fuck worked.
It's over.
Walking in the rain,
The scent of flowers,
Brings your memory again,
But minus the debilitating pain.

By the way . . .
Charlie died of a heart attack,
And the ambulance which took you away,
Had to come back.
I made a date with the hot EMT guy,
For tonight.
He's taking up the slack.

Death is fucking me again.
Death is fucking coming,
Filling up my pussy, filling up my brain.
Death is fucking coming in me.
Soon they'll bring the strait-jacket for me,
But I'll enjoy being deranged until then.

Everything ends,
Life, love, happiness—
Only sadness remains.
But I'd appreciate a warning from the reaper,
Maybe even a letter,
Stating her intent,
To separate true lovers again.

PART 6: GODDESS GAMES

I have been accused of nothing, but convicted of everything
— Felix Johnston

CHAPTER 86

Felix looked around her room of cats. The felines superglued to her walls and ceiling gazed back at her. All their expressions were placid,— she'd just fed them—halfway between sleepy grins and bemused stares.

She smiled. *It's time,* she thought with pleasure. *Time to get this show on the road. Time to get this over with.*

She crossed to her front door and peered up into the sky at the Sunt. The massive vagina-sun dripped light from its slit, bathing the skin sky in a rosy glow that made the pink expanse seem freshly-bathed.

Felix nodded. "I set my trap, but you didn't take the bait," she told the sky. "Fair enough, Old Man, you've set the rules of the game so far—but that's about changing. If you won't come down to me, I'll come up to you."

She frowned at the Sunt. "Shine on, you sexy diamond!"

She reentered the room, enjoying the feel of its bristly floor against her bare legs. She flung off her fur robe and stood naked in the room's middle, her body glowing with a lambency that silhouetted her delicate bones.

Looking around at her slumberous cats, Felix clapped her hands loudly. "Wake up, pussies! It's time!"

CHAPTER 87

"Okay, Dill, keep up the good work."

Money Rich replaced the phone in its cradle. She sat back at her desk, pleased. On her right, framed like a painting in the office window, the leeched-seeming sun dropped into its evening grave beyond the cubist skyline. Smoggy sunset.

So far the robogoons had distributed most of Ned Thomas's (*that pedophile cocksucker bastard*, Money thought angrily, tears misting her eyes again) ground-up remains to his little victim's families. Dillinger had reported back that most of the parents were grateful for the closure the knowledge brought them. From Dillinger's account, there was weeping and tears, and a delicious outpouring of rage and catharsis amongst those who'd watched the accompanying DVD of Ned being ground to mince.

(One family, the Perkins, had kept their 'Ned Brand' cat food in their freezer as a souvenir. They intended holding a yearly remembrance on their daughter's birthday. Money hoped they didn't plan on eating the cat food then.)

That was that then. She was going to carry out a web-search for Ned's clients and send each a copy of the DVD recording and a warning: Stay away from kids, henceforth, or else . . .

She doubted she'd need to do any more.

She relaxed, poured herself a glass of wine. She sipped. The red liquid— a Cabernet Sauvignon—went down smoothly.

It was early evening. *Uncle Luigi should soon call from the Big Apple with news about our drug deal.* The thought of making more money licked her clitoris like a lover. Arousal tingled her thighs. That settled it: *Once Uncle Luigi's called, I'm quitting work for the day . . . going to bed for a long lovemaking session with*

Daddy. She could already feel the dollar-coated, cash-stuffed corpse against her skin, feel the delicious gold dildo stabbing up inside her. (And there was *much* better on the way: *The four money suits I ordered will shortly be delivered. I'll be covered all over by wealth myself while he penetrates me.*)

But till then . . .

She picked up the remote for her office TV, tuned it to *Jerry Springer*, turned up the sound.

***

"So," Jerry was saying, addressing a group of six seated men in slashed denim who looked familiar to Money, but she didn't remember from where, "let's get this right for our viewers at home. You're saying that all of you are actually women?"

"Are we women, Jerry?" The heavily-bearded, muscular speaker gestured with a brawny hand. His voice was rough like cowhide. "Labels are so restricting. Gender identity ain't something you can just put convenient tags on."

Smiling, Jerry turned to the audience. "Male and female works perfectly well for me."

The audience laughed. "For me too!" a fat woman yelled. "Tell 'em, Jerry!"

Jerry turned back to the man. "I'm sorry, guys, I couldn't resist that. But seriously, it's a bit difficult, isn't it—I mean, accepting you all as normal, seeing you with the appearance of one sex and equipment of the other." He paused for effect, then added: "Well, you must admit *it is* odd."

"That's why it's called 'genderqueer,' Jerry. We don't fit into any neat category."

"You're all queer alright!" a heckler yelled. Everyone broke out laughing again.

Two of the men gave the audience the finger. One raised his fists in a fighting pose. "Bring it on, bi—beep!"

"You're the bi—beep, bi—beep!"

Jerry calmed the room. "Okay, settle down, everyone." He looked back at his guests. "Okay, so how do you cope with the ladies? You're musicians—not everyday Joes, or Janes . . . if I may—like the rest of us. While on tour you must get loads of female attention, right?"

Nods from all six men. "You've no idea, Jerry," the youngest of the group, Poppy-Z, said.

(Watching, Money giggled and sipped more wine. *Okay, that's where I remember them from—Femina's backing band!*)

363

"Okay, so say you're on tour with Femina, and some hot mama keeps giving you the eye. Okay, now this before tonight when you're coming out publicly for the first time . . ."

Poppy-Z laughed, ran fingers through his dark hair. "Let's just say, all our strap-ons work extra-hard on the road."

Loud laughter exploded all around the TV studio.

Jerry turned to face the camera. "Now ladies and gents at home, these six gentlemen, better known as Ladies in Disguise, sex diva Femina's backing band, aren't lying. Our show's doctors have examined them and confirmed that yes—they're *all* women, they've all got female plumbing down there." He grinned. "Stay tuned, everyone, we'll be back after the break, when group keyboardist Tony Jones here . . ." he pointed to the heavily bearded man, "is going to show us—by stripping off—that he *really is* a lady in disguise!"

Raucous cheering. The screen cut to a commercial for Diet Pepsi.

***

Money switched channels to the news. A pretty blonde wearing a red dress was anchor.

"Residents of New York City are still uncertain what to make of the newest super-villain in town. No one knows too much about her at the moment, but people are already calling the young woman—who's so far robbed three banks with tremendous loss of life and damage to property—Suicide Girl. Here's CCTV footage from yesterday at the Wells Fargo Bank's Broadway and Grand branch."

Money put her wineglass down and watched intently. The anchorlady had stopped speaking as a video was replayed.

In it, a pretty tattooed redhead of about eighteen or nineteen years old walked into the banking hall. She didn't join a queue. Instead she pulled out a switchblade and yelled out (the sound was a distorted fuzz, but her words were printed onscreen): "Everyone, get down on the floor—this is a robbery!"

The people closest to the redhead quickly got out of her way. "Robbing a bank with a knife?" one man said, his words coming up onscreen. "She's either stoned or a member of al-Qaeda."

(Money didn't find that funny. Two good friends of hers had died in the 9/11 airplane bombings.)

The redhead was clearly incensed that no one was taking her serious. "I said, get your asses on the fucking floor!"

Two people laughed. Two security guards with guns drawn walked over to her. "Hey, miss! Put the knife down!"

Rather than comply with their instructions, however, the redhead put the switchblade to her neck and violently slashed her throat open from left to right.

Money winced as blood spurted from the girl's neck, which yawned open. Falling like rain, it splattered the marble floor. It ran down her front, soaking her t-shirt, outlining her breasts and nipples, revealing that she wasn't wearing a bra.

The bleeding redhead smiled at the stunned security guards, all standing frozen with their mouths open. "Fuck you guys, you should simply have given me some money. You're all gonna regret this." Then she collapsed to the floor, stone dead in the widening pool of blood.

Several women screamed. One fainted.

A little boy pointed at the corpse and giggled. "She's full of red stuff, mummy—is everyone like that?"

Money shivered. Onscreen, one of the bank guards unfroze and made tentative motions towards the dead girl. Then he froze again.

The corpse was bulking up, expanding. The dead girl's clothes ripped off her body, bursting at the seams as she swelled. Her skin turned bright red.

The dead girl sat up, stood up. "I told you assholes you'd all regret it, didn't I?"

Money flung a hand over her mouth and gasped. Her actions reflected those of the onscreen bank customers.

The previously dead girl now stood at least seven feet high, more likely eight. Her body was more muscled than anyone's Money Rich had ever seen in her life—grossly, hideously, so; every muscle hypertrophied beyond belief, like she drank anabolic steroids for milkshake—muscle definition to shame the entire pantheon of Mr. Universe winners. Her crimson form was totally naked (with a shrub of red pubic hair), but her sheer bulk negated the concept of sexuality. Her breasts were pancake-flat spreads on massive pectorals like concrete slabs. Her nipples looked like pinheads.

Her head seemed almost an afterthought now. It remained normal-sized despite her body's expansion, a mountain peak on the massive triangular neck that expanded out to her shoulders. Her teeth were large and blunt, her eyes a dull glowing orange.

She no longer had the dying gash in her throat.

Money felt a sudden gush of heat in her cunt. It wasn't sex; it was the power this creature—Money couldn't honestly think of her as a woman now—radiated. *She's a primal force come to life. Damn, if I had this chick as my bodyguard . . .*

The bank guards reacted. One raised his gun. "Just calm down, lady. No one needs to get hurt."

Suicide Girl laughed. "No one except you, you mean." She swatted the man aside with a hand the size of his torso. The CCTV camera angle shifted, tracking the guard as he flew all the way across the banking hall to smash into a wall. The impact exploded the man: When he slumped to the ground, he left a mess of blood and brain matter on the wall, along with a deep indent.

The other guard began shooting. The slugs bounced off Suicide Girl's body. Laughing, she reached out and grabbed the guard's head, popping it like a pimple. Hair and brain tissue squirted out between her fingers.

She spun round to face the cashiers. "Now where is my damn money!? And I want a lot of it!"

By now all the customers were screaming and fleeing the bank, blocking the efforts of arriving security guards to get in.

"Where is my fucking money!?" Suicide Girl punched the marble counter in front of her. The part she hit disintegrated to powder. The female cashier sitting behind it disintegrated also, her body ripped to pieces by chunks of fist-dislodged (and critically accelerated) flying masonry.

Money gaped, as, automatic gunfire ricocheting off her broad over-muscled back like she was made of Kevlar, the crimson amazon waded through the bank's walls, screaming, "Where is the manager!? I said—where is the fucking bank manager!? Or do I have to fucking kill everyone in this fucking building to make my fucking withdrawal!?"

The image dissolved back to the blonde anchorwoman. She (with a clearly dishonest attempt at gravity) said: "This last robbery cost the Wells Fargo bank two hundred thousand dollars in cash, as well as the death of fourteen staff and so far unassessed damage to vehicles and property. Now we cut to New York City Hall, where Mayor Priscilla Presley is currently holding a press conference on the Suicide Girl situation.

***

Money poured herself a second glass of wine. She'd wanted to finish watching *Jerry Springer* with the big reveal on Ladies in Disguise, but this was way more interesting. She could always TiVo a *Jerry* rerun.

Onscreen:

Flanked by city council members and stone-faced security men, New York City mayor Priscilla Presley—a slim well-preserved middle-aged brunette—regarded the mob of reporters facing her with a harassed expression.

"The public wishes to know, Mayor: What is your administration doing to ensure their safety in the face of this new menace?"

Mayor Presley cleared her throat loudly. "I'd first like to ask everyone not to panic. Now, to answer your question: We are currently making every attempt to apprehend this dangerous woman. No avenue to bring her to justice is being left unexplored. I can't reveal what the police have so far uncovered, of course, but I assure everyone that their investigations are making progress and that we believe an arrest will shortly be made." She forced a cool smile. "Yes, the Empire State News reporter?"

"Mayor," a thin man began, "with the death toll currently at twenty-nine, what advice would you give to citizens?"

"A good question. I would advise the obvious: keep well away from any young woman who holds a knife to her throat and threatens to kill herself. I believe this is the normal procedure with suicides. Call the police. I repeat—keep *well* away from her. Do not attempt to engage her in any way whatever."

"Thank you, Mayor,"

"The lady from the Post?"

Money tuned out the discussion. She couldn't get Suicide Girl's brutal display out of her head. *What stupendous power! Just incredible!* Money was more than a little pissed-off—in fact, she felt extremely cheated. *Why is it that the really cool criminals always go to New York? More TV face-time? Damn! What I could do if I had this chick working for me; but no, she has to go for Bright Lights, Big City. Soon we'll have Suicide Girl on Broadway—the musical.*

She tuned her mind back to the press conference.

"But rest assured, New Yorkers, your elected city government is leaving no stone unturned in our search for this criminal. Suicide Girl can run but she can't hide. Superpowers or not, our forces of justice are more than a match for her. She will be arraigned in our courts to answer for her crimes." The mayor coughed. "All branches of the NYPD are currently on high alert. Every reported sighting of this so-called Suicide Girl will be instantly investigated. We ask all citizens to be watchful for this female menace." She smiled coldly. "The city's webcop force are particularly desperate to catch her, preferably in her transformed state. They think she'll make a massive amount of cat food."

This last statement triggered a lot of laughter.

Smiling, Mayor Presley indicated a haggard little woman furiously waving her hand. "Jessica Loren from the New York Times?"

"Do you think it appropriate, Mayor Presley, to make cat-food jokes at this time?"

Priscilla Presley sneered. "It's not a joke, Ms. Loren. I assure you, the webcops do think Suicide Girl will make excellent cat food."

More laughter.

"But, surely, Mayor—"

Jessica Loren never finished her question, because Priscilla Presley suddenly disappeared. Vanished in broad daylight from behind her wooden lectern.

All hell broke loose. The government officials flanking the mayor took a baffled moment to confirm that Priscilla Presley hadn't ducked down behind the lectern, or somehow slipped between them unnoticed, then pandemonium reigned. Men and women began running helter-skelter. Security men were seen shouting into walkie-talkies and rushing the other city council members up the City Hall steps. All was confusion.

The gathered reporters, quickly realizing the news potential of Priscilla's disappearance, quickly set up cameras and began filming on-the-spot reports.

***

About to refill her glass when the New York mayor disappeared, Money froze. Slowly, keeping her eyes glued to the milling onscreen confusion, she set both wine bottle and glass down.

Oh, fuck, she thought. *Not today. Hell, no!*

She muted the TV, which had now switched back to in-studio (with NYC as a small inset window), and which was already showing the first of a predictably endless series of 'Mayor Presley Vanishes' special reports.

Money got up, walked over to stare out her office window at the sky. Evening cloaked the building-strewn horizon; a familiar dread cloaked her soul. *Shit! This can only mean one thing!*

Her cellphone rang, startling her. She walked briskly back to her desk and picked it up. "Hello, Freddie, Money here." She listened to the breathless rush of words that followed. "What!!!?" She sat down, breathing hard and angrily. "The bitches were in the hotel the whole time? . . . You didn't open the email? . . . Yes, I know that! . . . One's dead? . . . Which one? . . . Good!!!"

She calmed herself, refilling her wineglass while speaking, her eyes occasionally flickering to the TV screen, where perplexed studio panel discussion was being intercut with replays of the astonishing scenes from New York City Hall.

Money sipped some wine. "Okay," she told Fred coldly, "first of all, please accept my honest condolences on Uncle Luigi's death. He was a great guy—we'll all miss him." She paused. "But . . . I expect *you* to clean up this mess. No one steals from me and lives to enjoy their ill-gotten gains. Now listen, here's how we're gonna handle it . . ."

CHAPTER 88

The Black Hawk helicopter hummed across the neon-lit landscape with its profusion of hand-leaved trees. The purple sun flickered like strobe-lighting.

The throb of the chopper engines, the monotonous sound of its propellers (like sped-up train wheels), the machine's vibration as it flew, made Ash feel like she and Skunk were meat in a grinder, or churning digestive juice in a metal monster's belly.

Skunk pointed. "There! That's the Everywhere Freeway."

Ash saw where she meant. Up ahead, a gray line on the distant horizon intersected their current course.

She relaxed back into her pilot's seat, relieved to have a landmark to navigate to. The landscape they'd been flying over was depressing. Its dark gloom wasn't what she needed at this time. Over and over again, she kept reliving that horrible moment when she'd found Raye dead.

How did Ash feel? Like her heart was literally broken. Skunk's comment about feeling soulless made perfect sense now. At the moment, flying the helicopter or crashing it? Both seemed one and the same.

I'm overreacting, she realized with a start. *Yes, I loved Raye with all my heart and now she's gone. But committing suicide won't bring her back again. What the hell is wrong with me?* Her eyes widened a tad. *Oh, it's this goddamn neon disco-scape.*

The landscape wasn't just depressing. Worse, it was perplexing—mind-bending. Left and right of Ash as she flew the chopper, she caught glimpses of other skies and suns, in palettes of unlikely colors—blue/green; red/white; yellow/brown—juxtaposed to this night/neon one, each linkage seemingly an impossibly smooth transition. Simple as exiting one room into another. Just like . . .

369

Just like entering Endless Street's Nighttime Zone, she realized.

"Where exactly are we headed?" she asked.

"A close friend of mine lives across the freeway."

Ash didn't question her further. It was somewhere to head for.

She became aware of a different ambience in the cockpit. It finally hit her what the change was. She glanced at Skunk for confirmation. Yes, she'd now switched off her vibrators, and removed the one in her vagina.

Ash corrected the helicopter's course, glad she didn't have to listen to her companion groaning out her latest orgasm.

***

Close up to the Everywhere Freeway, they flew over a high cliff bordering a black sea. Atop the cliff stood a solitary white house.

"Who in the world lives out here?" Ash asked. "The unfriendly ghost?"

"Fred's girlfriend Vola," Skunk replied. "She's quite the hen, but dynamite in bed."

"You would know, wouldn't you? I won't ask how." Her expression turned worried. "Hey, wait! Fred . . . comes up here?"

"Don't worry about it. He'll never find us."

"How can you be sure?"

"Bizarro is endless, and has strange linkages. Some planes transect others, some overlap. He could be standing right next to us and not see us."

"Didn't seem that way down in Endless Street. We saw everything."

"You only *thought* you saw every—"

"Hey!" Ash yelped. "What's this on my body?"

Skunk hid a smile. Ash's arms, legs, and face had suddenly become mottled with brown and gold.

Ash stared horrified at her weird-colored hands on the whirlybird's controls, then at Skunk, who still looked normal. "What's happening? My skin's scaly, like I'm turning into a snake. My nails are black like claws."

"Good thing you can't see your tongue."

"Huh?"

Skunk grinned. "Just joking. Don't fret over it, it's just an effect of the zone—think of it as ultra-realistic body-painting. It'll clear up in a moment. Look—it's already started fading." Her amusement became full-blown laughter. "Good thing we're not walking, or in a car. Then you'd *really* have something to get pissed-off about. You should ask Fred about that."

Ash didn't reply; she found the effect too realistic to joke about. She counted seconds while the snake patterning faded completely off her skin, then almost immediately afterward noticed something else that was odd, this time outside the chopper:

"Hey, where the hell's that?"

"Do you mean the checkerboard landscape with the huge castles and warring knights and the yellow-brown patchwork sky overhead, or the vista of burning buildings beyond it?"

"The first. No, both."

"The checkerboard place is Chessland; loads of chess-pieces come to life. The burning place is Hell—a version of New York City. Fucked-up like nothing you've ever seen in your life. A branch of the Everywhere Freeway leads to it, if you'd like to visit sometime. Or, we could detour over there now for a quick peek."

"No thanks!"

***

They'd reached the freeway The helicopter floated over it like a Made-in-the-USA metal angel.

"Widest road I've ever seen."

"You ain't seen nothin', darling. Close to Bypass Station, it expands to almost city-width."

"I really don't want to see that."

On the freeway's other side, the neon darkness ended with the abruptness of death by a gunshot wound to the head. Suddenly the sky was rosy pink.

Healthy pink, Ash couldn't help thinking. The ground below was a flesh-toned desert with bruise-purple dunes at its farthest reaches.

Then she saw the shining vagina dominating the sky ahead.

"HOLY SHIT!"

Skunk grinned at her. "Don't let the Sunt freak you out, we're almost there."

"Not freak me out? The sky were flying through can't be skin like it looks, and—"

In a seamless transition, Ash was suddenly no longer piloting the Black Hawk helicopter, but instead driving a white BMW sedan along a normal two-lane highway through the flesh-toned landscape.

Her head threatened to burst. "What just happened?" she asked in a tight, cold voice.

"Take it easy. It's a normal transition around here. Some sectors alter your vehicle to their optimum mode of transport. Helicopters clearly aren't welcome beyond this point."

Ash glanced up through the car's windshield. The vagina-sun dominated her vision, the surrounding sky looking like thighs flanking it. It was too much. She did the only logical thing, pulled over to the roadside and parked. She leaned back, head on the headrest, breathing heavily.

"I really don't need this now," she said softly. Then: "The money—is it gone too?"

Skunk shook her head. "It's still all here, in the back."

Ash heaved a deep sigh. "That's a relief. I'd kill myself if I'd just been through all that for nothing."

"Just relax," Skunk said, reaching across a hand and stroking Ash's cheek. "Just relax."

She slid the hand lower, into Ash's T-shirt, in turn cupping and stroking her breasts.

Ash didn't stop Skunk's explorations. Her body trembled from the other woman's caresses.

***

They fucked outside on the BMW's hood. Skunk took Ash gently, like she was a virgin.

"No," Ash said, when Skunk made to insert a vibrator into herself, "I don't want your monsters—I'm too vulnerable right now—I just want you."

Skunk smiled down at her. "This is long overdue. I've wanted you too since I first set eyes on you."

"You've already had me," Ash said, with a hint of sadness.

"From a distance. Not like I will now I have your consent."

Ash, her back on the windshield, her thighs spread wide, knees locked, bare feet flat on the hood, yielded to Skunk, melting like butter when the other woman tongued her clitoris and slid saliva-wet fingers into her.

Arms motionless by her sides, she wept while Skunk fucked her, tears streaming down her cheeks.

It's over, she thought. *We fucking did it.* And yet, her triumph was empty—there was no Raye to share it with.

Just as depression threatened to swamp her, she heard a click and the hum of a vibrator starting up, then another.

Next, Ash felt her labia spread wide. She gasped as Skunk slid the vibrator into her dripping sex. Her sensations kicked up a notch; she flooded with moisture. The vibrations seemed to pulse from her vagina through her entirety—not just her body, but also her mind and soul. Her depression fled her with scared fluttering wings.

She gasped again, moaning and biting her lip, when Skunk spread her buttocks and pushed the second vibrator into her anus.

She reached for Skunk. Skunk pushed her hands away. "Don't move. Just let me love you."

Ash nodded and lay limp again.

The hood dipped as Skunk climbed fully onto it. She licked up Ash's body, her tongue first wetting Ash's red pubic hair, then sliding—inch by excruciating inch to Ash's navel. Up her rib cage, teasing the underside of her breasts.

Ash orgasmed when Skunk's lips reached her left nipple. Still crying profusely, the feeling exploded through her like she was Dresden being bombed during WWII. It was indescribable, like she'd big-banged and become a personal universe. She was the sun—Sol—being born. She was the nine chunks blowing off it to form planets; she was life beginning in Earth's seas, the first woman and man, Eve and Adam; she was Jehovah's ten plagues over Egypt, Moses parting the Red Sea . . .

Her celestial glory contracted back to Skunk licking up her neck, sucking on her voice-box, tongue slithering up over her chin, biting her lower lip, teasing the soft flesh . . . then they were kissing each other, their tongues warring for dominance of salivary oral caverns.

Ash stared deep into Skunk's eyes, feeling a love unknown before, a rush of emotion that swamped her. Her flow of tears finally dried.

Skunk pulled away, looked down at her. "I'm loving you," she said, "like only one woman can love another—a blending like milk being mixed. Yin and Yin, two dark spiral halves forming a delicious, if imperfect whole. But then, who's to say what's perfect or not?"

She dropped her lips back over Ash's, dropped her hands back down to manipulate the vibrators plugging her orifices. The vibrator in Ash's rectum was just about popping out. Skunk slid it fully back inside her.

Another orgasm raged through Ash. Then another, then yet another. Soon, her gaze riveted on the vagina-sun overhead, she was screaming with pleasure. And still Skunk made love to her on the hood of the white car— its doors open wide like it was a bird in flight—an endless fuck continuum.

Finally, the pleasure became too much for Ash. She felt it rip her apart at her seams. With a last ecstatic scream, she fainted.

CHAPTER 89

Femina – Ghosts

Each time you fuck me,
The ghosts of my previous lovers raise their deformed heads,
Threatening to turn my bed,
Into a cemetery,
And my womb into a temple of the dead.

The pleasure of me fucking you haunts them,
Taunts them.
The liquid ghosts,
(All that dead come,
That went nowhere, became no one;
All the pleasure we shared, that became no bond,
Strong enough to keep us together, so we each moved on.)
They disapprove of you,
But that means nothing,
(I approve of you!)
What does is this present glorious stuffing,
This ecstasy-like-suffering.
The ghosts shriek with rage,
As you plow me with glee,
And turn my each sexual page,
Oh so tenderly.
They scream: "He used to be me!"

Fuck them, those memories refusing to fade!
They're each filling other women's cunts now,
But still lay claim to me.
We fuck!
The ghosts are persistent,
Their jealous voices insistent:
"He's crap! I did it better!"
"So," I retort, "why aren't we still together?"
Sorry, I know that's unfair,
We're not comparing in-bed performance here,
And concerning disappointments,
In me you had your fair share.
We really parted because we didn't care,
Enough about each other,
To sail together,
Through stormy emotional weather . . .
But you started it,
Assholes of my mental shit.

The ghosts don't like you one bit,
I think your penis just poked one in the cheek.
Die, you fucking memories!
(Memories of fucking?)
Vamoose with your lies!
Begone! Or little Johnny's shortly going to jism your eyes!

You spurt your seed in me,
And the ghosts they flee.
They depart, bereaved.
Still, nothing is achieved,
'Cos I know,
Once . . . if . . . *when* you go,
You'll leave behind your own ghosts.

CHAPTER 90

Fred put the phone down and frowned grimly at Lana. "Money sends her condolences over Big Tony's death." He pointed to the two cases. "She says to give you the drugs so the Philly guys know we're a reliable source." He looked pointedly at Lana. "You don't breathe a word about what happened here."

Lana Petrova, visibly shaken and still sticky with webcop web-silk, nodded slowly, then asked, "And the stolen cash? What will you do about that? Two million dollars is a lot of money to lose."

"I'll look for it. She's holding me responsible for finding it."

Lana scowled. "That is bullshit. You didn't rob yourself."

Fred smiled. "Someone has to be held responsible. Don't worry your head about it. It won't really be me looking. You know how Chicago operates—they'll contact everyone everywhere. Those two women won't be safe anywhere on the planet." (Fred, however, momentarily wondered if Ash and Skunk were still on the planet, or if they'd somehow found their way to Bizarro. It was highly unlikely—but the monster. . .) He pointed to Raye's corpse, then Eddie's. "In a way, these two got off lightly."

Lana shuddered. "I will be going then."

Fred nodded. "Yes, do, before the cops come." He retrieved Big Tony's gun from under the desk, placed it atop it. He frowned. "You know, Lana. I never wanted to be a gangster—just an honest man doing an honest job—"

"Our fate chooses us," she said. "I too have led a checkered life. Once I was popular in Mother Russia, then I was no one. Here too, in wonderful America, I loved Tony, and now he is gone." Tears brimmed in her blue eyes. "Where did he go, Freddie? My big strong American lover. Where did my Tony go!?"

She burst into tears.

Despite hating her for all the humiliation she'd been party to putting him through, Fred couldn't let Lana Petrova weep uncomforted. He stepped close, wrapped her in his arms. "There, there—it'll be okay. You'll see."

She wept into his shirt a while, then they separated. She wiped her eyes, smiled sadly. "I'm not sorry for how I made fun of you with the dog, because it was fun. And you came good when it sexed you. Orgasm is orgasm—all is wonderful, whether with man, woman, or animal. But I promise not to do it again, okay?"

Fred managed a smile. "Since you put it like that . . ." Then he remembered. *Oh, yes, the dog!* "Hey, Bitch! time to go home!"

At the mention of her name, the previously forgotten Doberman raised her head from where she'd been napping atop the dead shark.

"I'm really going to have a time explaining how that fish got in here," Fred said as Bitch shook herself to her feet.

"You will need to think very good," Lana said. "The other one downstairs is much bigger than this—like it came from the Spielberg movie. When it crashed beside me, I thought the world had ended."

Fred gaped at her. Another shark? He rushed to the window, peered down into the street. "Holy shit! It looks like someone opened it up and filleted it." His voice became grim. "And also like it was eating someone when it died."

He turned back into the room, snapped his fingers at the dog. "Okay, girl, time to go home. Cops'll be here soon."

Bitch leapt down off the shark. Rather than head for Lana, however, the dog rushed to Fred's side and sat down. She began nuzzling his leg.

"No, no, little doggie," Lana said, extending a hand to Bitch, "you have sucked enough human sex organ, drank enough sperm. Come home now. I will find you a nice strong hound to sex with."

She stroked the Doberman's head. "Let's go."

The dog refused to budge. She dug her feet into the bloodstained carpet and growled threateningly at Lana.

Fred colored with sudden realization. *She wants to stay here? With me? True, Felix told me to look after this dog, but . . . Shit!*

Lana's smile turned impatient. "Come on, Bitch, you cannot stay here and be sucking Freddie all day long. That joke is over." She reached down and grabbed Bitch's collar, then shook her head at Fred. "I never liked how Tony refused to use a leash on this dog. Discipline is essential with animals or they take one for granted, and a cocaine-addict dog is even—" her face clouded with sudden pain. "YEEEOOOOW!!!"

She and Fred both gaped at Bitch. The dog had sunk her fangs deep into Lana's left hand and was shaking it fiercely. Blood welled from the tooth punctures. Lana squeezed her eyes shut and let off another loud scream. She began jerking her hand to free it.

Fred tried to prize Bitch's jaws apart. It was no use—the dog clamped down tighter each time he achieved any separation between her teeth.

Meanwhile, she was severely mangling Lana's left hand. The beautiful Russian blonde had stopped screaming. Her face, however told a tale of horrible pain, agony she was barely holding in check. Blood now spurted freely from the widening wounds in her hand. Bitch's mouth was painted red. Fred put all his energy into another futile attempt to get the Doberman's teeth out of Lana's hand.

Then Lana grabbed the pistol on the desk.

"Stand back, Freddie," she said coldly.

He pulled his bloody hands off Bitch's jaws, stared at her in alarm. "Lana don't!"

"Shut up, you fool! I am not dog food." She placed the gun muzzle against Bitch's sloping forehead, pulled the trigger.

Boom! Bitch's head exploded.

The dog instantly collapsed. Lana dropped the pistol. She and Fred finally got Bitch's teeth out of her flesh. Fred winced at the semicircle of deep punctures that still bubbled blood.

Lana stood up. She kicked the dead dog violently. Twice. "Stupid mutt. Now I have to take rabies shots." She looked coldly at Fred, her frigid gaze tinged with worry. "You don't have AIDS, do you?"

He stared at her perplexed. "Huh?"

"You ejaculated in the stupid dog's mouth. Maybe your come is now in my wounds."

Fred kept a straight face. He shook his head. "No I don't have AIDS."

"Good," she replied, without the slightest hint of irony.

Fred bandaged Lana's hand with one of Uncle Luigi's handkerchiefs. He nodded at it. "Best you get that to hospital . . . quick."

Her beautiful reddened lips twisted into a sneer. "I'm not a wimp. I have survived greater pain than this. Now the bleeding is stopped, I will deliver the drugs home first and set up the collection, *then* I will go for treatment."

Fred nodded grimly. "As you wish, lady." He plucked the desk phone from its cradle. "I'll get Edmond up to carry the cases downstairs."

He spoke to Edmond Flourish: "Yes, right now; have Jody man reception. Tell the guests we apologize for the disturbance—the rest of their stay is on us. . . . What!? . . . Ed, I'm in no mood for jokes; Uncle Luigi's dead, Big Tony too. . . . No, he wasn't shot. . . . *No,* he didn't have a heart attack either—you'll see for yourself when you get up here; just hurry up. . . . What? . . . You're weren't joking?"

He hung up then stared at Lana, clearly perplexed over something.

"You look like you just saw Elvis's ghost," she said, wincing with pain.

"Worse than that. The King's widow just vanished into thin air in broad daylight. In front of a hundred witnesses."

Lana's eyes widened. "Mayor Presley? Disappeared? You cannot be serious."

"Edmond says it's on all the TV channels." He shrugged. "Today just got a whole lot stranger."

CHAPTER 91

Femina – Get Between

Once you see my pubic hair,
(You just want to) Get between my legs.
How come you're never scared,
(All you want's to) Get between my legs.
And honey, what will you find there?
(Treasure, treasure and pleasure.)

I stand up, I turn around,
My panties float down to the ground.
You devour me with greedy eyes,
When you want a fuck you never criticize.
You just want, you just want . . .

All the guys say:

I want your sexy thing,
That musky smelling scene,
Your superlative thing.
I'll treat you like a queen,
Buy you cars and diamond rings,
Just let me have that one thing.
I NEED to have your thing!
Can't live with your thing!

Living without your thing,
Is driving me insane!
I've got to ride your thighs,
(Wow, girl, your ass looks like the moon!)
Up to the sexy skies.
(Damn, girl, I hope I don't come too soon,
Hope I don't metamorphose into a buffoon,
Once I'm enclosed in your tight cocoon!)
I gotta get right in-between,
Gotta get in-between,
Gotta be a sex machine,
Digging on that old-school scene!
I need that tight, sweet, soft, slick,
I know you're oh so sensitive,
Down there,
Oh, come here, baby, let me have a lick—
Of your pussy, babe!

Once you see my pubic hair,
(You just want to) Get between my legs.
How come you're never scared,
(All you want's to) Get between my legs.
And honey, what will you find here?
(Treasure, treasure and pleasure)
But you could have an STD,
I want safe sex, safe sex.
Condoms? Damn, baby, you really came prepared.

All the girls reply:

You want my sexy thing,
My squishy sexy thing.
You treat me like a queen,
(Oh, you've got ways and means!)
Just to get your penis in-between.
You want to ride my hips,
(Like my thighs are horses,)
Glide inside my lower lips.
(Sucked in by nether forces,
That you guys can't resist!)
I'm wise to all your tricks,
And the reason you want this—
Us to have a 'relationship.'

You want my punany,
You want this fine pussy?
You want to enter me,
And fill me up with come?
I'll let you enter me,
Because you're so damn handsome,
And I like having fun.
Wow, I love the way you make me laugh,
So yes, you *can* fuck me in the bath.
Yes, get me soapy wet,
(You like the scent of my bubble bath?)
I love the way you spread my ass.
(Gripping those cheeks hard with both hands!)
You like this pussy, babe?
Is it everything that you dreamed?
See how you're moaning now,
Now that you're in-between?
I like the way you fuck it,
You like the way I work it.
Oh, God, I think I'm coming!
Not think . . . I am coming!
You too, boy? Yes pump it in!
Give my cat her dose of cream.

All the fat girls say, hi!
All the skinny girls say, hi!
Newsflash, girls:
It doesn't matter what you look like,
Guys still want what's between your legs.
Young, old, pitch-black, or milk-white,
Guys are willing to die,
To achieve what's between your thighs.
Yeah, they'll chase that pussy into the sweet by and by,
Gunfighters in the afterlife,
Fighting angels to survive.
They gotta have it!
(Have what, Femina!?)
They gotta have it!
(Have what, Femina!?)
Men gotta have pussy!
'Cos pussy is Forever!
Pussy is Forever!

Redhead, brunette, black-haired, blond,
It don't matter once you've got a cunt.
That's all guys really want,
Your brains are redundant.

Tall, short, fat, thin,
Rich girl, poor girl, beggar, thief,
Satanist or 'Born Again,'
Hare Krishna or atheist;
Guy's don't fuck your religious beliefs,
Your good deeds or personality,
Just your delectable fanny.

Pretty, ugly, frumpy, lumpy,
Bow-legged Louise,
Or knock-kneed Shelly;
Guys don't care 'bout such minor shit,
They just wanna get down with your hidden bits.
Fucking you hard while they squeeze your tits.

Fat ass, no ass,
Farm girl slob or catwalk class,
Airhead or Mensa IQ,
Anorexic, BBW;
Penis really likes you.
Yeah, penis REALLY likes you.

You could be a super athlete,
With toned arms and legs,
Or quadriplegic in a wheelchair,
Autistic—emotionally challenged,
With a mental age of twelve.
No matter, once you've a slit down there.
It's alright now, you vulnerable girls,
(No need to spend so much time reading you become a bookshelf!)
Penis loves you even if you don't love yourself.

Tramp girl stinks like a garbage dump,
And her armpits look like mangrove swamps,
Infested by sci-fi worms.
Crotch got so much hair, it looks like a hamster,
But her boyfriend, he just wants to hump her.

Don't worry, honey,
Just spread those cheeks,
This is one beauty contest all girls win.
All pussies are grey once the lights dim.

The Dark Side of the Fuck:

Even when you've got breast cancer,
Some guys still wanna grab ya,
Even cervical cancer.
 (Say what, Femina?)
It's true! Morbid but true!
They still want to put in you!
Guys'll do anything for a screw!
Some men are dogs, rabbits, pigs.
"Honey, let me get this straight:
You still find me pretty despite chemotherapy?
What? That's what *true* devotion is?
It's called 'for better or worse sex?'"
Your hair falls out, they'll jerk off with it,
Instead of taking you shopping to buy a wig.
Your teeth fall out, and they'll ask for head!
I'm trying to get inside guys' heads,
Their sex drive makes no sense.
Just flash your ass and spread your legs, and . . .
They'll fuck you to death on your hospital bed,
Fuck you into the grave on your dying bed.
What the hell is wrong with the opposite sex?

Coda/Reprise:

The girls are pleading:

Oh, guys, please have mercy,
Have mercy on poor pussy.
She tries her utmost best,
But she really needs a rest.
She doesn't mean to be a tease,
She does her best to please.
It's just biology,
We need understanding.
Give pussy TLC.
Pussy needs TLC.

But the guys are replying:

Screw that pussycat!
We'll never let vagina relax!
We're telling you that for a fact!
We gotta have, gotta have, gotta have . . . !

CHAPTER 92

When Lana had departed after Edmond Flourish (who'd left stupefied by the inconceivable mode of Uncle Luigi's death), Fred sat on the office desk and reflected. Edmond hadn't yet called the cops, he'd been unable to during the robbery—for some reason all external communications had jammed, and afterwards, he'd been waiting for Uncle Luigi's instructions. Which was smart, Fred reflected; it gave him time to tidy up a bit.

Owning the Hotel Bizarre (as Luigi's Rossi's sole heir) didn't excite Fred one bit. It would have, but for the mob connections. Money Rich, to be precise. And now her two million bucks was missing . . .

"Oh, fuck!" he said aloud. "Ashley Status and whoever you are—monster-vagina woman—you'd better run and never stop running, 'cos once you decide you're tired . . . you're fried."

He felt no anger toward Ash. Nor any sense of debt. *Yes, she kept the other skinny woman from killing me, but I saved her and Raye's asses too—at least I tried to. If I'd told Uncle Luigi they were here, they'd be back in Chicago now.* A lump caught in his throat. *And Uncle Luigi would likely still be alive.*

He regarded Raye's corpse, wincing on remembering her as she'd been—plump, pretty, and vivacious. *Not staring emptied-eyed at nothing like now, her mouth open wide like a blow-up sex doll. And no burial? The webcops are definitely gonna make pet food out of her. A damn shame!*

And beside Raye's corpse lay Bitch—the dog's head even more exploded than the brunette's.

Fred stood up. The office was too depressing. He walked out into the corridor, found little difference—there were corpses here too. Even more of them, male bodies broken and mangled like God had smashed them with a hammer.

Fred stared glumly around the corridor, at the gaping holes in the walls, at the dislodged, scattered masonry, at the ripped and warped exposed patches of the hotel's steel skeleton. At the blood splashed everywhere. *Yep, we've a hell of a lot of cleanup to do once the cops have been and gone.*

He looked around a moment longer, then decided: *Screw it! I need a lift!*

There was a small vial of coke in Uncle Luigi's desk. Fred returned to the office to get it, then instantly leapt back into the doorway in alarm and stood there shivering, the blood draining from his face.

Not again.

Bitch's body was altering. The dead Doberman pinscher's spilled brains were slurping back into her head, her destroyed skull repairing itself over them. Worse/odder still than the knitting skull, the dog's body was visibly growing larger, her limbs getting longer. She was also losing her fur, except on her head, which, once the skull was completely repaired, sprouted long black hair. The face flattened, the ears shortened . . .

Fred's mind wiped clean of all thoughts of cocaine. Horrified, he jabbed a finger at the ongoing transformation. *The dead dog—Bitch! Sh . . . sh . . . she's be . . . be . . becoming . . . a human woman!*

***

The transformation on the office floor ended. The woman who'd been Bitch opened her eyes and got to her feet. She looked around and saw Fred.

She grinned at him. "Hi, Freddie."

Fred gaped back speechless at her. She was almost as tall as himself and very pretty. She was of course naked. Her body was very well built, small-breasted and athletic, with almost canine muscle definition. Her night-dark eyes, prominent cheekbones, Roman nose, and milk-chocolate skin suggested Native American ancestry.

She kept grinning at Fred like she was expecting him to say something.

He found his voice. "Who . . . who . . . who are you?"

She extended her hand for a shake. "Rebecca Johnston. LAPD narcotics department."

Fred shook her hand. She stretched and groaned. "Please don't ask me to explain how I became a dog."

Fred nodded. "Okay."

Rebecca Johnston sighed, a long exhalation of breath. "You have no idea how long I've been waiting for someone to kill me so I can become human again. The rules say I can't commit suicide. If I do, I simply transform into another mutt. I'll be forever grateful to Lana Petrova."

The color slowly returned to Fred's face. "What are you talking about?"

She waved a languid hand. "I'll tell you later." She pointed to Raye's corpse. "Help me get her clothes off."

"Don't bother," Fred said, with more confidence. "You look about Femina's size. I'm sure she'll have something that'll fit you. Or one of her backing singers will."

Rebecca turned from the dead woman. "Okay, lead the way." She smiled at Fred, placed a soft hand on his shoulder. "Don't worry, baby, I really like you. We're gonna have some great times toge—Damn!" She grabbed her head, clamped her eyes shut and grimaced like she was in great pain.

"Are you okay?"

The pain left her face. She opened her eyes. Fred immediately noted all the playfulness had left her. "What's the matter?"

Rebecca smiled sadly. "Nothing you'd understand. *It's time.*"

"Time for what?"

She gave a forced laugh, stroked his cheek. "You're real cute, you know. That's why I started giving you blowjobs." Her expression turned dead serious again. "Freddie, I gotta go—it's time. Hold a rain check for me on those dates—I might see you again."

He had no idea what to think. He didn't *want* to think. "What are you talking about?"

Rebecca leaned forward and kissed him tenderly on the lips. "See you around, baby."

Before he could reply, she faded from view. One moment she was there, the next, like darkness melting into light when drapes are opened, she was gone.

Fred stared in confusion at the empty spot where she'd been just moments before.

Then he stared down at the empty spot on the carpet where Bitch had recently lain. He shrugged, grinned. *Yeah, that's right—I just had a discussion with a dead dog that became a gorgeous Indian woman with the hots for me, and then she vanished before my eyes. Oh, yeah, I'm keeping this to myself. I'm not breathing a . . . hold on a minute, didn't Edmond just say Mayor Presley also just disappeared?*

The office phone rang. Fred picked it up.

"Yes, Edmond? . . . *What!?* Femina just vanished from the lobby!? . . . Leaving all her clothes behind?"

CHAPTER 93

Now, as Ash steered the white BMW down the highway, she was much calmer. Indeed, she felt radiant, like the sex—incredible, she disbelieved just how incredible—had purged her of her demons. She felt renewed, strong enough even to go through the just-concluded robbery again. At the moment, Raye's tragic, traumatic passing was a distant, passion-obscured event.

She grinned at Skunk, reached across to squeeze her thigh. She was grateful for this gift the woman had given her.

"Thanks," she said with deep feeling.

Skunk smiled tightly back. "We're almost there. You can just see it in the distance."

Ash smiled understandingly. She knew why Skunk was so tense. *See? You shouldn't have refused to let me fuck you in return when I came out of my faint. No problem—I'll do you too when we reach your friend's house. It'll be the best sex you've ever had.*

She squeezed Skunk's thigh again, then refocused her attention on the road ahead, the grey line that continued into the interminable distance.

She relaxed back in the BMW's bucket seat and shifted gears, thrilling in the rush of power and acceleration as the car surged forward, a white beast eating up the highway.

Occasionally, she grinned up at the vagina-sun gleaming benediction down on the world—on her.

***

A hulking gray blur appeared suddenly on their left, travelling parallel to the BMW at immense speed. Ash braked just in time as the gray object swerved across the road. She stared at it, blinking in wonderment as it dug itself into the ground on the other side.

It was . . .

"That is a metal fish with legs," she blurted out as the monster's armor-plated tail vanished belowground. "*Lots* of legs. And it's so huge—bigger than an airplane!"

Skunk gave a preoccupied nod. "It's a meta-whale. Harmless enough, but a nuisance because it has an attraction to roads. And it goes without saying that you don't want to crash into one—be like ramming into a tank." She gestured over at the gaping chasm in the earth the behemoth had left in its wake (large enough, in Ash's opinion, to tip a house into). "This one's clearly lost—they're normally found in the sectors north of here, close to Bypass Station, where there's roads galore." She shrugged. "It'll keep flipping around and digging everywhere up till it finds its way home again."

Ash nodded. "Skunk?"

"Yeah?"

"Is the ground inside that hole raw meat, or is that just my imagination?"

Skunk pointed ahead. "What difference does it make? Just drive."

Ash scowled, then set the car in motion again.

They rolled. Their destination—a solitary windowless roadside shack on their left—came suddenly into view like it was rushing to meet them.

Ash parked, and they got out. "Your friend lives in this hovel?"

Skunk gestured impatiently. "Come on, Felix is waiting."

"Felix?"

***

Standing amidst the cats plastered to Felix's walls and ceiling and the bristling furry floor, Ash tried to make sense of what was going on. She set her mind-chip to record everything—she hoped this video would turn out better than the last one had. She had a claustrophobic feeling that the myriad felines were recording her in return.

"Hello, Ash," Felix said. "Nice to see you again."

"Hi," Ash replied, without looking at the nude old woman. She was gaping at the second woman in the room, also naked. "Mayor Presley? *Priscilla* Presley? What on Earth are *you* doing here?"

The New York Mayor smiled. "It's time," she replied simply.

Ash looked at Skunk. "What is going on? What do you want with me?"

Skunk grinned back at her. "Nothing. I just needed transport here." She grinned. "The sex wasn't bad either, was it? Sort of payback for tricking you to bring me."

"But the robbery . . . the money?"

"The plan was a genuine one. I had no idea . . ." she gestured around the room, "that *this* would happen." She shrugged helplessly. "One project has just superseded another, is all. The money's all yours now."

Ash nodded slowly. "Thanks." She looked bemusedly at each woman in turn. "Can you please explain what you're all doing here? I know Felix and Skunk, but Mayor Pres—"

The door creaked behind her. She whirled around as it opened. Femina and a woman she didn't know walked into the room of cats. Both were buck naked.

"Sorry we're late," the blonde singer said. "Nosy got lost." The other woman, pretty with Native-American features and long jet-black hair, waved to Ash.

"Hi, Nosy," Skunk said, "I thought it was you stuck in that dog."

"Is it *really* time?" Rebecca Johnston asked Felix.

The old woman nodded back. "Yes."

Ash looked around the five women, noting that Skunk was now also completely nude. She sensed something odd in the air. "Could you ladies please stop being so cryptic, and explain what's—"

Understanding hit her then, like it had always been there. She looked at Femina, then at Felix. She now remembered how the first time, when she and Raye had met Felix, the woman had seemed familiar. Now she knew why. *She . . . she looks like an old version of Femina. And . . .* She looked from one woman's face to the next, comparing. The bone structure was the same, the lips had the same width and fullness, they all had the same eyes, the same chin . . .

"You're sisters?" she gasped.

Felix nodded. "Yes, we're sisters. Permit me to introduce the family. She gestured around with a hand, starting from Mayor Presley. "Bossy, Furry, Stinky, Sexy, and Nosy."

Ash nodded. "You ladies sound like a politically incorrect version of the Spice Girls."

Priscilla Presley laughed. "They're just our fun names for each other. I'm Bossy 'cos I'm in government."

"She's our overachiever," Rebecca said. "I'm a cop, so 'Nosy.' The reason for Femina's, Felix's, and Skunk's nicknames must be obvious."

"There's also 'Greedy'," Skunk said. She gave Felix an enquiring look. "Is she coming?"

"Forget her," Felix replied, with a hint of anger. "We're more than sufficient without her." The cats on the wall all bristled and spat in support of her anger.

"I'm not sure of that," Rebecca Johnston said, her voice a little nervous. "You know what she's like when you don't include her in things."

"I'm with Furry," Priscilla said. "You know the saying about too many cooks?"

Ash admired Priscilla Presley's body. For an older woman the NYC mayor looked great—almost no cellulite, and her breasts were fantastic. (She choked down her urge to grab them and suck their nipples.) *I need her plastic surgeon's phone number.*

She pulled her thoughts away from Priscilla's breasts. "Look," she said helplessly. "You've lost me again. It's time for *what?*"

"Time to ascend into Heaven and dethrone God," Femina said in a cold voice.

Ash checked her face to see if she was joking. *No, she's absolutely serious. She means it.*

She looked to the other women, saw no hint of a shared joke. "You want to dethrone God," she said in a quavering voice. In her mind she thought: *Oops, I've just stumbled into the funny farm.*

"We're not mad," Priscilla said. "We're goddesses."

"Goddesses?"

"The Female Commission, to be exact," Femina said. "A secret group dedicated to the emancipation of all women worldwide." She looked ceiling-ward. "The Patriarch up there has been on the throne for way too long."

"I will ascend into Heaven," Felix intoned quietly. "I will exalt my throne above the stars of God; I will sit also upon the mount of the congregation, in the sides of the north; I will ascend above the heights of the clouds—I will be like the most high."

"This is certain to end badly," Ash said.

Felix's eyes narrowed. "Why?"

"You're quoting the Bible—Satan . . . Lucifer—I remember that passage from Sunday School. We all know how that revolt ended."

"Stupid devils," Felix said. "The prong-headed fools weren't prepared."

"Look," Skunk said nervously, "Nosy's right. Maybe we should ask Greedy's assistance. You know how supremely resourceful she is. And with her, we'll have a full complement of our abilities—"

"We're not going to Heaven to *rob* God, we're going there to kill him, or at least kick him out of office."

"Forget Greedy," Priscilla said. "We do this ourselves."

"Who's this 'Greedy' sister of yours you keep making reference to?" Ash asked.

CHAPTER 94

Money Rich sneered at the video image on her laptop screen, projected in high-definition from Felix's house in Bizarro. Her five younger sisters talking big as usual, without being aware she was listening in.

And once again scheming on how to exclude her from The Project.

She shook her head. *Don't you chicks ever learn? You can't teach your grandmother to suck eggs!*

And the other woman with them? Ash . . . Ashley Status?

Money's amusement turned to anger. Ashley frigging Status? *Oh, so you've turned up here too? Killing Daddy wasn't enough, you little piece of shit?*

Money felt suddenly tense. This would never do. She got out a handful of bills from her purse. She spread her dollar-sign-decorated thighs, slipped her stitched-fifty-dollar panties aside, and slowly slid the cash back and forth over her vagina, relaxing into an oasis of delicious pleasure.

Oh, yes. That's world's better. An icy smile on her face while she masturbated, Money returned her attention to the six women in Felix's house.

CHAPTER 95

The five goddesses formed a circle around Ash. They held hands.

"Transform!" Felix commanded.

All the cats in the room instantly became vaginas. Walls and ceiling were now a seamless furry patchwork expanse punctuated with thousands of sexual openings. The floor also transformed, its bristly coating becoming normal pubic hair. Now it too was covered with vaginas that glistened with lubrication and sucked at the feet of the women.

The room filled with female musk, woman's clean natural perfume. The scent was the perfect aphrodisiac.

Chills of fear went through Ash. At the same time, however, a gush of vaginal heat burst up through her loins. She was filled with a sudden desire to be one with these great women.

"Pussy's true form is now revealed," Felix said.

"And She saw that it was good," Priscilla said.

"Now!" Femina yelled.

The goddesses instantly broke apart. Taking a wall each and leaving the ceiling to Felix (who floated up towards it like a feather on an air-cushion), they began sexing the vaginas coating the room. Each goddess directly stimulated six vaginas at once—one with her mouth, two with her hands, two with her toes (wiggling them deep in the sexual openings), and one with her own vagina, grinding her crotch over the wall, while the opposite sexual organ rose up in a hump of pubic fur to grind back.

The women moved all over the walls, stimulating from one set of cunts to the next. They crossed the furred surfaces like spiders (with hands and feet in the vaginas), climbed them like the orifices were ladder rungs. Felix likewise traversed the ceiling upside-down, sucking and licking and fist-and-foot-fucking it.

As they worked, the room grew brighter, the vaginas glowing as they were stimulated.

***

Felix took a break from fucking the ceiling to peer down at Ash. "Hey! get your kit off and get busy on the floor!"

Ash, understanding what Felix meant, shook her head in horror, suddenly extremely embarrassed. "Oh no, I couldn't possibly."

Skunk plucked her lips away from a vagina that was desperately kissing her back. "Do it!" she moaned, her eyes half-rolled back in her head. "This is the *real* reason I brought you over—there's supposed to be six of us sexing the room. Without Greedy, we're one short."

Ash's embarrassment left her. Her body felt hot like she'd been baked in the sun. Her pussy had a fire in it. The seemingly thousand vaginas on the floor were friendly mouths begging her to talk to them. To tell them she loved them. The room's pungent musk filled her nose, convincing her it was the right thing to do.

She nodded, began unbuttoning her top. The next moment her clothes disappeared off her body and she was falling forward onto the pubic floor. She smacked down onto the soft flesh, her mouth automatically sealing around the closest labia beneath it, her tongue dipping deep into the tunnel, tasting the female nectar. The pungent smell of vagina covered her like designer perfume; her last reservations dissolved away in it. She stretched out her hands and feet, dipping fingers and toes into vaginas and loving the floor. A vagina humped up and rubbed itself against her own sex, slippery and slithering like scissoring with Raye, with her other girlfriends. Pleasure thrilled up her cunt.

She understood what they were doing—they were powering up the room. And she knew now, that the goddesses—Felix, Priscilla, Skunk, Femina, and Rebecca (in descending order of age revealed to her)—weren't insane at all. It really *was* time for a change, and they'd bring it about. They'd pull off the divine coup d'etat. They were powerful enough, stronger than Lucifer and his incompetent angelic mob. They would dethrone God—the ancient patriarchal tyrant bastard.

Ash loved the room's cunts with passionate abandon, feeling like she was a thousand women at once sharing a thousand orgasms. She was the goddesses and they were she. She was in their vaginas and they in hers.

She and they crawled over the vagina room together, loving it, loving it, loving it, and it grew brighter and brighter and brighter and brighter.

And she came and dissolved into an ecstasy unimaginable. And fainted from the Heavenly bliss of it.

CHAPTER 96

Ash awoke. Her body felt dead, leeched of every iota of energy. At the same time she felt incredibly fulfilled, which oddly, was energy in itself.

She still lay on the floor of the vagina room, but something now felt different. She sat up, looked around.

With a shock, she realized that she was alone in the room. The vaginas on walls, floor, and ceiling, now pulsed with blinding light like she was inside a nuclear reactor. Spears of white brilliance crisscrossed the room in a web like the cunts were lasers.

At first Ash thought the goddesses had betrayed her, left her in danger, to be roasted in the hot glare. Seeing the door ajar, she leapt up and grabbed her clothes.

Then ghostly blue words appeared in midair between Ash and the door.

She whispered them:

"Thank you, Ashley Status. We were waiting for you to awaken. We are now fully powered up and ready to travel to Heaven. You, being mortal, cannot accompany us. But we are grateful to you. Exit the room and go in peace. Farewell."

The words dissolved. Ash scrambled toward the door. Just as she was about opening it, another set of words appeared:

"Head towards the Sunt. In Vagina there is always safety."

Somehow, Ash had the feeling Femina had written this last. *But where are you all?* she wondered.

***

Ash stepped outside, then turned around.

Then she gasped, almost dropping her clothes in shock. *Oh, my gosh!*
She quickly moved well back for a good look.

There was no house anymore. In its place, and rising out of the ground, was a gigantic silver woman. The door in the woman's crotch (from which Ash had just exited) disappeared.

The silver giantess emerged fully from the ground. She was at least a hundred feet tall. Her nude body glowed with lustrous radiance. Her beautiful face shone with a glory almost too terrible to behold. Everything about her—her arms and legs, her breasts, her buttocks, her feet, her shimmering pubic hair—was perfect.

She rose higher, her limbs moving slowly, a smile dancing on her lips. Her motions were erotic, and also suggestive of immense power, as if her loins housed orgasms capable of destroying the universe with their ferocity.

Filled with sudden humility in the presence of such divine awesomeness, Ash fell on her knees before the ascending silver figure and worshipped.

Now God is a woman, she thought, *and she's damn pretty too.*

She got back to her feet. While pulling on her clothes, she pondered what had happened. *Clearly, making love to the vaginas in the room caused the goddesses to fuse into this . . . super-goddess now ascending.* She tapped her head and grinned. *And I'm recording all this!*

She stood a while longer watching the silver woman slowly rise towards the Sunt, then walked over to the white BMW.

She grinned at the money on the back seat. "Yeah, things haven't really turned out that badly after all."

She got in and drove off, spinning the car around, so it was heading back the way she and Skunk had come, towards the Everywhere Freeway. She stepped on the gas. *Best I get a move on.*

It wasn't that Ash wanted to disregard Femina's advice about driving toward the vagina-sun, but she currently had no idea where she was. She aimed to convert the BMW back into a helicopter again, then fly around a bit and see if she could find her bearings. If that failed, she'd fly back to the elevator hut, ride the cage down to Endless Street, hide out there.

A sudden memory of Raye made Ash immensely sad. Tears filled her eyes again. *Oh, shit, baby! We're rich, and you're not here to share it with me!*

She wiped her eyes. Then she became aware of something odd beside her on the car's front passenger seat.

She looked at it. It was another floating message. Large smokey green letters read:

"Payback's a . . ."

The words coalesced into a dollar sign.

Ash realized she'd taken her eyes off the road. She looked quickly forward again at the impression of something building-sized lurching up just ahead of her.

She tried to swerve out of its way, but it was too late, the creature was too big, moved too fast. It seemed like an entire apartment block—a metal-plated gray apartment block with a hundred legs—obstructed her way.

The BMW slammed into the meta-whale.

Its airbags instantly inflated, protecting Ash, but the impact stunned her. She sat groggy, helpless to prevent the next lightning-fast occurrence.

Like a monstrous support column falling, one of the meta-whale's passing feet stomped on the BMW's crumpled front end, completely flattening it.

Ash screamed and kept on screaming. The mangling had shattered both her ankles and shins, and also locked her legs in the compress of metal that had been the vehicle's engine. The meta-whale vanished into the ground again.

Both airbags deflated.

Her eyes wide with agony, Ash suddenly smelt spilt gasoline. She saw smoke, then licking flames. The shattered engine was on fire!

In a panic, she tried to open the car's doors, but their controls were totally damaged. Even the glass wouldn't wind down.

She fought to free herself, but her legs . . . oh, the pain was so excruciating it paralyzed her. She collapsed back in her seat, scared to move . . . scared to even breathe. She felt the blood draining from her legs, felt herself weakening as it went. But she wasn't bleeding to death fast enough, not quickly enough to die before the car caught fire, became a raging inferno.

She began praying to the ascending super-goddess to save her, then stopped and sneered. *That lady's got bigger fish to fry that rescuing little ol' me.* Looking back out the window, she just made out the rising silver toes. *Go for it, girl!*

Another burst of pain from her destroyed feet and the fierce spreading heat wiped out Ash's energy. She collapsed back into her seat again. *Hey, screw this!* she thought calmly. *If I'm going to die, I'm going out with dignity.*

She sat calmly, enduring the excruciating pain, awaiting her bitter end. She was aware that her legs had stopped bleeding—the fire had cooked the blood in them.

The flames flickered up around her legs. She beat them out, wincing, gritting her teeth, refusing to vocalize her agony.

Smoke filled the car. Ash choked on it, her vision now obscured. *Damn this! I've no fire extinguishers in my muscle-purses—just loads of explosive stuff. But then, I never expected this to happen to me. Only good thing is, inflatables don't blow up till you blow them up.* (She scanned the airwaves with her mind-chip, but found only static—no help out here.) *And it looks like I'll be blowing up soon enough.*

To neutralize the pain of her hurting body, Ash slid fingers into her cunt and began masturbating hard and fast. It helped. A rush of liquid wellness went through her, like her vagina was flooding the burning car with dousing water. She concentrated hard, working to reach one last final climax.

Just before the BMW exploded, Ash remembered the money—the two million dollars in cash on the rear seats. With a pleased sense of achievement, she turned for a final look at it.

"Oh, fuck!" she gasped, pissed-off by the irony of everything. The two cases of money had vanished.

"Oh, fuck!" She gasped again as she reached orgasm, her pain completely blocked out for a glorious physical moment.

Then the car became a fireball, spewing plumes of black smoke across the pink landscape.

Above and beyond it, the silver goddess continued to rise.

CHAPTER 97

Femina – Goodbye!

I died with Pride,
Never begged for mercy,
Never cried,
Just like I lived my life.
Fuck you, if you wanted me to beg,
Won't ever happen,
I got too much self-respect.

Goodbye, cruel world,
I did my honest best.
Might not have been good enough,
But I ain't got no regrets.
I've had the life I wanted,
You guys can live the rest.

CHAPTER 98

Money Rich smirked at the fiercely burning car with its roasting inhabitant. "Fuck you, Ashley Status."

She forgot the dead woman, scrolled the laptop's view to the rising combination of her sisters in their 'Female God' avatar. *They actually did it. Well, almost.*

The monitor showed the scene with HD clarity. The silver goddess had reached the Sunt. Money grinned. (The Sunt was essential to her sisters' plans—the final source of power they needed.)

She waited till Female God was stretching out her hand to grasp the vagina-sun, then poised her cursor over the Sunt, clicked on it, and dragged-and-dropped it into a recycle bin that had suddenly popped up onscreen.

Over the desert, the Sunt disappeared.

Female God's silver face wrinkled in surprise.

Money next double-clicked on the silver deity herself. She selected 'Dissolve into component parts' from the dialog box that appeared, and hit 'Enter.'

Then she relaxed back into her chair and resumed masturbating, watching the screen with an amused smile.

***

Out over Bizarro, up in the skin sky, Female God exploded.

After a moment when she became transparent as water, she broke apart again into the five sisters and thousands of cats, all of whom fell together out of the sky.

Money laughed at the five women who were picking themselves off the ground (clearly wondering what had gone wrong), while the cats landed on and around them. She tapped a key combination on her laptop and the connection became two-way, a huge rectangle appearing in the air above them with her face in it.

She waved down at her sisters. "Hi, girls. Going somewhere without me!?"

"Greedy!" all five yelped at once. Their faces turned different shades of angry and embarrassed. Then they all calmed somewhat.

(Now, seen through the laptop by her sisters, Money Rich looked different. No longer was a she a beautiful twenty-something redhead. Now she looked immeasurably ancient—eons old. So old, the wrinkles in her face seemed living things. Her stringy hair was the barely-pink color of a red dress faded through years of compulsive overuse, of blood dissolved in water.)

"Sis, you messed up The Project," Rebecca said. Her face however showed relief.

Money shook her head, her jade gaze cool reproof. "No I didn't. I saved your impatient precocious asses from getting embarrassed. Not to mention I've also just saved you five from taking the ass-whipping of your endless lives." She sighed. "I've told you girls time without number—we're not ready yet. Which part of 'not ready' do you have difficulty understanding?" Then she frowned. "Sexy?"

Femina ran guilty fingers through her blonde locks. "Yes, oldest sister?"

"Whose idea was this?"

Femina and Rebecca instantly pointed to Felix. "Hers."

Felix scowled with disgust at the betrayal. "Yes, *I* summoned everyone. I'm tired of watching and waiting—it's all we ever do. Meanwhile womankind suffers endless abuse."

Money laughed softly. "And of course, you left me out 'cos I'd say no." She made an expansive upward gesture. "If *I* could stop you this easily, what do you think *HE* would do when you got up there? He'd have had you all for lunch, then fucked your uppity asses for desert. And where'd we be then? Where would your precious womanity be?" She shook her head in disgust. "Furry, you just *look* old. Your brains haven't atrophied yet—use them occasionally."

Felix grimaced like she'd drunk prune juice. "With the Sunt's power we'd have been invincible."

Money sneered. "Fuck the Sunt."

"Can I have it back?"

"I trashed it—it's too obvious. Use a normal sun from now on. Make it a pink hole if you want vaginal symbolism."

Felix's eyes clouded with rage. "How dare you destroy my sun, you money-hungry bitch!? You stupid—" She spat at Money. The gob of sputum flew up through the laptop monitor to splatter Money in the eye.

Money's face darkened. She reached a hand through the laptop screen into Bizarro and slapped Felix hard across the face. Whack! Her sister reeled back, then tripped over a cat and landed hard on her backside, her aged vagina gaping between spread thighs.

Money withdrew her hand, wiped the sputum from her eye. Breathing hard, Felix glared up at her face in the sky.

"Hey!" Priscilla Presley said. "There's no need for that nonsense!"

"Shut it, Bossy; it's time Furry learnt her place. Her spitting on me is way out of line."

Priscilla scowled. "*You* should be called 'Bossy'—you're always pushing the rest of us around." Then she smiled sweetly. "Name change, everyone? I'll simply be 'Polly' from now on."

Rebecca made a face. "What kind of nickname is Polly?"

"She means from 'politics,'" Skunk said, bending to help Felix up. She looked angrily up at Money. "And I agree—you can't hit us like we're kids."

The others nodded.

"I suggest you five act like adults then."

Felix got to her feet again. She looked around at her confusedly milling, meowing, cats, then snapped her fingers twice.

The cats instantly reformed into her house a short distance from the sisters.

That done, Felix glared angrily up at Money, her cheek angry red where the older woman had hit her. "Don't you dare lay hands on me again!"

Money shrugged back dismissively. "Don't you ever sass me again."

Skunk turned to Priscilla. "No. You remain as 'Bossy.' *She* remains 'Greedy' 'cos we know she hates the name."

"Okay, ladies, enough—"

Money froze midsentence, pulled her lips back over her teeth in a grimace and shut her eyes.

"This takes the cake," Felix said. "She's wanking while talking to us? How patronizing can you get?"

Femina and Skunk giggled. "When a girl's gotta come, she's gotta come," Femina said.

"Hey, hurry up your orgasm!" Priscilla yelled. "We're talking business, not pleasure!"

Rebecca grinned broadly. "I guess she's human after all—oh, we're not human, are we?"

Money opened her eyes and sighed, her expression now relaxed. "You girls always stress me out." She stuck a hand through the laptop into

Bizarro again, jabbing a finger at the five goddesses. "Do you get the point?"

"Your finger's dirty," Femina said nicely.

"Oh." Money pulled the finger out, licked the pale creaming off it, then poked it back through the screen. "Now, do you understand? I'll lay it out again for you, since Furry particularly, has grammar-comprehension issues. We do not move on Heaven till I say we're ready."

"Why does it *have* to be *you*?"

Priscilla looked sharply at Felix. "Cool it, Furry."

"Understand this," Money continued. "*I'm* running this show. *I* say when we're ready to fuck with God. And then, the six of us, not five—I honestly can't believe you had someone else service *my* floor, and that bitch Ashley Status of all people; no, forget that shit—the *six of us* will ascend into Heaven and defeat the Almighty." She looked around, her immeasurably old face severe. "And then, I assure you *we will* succeed. But you need to be patient." She looked pointedly at Felix. "Dig, cat lady?"

Felix rolled her eyes. "Okay, I'm sorry we went early. It's just so soul-destroying having to keep watch—"

"We're sorry too," Priscilla interrupted her. Skunk, Femina, and Rebecca nodded contritely.

Money smiled. "That's okay. Just a little misunderstanding between sisters." She clapped her hands. "Okay, everybody, back to work. Hey, Sexy?"

"Yes, oldest sister?"

"Title your next album *The Abolition of Man.*"

A demure bow; a grimace; a questioning look. "That sounds horribly misandric."

"Don't worry about it. The ultra-feminist lobbies already criticize you for being too male-friendly anyway. This title will win them over. Just keep the songs your normal mix of lust, cunt, undying love for cock, and hatred of men. Keep everyone guessing."

Femina nodded. "Yeah. I do love guys, but they've really got to be put in their place—level with us."

"And, Sexy? You and Bossy both say you were abducted by aliens. Always works."

Priscilla heaved a sigh of relief. "I've been wondering how to explain leaving so abruptly." She smiled. "Okay, ladies, time I was going. I've a whole city in panic, looking for me."

"Gotta leave too," Femina said.

Both women hugged their other three sisters, then faded from view.

Felix gasped. "Bossy forgot her clothes in my house! She's going to reappear in public naked. Sexy too, but *she's* used to being in the buff."

Skunk licked her lips. "Oh, she's going to cause a sensation."

The four sisters considered this, then they burst out laughing.

"Bossy's got a hot bod," Rebecca said. "It'll be a good sensation. Give the Big Apple something to talk about for a while. The entire USA in fact."

Skunk looked at her youngest sister. "I'm staying here, want to hang out with Furry awhile. You coming too? Catch up on old times? You've been out of circulation like forever."

Rebecca Johnston shook her head. "Nah, got me a hot date."

Felix raised her eyebrows. "Out here in the middle of nowhere?" Then she grinned. "Oh, him! You'd better come over to the house for some clothes then. You can have Bossy's."

Rebecca preened herself. "Nah, leave 'em. I need to make a great second impression on the guy."

She hugged the other two, waved to Money up in the video window, then set off down the highway towards the Everywhere Freeway.

Skunk watched Rebecca's hips sway as she left them behind. "That ass is so hot. Nosy really should cover it up."

Money laughed. "I think she was a dog so long she's forgotten nakedness isn't a fashion statement."

The rectangular window dropped lower, shrinking as it came. Finally, it was normal laptop-monitor-sized and floating at the height of the goddesses' breasts.

Skunk and Felix walked back to Felix's house, talking to Money in the floating window.

"I'll let you in on a secret, Furry," Money said. "One major reason we aren't ready yet? You need more cats."

"How many?"

"Three million."

"Three *what*? What the hell for?"

"See why I told you to wait for me? I saw God fight once. Old Guy's like the Shaolin Master of Eternity. Like ten billion Bruce Lees using nuclear weapons as nunchaku. No way you want to mess with Him without being *totally* prepared."

"Hmmm. But *three million* cats, Greedy. That's *a lot* of pussy-power. I'll end up with a mansion out here."

"Wherever. Just start collecting the furballs."

***

"Hey!" Skunk said. "Before I forget: that necklace you're wearing is rightfully mine."

"This one? Kate Rose's?"

"Yes, that one. Hand it over. Eddie loved me. He'd have wanted me to have it."

"Sorry, sis. You know what they say. Finders keepers . . ."

"That's why we call you 'Greedy.' Can't you keep your fingers to yourself just for once? Give it back! You don't need it for protection anyway."

"Neither do you, Stinky. I just like the way it looks. Sweet green— matches my eyes to a treat. Okay, okay, stop looking so pissed-off. I'll sell it back to you. You got thirty million dollars?"

"What!? It cost you twenty-four!"

"So? I'm a businesswoman. Girl's gotta make a profit."

"Screw you! You can keep the damn thing!"

"Ha ha ha! Thanks, sis!"

"And, hey! What's the deal with you wearing clothes made from money all of a sudden? There's famine in the Third World you know."

"Yeah, and the necrophiliac thing with the stuffed corpse? You going senile or what?"

"Senile? Me? Ha ha ha! You girls will never understand what that gold penis feels like—"

"We *don't want* to feel it, Greedy."

"No, we friggin' don't."

"Whatever."

CHAPTER 99

Fred stared at the burnt corpse in the gutted BMW. Without being told, he knew it was Ashley Status. He just felt it in his heart.

He winced. *I hope she didn't suffer too much before she died.* It seemed inconceivable to him that she hadn't, but . . . maybe the smoke had suffocated her first.

A few flames still fluttered on isolated patches of the car. Thin, adamant smoke trails rose like from an extinguished campfire. The stink of roast flesh mixed with that of burnt leather and rubber in his nostrils.

(Beside the road was a massive hole like a mineshaft entrance. Its edges were ragged bleeding meat. Fred refrained from looking at it too often. The implications of its size scared him. Scarier still were the massive footprints beside it. He'd passed several other such excavations on his drive over.)

From pure force of habit, Fred searched for the money in the BMW, even jimmying open its trunk. (While searching, he noticed the hole in the left side of the skeleton's charred skull. A matchbox-sized excavation filled with melted wires. *She had a mind-chip?*)

When he'd done searching, he laughed at himself. *What was I thinking? Two cases full of paper would just be additional fuel for the fire.*

He walked away from the burnt car towards his blue Aston Martin. He was uncertain what to do now. He'd been on his way to see Felix, to plead with her to PLEASE STOP(!) doing her goddess tricks around the Hotel Bizarre—Femina's sudden disappearance had caused even more of a stir than the explosions from the robbery. Her band was in panic, the police had taken statements from everyone, and . . .

And it would be VERY nice if Femina could be returned home immediately.

That had been his intention, till he'd seen . . .

He still questioned his sanity on this. First there'd been a gigantic silver woman floating in the sky and reaching for the vagina-sun. Then the Sunt had disappeared. Next the silver woman had exploded, and it had seemed to rain several objects for awhile. Then a large mirror with a gnarly old woman's head in it had appeared in midair. Then a hand . . . And now, the mirror too had just disappeared—falling from the sky and shrinking as it fell.

Fred was certain all this was happening over at Felix's house. So he was no longer in a hurry to visit her. *I think I'll just go see Vola instead, then maybe later . . . Hey! What's that?"*

'That' was two brown objects a short distance in from the highway beyond his car. Heart beating fast, Fred ran across to them. He practically wept on seeing the two pigskin cases. He opened them. Both were packed full of rubber-banded wads of hundred dollar bills. Fred looked up from the money, back over at the burnt-out BMW. *How in the world did these get over here? There's at least a hundred yards between the car and . . . Unless, she came out here to bury the money and forgot something and went back to get it, and then . . .*

He let his suppositions go. *What matters is that the cash is safe. Money Rich will be delighted. No, she'll be orgasmic.* (Fred had heard a few odd rumors about her.)

He snapped both cases shut again and picked them up.

Walking back toward his car, Fred suddenly saw he wasn't alone on the road anymore.

A naked woman was approaching him from the direction of Felix's house.

He walked faster. Not expecting trouble, he'd left his gun in the glove compartment. And now, with all this cash . . .

Then, close to his car, he saw who the approaching nude was.

"Rebecca? Rebecca Johnston?"

She grinned at him. "In the skin, baby."

They reached the Aston Martin at the same moment. Fred dropped the cases on the convertible's rear seats, then turned to Rebecca again.

"Rebecca . . . what are *you* doing out here? Hey! Are you connected with the missing Mayor and Femina?"

"You don't want to know."

Fred rolled his eyes skyward for a moment. *What a trite comeback.* Then he grinned. *Yup, she's right. I really don't want to know. Maybe tomorrow; next year even. Just not right now.*

Ravishingly beautiful, Rebecca's nakedness chilled and thrilled Fred. He feasted his eyes on her lovely face with its crowning drapes of black-as-night hair, on her delicately muscled body—the high conical breasts, the flat belly, the wasp waist, the just-right hips, the delightfully sculpted pubic mound with its raven bush . . .

She pirouetted in a slow circle for him. Fred's breath caught in his throat. His crotch tightened. *Oh my God! That ass, those thighs, those ankles . . . Holy shit!*

"Exactly," Rebecca said.

"What?"

She grinned. "Just thinking aloud. Happens occasionally." She flashed her eyes at him. "Do you like what you see, Freddie?"

He nodded quickly, not trusting himself to speak lest he slaver saliva everywhere. Then remembrance/guilt flashed through his mind. *But, Vola . . .*

"Fuck Vola," a soft voice said in his head. "And I don't mean literally. Your bird woman is out. I'm in."

I didn't just hear that, Fred thought.

"You did," Rebecca said.

He gaped at her in horror. *Hell no, not another one!*

She grinned. "Yes, Freddie darling—another one. You appeal to us goddesses. She slipped her arm through his. "And since you clearly like the merchandise . . . I'll put it this way: I haven't had sex in four years— screwing that house back there doesn't count. You get the idea?"

Fred nodded. *Screwing the house?* He shrugged it off. He smiled as Rebecca Johnston got into the car, running appraising eyes over her exquisitely toned curves.

"So where are we going, darling?" he asked when she was seated.

She grinned. "Well, I've already got me a nice hard man. Just find us a nice soft bed somewhere."

They sped off.

CHAPTER 100

Femina – Almighty Cunt

You will die in my cunt,
Like your semen does in my womb.
I am an unforgiving God,
You will pay for the crime of penetration with your life.
I show no mercy,
I take no prisoners, (though I be your loving wife).
I will resurrect you and kill you again,
And again, and over again.
This is my predestination, and your glory,
Your shame, your pain.
The real never-ending story,
Through human eons unchanged.
Darling,
You will love me,
And hate me.
You will despise me,
And crave me.
You will worship me,
Cherish me,
Proclaim me as the one and only,
Man's true Deity,
The one you MUST HAVE and truly want,
Almighty Cunt.

Your strength will melt like chocolate,
In my unknowable depths.
In my southern mouth,
Vanishing under quicksand,
In my swampy delta . . .
You will gasp your last dying breath.
Your pride is your trouser snake,
But I bend it to my will.
It bites me, but I AM antidote!
Its barefoot-and-in-the-kitchen venom evaporates in smoke.
You will break,
Like rotted wood,
Once you have a feel,
Once you see me revealed.
(You may even come prematurely,
If I bend over in high heels.)
Your cock is only as good,
In bed as I let it be.
(A truth eternally misunderstood,
By both Adam and Eve,
Of course, I mention the original He and She figuratively.)
Whatever you really feel,
You WILL accord me the proper respect,
Or live in regret,
Of the hot loving you won't get,
Ruing the day you offended me.
I am your rising and setting sun,
The ONLY fucking one,
Almighty Cunt.

However hard you are,
Is far from hard enough.
Stop talking tough,
I render even presidents and kings soft,
And afterwards all shower me with praise and gifts and love.
I am all in all, there is nothing more to want,
Besides Almighty Cunt.

You may fuck me real HARD,
(Really slam this ass!)
Plumb me with your dong,
All day and all night long.

VAGINA MUNDI

You can make me bleed,
Pump me full of good or retarded seed,
Freeze me with insecurities,
Even plague me with disease,
But you can never overcome me,
Never break me,
Never bring me to my knees.
For I am what I am,
The eternal, unchanging essence of woman,
And you . . . you are just a man.
To believe anything else is delusion,
Testosterone-fuelled illusion,
Of a machismo Neverland,
That never was, and never will be.
Mere mortal man,
I transcend all your plans,
Forsake your masculine folly,
I am your reality,
Show me true fealty.
I am the sex you want,
And can't ignore,
(Bow low and implore,
Yes, get down on the floor and fucking beg for more,
'Cos you KNOW you want more.)
This hole so tight, so slack, so soft,
Never rough,
The excruciatingly gripping flesh velvet glove,
That you love.
THAT YOU LOVE!!!
Of which you can NEVER have enough,
Almighty Cunt.

Worship at my opening,
You neighborhood dog of lust.
I turn your strength to weakness,
See how breathlessly you thrust,
Panting like you'll burst.
I AM simply too much!

Penetrate me deeply,
Slide in as far as you can,
Search for sweet truth within me,
You mere mortal man.

(Why can't you understand?
Sex is nature's jigsaw,
Woman eternally puzzling man.)
Leave your prejudices in me,
Shed your myopic points of view,
They were valid before you fucked me,
After me your opinions are renewed.

Like it or not, you will love me,
Worship and praise me,
Cleave unto me blindly,
Profess your undying loyalty,
To my orifice alone,
The all-conquering vagina,
Queen glorious clitoris on her throne,
As you die!

(Draw your last feeble breaths.
I, WOMAN, will fuck you to death!)

Yes, die as a hero,
A besieging knight,
Of the ass table,
Tonight,
Across the labial drawbridge,
In the eternally vernal paradise,
Within the castle of my thighs.
And as you lie,
In your grave,
Darling toy boy, Casanova, sex slave . . .
Watch my pussy phoenix rise.
Forever, I rise.
I rise,
From the ashes of Patriarchal lies,
To soar unbound through gender skies,
Reflected glorious in masculine eyes,
True femininity as it was designed.
I have overcome the restrictions,
Discriminations, ContraDICKtions,
Rape Culture, emotional vultures,
Biology and emotional ties,
Mother-transmitted traditions of prescribed compromise,
Peer pressure, religious fervor, Political alibis,

For a second-class-citizen female life.
LIES, GIRLS! ALL LIES!
And now I realize,
As I redefine my desires on this maiden flight,
That proclaims my freedom,
All women's freedom,
As I swoop back down to lie by your side,
Glide in and softly alight,
This world is MINE.
YES! MINE!
I AM WOMAN!
I have . . . I am . . . what men really want—
The primal force that can never be overcome . . .
Almighty Cunt.

And you better believe it, brother.
Me and my sisters know we've got THE POWER!
We'll fucking get what we want!
We're backed by . . .
Almighty Vagina.

The End

ABOUT THE AUTHOR

Wol-vriey is Nigerian, and quite tall.

He currently resides in a state of uneasy stalemate with his threatening-to-thin-beyond-redemption hair, and believes there actually are things that go bump in the night.

Wol-vriey recycles the ridiculous into reasonable reality for the reader.

His WEIRRRD philosophy?

WEIRRRD = Warp/Write Everything into Realistic Ridiculous Readable Distorted Dream Dimension Descriptions.

Wol-vriey blogs at:

http://oddityfarm.wordpress.com

OTHER GREAT TITLES FROM

Burning Bulb
PUBLISHING

WWW.BURNINGBULBPUBLISHING.COM

ANTHOLOGIES
BIZARRO AND TRANSGRESSIVE FICTION

THE BIG BOOK OF BIZARRO

The Big Book of Bizarro brings together the peculiar prose of an international cast of the most grotesquely-gonzo, genre-grinding modern writers who ever put pen to paper (or mouse to pad), including:

NIGHT OF THE LIVING DEAD horror writers John Russo & George Kosana; HUSTLER MAGAZINE erotica contributors Eva Hore, Andrée Lachapelle, & J. Troy Seate and established Bizarro genre authors D. Harlan Wilson, William Pauley III, Wol-vriey, Laird Long, Richard Godwin and so many more!

From Alien abductions to Zombie sex, The Big Book of Bizarro contains OVER FIFTY STORIES of the most outrélandish transgressive fiction that you'll ever lay your capricious and curious hands upon!

WARNING: This book may be one of the most controversial and dangerous books you'll ever read.

WESTWARD HOES

Nine outlaw writers rode into town from obscurity to pen nine tantalizing tales of horror and fantasy, and leaving once they branded their own personal marks on the weird western genre and became living legends of the American Frontier experience.

Like drunken Indian scouts, the writers fervidly tracked down and captured the Western genre, tore off its fashionable veneer and ravished its exposed essence.

So belly up to the bar with your favorite soiled dove and enjoy perusing these thrilling tales of Old West debauchery, danger and desire; compiled by the publisher of The Big Book of Bizarro and featuring the bizarro novella *Big Trouble in Little Ass* by Wol-vriey.

Burning Bulb
PUBLISHING

ANTHOLOGIES
BIZARRO AND TRANSGRESSIVE FICTION

THE BIG BOOK OF BIZARRO SPECIAL KINDLE EDITIONS

OTHER AWESOME COLLECTIONS

GARY LEE VINCENT'S
DARKENED
THE WEST VIRGINIA VAMPIRE SERIES

DARKENED HILLS

When evil descends on a small West Virginia town, who will survive?

Jonathan did not start out his life to become a rambler, it just worked out that way. William was a troubled youth with something to hide. Both were from Melas, a small town tucked away in the West Virginia hills... a town where disappearances are happening more and more frequently.

After the suicide of a wanted serial killer, the townsfolk thought the nightmare was over. But when a centuries-old vampire is discovered they find out the hard way it's just getting started. Dark secrets can only stay hidden for so long and when the devil comes to collect, there will be hell to pay. Can Jonathan and William find a way to stop the vampire before it's too late? Find out in *Darkened Hills!*

DARKENED HOLLOWS

In the heart-stopping sequel to the award-winning *Darkened Hills*, Jonathan and William must return to West Virginia to face possible criminal charges stemming from their last visit to the damned town of Melas, where both had narrowly escaped the clutches of a vampire seethe.

And as livestock start mysteriously getting murdered with all of their blood drained, worried farmers are searching for answers - leaving the local Sheriff and his deputy racing against time to learn the cause before a more violent crime is committed.

Burning Bulb
PUBLISHING

WWW.DARKENEDHILLS.COM

GARY LEE VINCENT'S
DARKENED
THE WEST VIRGINIA VAMPIRE SERIES

DARKENED WATERS

When the world goes to hell, the chosen must arise!

As Talman Cane orchestrates a flood of epic proportions in this third installment of the *Darkened* series the towns of Melas and Tarklin are caught completely off guard by the deluge. Hell-bent on finishing what they started, the evil brothers return to the lunatic asylum to take care of the witnesses and add to the ever-growing army of the undead.

Aided by Lucifer himself and the insane vampire demon Legion, the stage is set to channel all of the forces of hell to come forth. In an all-out race to survive, Jonathan, William, and Amanda soon discover they are up against impossible odds as Lucifer opens the Gateway to Hell, ushering in the zombie apocalypse and the End Times.

DARKENED SOULS

Melas and the Madison House are about to be rebuilt.
True evil is about to be reborne!

Young ex-priest and vampire-killer William is drawn back to the West Virginian town that almost killed him, where his vampire arch-enemy Victor Rothenstein still stalks the earth.

The town of Melas lies destroyed after the battle of the End of Days. But why is wealthy Jackie Nixon so eager to rebuild it using the bone dust of murdered souls?

Terrible evil has visited before, but the Gateway to Hell is about to be reopened in a horrific climax. And this time – it's personal.

www.DARKENEDHILLS.com

Burning Bulb
PUBLISHING

WEST VIRGINIA-THEMED HUMORROROTICA
BY RICH BOTTLES JR.

HELLHOLE WEST VIRGINIA

From the heights of Mothman's perch high atop the Silver Bridge in Point Pleasant to the depths of Hellhole Cavern in Pendleton County, evil lurks within the shadows as the sun sets upon the haunted hills and hollows of West Virginia.

Bizarro author Rich Bottles Jr. blows the coffin lid off horror genre clichés with this tour de force cast of Eco-friendly vampires, beach-yearning zombies and sex-starved she-devils.

LUMBERJACKED

If you are easily offended or do not possess a truly depraved sense of humor, this story may not be the light summer reading fare you desire. As for the four feisty female freshmen stranded on top of West Virginia's third highest mountain, they have no choice but to experience the sick, twisted debauchery and perverted mayhem described deep inside the tight unbroken bindings of this horrific missive.

Lumberjacked takes the reader to a nightmarish world where character development and aesthetic integrity are prematurely cut short by the swinging axes of maniacal lumberjacks, who are hell bent on death and destruction in the remote forests of Appalachia. And at the climax, when paranoia crosses over to the paranormal, Lumberjacked makes Deliverance look like a family raft trip down the Lower Gauley.

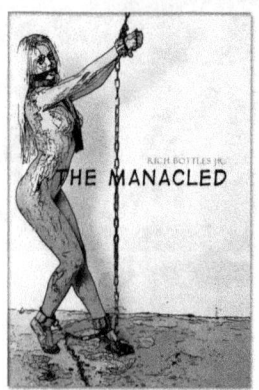

THE MANACLED

What happens when twin brothers lease out the former West Virginia State Penitentiary with the false purpose of filming a documentary on supernatural phenomena, but their true intention is to make a pornographic movie?

Chaos ensues as the disturbed spirits of murdered convicts, along with the reanimated dead from the neighboring Indian Burial Mound, take their vengeance on the unwary and undressed trespassers.

Zombies, ghosts, mobsters and porn collide in this bizarre tale from horror author Rich Bottles Jr.

Burning Bulb
PUBLISHING

WOL-VRIEY
BIZARRO AND TRANSGRESSIVE FICTION

Burning Bulb
PUBLISHING

BOSTON POSH

In 2028 AD, the USA is a nation ravaged by hungry dragons and dinosaurs. In Boston, Massachusetts, private eye Bud Malone is hired to rescue a kidnapped heiress. But nothing is as it seems. Malone works to unravel a tangled web involving Boston Chinatown, a 200-year-old woman with a 9-year-old body, white robots, a human-liver-eating psychopath, a golem, a porcelain dragon, and a snake goddess with a crush on him. There's also a woman obsessed with chicken sex. Then Malone meets Posh Lane, a gorgeous call girl who's desperate to quit her pimp. Romantic sparks ignite between Posh and Malone, but Posh's past suddenly catches up with her in a BIG way. To save Posh, Malone agrees to run a quest for Earth's new rulers, the Forks. But, Malone has no idea that agreeing to the Fork's odd request will send him on the weirdest trip he's ever been on in his life.

VEGAN VAMPIRE VAGINAS

The biggest bank heist in US history. And Tom Palmer can't remember pulling it off. And no, this isn't your standard case of amnesia. After a one-night-stand gone horribly wrong, Boston salesman Tom Palmer wakes up with a vagina implanted in his left hand. Then his day gets worse:

Tom is transported across space-time to a nightmare version of Boston, one where the Bizarro virus has transformed half the population into cannibals. Worst of all, Tom discovers that in this new Boston, he's the infamous gangster Pussypalm, wanted for robbing the Federal Reserve Bank of Boston a year ago. He also learns that the vagina in his hand is prophetic, i.e. it talks . . . after sex. With 130 people left dead during his bank heist and six billion dollars missing, Tom knows he's living on borrowed time. It is in his best interests not to remember anything. Because once he does . . .

VEGAN ZOMBIE APOCALYPSE

In the post-apocalypse worlderness, zombies rule the earth. They're allergic to meat, and brains literally make them explode. Zombies now eat blood potatoes, parasitic tubers grown in the flesh of humancows corralled in maximum security farms. Two fugitives meet in the ancient ruins of Texas. The first is Soil 15-f, a womancow who's escaped her farm a week before she's due to be killed and her blood potato crop harvested. The second fugitive is Able Kane, former head necros food technician, now sentenced to death for heresy. But Soil is no ordinary humancow. Unknown to herself, she's the vegan zombie agricultural revolution, and the zombies desperately want her back. And the necros equally desperately want Able Kane dead. He's fled with a forbidden discovery which will reshape the world for the worse if used. And Able is just hardheaded/misguided enough to use it.

MINOR CONFESSIONS OF AN ANGEL FALLING UPWARD

by Planner Forthright, as edited by Joey Madia

Confession. Revelation. Rant. *Minor Confessions of an Angel Falling Upward* is all of these... and more. Set in modern times and spiraling back to the swirl of Pre-Creation, this postmodern blend of genre-bending pop-prose and socio-political commentary is a classic tale of the (anti-)hero's quest for Reason and Redemption in a Universe gone mad.

Who is Planner Forthright? A fallen angel made Man. A once-winged evil with un-Divine purpose on this Plane. A cannibal prince chosen to inherit a castled landscape of destruction and despair. An Alchemist of sorts—a mental magician; a mortar-and-pestle wizard converting carbon lies to golden Truth, whose language is his own. A Vampire by nature and condition whose been walking the waters and thorny highways of our planet for over 40 years. And he's seeking a way out...

PASSAGEWAY

by Gary Lee Vincent with illustrations by Andy Hopp

When an archeological dig goes horribly wrong, the team is trapped in an alternate world where evil awaits them at every turn. Find out who will survive the *Passageway!*

From Gary Lee Vincent, the author of supernatural vampire thriller *Darkened Hills*, comes an unforgettable tale that spans four continents and takes the reader to the very realm of Hell itself.

Skeleton warriors, zombies, other undead beings and werewolves are all very real inside the *Passageway!* In this Bizarro-genre tribute to H.P. Lovecraft and Indiana Jones, this deadly tale will keep you guessing and leave you breathless to the end!

THE TWELVE STEPS

by Zachary Crabtree

"A Man who Cannot Keep Awake Cannot Keep it Together." There is always something that pulls an alcoholic deeper into his unquenchable thirst – something degenerative to the human spirit. Indeed, there have been incidents in my life that carry tragic significance to me, yet I know they pale in comparison to the tragedies experienced by others.

When the jagged pieces of a disfigured past become a troubled, broken-up, glass-bottled mosaic in one's present life, all the innocent souls affected along the way become entangled in one's conscience; while the depression, pills, manic behavior and soul-searching coalesce in a series of twelve steps.

Alcohol affects the lives of hooligans, stubborn old fools, lovers, and families torn apart by drunk drivers – drunk drivers like me.

Burning Bulb
PUBLISHING

Bright little children, at school and at play,
until their minds are stolen away...

A Novel of Terror by

JOHN A. RUSSO
THE ACADEMY

THE ACADEMY

The Academy. It's every parent's dream, turning their little darlings into geniuses, superachievers, perfect little children.

And if there's a problem, the Academy fixes that too. It's a simple operation. Just a little device. Then a teeny pink scar on a tender little skull . . .

One boy knows the secret. Now he wants his mind back. But it's much, much too late. Too late for anything but the ugly feelings. The bad feelings. The messy sexy feelings. The knife-cold hatred, the murderous rage, for total, screaming, blood-drenching revenge . . .

www.TheJohnRusso.com

Burning Bulb
PUBLISHING

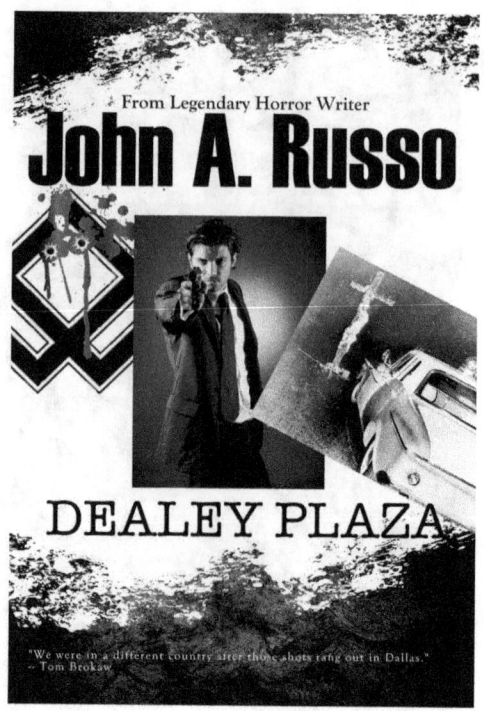

DEALEY PLAZA

From legendary horror and suspense writer JOHN RUSSO comes a harrowing tale where no one is safe!

Dealey Plaza is one of the most notorious places in America, and when youthful conspiracy buffs go there in 1964 to stage their own reenactment of the Kennedy Assassination, four of them are brutally murdered ~ the first victims of a hate-filled legacy that continues for four more decades.

The survivors of that long-ago Dallas trip, each of them now icons of the American way of life, are about to be honored ~ or killed.

Who will live and who will die? Will it be country-western star Lori McCoy? Her loving husband? Her scheming ex-husband? Or the case-hardened FBI agent and longtime friend who risks his life trying to protect them?

www.DealeyPlazaBook.com

Burning Bulb
PUBLISHING

THE FALL OF TOMORROW

Hopelessness... How do you protect your loved ones when Hell itself opens its insidious mouth?
Horror... Nightmarish Creatures invade your world and there is nowhere to hide.
Blood... How long can you hold out before they come for you?
Pain... Where do you run to avoid being eaten alive by monsters with a voracious appetite for your flesh?
Screams... While you selfishly run for your own life.
Questions... Who is to blame? Where did they come from? How many people survived...and how does the human race find the means to fight back?

THE FALL OF TOMORROW is man's last tale of desperation told by those that are striving to salvage some hope against a ravenous bastion of evil beasts bent on ruling our world.

"David Fairhead writes compelling stories that offer very human characters and very inhuman monsters. There is no subtlety in Fairhead's imagination - he is simply dying to scare the hell out of you."
- Nelson W Pyles - author of DEMONS, DOLLS AND MILKSHAKES

Burning Bulb
PUBLISHING

ELVIS PRESLEY, CIA ASSASSIN

"I can guarantee you. Read this book and you'll never look at Elvis the same way again!"
~ Douglas Brode, author of ELVIS CINEMA AND POPULAR CULTURE

SOON TO BE A MAJOR MOTION PICTURE

In 1970, singer Elvis Presley secretly met with President Richard Nixon. This new comedic novel imagines that Presley became a Central Intelligence Agency operative, eventually moving up through the ranks to become a skilled assassin.

Presented in an oral history fashion, the book tells us about Presley's secret transformation by the people who knew him best.

Did he fake his death in 1977? Was Presley involved with the Watergate scandal? The Iran hostage crisis? Communicating with aliens?

Read this book to find out the answers to these and many more questions.

Burning Bulb
PUBLISHING